MURDER
REUNION

Murder Reunion

Spiderwize
Remus House
Coltsfoot Drive
Woodston
Peterborough
PE2 9BF

www.spiderwize.com

A CIP catalogue record for this book is available from the
British Library.

The views expressed in this work are solely those of the author
and do not necessarily reflect the views of the publisher, and the
publisher hereby disclaims any responsibility for them.

All characters in this publication are fictitious and any
resemblances to real people either living or dead are purely
coincidental.

ISBN: 978-1-911113-88-1

MURDER REUNION

LIZZIE HILL

Contents

PART III – TENSIONS

PART IV – MURDER ENQUIRY

PART V – AFTERMATH

PART I – REUNION (SECOND HALF)

Prologue

It was a glorious September day with hardly a cloud in the pale blue sky. The sun was warm on her skin as she walked briskly through the crowds of ambling shoppers to her apartment a short distance from the office. She had butterflies in her stomach and was smiling like a Cheshire cat as she thought about her secret tryst with 'him' last Tuesday lunchtime. She wanted to skip and twirl around and tell the whole wide world that she was in love and was going to spend the afternoon loving and being loved, that no one else mattered except the two of them.

Shivers of delight ran up and down her spine as in her mind's eye she could see him naked, smiling, as he pranced past the bottom of the bed disappearing through the door to the en-suite, leaving her trembling with satisfaction, too weak to move, wanting the moment to last forever. She felt heady as she recalled the power of the water surging through the shower and his rich baritone voice filling her ears as he sang loudly, "All I need is the air that I breathe just to love youuuuuu…"

She hummed the song all the way to the third floor and although the sound was amplified in the lift it did not inhibit her, it merely enhanced her growing excitement.

While opening the door to her apartment her mobile phone bleeped, indicating a text message. Distracted, instead of securing the door as she would normally have done, she rummaged around in her handbag to retrieve her phone. She read the message while walking towards the lounge; it was from him.

"Stuck in London, train delayed, bad reception, ring u l8r soz Luvu xxx"

Her heart sank and her eyes stung with tears of disappointment and the pain of longing. She closed her eyes as she fought to control her emotions.

Suddenly the hall became cold and dark. She sensed danger and shuddered as a feeling of terror engulfed her, making the hairs on the back of her neck stand up. Fear coursed through her body. She slowly turned and saw a dark silhouette filling the doorway. There was no escape. She looked up and their eyes locked for what seemed like an eternity, but in reality it was for no more than a few seconds. Not a word was spoken.

Then the figure lunged at her, powerful like a panther, hands clasped around her throat, pressing on her windpipe. She landed heavily on the floor and her assailant landed on top of her with a thud, forcing all of the air from her lungs. Everything was in slow motion. She could not catch her breath. 'I CAN'T BREATHE' she wanted to scream out, but the words would not come.

Gathering

January 10th, 2010 fell on a Sunday and 'The Flakes', the name Piers had chosen because it snowed the first day they met, decided to hold a Sunday lunch reunion, where else but at their favourite haunt, The Toby Jug, a pub and restaurant affectionately known as 'Jugs'.

Bev, who had organised the event, was the first to arrive; her husband Colin had given her a lift into Manchester city centre. She bought herself a Diet Coke and, like a homing pigeon, made her way to the familiar corner where, after hauling herself up and swivelling to balance, she sat on a high wooden stool, looking out of one of the long, ceiling-high windows at the grey, snow-laden sky. Almost immediately, as if to pay homage to the first meeting of 'The Flakes', it started to snow.

As she watched the snowflakes twirling slowly in a graceful downwards spiral to their inevitable extinction on the pavement below, she reflected on the times she had been in Jugs over the years, probably even sat on the same stool and experienced a range of emotions from laughing until she had cried to crying until she had laughed and everything in between.

The place was all but deserted (which was a far cry from her Manchester city working days!) Nevertheless, she was able to visualise it heaving with people. In her mind's eye it was warm and brightly lit, she could see familiar faces standing in groups around the tables in deep conversation,

1

interspersed with bursts of raucous laughter; others were pushing past each other or fighting their way to the bar. It was so noisy everyone seemed to be speaking at once; she could almost smell the combination of alcohol and the now outlawed cigarette smoke. Suddenly a wave of nostalgic sadness overwhelmed her and, not for the first time, she wondered if this reunion was a good idea after all.

Rachel decided to drive but was barely able to concentrate because her mind was in such a whirl. She had mixed feelings about her time working in the city, so much so that this was her first venture there since leaving to work nearer to home, five years previously. Ironically, the fresh start she had hoped for had eluded her through the bizarre coincidence of working for someone directly linking her to the past, which added to her reluctance to go to the reunion. Yet she had felt obliged to make the effort and, if she was honest, curiosity had gotten the better of her.

Initially she had intended to park in the nearby multi-storey car park and walk to their meeting place, but at the last minute, due to the rapid deterioration of the weather, she decided to drive past to check out possible parking spaces and was pleasantly surprised to be spoilt for choice. She managed to park opposite the main entrance but stopped short of climbing out of the car when she caught sight of Bev's shoulder-length light-brown hair and forlorn face, framed by a window with familiar pale green curtain swags. She was sitting where they used to sit Monday lunchtimes, when they had shared a bowl of chips, drank Diet Coke and generally caught up. Now Bev looked like a small child peeping out of the huge window, the falling snow adding a poignant air to the picture. The faraway look on her face showed she was clearly lost in thought. Rachel was struck by the sadness of her expression and then became conscious that her own face probably mirrored that of her friend's. The memories came flooding back and she felt compelled to remain in her car and gather her thoughts before joining the others.

Although the invitation was specifically sent to Lucy it was expected that Ben would accompany her because they usually went everywhere together, they even dressed alike as their blue weatherproof coats, scarves and gloves bore witness. The train from London to Manchester was almost empty and they sat in companionable silence, enjoying the gentle rocking of the carriage. Lucy's broken relationship and Ben's lack of a training contract had brought them together and in turn forced them to move away from Manchester for a new beginning. Making the move together had taken their families and friends by surprise, but if others thought them an unlikely duo they had absolutely no regrets; life was good, very good. They gave each other joy, a sense of adventure and the promise of more.

Returning to Manchester was a regular trip but on this occasion they were in particularly high spirits and really looking forward to catching up with 'The Flakes', finding out everyone's news and telling them about their continuing adventures in the West End.

At first Piers was all for the get-together but, by the time the festive season had ended and the usual post-Christmas anti-climax had set in, the euphoria for a reunion had almost evaporated. In fact, he would have cancelled except for a vivid dream in which he had found himself in 'Jugs'. He could not remember anything else about the dream other than a feeling of complete happiness which compelled him to turn up.

He had decided to catch the bus as suggested by his wife, who had added, sarcastically, that way he could enjoy a celebratory drink… or two. She had said reunions were a waste of time and she was far too busy to drive him into the city. He knew that that was just an excuse; really she did not want him to go because she did not want the past raked over.

He was surprised by how many were on the bus. There were three girls, he guessed in their early twenties, talking excitedly; three men all different ages, who he assumed were workmates as he had heard them moaning about the hours they had worked over Christmas; an elderly woman sat on her own at the front behind the driver's cab, her deep-red coat matching her trolley bag which was resting against the seat next to her; two middle-aged couples, clearly a foursome, chatting away; and two elderly, cloth-capped men, sitting in the middle of the bus on opposite sides, staring blankly at their steamed up windows, who could easily have passed for a couple of bookends.

Piers sat on the back seat centre left where he had a clear view of the motorway through the front window. He was amazed by the volume of traffic for a Sunday. *Thank goodness the traffic is free flowing* he thought, and then his mind drifted back to his time working at Stepwells, the city centre law firm where 'The Flakes' were formed.

A loud bang startled him out of his reverie, it sounded as if it had come from under his seat. This was immediately followed by a smell of burning and he strode quickly to the front of the bus to inform the driver he thought the vehicle was on fire. The driver looked into his wing mirror and saw a plume of black smoke belch out of the back of the bus. At the same time the driver of the lorry behind sounded his horn in warning. The bus driver drove on to the hard shoulder and asked everyone to evacuate the vehicle while he contacted the bus company to organise a replacement.

Piers led the way up to the shrubs on the grass bank the driver had pointed to. He turned to see the others dutifully following him and scanned the wintry sky, simultaneously hunching his shoulders and turning up his black trench coat collar, pulling it tight around his neck, wishing he had worn his woollen hat. They all gathered just as light snow started to fall and began jigging up and down, rubbing their hands together in an effort to keep warm. Piers joined the three dithering young girls huddled under an umbrella and in his best Bruce Willis voice said, "'Catch a bus,' she said, 'enjoy yourself and have a drink,' she said, 'that way you'll have no need to worry about driving the car.' She could have warned me the bus might blow up!"

This made the girls giggle and was all the encouragement he needed to launch into his stand-up comic routine. "There was this man who was trying to get on an overcrowded bus but was pushed off by the people inside. 'There's no room,' they shouted, 'it's full up!'

'But you must let me on!' protested the man.

'Why, what's so special about you?' they demanded.

'I'm the driver!' replied the exasperated man."

The girls groaned at the joke which drew the attention of the others and pretty soon he had a captive audience. In an Irish accent he told another joke.

"A group were touring Ireland. One of the women was a miserable curmudgeon, constantly complaining. The bus seats were uncomfortable, the food was terrible, it was too hot, it was too cold, moan, moan, moan. When the group arrived at the site of the famous Blarney Stone the guide explained, 'Good luck will be followin' ya all ya days if ya kiss the Blarney Stone,' he paused before continuing. 'Unfortunately it's being cleaned today and so no one will be able to kiss it. Perhaps we can come back the morrow.'

'We can't be here tomorrow,' the nasty woman shouted, 'we have some other boring tour to go on. So I guess we can't kiss the stupid stone.'

'Well now,' said the guide, 'it is said that if you kiss someone who has kissed the stone, you'll have the same good fortune.'

'And I suppose you've kissed the stone,' the woman scoffed.

'No, ma'am,' the frustrated guide said, 'but I've sat on it!'"

The group laughter was music to his ears and he managed to keep the freezing passengers entertained until the replacement bus turned up, approximately fifteen minutes later. They quickly boarded the warm vehicle and soon settled down for the final leg of their journey. Piers found it amusing to observe that the passengers, himself included, had all returned to their corresponding seats, as if nothing had happened. All that is except the original driver, who was duty bound to stay with his defective bus until the rescue service arrived.

As the chill left Piers' body his thoughts returned to the beginning of The Flakes and the ghosts of his city past.

Bev saw Rachel walk through the entrance and waved her over. "Hello you!" they said in unison as they embraced in greeting.

"It's so good to see you," said Bev, "you're looking really well."

"And you," replied Rachel. "How are you? How's Colin and the kids?"

"Oh I'm fine, ticking along as you do. Anyway, first things first, do you want a drink?" Bev moved to get off her stool but

Rachel stopped her. "No, no, I'll get my own drink. What can I get you?"

"Nothing, I'm fine for the moment thanks."

"Well what about a bowl of chips, you know, for old time's sake?"

Bev laughed and said, "Better not, it will spoil our meal."

Rachel laughed in agreement and moved to the bar to buy herself a drink. She was served much quicker than she remembered back in the day and before they knew it she had returned to Bev to continue their conversation.

"The kids are going great guns, Fiona's at Leeds University studying for a media degree and Jonathan's working in an architects' office as a trainee, they're paying for him to go to college on day release to learn C.A.D, Computer Aided Design, whatever that means. Unfortunately, it's the same ol', same ol' for Colin, he still hates working at the Job Centre but at least he's earning."

The mention of Colin seemed to put a damper on her spirits, so Rachel quickly changed the subject and asked how her job was going. Immediately Bev's eyes lit up as she spoke excitedly about David, her boss, how handsome he was, the laughs they had and she spoke at length about his amazing jet-setting lifestyle. Rachel listened intently, noting the sparkle in her eyes. She recalled seeing that same look in someone else's eyes, a long time ago; it was the look Nick had when speaking about Andrea. In that moment she realised Bev was in love with David, which probably explained the sad expression on her face when staring out of the window a short while earlier. Suddenly she felt sorry for her friend. Nevertheless, they carried on chatting and catching up on each other's lives while waiting for the rest to arrive.

A commotion drew their attention; it was Lucy and Ben, who had burst through the double doors of the pub shouting, "Hello Flakes!" at the top of their voices, throwing their arms wide open as if performing in a pantomime. Customers and bar staff alike watched in fascination as they rushed over to the girls in the corner, crushing them in a joint bear hug causing all four of them to fall about laughing. Then they bounded over to the bar to order their drinks.

"They're like a couple of big blue Labrador dogs bouncing all over the place."

Rachel laughed at Bev's apt description. It was good to see the two of them so obviously happy with each other. Back in their Stepwells days she had been very concerned to see how hurt Lucy was when she split with her previous boyfriend and worried that she had jumped into a relationship with Ben too soon; seeing them now banished any lingering doubts.

Piers recognised Lucy's inimitable high-pitched giggle before he actually saw her standing with the others in 'their' corner. Immediately he was transported back to a time when life was good and full of promise. He pictured the young man he was, all laughter and curls, surrounded by giggling girls, his for the asking. Oh how he had loved that young man. He longed to shake his hand and tell him how much he admired him and give him the benefit of the wisdom he had gained through experience and protect him from life's harsh realities. Now he did not know where the young man had gone to, and, more worryingly, where his middle-aged counterpart had suddenly sprung from!

He remained by the pub entrance observing the group. Lucy was centre stage doing most of the talking, pausing to join the occasional group laughter. *Some things never change,* he mused. Her blonde hair was short and curly, just like his used to be. His cousin Ben had not changed one iota; he still looked 25 going on 50. Piers was surprised to feel a pang of envy at Ben's rosy-cheeked face and jovial expression, a feeling he would never have anticipated with regard to nice but boring Ben. *How some things completely change!* he thought. Bev looked slightly jowly and Rachel had piled on the pounds, but both were still attractive.

As he made his way over to the group Lucy was the first to spot him. She waved and shrieked, "You've lost your curls!" Turning to the others she proclaimed loudly, "Oh my God he's lost his curls!"

"Sure have and you've obviously found them!" Piers counteracted, patting her on the head before giving her a crushing hug and slobbering kiss. He pretended to play-fight with Ben before shaking his hand and slapping his shoulder, then he hugged and kissed Bev and Rachel.

"Oh it's so good to see you all."

They all echoed his sentiments and he went off to buy a round of drinks. Lucy offered to help carry them.

"So Hun, how are things with you and Ben?" Piers asked Lucy while the pretty barmaid sorted his order; he was sure he had seen her before but quickly dismissed the thought, concentrating on Lucy instead.

"We're really, really happy; it's a fun relationship with plenty of *steamy* sex."

"Now why doesn't that surprise me? After all, steamy sex is a family speciality!" laughed Piers. "So you're really, really happy are you?" He looked directly into her aquamarine blue eyes, as if checking for a sign of uncertainty.

"Yes, hand on heart, I'm happy." She met his probing stare. "Very!"

"Good, that's what I like to hear."

"And what about you, are you really, really happy?" It was her turn to look him in the eye but in her case with a hint of a smile playing across her lips.

"Oh, tickety-boo, tickety-boo."

Before she had chance to question him further the barmaid smiled and handed him his change and he scooped up two pints for Ben and himself. Lucy picked up the drinks for the girls, trailing after him to their corner.

"Anyway, how are you two enjoying life in the West End?" Piers directed his question to Lucy.

"Hmmm," she paused for effect then launched into her well-rehearsed spiel without stopping for breath. "As you know I'm working in the West End for the Ventura Theatre Company. I help organise everything from booking the shows, selling tickets, hiring and firing staff in the bar, catering and cleaning. There are no set hours and sometimes it feels like I'm working 24/7 but then I have time off in lieu, which really suits me, I get to do my own thing! It's the best job ever, so exciting and I meet famous people and have free tickets to the shows."

"Wow! Who have you met?"

"Ooh loads, Elton John and his husband David Furnish, Phil Collins, Jerry Hall and Marie Helvin, Joanna Lumley, Sean Bean, Timothy Dalton, oh and a few days ago I saw Lee Mead, Denise Van Outen's husband, he's gorgeous. I've also seen film stars on the red carpet for opening nights in Leicester Square."

"Oh go on then, tell us who," Piers said rolling his eyes.

"Well, Brad Pitt!" She grinned at Rachel knowing how much she liked him, and her grin widened as Rachel's jaw dropped. She turned back to Piers as she continued, "Tom

Cruise, he's smaller than I thought, but still shaggable and so is Justin Timberlake!" Lucy clearly loved life in London.

"And what about you Ben, are you enjoying your job and life in London?" Bev asked.

"Erm, a love hate relationship if I'm honest, I love London but hate my job."

"Why do you hate your job?"

"Actually the job is okay if I could be allowed to get on with it, it's the prat I work for who I hate. He's rude, arrogant and dictatorial. It's bad enough I have to put up with that attitude at home, let alone at work!" It took Lucy a second or two before the insult registered, then her mouth dropped open in shock and Ben brought his elbow up to protect himself from her indignant slap.

After they had finished messing about Lucy turned to Bev and asked, "Are you still working for that property investment group in Openshaw?"

"Oh yes," she said wistfully, "it's a brilliant job and Mr Fellows is a dream to work for, I love my job, I just hope it lasts…" Her middle distance stare caught the group's attention and it was a few seconds before she was back with the others, who continued to watch her intently. Lucy broke the spell by asking why she was concerned it would not last, sensing there was some juicy gossip up for grabs. *Perhaps it is not just her job she loves,* she wondered.

"Just too good to be true," Bev replied, "too good to be true." Her voice trailed off and she looked down, but not before her eyes revealed her sadness.

There was an awkward silence, the flow of conversation faltered to a natural break and they carried their drinks into the room at the back of the building, settling down at the oblong dining table.

"I can't believe it's been ten years since we first met," Rachel began, "I can still remember how I felt, both nervous and excited, when my dad drove Lucy and me into the city to see Phil Allen at Aspect. Do you remember all those furtive phone calls beforehand, Lucy, so that old face-ache, the little barrel of an office manageress of the dump we worked at, wouldn't cotton on? Wasn't she vile! You know I can't even remember her name now."

"Maud 'Heifer' Armstrong!" answered Lucy.

"That's right, the 'Old Heifer'!" They both dissolved into a fit of giggles.

"Remember when she hid my car keys in the office on Christmas Eve and I had to ring my dad to bring my spare set?" said Lucy.

"Oh yes, I remember. And then they miraculously appeared on top of the filing cabinet when we returned to work after the Christmas break. She was such a bitch; thought you were getting it on with the boss!" Rachel laughed again.

"I'd never be that desperate, ugh he was such an ignorant bastard!" scoffed Lucy.

"It's weird how we all moved on from Stepwells around about the same time. In fact, come to think of it, most of the people we started with have moved on," Piers said, then continued, "At the time I couldn't get away quick enough but in hindsight it wasn't such a bad place to work, the money was pretty good and to be honest I was probably at my happiest there." He turned to his cousin. "Thanks Ben, as I've said before, I'll always be grateful to you for recommending the firm."

"I agree, it wasn't a bad place to work, I miss the gossip and the different characters. I don't miss O'Dwyer though, she had it in for me from day one. The way she used to fawn over the clients and make silly small talk while batting her false eyelashes! Ridiculous," said Rachel.

"Remember the Husslebeas and that tattoo?" Lucy said and everyone started to laugh again.

"Oh, oh, remember that big girl, you know, the one who sometimes sang with that beanpole of a bloke, what's his name?" Ben thought for a second. "Catchpole that's it, that's his name and she's Donna somebody-or-other. Do you remember she tripped up as she climbed on the stage and went arse over tit, and she hadn't got any knickers on!"

"Trust you to remember that." Lucy playfully punched him pretending to scold him but joined in with the laughter too.

"Those were the days," said Bev. "Yes, it is strange how we all left just after the murder. Almost as if it was the catalyst to us all moving on."

"Yes," agreed Piers, looking into his almost empty pint glass, lost in thought for a long moment. Then, in a faraway voice, he added, "A story is waiting to be told."

Murder Reunion

PART II – NEW BEGINNINGS

New jobs

Ten years earlier

Lucy and Rachel left the comfort of their cosy court jobs when the boss appointed a new manager from outside the Magisterial Service, quashing any chance of staff promotion. This development predictably caused morale to plummet and people to move within or even outside the service. Lucy was extremely angry as she had effectively been running the court office for a number of years on the understanding that she would replace her manager who was nearing retirement. As change was inevitable Rachel decided to meet it with change and joined Lucy by working for a criminal defence lawyer, Douglas Markham.

Middle-aged, sandy-haired Markham was an affable chap, popular with defendants, police and court staff alike and because one of Lucy's duties was to process Legal Aid applications she had built up a good rapport with him. He was a sole practitioner who said he was moving into brand spanking new offices.

The new offices never materialised and the job turned out to be nothing more than a 'sweat shop' in a dangerous environment. They were expected to work long hours in cramped offices with security bars welded to the windows to prevent burglary, but *unbelievably* the offices were above a bakery, without a fire escape! The only means of escape were stairs opening out into the street, at the foot of which bags of shredded paper were piled high awaiting collection! One carelessly discarded cigarette was all that was needed and… it did not bear thinking about. Manchester city centre working soon beckoned; they signed up with Phil Allen, a recruitment agent. The only fun they had was furtive phone calls arranging interviews.

"Lucy is that you? Can you talk?" enquired Phil. "Is Rachel with you?"

"Yes she's here," whispered Lucy.

"Good, can you both come for an interview on Tuesday night at 7.00pm?"

Lucy silently mouthed the day and time to Rachel who nodded her agreement.

"Yes, we'll see you then," Lucy quietly confirmed.

"Great, looking forward to meeting you both at last," Phil said, ending the conversation.

As they made their way to the meeting with Mr Allen, they were both excited and apprehensive. The towering office blocks with lights blazing from windows on each floor were a world away from what they were used to working in, and the city centre seemed so glamorous with its numerous shops, inviting restaurants and people milling about. Phil Allen, the archetype 'grey suit', was saved from being dull by his friendly smile, which, once the typing test was over, put them at their ease. Two days later Mr Allen rang to say he was delighted to have lined them up for an interview at the same place, Stepwells, a legal firm based in the city centre.

For the interview Lucy straightened her naturally curly blonde hair and wore her navy blue suit. Rachel wore her favourite grey suit and bound up her wavy, chestnut coloured hair in a chignon. They both looked very professional. The interviews at Stepwells went well, despite the surprise spelling and grammar tests and they left feeling quietly confident. A few days later both were invited to a second interview. Rachel asked to be considered for a general secretarial position because she wanted to get a feel for the place before working for anyone specific; working in the 'sweat shop' had made her wary. Lucy was quite happy to be assigned to someone from the outset. They were both offered jobs and the next day handed their notices in, which was one in the eye for Maud, the 'old heifer' of an office manageress. Rachel was still minded to tip off the Health and Safety Executive about their appalling working conditions but thought better of it, not wishing to prolong her involvement with the wretched firm.

Their start day was the 10th January 2000.

Hayden could feel bile in the pit of his stomach starting to rise; soon it would be at the back of his throat and he would have to use all of his willpower to stop himself gagging. The muscles in his skeletally thin face contorted and a familiar look of scorn enveloped his face as he watched his mother slam the cutlery and condiments down on the table. *How could that have given birth to me?* he asked himself for the umpteenth time, just as she looked directly at him and for a split-second he thought he had said it out loud. He continued to watch his mother as she wobbled back into the kitchen. She quickly reappeared carrying their dinner plates piled high with chicken and vegetables, swimming in a rancid liquid. He could not decide which he hated more, her cooking or her. All he knew was his loathing of her was increasing and caused his rosacea condition to flare up. He looked askance at his father. There was a time he had felt sorry for him but no more; he was a wimp. He resented the fact that he had inherited the worst of both of them; her florid colouring and his lanky skinniness and sharp features and he hated his frizzy, grey coloured hair, which seemed to have a mind of its own.

While forcing himself to eat his meal he thought about his immediate future. *Well I know there's sod all I can do about my appearance but there's one thing I can do and that's make sure I'm not lumbered with looking after them in their old age. Come the New Year I'm going to make enquiries about moving to Manchester, I've had enough of Leeds anyway, particularly since discovering Louis has been using me. He wasn't interested in me at all, just gave me work because he didn't want to load his 'secret girlfriend' down, well that is one secret I'll make sure is out in the open, huh! I'll teach him. Nobody, but nobody messes with me and gets away with it.* He decided to accept his Uncle Rhys's offer of accommodation.

Back at work after the Christmas break Hayden spent his lunchtime trawling the internet for recruitment agencies in Manchester. He chose ASPECT, an agency specialising in 'Administration, Secretarial, Personnel, Executives, Clerical and Training' jobs. He arranged an interview with Phil Allen of the company for the following Friday, pre-booked the train tickets, started complaining on the Wednesday of headaches, on Thursday feigned stomach cramps and on Friday no one was surprised when he called in sick. The agency tests and interview went very well, as he had expected, and, in view of the distance involved, Phil pulled strings to get him an interview at Stepwells for that afternoon.

Stepwells' offices were in a prime corner location in the legal square of Manchester. The building was a solid turn of the century structure. It looked a little like a medieval fortification with its grey stone exterior and long narrow windows. Only the huge smoky-coloured glass entrance doors gave it a sense of modernity. Hayden was particularly impressed with the foyer with its marble flooring, high ceilings, quality leather chairs and plain, low level, solid wooden tables, with the daily papers scattered on them in a seemingly casual manner. The pièce de résistance was several alabaster busts housed in individual alcoves. It reminded him of a museum; he loved visiting museums. The uniformed commissionaire just added to the air of opulence.

Hayden strode confidently over to the commissionaire.

"Good morning I'm Hayden Rhys Husslebea." He waited to see if he recognised his name, but he clearly did not so he added in clarification, "I have an appointment with Ms O'Dwyer at 11.30 this morning."

"Good morning sir, please take a seat," the commissionaire replied, his open hand drawing Hayden's attention to the seats. "I'll let Ms O'Dwyer know that you are here."

Now this is my kind of place Hayden mused as he waited. Ms O'Dwyer appeared almost instantly.

"Good morning, Mr Husslebea I presume." Gillian O'Dwyer smiled in greeting and Hayden was relieved she did not offer her hand; he hated shaking hands.

They took a lift to the second floor and she lead the way along an expensive beige carpeted corridor to the interview room, which was very plain except for an abstract painting of what looked like the Manhattan skyline at night. Ms O'Dwyer and another young woman called Mrs Wentworth conducted the twenty minute interview. He was confident it went very well, that they were impressed with his CV and his camp humour made them laugh; it was a foregone conclusion he would get the job, the telephone confirmation was a mere formality. Afterwards he caught the bus to Uncle Rhys's.

He was surprised to be called back for a second interview, figuring that the first interview was more than adequate. Nevertheless, he did as requested reasoning that the second interview was merely a jobsworth for someone and a few days later was pleased to accept a job offer. He was also pleased with his parting shot on the last day at his current firm. His timing, as usual, was impeccable; having waited until the office was full he made a point of shaking Louis's hand vigorously, thanking him profusely for all his help and support and wishing him and his boyfriend a happy future. A self-satisfied grin stretched across his face at the memory of Louis's shocked expression and red face.

His start date was the 10th January 2000.

His name was Piers Smallman; the surname suited his five foot seven inch chubby frame perfectly, which, together with his baby blue eyes, wide full mouth, dimples and curly blond hair gave him a cherubic look. His lack of height certainly did not diminish him in the eyes of the girls because he was never short of female company; they considered him cute. In fact as far as he was concerned the taller the girl the better. He was excited at the prospect of working at Stepwells, it was a good career move, a firm with a reputation for quality work but also known for its social life.

His start date was the 10th January 2000.

Hospital

Laid flat on his back in an almost empty hospital ward was not quite how Nick Turner had planned to welcome in the New Millennium; a different kind of laid was what he had had in mind. He would have kicked himself for his stupidity had it been physically possible.

"Stupid, stupid, stupid!" he voiced his frustration as the events of the previous day ran through his mind yet again.

"Why did I insist on trying out Dave's new bike? What a prize prat skidding on black ice and smashing into a brick wall. Idiot!" he angrily chastised himself through gritted teeth.

It was so cruel that Nick, the ultimate party animal, should be incapacitated at this 'mother of all' party times. It was not without reason that he was nicknamed 'Farrelly' after Colin Farrell, a movie star who was also known for being a womaniser. He understood and liked the comparison, a mop of dark brown hair, beady nut-brown eyes, worked hard, played hard and was not afraid to take chances. Frankly, he considered himself more attractive, not least because he stood a few inches taller at 6 foot 1 and was bigger built. It was no secret that he liked the girls and as long as they were willing he was only too happy to oblige, and willing they certainly were. Yes, he knew 'what every woman wants' and it was not Mel Gibson!

He realised he was lucky to have sustained just a stable fracture to his spine for it could have been much worse. The consultant was confident it would heal quickly. Football and boxing classes had kept him fit and the pretty nurses were helping to keep more than his spirits raised, especially the little redhead who was particularly attentive. He may have been temporarily rendered helpless but the Turner magic was still working.

People

The three years leading up to the New Millennium had been exceptionally good and Stepwells had undergone rapid expansion but there was still a need for more staff. Lucy Penikett, Rachel Dawes, Bev Jelf, Hayden Husslebea and Piers Smallman made up the first batch of recruits.

Stepwells' building was four floors high, staffed by approximately seven hundred people. In fact there were more employed in the photocopying department than in the whole of Lucy and Rachel's last firm, it was very daunting; thank goodness they had each other for moral support.

The initial week was training. There was a lot to take in but it was a relaxed atmosphere and the group enjoyed a few laughs, mainly listening to Piers, who took on the mantle of classroom clown and was very entertaining with his perfectly timed wisecracks. He decided to call the group 'The Flakes' on account of it snowing quite heavily the day they started.

Halfway through the first training session Piers set the pace.

"Experts say that every home will have a computer. Great, then our personal lives can be just as screwed up as things are at the office." This was followed by group laughter.

Lucy was the first to admit she had made a mistake on the computer; she had somehow managed to delete the entire training programme from her system! "To err is to be human but to really screw up requires a computer," Piers proclaimed in his best theatrical voice to more laughter.

At the end of the session the trainer asked them to complete the computer training log.

With a cheeky wink at the trainer Piers said, "Go ahead and put it on the computer, at least you'll know where you put it even if you can't find it again!" The trainer joined in with the group laughter. Later that evening she laughed a lot in Piers' apartment.

Lucy had been assigned to work for two people, Maggie Rollaston, a junior lawyer and, Ben Tranter, a trainee lawyer. There was quite a lot of work to greet her but she was used to hard work from her 'sweat shop' days so she just rolled up her sleeves and got stuck in.

Meanwhile, Rachel had to report to Gillian O'Dwyer who was the personal assistant to a leading partner. She immediately put her foot in it by calling her Gill.

"It is Gillian, thank you," was the snotty response.

The rest of the afternoon Rachel spent twiddling her thumbs as Gillian did not give her any work. Instinct told her she was not going to gel with Gillian.

"I'm just mixed up. I don't know what I want," Bev moaned to her husband Colin through the bedroom mirror as she used the curling tongs on her hair. "I know at Stepwells Frank Hunter was a nightmare to work for but I miss the buzz, I miss his fast-paced-working-on-the-edge style. He's agreed someone else will do the routine work while I can concentrate on the things that really interest me. I just know that even if I don't return to working for Frank, I can't stay where I am, the man is a complete moron, he hardly gives me any work and what he does give me, bores me. I'm going to give Frank another shot."

That was the end of their discussion and he had not said a word! Colin wished Bev would settle down, he had enough on his plate without worrying about his wife's job. She should try working at the Job Centre for a week; she would soon know when she was well off. Women!

"Hi I'm back," announced Bev to anyone within earshot. "I know, I know, you must think I'm mad but I missed the buzz of this place, sad cow that I am. Frank has said things will be different. I'm just soooo glad to be back."

Not everyone was soooo glad she was back, she had ruffled a few feathers before going, particularly Gillian's, whose mood matched the colour of her shoulder-length, smouldering red hair. Interesting times lay ahead.

By the third week Lucy had her two eating out of her hand and was really enjoying herself, whereas Rachel wished she had plumbed for a set job rather than float. Everyone had their own way of working which was hard going and while most were grateful for any help they received, her fourth and fifth weeks were spent working for an absolute bastard. He was impatient and expected her to know instinctively which files he was referring to, definitely a 'crystal ball' job. Unfortunately he was also head of department and obviously new recruits were a waste of his precious time! He was so petty, asking everyone in his team if they wanted tea or coffee for elevenses and pointedly ignoring Rachel. She hated working for him and he undermined her confidence to the point where she wondered if she would be allowed to complete her probationary period, let alone be kept on.

Hayden quickly settled into a routine at work and enjoyed living at his uncle's home. He had chosen to be a float secretary and had immediately been assigned to work in the Litigation Department for twelve months, of which nine months were covering a secretary's maternity leave. He liked litigation work, indeed, if he had had the opportunity, he would have liked to have been a barrister as arguing the point and cutting comments were things he excelled at.

He also liked the idea of being the only male doing predominantly female work. He loved to make the young girls laugh with his outrageous stories and camp comments. Occasionally he would wear something shocking, like bright pink socks, just for the hell of it. He picked up the working practices easily because it was more or less what he had been doing in Leeds, and he knew he was popular among the lawyers from a novelty aspect. He quickly built up a reputation as a good worker and knew who to curry favour with and how to deal with those who objected to him or annoyed him. *Oh yes, Mother has done a good job of teaching me to be spiteful! All in all this was a good move.*

Uncle Rhys was Hayden's mother's younger brother who fortunately, from Hayden's point of view, was nothing like her. He was an accountant, single and lived alone in a traditional semi-detached house with a square bay window and a small front garden surrounded by a three foot high wall. The house and garden were in need of a good overhaul but it would do until Hayden could get settled and find his own place.

There was a bus shelter two doors up from Uncle Rhys's house where yobs gathered most evenings. They would shout and laugh loudly, drink and smoke and throw litter on to the nearby gardens, including his uncle's. This irritated Hayden more and more until eventually he had had enough and reported them to the police, the Local Authority and his MP. He also wrote a letter of complaint to the local newspaper. Unrealistically, he had expected to see signs of law enforcement the following night. Disappointed and annoyed at the lack of police presence he rang the Local Authority and police again.

Two days later he rang them again. It took just over a week of complaints but eventually Hayden got his way. He spotted a police car driving slowly past one evening at the time the yobs normally congregated. At first the yobs sniggered and jeered but after a second slow drive past they walked off down the road and out of sight. Hayden was well pleased with the outcome. *Complaining does work if you are persistent enough, as I know only too well.* He had made complaining a work of art.

For his first training seat Piers was assigned to Frank Hunter's team specialising in Commercial Property Law. Hunter was very much the alpha male; his name suited him very well, for once he set his sights on a new client he always succeeded in capturing them. He was a lean, mean, money making machine, the most focused person Piers had ever come across and unfortunately seemed to be devoid of humour, which was Piers' strong point. Nevertheless, although he found Hunter rather intimidating, he liked his no nonsense style, his very precise instructions, realised he could learn a lot from his first seat and was excited and eager to get into the swing of things.

Long-legged, fair-haired Peter Richardson was not easily impressed, in fact he considered himself to be intellectually superior to the majority of those within his legal circle including his clients. Of course he was careful not to show his superiority, preferring to act the clown. Only Gillian truly knew how he felt and they would often giggle hysterically at the responses he elicited to his double entendres. So when Peter found himself opposite Simon Miller, of Inglemead &

Noakes, on a complicated, protracted property deal in London and found Miller to have a mind as sharp as his own he was impressed. Impressed enough to offer him a position in his team with a promise of partnership after a suitable period of time, without following the firm's protocol of discussing it with his contemporaries first.

The timing was superb for Miller because, unbeknown to Richardson, he had just had his application for partnership turned down for the second time and was on the verge of approaching other firms to further his career. Unlike Richardson he had made some discreet enquiries about Stepwells and more importantly about Richardson before negotiating the final stages of his contract offer, which was very fortuitous because he discovered Richardson was known for not promoting within his team, so he made sure a clause was included guaranteeing an offer of partnership within twelve months of joining Stepwells.

Richardson was rather taken aback by this demand but could not help having a sneaky regard for Miller's astuteness and considered this only served to underline his own astuteness in offering him a position in the first place.

Miller was due to start on 26th June 2000 but decided to book a last minute holiday, delaying his start date by two weeks. Richardson was quite irritated by this setback, not least because he had authorised a team night out at Browns as a 'welcome to the team' surprise. It would not be the only time Miller dictated the tune.

Nick Returns

Nick felt unusually nervous; he had hardly slept a wink and there were butterflies in his stomach. *Pull yourself together man, anyone would think it was your first day at the firm,* he chastised himself in the bathroom mirror. *Thank God I spent the night in my own bed and not in my sexy little nurse's for once.* He took a few deep breaths and decided the quicker he got back to work the better. He dashed around his small terraced house like a madman, getting dressed and collecting his things. He double-checked he had got his wallet, identification card, bus pass and keys before pulling his front door to. He sprinted down the road and just managed to catch the bus into the city centre.

"Hi Nick, it's good to see you back," beamed the pretty blonde on reception. *I really must try to remember her name,* he made a mental note as he returned her smile. On the way to his room several people shouted, "Hello Nick" or similar terms of greeting. He hung his jacket up and made his way to the kitchen. He was surprised to see Sarah in there, she was normally in later.

"Hi Sarah, how come you're in so early?"

"Oh, hi Nick, good to see you back. I take it you've fully recovered from your motorbike accident?"

"Oh yes, couldn't wait to return." Although his response was said in a sarcastic manner he really was glad to be back.

"We had yet another office move over the weekend. The powers that be only told us on Friday. God knows why they are so adamant we should keep moving about. Anyway, that's the reason I'm in so early, to check I have all of my things and to get organised, yet again! Wouldn't want to do an O'Dwyer! Remember when she sent crates to the fourth floor section three, instead of third floor section four?" They both laughed at the memory. "It was hilarious at the time, but makes me quadruple check before, during and after every move. Have you seen Andrea yet?"

"No, is she alright?" He felt his heart lurch at the very mention of her name. He had been surprised and unsettled at how much he had missed her over his seven weeks off work. She had visited him a couple of times at the hospital and his need to see her, just to talk with her, was like a dull ache he could not ignore. His feelings for her had changed from friendly colleagues to something much deeper in the two years since they had started at Stepwells on the same day and sat by each other in the introductory training lessons that took place during their first week. Although Nick was a solicitor and Andrea was a trainee Legal Executive the training classes included all newcomers irrespective of their status. He decided he would have to tell her how he felt even if he did risk rejection.

"She's been moved to the other side of the floor. She's not happy about it and thinks her boss, Chris 'Always' Wright has asked to move away because Richardson has appointed a new guy to the team, which has scuppered his ambition. Anyway, he's Simon Miller from London, apparently on a promise of a partnership and rumour has it that he's insisted the promise be written into his contract!"

The feeling of butterflies in Nick's stomach was replaced with nausea. He needed some fresh air to collect his thoughts and headed off to the fire escape for a cigarette while he processed the devastating news of the appointment of Miller. *Some welcome back!* While smoking he decided to email Andrea, inviting her to lunch to find out more about what had happened while he was away and more importantly to tell her how he felt about her. They agreed to meet just around the corner from Stepwells, to avoid Gillian's ever watchful eyes.

As Andrea walked towards him, his heart quickened at her beaming smile. He thought there was something different about her, but could not work out what; it was a sort of glow outlining her. Then she held out her left hand, waggling her fingers and said in an exaggerated posh voice, "The water in our cellar is this high!"

He saw a sparkle of light. "Is that an engagement ring?"

"Oh yes," she beamed.

Nick felt a sharp pain in his chest which took his breath away.

"Kevin got down on bended knee in La Gavroche restaurant on our early St Valentine's Day, Saturday just gone." She beamed as her news sank in before continuing. "I had no idea he was planning to ask me. The place was packed and when I said 'Yes' everyone in the restaurant started to clap and shout 'Congratulations'. It was so wonderful I burst into tears. We've already set the date; Saturday 7th October this year, on his birthday, so that he doesn't forget!"

As Andrea continued to tell Nick her news and plans for the future he felt light-headed and could not take in what she was saying, it was as though she was drifting away from him. *This is disastrous* he thought, but somehow managed to congratulate her.

"Kevin is a very, very lucky man. I hope he realises and makes you happy." He hoped he sounded genuine for her sake but could not wait to get away from her so he could think things through. He felt a gnawing emptiness. *I would make her happy, very happy.*

Rachel

Rachel felt a huge sense of relief when her stint of working for 'Mr Crystal Ball' was finally over. Her next assignment was to work for two young men, Nick Turner and Ken Grainger. Nick was without a secretary and Ken's secretary, Sarah, was on holiday. They were both easy to work for, although their style of work was totally different, Nick manually altered documents for typing, whereas Ken dictated amendments on tape, but their work was clear and as such a complete and welcomed contrast to 'Mr Crystal Ball'. The mere thought of him made her shudder. *Huh!*

At the beginning of April Gillian spoke to Rachel.

"How are you finding working for Nick?"

Still smarting from the episode with 'Mr Crystal Ball' Rachel defensively asked, "Why, has he complained?"

"Oh no, quite the opposite, he's asked me to ask if you'd like to work for him permanently, he didn't ask you personally in case you didn't want to work for him and felt embarrassed to say so."

Embarrassed? Rachel was delighted. At last someone had recognised her potential to be a good secretary and it was one way to avoid being assigned to 'Mr Crystal Ball' again. She accepted, despite the faint ringing of an alarm bell in her mind; they had had no interview, had barely spoken and she knew nothing about him. Nevertheless, against her better judgement, she pushed these doubts to the back of her mind.

After a few teething problems, one being sitting near to Gillian, Rachel settled into a routine and began to enjoy

Nick's work. He seemed to instinctively know her capabilities and she quickly built up a good rapport with his clients, family and friends. She shrugged off the fact that he invariably left work on her desk when she was not there, which must have been deliberate timing because she hardly ever left her desk. Conversely he would leave encouraging notes attached to the files which she found quite sweet. "Thanks Rachel for all your hard work", "Excellent", "Well done", "Your hard work is very much appreciated", etc.

Bev

Bev noted Gillian's failure to welcome her back and sensed there was a problem festering and decided to try and smooth things over, so mid-morning she went over to her desk.

"Hi Gillian, are you free for a coffee lunchtime today?" asked Bev.

"Oh, yes, yes of course," agreed Gillian, who was taken aback and rather perplexed. *I wonder what she wants,* she thought after agreeing to meet in Starbucks.

Later in Starbucks, Bev opened up the conversation by saying, "I gather Nick's got what he wanted."

"What's that?" Gillian enquired.

"I understand he was looking for a mature secretary, one who would just get on with his work and not be a distraction. Well she's certainly mature and you could hardly call her a distraction!" Bev giggled.

"Yes she was a surprise choice considering his reputation for the young ladies. I wonder how long she'll last? I'm not keen on 'Luce' either, I think 'Loose' would be a more befitting spelling because where *does* she get such disgusting joke emails from? How she manages to get them past the censor I'll never know! She'll be out of a job if she's not careful."

"Have you heard of her latest tease?" Bev continued.

"No. What's she up to now?"

"She pretended to be a swinger and propositioned one of the lads in the post room, the young one with the brown curly hair."

"No! You're kidding. She didn't!" exclaimed Gillian. "Well I never! She's unbelievable! Did he agree?"

"I don't think he could, he was speechless." They giggled in unison.

It has not taken her long to get back into the thick of it thought Gillian as they made their way back to the office.

Lucy

Lucy quickly got to grips with Stepwells' sophisticated system and churned out the work. Occasionally people would try to take advantage but she would soon put them in their place. She was not afraid of hard work but would choose whether she helped out or not; she certainly would not be put on, her 'sweat shop' days had at least taught her that much.

She also became known for emailing jokes and pictures that were highly amusing but borderline censorship. Although Maggie considered her common she could not help but admire her confidence and ability to get the job done.

Lucy was all about having fun and would do outlandish things just to make people laugh such as flapping her blouse at Ben, giving a quick 'whey hey' flash of her bra just to embarrass him. Poor, shy, ordinary Ben, he did not know where to look and everyone around him fell about laughing at his red face. Nevertheless, he was seriously attracted to Lucy; she was everything he was not: confident, funny, bubbly, spontaneous, sexy, and did not seem to care what people thought of her. She was exciting to be around and he could not get enough of her, but unfortunately she had a boyfriend.

Ben and Piers grew up together, their mothers were sisters. Ben was as shy and introvert as Piers was self-assured and extrovert and, like a moth to a flame, Ben was drawn to him, although he sometimes felt inadequate. Nevertheless, when he found out that lunchtimes, and occasionally after work, Lucy would meet up with friends, Ben asked Piers to go with him. Asking Piers along did the trick because they soon became part of Lucy's social scene which suited gregarious

Piers very much, he loved playing to an audience, especially a female audience.

Bev and Rachel

Although Bev quickly settled back into the routine of working for Frank Hunter, she was finding it difficult to cope with the mood swings and jealousy of her husband Colin and desperately needed a trustworthy friend to talk to. She was on friendly terms with most of her colleagues but unsure as to who to trust because gossip was rife in the office. She had noticed that Rachel kept herself to herself and telephoned her.

"Hi Rachel, Bev here, are you free this lunchtime for a bite to eat?"

"Oh hello," answered Rachel, surprised. "Yes that would be nice, thank you. Where do you want to meet?" She was pleased yet curious about the reason behind the invite.

"I thought we could meet at The Toby Jug, you don't usually have to book in advance."

"Okay then, see you outside at just after 1pm."

Rachel crossed the road to join Bev who was waiting outside The Toby Jug as arranged.

"Thanks for agreeing to lunch, I've been meaning to meet up with you to see how you're settling in," said Bev as she led the way inside. The place was busier than she had anticipated and the only seats available were two high chairs in the corner near to a wide shelf. They settled for them and quickly decided on a glass of Diet Coke and a bowl of chips each. Bev placed their food order at the bar and returned with the Cokes and a wooden spoon with number 18 painted on it to display in the small empty wine bottle on the shelf. After three awkward attempts she eventually managed to climb up on to the chair, where they both collapsed in a fit of giggles at her ungainly efforts, which certainly broke the ice.

After composing herself Bev said, "So how are you getting on?"

"I'm really enjoying myself. I've only worked in small firms before so Stepwells is quite a culture shock, but I find it quite exciting, learning new skills, getting to know different people," Rachel enthused. She paused before asking, "Why did you leave Stepwells before?"

"Oh various reasons, things were getting me down at work and at home. Between you and me, I could have done with a few months off work but couldn't afford to be without a regular income, so I decided to jump ship on the basis that a change is as good as a rest. A decision I quickly came to regret."

"Oh, why was that?"

"Believe it or not I wasn't busy enough! Fortunately, I'd kept in touch with Frank Hunter and told him I wanted to come back. He pulled a few strings and hey presto, six months later thank God, or should I say thank Frank, I'm back."

The food arrived and between dipping their chips in mayonnaise and eating them, they started to get to know each other and formed a close, supportive friendship, with Monday lunchtime becoming a ritual of sharing a bowl of chips, drinking Diet Coke and generally catching up.

By their third meeting Bev felt confident that Rachel could be trusted and told her about how she had fallen in love with the lead singer of a band gigging at the pub where she worked part-time to finance herself through a personnel course at college. James was tall, dark, incredibly handsome and swept her off her feet; being involved with the band was awesome.

Despite her parents' disapproval because he did not have a proper job and was a West Indian, they got engaged after three months. Sadly, six months later James broke her heart by finishing with her because the band had accepted the opportunity to be a supporting act to a top rock band on a world tour. Distraught, she quit college, quit her part-time job and took a secretarial position at a local firm. She got in with a couple of girls and at every opportunity was out partying and drinking, which helped her forget James and lose her inhibitions, but her life was spiralling out of control. Drinking meant she did not care.

Then at a family wedding her 'knight in shining armour', Colin, rescued her from herself. A stocky man, with short, wavy blond hair and a strong jawline. She found him easy to talk to and before long they were an item. He did not sweep her off her feet but was steady, reliable and more importantly her parents approved. He adored her. Within months she had accepted his proposal and at 24 years of age became Mrs Colin Jelf. Two years later they had a daughter, Fiona, almost three years later they had a son, Justin, and life rolled on. Fiona starting at senior school suddenly made Bev realise she was in a rut and so it was she changed her job.

Moving to work at Stepwells was so exciting, there was a real buzz about the place. For the first time in years she felt truly alive and embraced all that the firm had to offer. Frank Hunter was her boss and part of her role involved organising team/client nights out. One client was particularly attentive, constantly telephoning her, laughing and flirting, which she reciprocated. On the next night out his compliments led to drinks, a dance, a mind-blowing kiss and an invite back to his place. The only thing that stopped Bev in her tracks was her son's face with a stern expression suddenly springing into her mind's eye. This brought her to her senses and instantly cooled her ardour. The client was understandably annoyed, Hunter was astonished at their public display on the dance floor and her cheeks burned with embarrassment. She also realised something was obviously lacking in her marriage.

Colin noticed a change in her and became suspicious and possessive, turning up at the office at different times as if trying to catch her out, so, although she loved working at Stepwells she decided the best thing to do was to move jobs. Unfortunately, within weeks she realised her mistake and six months later, 10th January 2000, she returned to Stepwells.

Colin was not happy about her moving back to Stepwells and it did not help that he was under pressure in his own job working at the Manchester City Employment Exchange.

However, feeling able to talk things over with Rachel finally helped diffuse the situation at home with Colin.

Rachel was more than happy to be Bev's confidant, she admired her ready sense of humour, her self-confidence and found her interesting to listen to. Likewise she opened up about her ordinary, humdrum life, in which she was happily married to Ray, who ran a small haulage firm. They were the proud parents of Isabel, who worked for the local authority and Kate, a trainee-teacher. Rachel agreed to return to full-time work when her husband's firm lost a lucrative contract and his earnings dropped dramatically overnight. After a couple of jobs, one where her fixed term contract ended and another she left for various reasons, not least that it was unsafe. Then she landed at Stepwells which, most definitely could not be accused of being humdrum.

Nick

Nick had a way with women and a reputation for being one of the lads. His devil-may-care attitude added to his allure; basically the girls wanted to be with him and the lads wanted to be like him. When it came to his personal life Nick refused to be answerable to anyone. He particularly enjoyed the chase, sometimes more than the actual conquest. In fact if a girl proved to be too easy he would quickly move on to the next one, as in the case of Faye Devlin.

It was a known fact that if a bloke bought Faye a few drinks after work he was guaranteed an invite back to her place and, never one to miss an opportunity, Nick put this to the test on the next team night out. Throughout the evening he bought Faye drinks, ordered a taxi to take her home and spent that night and the next couple of weeks at her place, enjoying an intense, purely sexual relationship. She was certainly a willing and surprisingly demanding partner. When he decided to end the relationship he assumed she had had as much fun as him and did not need an explanation and so at the next team night out, without a second thought, he turned his attention elsewhere.

Faye was absolutely devastated at how insensitive he was towards her. She felt utterly humiliated when he turned his back on her in front of everyone and started chatting to another girl. She cried for days and had a week off work, vowing she was finished with men for good.

Stepwells

Stepwells' essence was clearly work hard and play harder, as every three months there was a team night out and it was an unspoken rule that all should attend. Lucy and Rachel were eager to join in on their first team night out; they found it exciting working in the city, certainly after recent work experiences which were no play just work hard and even harder; they wanted to make up for lost time. This time The Toby Jug was the chosen venue as it had a private function room at the back. It housed a huge collection of Toby Jugs, (hence the name), of all shapes and sizes, displayed on picture rails or hanging from ceiling beams. The restaurant and function room were wood-panelled which gave it a 'Ye Olde Worlde' charm.

Rachel was disappointed because Nick failed to turn up at The Toby Jug; she was hoping that in a more relaxed atmosphere they would be able to finally break the ice by having a friendly chat. Sadly it was not to be, so she made the most of the evening by linking up with Lucy, Ben, Maggie and some of the others, joining in with their laughter as they decided which Toby Jug resembled the partners and other hierarchy of Stepwells. This game, together with the free-flowing alcohol, proved to be hysterically funny.

After about an hour most of the group moved into the function room and helped themselves to the buffet food and yet more drinks that Gillian had organised and Peter had paid for on his expenses card. Towards the end of the evening Peter asked Rachel where Nick was and, judging from the expression on his face, was annoyed by his absence.

"Hi Faye, Nick here."

Faye's heart had skipped a beat at the sound of Nick's voice but she had the presence of mind to enquire, "Nick? Nick who?"

"Nick Turner." He sounded slightly indignant that she did not recognise his voice but continued, "I was wondering what you were doing tonight and if you fancied coming out for a drink?"

"Who with?" After eight weeks without contact she was suspicious as to why he was inviting her out now.

"Me and Jonathan, a client of mine, I would like to introduce him to you."

Her suspicions were well founded and turned to fury. "So sorry but I can't, I've got to wash my hair. Try Prospect Street, that's where the prostitutes hang out!" she slammed the telephone down. *Fuck you Nick, fuck you! S*he burst in to tears.

"Ah Nick," said Gillian, the day after the Toby Jug night out. "I thought I'd just mention to you that Peter is really impressed with Rachel's work. She just sat there the other day and quietly worked her way through the 27 tapes you'd done over the weekend. He couldn't believe how fast she worked. How are you getting on with her? I've noticed you never seem to speak to each other?"

"She is a good worker but to be honest I just don't know what to say to her. I find her very aloof," complained Nick.

"No, no, you've got that wrong, she's just reserved," countered Gillian. "She's got children, ask her about them, ask her about the jobs she's had before. It's not like you to be so uncomfortable with a woman. The Turner magic on the wane is it?" she teased, before adding, "I'm sure you'll find something to talk about." The tone of her voice sounded like a command and he knew only too well she was speaking at Richardson's behest.

The following Monday, Bev and Rachel met for lunch as usual, when, amongst other things, they discussed the night out at Jugs.

"Richardson seemed annoyed that Nick had not put in an appearance," said Rachel.

"That's rather par for the course I'm afraid. Nick's inclined to be a law unto himself," Bev said. "He's one to push the boundaries, certainly not one to toe the line. Richardson is constantly trying to control him, with the aid of Madam O'Dwyer, of course, who relishes putting the pressure on! Oh the games people play. Anyway, time to go back and play some more."

Summer Intakes

During the summer of 2000 the economy was booming, Stepwells was inundated with work, particularly in the building sector, its legal mainstay, and consequently it was still taking on staff.

Jennie had passed her legal secretarial course with flying colours and had signed up with ASPECT Recruitment Agency. After the usual secretarial tests Mr Allen, the manager at ASPECT, arranged an interview at Stepwells, which Jennie sailed through.

"Good girl, I knew the interview would go well," said Zac. "Get yourself ready and we'll celebrate in style and you can tell me all about it. The black and white dress I bought you would look nice." Jennie beamed at him. "Aw Jennie babe how could they resist you? Come here and let me show you my appreciation, we've got an hour before we need to leave the apartment."

Afterwards he watched her getting ready. She had really blossomed in the two years since moving in with him. He could tell she was happy as she was always smiling, never moaned or made demands and they would often end up giggling over nothing. He was happy too. He knew they looked good together; her slender figure and ethereal quality contrasted beautifully with his finely honed 6' 2" frame, olive skin and inky black hair. She wore her natural white-blonde hair long and the minimum of makeup. She had the sweetest of natures, a childlike quality that belied her age and an innate sexiness. One of the nicest things about her was that she did not realise how attractive she was, or the effect she had on other men. He knew, he had seen other men ogling her and felt smug that she was his, a fact he pointed out to her every now and then. Not that he needed to remind her because he knew she adored him, he had done a lot for her. Yes, he was well pleased with how his life was panning out.

Jennie's start date was Monday 26th June 2000.

At 5' 7", slender, with cascading hair and cornflower blue eyes, Jennie caused quite a stir amongst the men at Stepwells, even those old enough to be her father. She seemed oblivious to their stares but Gillian was not, she had clocked Peter and Nick's jaws drop in unison and had teased them unmercifully, taking great delight in pointing out they were both old enough to be Jennie's father, a comment she knew was guaranteed to rattle Nick's cage knowing his fear of aging. Men's apish behaviour around pretty young girls never ceased to amaze her, they could be so tiresome. She considered it fortunate for the team's wellbeing that Jennie was assigned to Frank Hunter's team. She resolved to keep a close eye on young Jennie's progress.

Grace Zeglinski had been temping in the city for the past ten years. She considered Phil Allen, her recruitment agent, to be very charming and handsome; his mousy coloured hair had turned white at the sides giving him a distinguished air. She thought him to be excellent at his job as he always found work for her when she needed it. She was single and lived with her elderly mother, her father having died twelve years previously. Temping suited her very well, giving her precious freedom to do things for her mother and herself, such as doctor's appointments etc without people knowing her business. She hated people knowing her business.

For her first day at Stepwells, 26th June, she chose to wear her slate grey suit and white blouse, which complimented her grey, shoulder-length bobbed hairstyle perfectly. Although it was obvious she was in her mid-fifties she thought she looked good for her age, she had managed to keep her trim figure and was thankful her bitterness and loneliness had not left their mark on her face. She had never worked at Stepwells before but was quietly confident she would quickly get to grips with its system, because the city centre firms were all much of a muchness. *Maybe I'll meet Mr Right at this new place?* she mused.

Just as Grace had anticipated, the working practices at Stepwells were more or less the same as those of the other leading law firms she had worked for. She was assigned to work for Simon Miller, who was in his early thirties. He was moving from a London firm and was due to start at Stepwells two weeks after she had started, which suited her very well as it meant she was able to get to grips with the firm's house styles and set up her own working routine without unnecessary interference.

Grace enjoyed working at Stepwells and settled in very quickly, particularly as Gillian had taken her under her wing and was quick to praise her to Mr Richardson. She eagerly awaited Simon Miller's arrival and was pleasantly surprised at her first impression of Mr Miller, who wore dark framed rectangular spectacles remarkably like hers. His air of confidence and boyish charm quickly won her over and she thoroughly enjoyed teaching him 'the ropes', impressing him with her organisational skills gleaned over the years. Although they were supposed to be part of Richardson's team, the reality was because Simon was due to be promoted to partnership the following year, having brought his own client base with him, they were more or less left to get on with their own work, which was just perfect; she was not a team player.

Paul

Paul Brown felt as miserable as the January day was cold and wet, he was frustrated and bored with his empty life until he noticed 'him' on the underground. Group laughter had first drawn his attention, then he noticed the man whispering something to two young women who were standing on the platform which caused them to laugh hysterically. Paul edged nearer to the trio and overheard 'his' caustic comments about other people waiting for the train.

"My God would you just look at the state of that! That thing in the bright orange crop top with the love handles hanging over the top of her trousers, she looks like a huge satsuma with the peel hanging off."

The girls sniggered.

"I bet her Chinese tattoo says 'Wide load!'"

The snide comments just rolled off his tongue, all the more amusing because of his high-pitched nasal voice.

"If I was that bloke with her I'd have my eyes tested."

Oh he is funny thought Paul as he tried to suppress his own laughter. He envied his ability to make people laugh like that, it was a gift.

That was the start of Paul's obsession.

For weeks afterwards his routine was to arrive at the platform a quarter of an hour earlier than he needed to and wait for 'him' and his entourage of girls to arrive. They always congregated at the same place, standing on the platform, chatting and laughing, while waiting for the train to arrive. By getting there before them Paul was able to secure one of the few seats nearby, fortunately near enough to hear most of their conversation.

There was one hair-raising occasion when 'he' suddenly turned and looked directly at Paul, a very intense, quizzical look. His piercing grey eyes seared through Paul's pale brown eyes to somewhere deep within, a look that said 'I am aware of you, I know your game', a look he could not erase from his mind's eye, which sent a quiver of excitement coursing through his veins each time he recalled it. And he recalled it often. From then on, each morning, he bought the Sun newspaper and pretended to read it while continuing to eavesdrop, careful not to be caught observing the subject of his interest again.

He had heard one of the girls call him Hayden and thought the name suited him, it sounded very sophisticated. He was fascinated by his sharp wit and air of confidence and admired the flamboyant way he dressed, particularly his multi-coloured waistcoats, wing-tipped shoes, sometimes a dickie bow, sometimes a loud tie. He also thought it stylish that he wore different coloured rimmed spectacles to coordinate with his clothes. He envied how his clothes fitted his slender figure, so different to his own bulky frame and how he kept his hair cropped short and left a thin line of facial hair which enhanced his high cheekbones and square jawline. He thought about Hayden more and more, until his fascination became all consuming.

One morning there was no sign of Hayden or the girls. As each minute passed he felt panic rising and the tension in his throat tighten. He wiped his sweaty palms on his trousers and checked his watch for the umpteenth time while pacing backwards and forwards, scratching his head. Suddenly he felt a rush of relief as he heard Hayden's distinctive high-pitched voice coming down the escalator and his panic started to subside. He followed them on to the train and heard the slim, dark-haired girl thank Hayden for the coffee, insisting that the drinks were on her the following morning.

He was desperate to find out what Hayden did for a living, imagining him to be some fancy hotshot lawyer in a big city law firm, the kind you see in the movies verbally destroying the opposing side's case while reducing the jury to fits of laughter. He followed him and was not surprised, therefore, when he saw Hayden walk through the doors into Stepwells' foyer.

Overnight he hatched a plan, he would pretend he had found a silk cravat outside on the pavement, the sort he felt sure Hayden would have chosen. He would take it to the commissionaire saying he had seen a man drop it outside, hoping it would lead to more information about him. It worked like a dream. The commissionaire asked him what the man looked like and after he had described him the commissionaire said, "Oh that must be Hayden Husslebea, our male legal secretary."

Not only had he found out what he did but his surname too. He liked his surname, it was better than his own boring Brown.

The next morning Paul was up bright and early and feeling very optimistic, he had made some life changing decisions during the night which were all down to Hayden. Although Hayden did not know it, he had inspired him and shown him the way. He hoped one day, very soon, he would be able to tell him personally. The thought of their first conversation sent a tingle of excited anticipation down his spine. Paul had been in a rut for far too long: dead-end job at the call centre, boring appearance, boring name and boring life. *Today is the day of change* he declared to the silent shadows of his sparsely furnished room.

Before going to work he called into the ASPECT Recruitment Agency to enquire about the legal secretarial training course they were advertising on a billboard outside their premises. Jayne, a tall, willowy, doe-eyed girl with short, curly, light brown hair and a warm smile, instantly put him at his ease, poured him a coffee and chatted about the six week course they were piloting. Half an hour later he had signed up. As luck would have it his first session was the following day.

He sailed through the course; working at the call centre had its compensations because typing in the customer details, requests and complaints had helped with his touch typing and working the late shift enabled him to attend the course. He found the basic introduction to law fascinating, so much so that from his lessons he went straight to the library and began reading law books. It was in one of these books he discovered that he could apply to the local Magistrates' Court to change his name. Thus it was, by week six of his course, he was officially known as Paul Husslebea.

Jayne was astonished at how quickly he had learned everything and had no hesitation in recommending him for a legal secretarial position at Stepwells.

His start date was Monday 18th June 2001.

"Oh Hayden, you're wicked," said Sarah Price through tears of laughter as she witnessed one of the more uptight female solicitors dash to her telephone, yet again.

"That'll teach her to keep wasting time," Hayden sneered after he had replaced the receiver. "You don't know how wicked I can be sweetheart. I'll make sure she stays at her desk. I just press the stop button when she picks up the receiver but continue talking so that she doesn't get suspicious. Anyway, let's face it she's too thick to realise it's me making the silent phone calls. I used to do the same when I was on the fourth floor. You know that associate in litigation, who looks like he's got a nasty smell under his nose, Gerry somebody or other? Well one day, after my third silent phone call of the morning, he exploded just as the senior partner was walking by. I nearly choked it was so funny. It's a power thing, never fails, better than sex, sweetheart. You should try it sometime." *Oh no, she does not know how wicked I can be*, thought Hayden.

"What! Oh no! I don't like the idea of another male secretary. There's only room for me!" protested Hayden after Sarah had informed him about the new appointee.

"Hmm I didn't think you'd approve. In fact there's more, he shares your surname, he's called Paul Husslebea."

"What!!!" Hayden exploded. "Is this some kind of joke? Is this a piss-take? I'm going to personnel to find out what the hell is going on!" and he flounced off towards the lift, his face looking like thunder.

Browns

The latest team night out was at Browns, a small, exclusive, dimly-lit nightclub, with soft brown leather sofas and occasional tables dotted around the edge of the dance floor. The restaurant area was sectioned off by a trellis partition. This time Peter Richardson and Ken Grainger were treating their teams to a sit down meal. Rachel was a bit late getting there and was quite taken aback when Nick made a beeline for her, giving the impression he had been waiting for her. He put his arm around her shoulders, bought her a drink and generally made a fuss of her in front of the small group he was standing with. She was very flattered but uncharacteristically shy. Her instinct told her things were not right but again she chose to ignore things, that and the fact he had obviously had a few drinks.

Just before the meal Nick disappeared. Rachel tried to save him a seat next to her but by the time he reappeared Ben and Piers were sitting either side of her. She was really shocked when Nick dragged Piers off his seat proclaiming, "Rachel's my secretary, go and sit next to someone else's." For once he was very talkative. "I'm really pleased with your work and my clients are very impressed with how professional you are, my only concern is that I'm going to lose you to someone else."

Rachel could hardly believe her ears. *At last the ice is melting.* "Oh no Nick, I love doing your work, you've no need to worry, but we really do need to talk to one another."

"Yes I know, I know, I must find time," Nick concurred as he took a big swig of his pint of beer before being drawn into a conversation with Richardson.

As a rule Piers was good-natured and did not take offence easily. Being vertically challenged he had learned early on in life that it was better to see the humorous side of most situations, and he generally turned life's knocks into a joke, but Nick manhandling him out of his seat in front of everyone had really rattled his cage. After the meal, instead of mingling with the crowd as he normally would have, he stood at the far side of the bar nursing his pint, looking decidedly grumpy.

Faye had clocked Nick humiliating Piers and went over to him. She empathised with him, she too had been a victim of Nick's. In her case he had turned on the famous "Turner magic", wined her and dined her and then, with his sensuous 'dark chocolate' lilting Welsh accent, had charmed his way into her bed. They had enjoyed an intense, short-lived, passionate fling before he unceremoniously dumped her. Not even a "it's been nice knowing you but..." speech, he had simply turned his back on her at a work's do and focused on his next intended conquest. Although she was aware of his reputation for being a player, she had started to fall for him and still felt devastated by his callous disregard for her, flabbergasted at his barefaced cheek when a few weeks later he had tried to fix her up with one of his clients, as if she was the firm's prostitute.

"Hi Piers, are you okay?"

Piers did not say anything, he merely grunted and shrugged his shoulders.

"Nick can be rather insensitive at times, as I know only too well," under her breath she muttered, *"the bastard."* She ordered another glass of red wine and stood side-by-side with Piers, in silence, each lost in thought, sipping their drinks like a pair of automatons.

After the meal most of the team piled onto the dance floor. The band was playing a good mix of lively rock and pop songs. It was hot, noisy and a carnival atmosphere. Everyone seemed to be caught up in the excitement of the evening, pouring all their energy into dancing, abandoning themselves to the music. Although the floor was packed somehow Nick manoeuvred himself to be opposite Rachel. He reached out and slid his hand around the back of her neck, gently but firmly pulling her toward him. She felt like a startled rabbit caught in headlights, not knowing what to do next. For a long moment time stood still. All she could hear was her heart beating, waiting for his next move.

Suddenly, out of the corner of her eye, she spotted the long, gangly shape of Gerry "the Lech" Catchpole staggering over, the worse for drink. He grabbed the back of her skirt while flinging his other arm around her waist, causing her to almost topple over backwards. She was outraged and pushed him away as hard as she could; he lost his balance and fell onto the stage, landing on the female singer who stumbled on to the drums and sent the symbols crashing to the floor. In those few seconds he managed to completely demolish the band; it was absolute pandemonium, followed by the deafening silence of the bewildered crowd as they waited open-mouthed for the band to recover from its unexpected onslaught.

Christ that was a close shave, what the hell came over me? Nick questioned himself. *Thank God that drunken idiot Catchpole grabbed Rachel; he saved me from making a complete fool of myself.* He was still thinking events through when he spotted the office 'angel' and quickly made his way across the room to her.

"Hi, I'm Nick Turner." He shook her hand. "How are you enjoying working at Stepwells?" *Now she's more my type, young and fresh, just ripe for the plucking.*

After composing herself Rachel scanned the crowd; she spotted Nick in the far corner with young Jennie Enderby, her long blonde hair unmistakable in the dim lights. Rachel's emotions were in turmoil, she was unbelievably angry with Catchpole and alarmed at her strong reaction to Nick's obvious flirting with Jennie. She felt nauseous and had an overwhelming desire to run away and hide. She hastily made her way to the toilets, thankful there was none of the usual queuing associated with ladies' toilets as she was desperate for the solitude of a cubicle, allowing her the chance to bring her feelings under control. She leaned back against the locked door and closed her eyes, willing her racing heart to be still. It seemed to take an age but in reality it was probably only a minute before she was able to rewind and analyse the events of the evening. Then the awful truth dawned on her; Jennie was a threat to her job. *I really like my job but seeing the two of them together I just know Nick wants Jennie to work for him instead of me.*

Having decided the best course of action was to go home, she was just making her way to the cloakroom booth to collect her coat when Richardson emerged from the shadows.

"Hi Rachel, are you enjoying yourself?" He did not wait for her reply but carried on. "I'm really pleased with the turn out tonight. It's always a good night here, don't you agree? By the way has Nick introduced you to any of his clients yet?"

Rachel shook her head.

"No, I thought not, we'll have to remedy that." Then he was gone.

Not for the first time Rachel had the feeling that Peter had been watching her.

Jennie's head was spinning; she had had a wonderful night and was overwhelmed with all the attention she had received and the many compliments she had been paid by various people. It seemed as if everyone wanted to be her friend, she felt like a star and was still on a high when she collected her coat and went outside to meet Zac. His car was parked just around the corner as arranged, but he was not in it. She looked down the street and then turned to look back in the direction of the club when Zac's face suddenly loomed at her, making her jump. He looked frighteningly angry. She thought he was about to say something but appeared to change his mind. He unlocked the passenger door for her, walked around to the other side and climbed into the driver's seat. He did not say a word during the drive home and she instinctively kept quiet. His stern look and silence, together with the direction he came from, made her suspect he had been lurking outside the nightclub as if he did not trust her, which puzzled her; she had never given him any cause for concern, ever.

Zac felt uneasy; his instinct warned him to keep an eye on Jennie, or more importantly the men she was working with.

Next

Although he had heard the rumours about Faye being an easy lay, Piers was still surprised to find himself in her apartment the morning after the team's night out at Browns. He lay in her king-sized bed listening to her moving around the kitchen; he could hear the kettle boiling and smell sausage and bacon as they sizzled in a frying pan. He tried to recall the previous evening. He remembered them standing in silence at the far end of the bar and could remember the ceiling spinning around while he lay in bed, but try as he might he could not recall what had happened in-between. Judging from the pounding in his head he must have got well and truly hammered.

Fortunately, Nick was not in work the following day, Friday, so by the time Monday morning came around Rachel had reasoned things out in her mind and put her overreaction down to too much wine and excitement. Common sense having prevailed she had hoped the night at Browns would open up the lines of communication between her and Nick, but he was as reticent as ever and she began to feel very despondent again when a couple of weeks later, out of the blue, he said, "Rachel some of my clients would like to meet you, will you be free two weeks on Thursday? I'd like to organise a night out for you to meet them."

She was bowled over, sensing refusal was not an option.

"Yes that night will be okay, thank you. I'll look forward to it."

Rachel was on a high for the next few days and tried on everything in her wardrobe, desperate to look her best, wishing she was thinner, a lot thinner! By the time the night came around she was feeling very anxious but relieved to learn that Maggie was also included on the night out, which was just as well because for the half mile walk from the office to the club Nick raced ahead at an impossible pace, and neither she nor Maggie could keep up with him. Nick and the clients were already standing in a group, drinks in hand, when a breathless Rachel and rosy-cheeked Maggie joined them. There was a long pregnant pause before a slim, dark haired man, with a soft, refined voice, said, "Hello, I'm Jonathan, I know everyone else here so, by process of elimination, I'm assuming you must be Rachel."

They shook hands but Rachel was mortified that Nick could not even be bothered to introduce her. Her confidence plummeted as the group all stared at her. She felt a mess and just wanted the ground to open up and swallow her.

"How did your night out go?" enquired Lucy the next morning.

"Hated it," Rachel answered.

"Oh, why?" Lucy's smile turned to a look of concern.

"Nick raced ahead of me, never introduced me to his clients, ignored me for the whole evening until it was time to get into my taxi home, then he insisted on giving me the taxi fare and a great big hug and kiss on the cheek in front of everyone in thanks for going out!" She snorted in frustration and then continued, "I just don't understand his behaviour at all; he makes a big thing about organising a night out for me, treats me like shit, leaves me feeling like an awkward teenager and finishes with a big show of affection!" Rachel could not disguise her exasperation.

"Oh Rachel, I can just picture the scene. Poor you! What a prat he is!" said Lucy unable to contain her laughter.

"Your secretary was a bit of a surprise given your penchant for young, leggy blondes. How old is she?" Jonathan enquired.

"Hmm, not sure." Nick reflected. It was not the first time he'd wondered at the wisdom of asking Rachel to work for him. "She's a good worker," he continued. "Besides, Richardson suggested a more mature woman would be beneficial for my career. He said I was too easily distracted by the younger girls and needed someone who just gets on with my work."

"I see," Jonathan smirked. "No, I can't see you being distracted by that one, more likely to get your arse kicked if you step over the mark. Rather you than me mate, rather you than me," he teased then changed the subject.

Although he had had a skinful Nick felt surprisingly sober in the taxi on the way home as he mulled over the night out. Jonathan's observation about Rachel had irritated him and he kept going over their conversation in his head, so much so that the first thing he thought of upon waking the next morning was their conversation. By the end of the day, although he understood the wisdom of what Richardson had said, he realised she was not right for him and he also needed to find out how old she was.

He discreetly tried to find out Rachel's age and was surprised at how difficult it was proving to be. He had decided against asking Gillian as she had a tendency to seize on any tiny thing and blow it out of all proportion and he did not want to ask anyone in HR in case he gave them the impression he might have a problem with an older secretary. In the end he asked his sister what he should do. She asked him a few pertinent questions about Rachel and after establishing she was married with children suggested Nick take her to lunch and mention he was under pressure from his parents to settle down because they wanted grandchildren, then he could casually ask how old she was when she started a family, from which he should be able to deduce her age. His sister's suggestion was perfect, especially as Gillian had mentioned that he and Rachel hardly spoke to one another.

Zac and Jennie

Zachary Thomas Owen's childhood on the outskirts of Leeds was one of fear and misery. He was the younger of two children, Michael being the eldest by 18 months. Their father, Thomas, was a long distance lorry driver and only home for part of the week, which was fortunate for the family because he was a violent man, free with his fists and feet, who would fly off the handle for no apparent reason, usually after he had been drinking.

Their mother, Sally, bore the brunt of his outbursts, more often than not protecting the boys. Zac would lie awake at night listening to the slaps and thuds from the next room and his mother crying and pleading with his father to stop. He would hold his pillow over his head in a vain attempt to block out the sounds and feel sick with anxiety, weak and helpless because he could not defend his mother, and afraid in case his father came after him next. Although he shared a bedroom with Michael neither of them mentioned what went on, which added to Zac's sense of isolation. He hated his father and vowed one day, when he was big enough, he would teach him a lesson.

He never had that chance.

One night, when Zac was eleven, after a sustained brutal attack on his mother by his father which rendered her unconscious, on instruction from his father Michael ran to their next door neighbours to ask them to telephone for an ambulance. Zac peered into his parents' bedroom. He could not see his father but could hear him moving around the room. He saw his mother lying on the bed on her back with blood all over her face. Thinking she was dead, he ran outside and was violently sick on the front garden.

It was a dark and dank morning, dawn was breaking as he sat shivering on the granite stone garden wall in his flimsy pale blue pyjamas, afraid to return to the house, oblivious to the cold and in a state of shock. Before the ambulance arrived his father stepped out of the front door. He was unshaven, dressed in his usual dirty brown leather bomber jacket, smelling of oil, wearing stained dark blue working trousers and steel toe-capped boots and he had his black duffel bag slung across his left shoulder. Zac's body instinctively tensed but he remained as still as the stones in the wall, merely glancing sideways underneath his eyelashes as his father walked towards him. Without pausing or looking at his son he carried on walking past and up the hill. As he turned the corner, in his thick Yorkshire accent he said, "So long son," before moving out of sight.

In that moment Zac knew, deep down inside, he would never see or hear from him again and felt nothing, just numb.

The ambulance came into view just as his father disappeared, as if he had planned it that way. Mrs Johnson, their small, chubby, neighbour with curly grey hair, beckoned the boys into her house explaining her husband would prepare their breakfast while she showed the paramedics upstairs to their mother.

Royal blue striped curtains with a frilly edge, plump yellow cushions tied to the chair seats with a bow, a matching tablecloth and several ornamental ducks in comical poses scattered around the pine kitchen made the Johnsons' home cosy and inviting. A stark contrast to their own home with its shabby cupboard doors hanging off, threadbare carpets and musty smell.

Mr Johnson, a tall thin man with wispy white hair and a happy face, was preparing breakfast as his wife returned to inform them that their mother was going to be alright but would need to stay in hospital for a couple of days and they would be staying with her and Mr Johnson in the meantime. The reality was there was no one else they could stay with as their father had effectively severed all ties with any extended family many years previously.

Zac was unsure whether it was the good news or Mr Johnson's cooking, but the sausage, egg and bacon breakfast was the most delicious ever.

Life continued to be tough, even though their father never returned. Money was tight and Michael assumed the role as head of the family, following in his father's footsteps by becoming a bully, mainly to Zac. By the time Zac reached thirteen he was four inches taller than Michael and after one particular bullying incident a vicious fight ensued, culminating in Zac being knocked out. Although he had lost the battle he had actually won the war, because Michael, surprised by the ferocity of the fight, never hit him again.

When Zac was fifteen Sally allowed her boyfriend to move in to their home. Within weeks he had made it clear he did not want the boys around and started laying down the law. At sixteen Zac had had enough of the situation at home and left to work with his friend Archie Fieldhouse at his Uncle Norman's building firm in Preston, near Blackpool.

He thrived on the hard work, enjoyed lively banter with his fellow workers who laughed at his quick witted one-liners. His impressive physique from working on building sites, renting his own apartment, together with money in his pocket, gave him confidence and made him popular, definitely with the girls.

In twelve months his life had changed completely and was very good indeed.

Early memories of Jennifer Alexandra Enderby's childhood were happy, carefree, sunny days, playing in the fields surrounding the large family home in Shropshire, riding her pony Shooting Star, as Alex, her father, guided her around the field. She adored her father and loved the name he had given her pony.

One particular star spangled memory stood out from all the rest, the fairytale evening her father was pointing out the North Star, the Great Bear and other star constellations. She remembered how they became so excited when a real shooting star whizzed across the night sky and he explained it was a magic star and whenever she saw one she should make a wish. Then he quietly sang, in barely a whisper, "Catch a falling star and put it in your pocket, never let it fade away..."

She felt very close to him that night.

Happy memories would came flooding back whenever she scanned the heavens looking for a shooting star and for a few precious moments she would be transported back to the fairytale, full of wonderment, feeling the warmth and security of her father's love. Inevitably, reality would kick in, robbing her of her fleeting happiness, and she would remember he was not her father and her sisters were her half-sisters. Her mother had had an affair with a man working temporarily in the village and Jennie was the result of the encounter. She had tried to pass Jennie off as her "father's" child, even given her the middle name of Alexandra after him, but as she grew up he became increasingly suspicious, particularly as she was so fair compared to the rest of them. She remembered the terrible arguments, her mother crying hysterically and her sisters pinching her and blaming her for the trouble.

When she was eight her parents divorced and her mother moved to Blackpool with Jennie and her sisters to open a small bed and breakfast hotel. She only saw her "father" a few times after moving. His visits were very distressing for them all and invariably ended in an argument with her mother. She hated her new life. Her sisters, who continued to hold her responsible for their change of circumstances, moved into rented accommodation together as soon as they could and had hardly any contact with their mother or Jennie.

Her mother became increasingly difficult to live with. She started drinking heavily, had numerous men friends and left Jennie to do all the chores. She felt like Cinderella with her wicked witch of a mother plus the two ugly sisters. She hated the way her mother's "friends" looked at her, leering; it made her want to vomit.

It was during a particularly upsetting incident that she met Zac. Her mother had been drinking all day, shouting her orders out as usual, but when Jennie pointed out she had got to study for her exams her mother became abusive, grabbed her handbag, slammed the front door so hard the house shook and headed off to her local, a pub in the next street. Jennie could not stop the tears rolling down her face; she was desperately unhappy with her life. She had no one to turn to and felt trapped.

She was in bed when her mother returned from the pub. Usually she staggered home with one man but this time there were two. Jennie lay very still in the darkness of her tiny, cramped room, listening. She could hear muffled laughter from the lounge and then heard the door open and her mother yell, "Jennie get down here now! Do you hear me, NOW!"

Jennie was alarmed. Her mother did not usually have anything to do with her last thing at night as she was normally too busy "entertaining". She quickly dressed and went downstairs. The scene that greeted her turned her stomach. Predictably, her mother could hardly stand, her eye make-up was smudged and her clothes and hair were dishevelled as if she had been rolling about in a field. The two men with her looked almost as bad and the room reeked of beer and cigarettes. Before she had time to say anything the elder of the two men leered at her and said, "Who have we got here then? A younger version of her mother? Your mother said you were a schoolgirl, you don't look like a schoolgirl to me."

He made a move towards her and she stepped back instinctively, ready to make a run for the front door.

"Leave her alone Norman, she's young enough to be your granddaughter you dirty bugger," the younger man said.

"Here, who are you calling a dirty bugger! I've a good mind to…" As he lunged at the younger man, who had deftly moved to one side, he toppled over and landed with a thud on his chest to the loud cackling laughter of her mother.

The young man wasted no time, he could see Jennie was afraid and said, "Come on, get your coat and bag, let's have a coffee at the café on the corner while these two sort themselves out." He threw them a look of disgust as he opened the lounge door to leave. They responded with loud drunken laughter. Jennie followed orders, glad to escape the house and its degradation.

She sat at a table in the front window of the café overlooking the promenade. The tide was out but she could still make out the white top crest of the waves in the distance. She saw her sad reflection in the window and her loneliness wrapped itself around her like a heavy grey cloak.

Completely lost in her misery she jumped when the young man appeared carrying two steaming cups of hot chocolate with a huge swirl of cream on top. She forced herself to smile at him but her eyes remained full of sorrow and tugged at his heart strings.

He felt a pang of conscience when he thought about his reason for going back to the hotel with her mother and Norman, his boss. The mother had said she had a lovely daughter at home who would "look after him" while she looked after his friend. She had patted Norman's face while winking at him, giving him the impression her daughter was also a slapper, but just a younger version. It was obvious his assumption could not have been further from the truth. She was waif-like, fair-skinned with white blonde curly hair and her big baby blue eyes were full of anxiety; hers was a fragile beauty and he wanted to shield her from harm.

They sat and talked until the early hours. At first she was reluctant to say anything, she just quietly listened to him but eventually he won her over. She relaxed and poured her heart out. By the time she had finished he had made his mind up that he would do whatever it took to look after her and get her away from her vile mother.

Twin Towers

Lucy sent a high priority email to her contacts at Stepwells,

"OMG, have you seen the news? Ken Grainger's just announced that the Twin Towers in New York have both been hit by terrorist kamikaze planes! It's unbelievable!"

The recipients all replied expressing their disbelief; "I know, it's really scary!"; "WTF!"; "What's the world coming to!"; "What next?"; "It's like something out of a movie!"

Dangerous times, putting everyday life into perspective... for a while.

Relationships

Piers had been seeing Faye since getting together at Browns on the last team night out but she was becoming serious about him, pressurising him to move in with her. She was an attractive girl, slender with light brown hair in a short elfin style which framed her face perfectly and she had a great sense of humour, but he was only with her for sex. It was not without reason she was known as 'Old Fayethful'; after a few drinks sex was guaranteed. She was incredibly naïve if she seriously expected him to make a commitment when she had been with so many of his mates! The sad thing was, if the circumstances had been different and she did not have such a reputation, he might have been tempted to move in. He made a mental note to finish with her soon.

Lucy Penikett took Paul under her wing as soon as he started at Stepwells. She was fun to be around, made the work seem easy and included him in her lunchtime gatherings, for which he was most grateful. Within a month he had settled in well and felt very optimistic about his future at Stepwells. He had yet to meet Hayden but had learned he was a creature of habit and could be found in the kitchen each morning at precisely 10.45am making a cup of echinacea and raspberry tea. He resolved to get himself a box of the same brew that lunchtime. The next day he made sure he was in the kitchen at 10.40am, in time to meet Hayden.

"Hi, I'm Paul Husslebea," he extended his hand in greeting.

Hayden physically balked at the sight and ignored the gesture saying, "I'm sure you are!" flouncing back out of the kitchen, teabag swinging from his tightly clenched fist.

Paul was baffled by his reaction, he felt humiliated and hurt. He was grateful that no one else was around to witness the bizarre encounter. He sat at one of the round, glass-topped kitchen tables sipping his echinacea and raspberry tea mulling over the scenario. Suddenly he had a brainwave. *I'll find out who Hayden is pally with and get to know them, and in time I'm bound to be moving in the same social circle. Problem solved.*

"Huh, let me sit down. I've just had an encounter with The Incredible Bulk in the kitchen!" declared Hayden.

"Eh? What on earth do you mean?" enquired a bewildered Sarah.

"Who else but that excuse for a male secretary, Paul Husslebea, that's who!" snarled Hayden. "Have you seen the size of him? He might have the same surname as me but thank God he looks nothing like me. I still don't believe Husslebea is his real name, he can 'Paul' the other one. As far as I'm concerned he's more like a Fattiebee! Huh! Gross." Sarah managed to contain her laughter… just.

A few days later Paul seized his opportunity to worm his way into Hayden's circle of friends.

"Hi, I'm Paul, I've just started working as a float secretary in Frank Hunter's team," he greeted Sarah by the photocopier.

"Oh hi, I'm Sarah and I work in Ken Grainger's team." She shook his hand without hesitation. "How are you finding working at Stepwells?"

"I'm really enjoying it, it's my first job as a legal secretary and so far I've found everyone really friendly and helpful, it seems like a good firm. How long have you worked here?"

"Oh, about four years. Yes, it is a good firm to work for." She collated her photocopying and headed back to her desk calling over her shoulder, "Catch you later." He thought how nice she was and was delighted to have made contact with one of Hayden's circle. *Only a matter of time,* he thought, *only a matter of time...*

Age

It was Lucy's turn to buy Rachel a lunchtime drink.

"I'll have the steamed milk with coconut flavouring please."

"I'm flaming mad!" hissed Lucy to Rachel as she set the drinks tray on the table. "Earlier this morning I walked into Richardson's office and overheard Maggie claiming the credit for the new review system I'd set up!"

"You're joking! Did you say anything?" enquired Rachel.

"Too right I did, I said, 'Oh Peter I was going to mention MY idea to you but obviously Margaret has got in first, what d'you think of it?' You should have seen her face colour up; she turned the colour of your blouse. By the way bright red really suits you, it brings out your red highlights."

"Oh, oh thanks."

"Richardson said he thought it was worth a try and thanked me for thinking outside the box. Nobody, but nobody, steals my glory! Huh! I'll have to watch her but she'll think twice about taking advantage of me again and she knew I was annoyed because I called her Margaret, she hates being called Margaret. Anyway enough of my problems, how are things with you?"

"Oh same old, same old, still indifferent. I reckon my age is the problem, not young and sexy enough.

"Don't put yourself down," Lucy chastised. "Getting the job done should matter, not age, because age is nothing but a number. Did I tell you about my school reunion? No? Well, David Law was our year's best athlete, good looking too; in fact I had my first real kiss with him." There was a faraway look in her eyes and the hint of a smile as she obviously relived the moment. "Anyway, when he was twenty five he died of a heart attack, no warning, nothing. One minute he was laughing with his mates the next minute he was dead. I was numb with shock when I found out and it's certainly changed my outlook. Now, you madam are selling yourself short. Invite Mr Turner for a coffee one lunchtime to break the ice."

"I know, I know," Rachel agreed. "I just can't gauge him, there's a tension between us which is getting me down. I wish I'd found out more before accepting his job offer. You're right, as always, I will ask him out for a drink soon."

"You know it makes sense," Lucy said, then changed the subject. "By the way I was in the Castle yesterday lunchtime, Gillian asked me to join her and a few others. It was in celebration of Peter's birthday. It's quite nice in there. How come you weren't invited?"

"Oh I was, but declined because I was meeting my friend Linda, from Coventry. She's in Manchester for a few days on a course for her new job in the Prison Service. Gillian said she was welcome to join the party but I managed to get out of it. It's bad enough having to work with her, there's no way I'm introducing my friends to her. Anyway how did it go? Got any gossip?"

"It was hilarious. We were all sitting around in a circle waiting for food and Gillian opened by saying, 'Now come on folks who fancies who?' What kind of question is that? I told her that I thought all the blokes at Stepwells were knobs and I wouldn't touch them with a barge pole. You should have seen her face it was a picture and the rest of the girls were in hysterics. Richardson and Turner gave me filthy looks, but you know me, I always speak my mind!"

"Oh Lucy, what *are* you like!" laughed Rachel.

"Then," continued Lucy, "Maggie teased Nick about his visits to Nymphs, saying the girls were prostituting themselves while he paid for it. You could tell, by the angry expression on his face, that he was livid. Then Peter defused the situation by announcing he'd asked for Hayden Husslebea to cover while Gillian's in New York, sending more shockwaves through the group."

"Oh no, not him! I've heard he's really disruptive and a bully," groaned Rachel.

"I know. Some people flatly refuse to let him work for them. Peter seems quite pleased though, but then he would wouldn't he, because I reckon he's quite camp and I'm never wrong about people. I tell you Mystic Meg has nothing on me. By the way, keep it to yourself about Husslebea working for Peter, Gillian was at pains to point out that he hasn't been asked yet, I wouldn't want to tip him off and spoil the fun!"

The following morning Rachel went to see Lucy at her desk.

"No need for me to invite Nick for coffee, he's just asked me to lunch today, what do you reckon that's about?"

"Hopefully it's to break the ice. As you know I go out with Maggie and Ben regularly. They are encouraged to take their secretaries to lunch every now and then to keep them sweet. Enjoy yourself. Where's he taking you?"

"The Tuscany Times."

"Oh very nice, that's pricy, let me know how you get on."

Two hours later they met in the downstairs toilets.

"How did it go?" enquired Lucy.

"The beginning of the end," replied Rachel.

"What on earth do you mean?"

"Well, while we were waiting for the food, Nick asked if I thought he should get married because his parents wanted grandchildren. I said, 'If you're having to ask me, then no.' Then he asked the question he really wanted to ask, 'How old were you when you started your family?' Lucy I wish I'd had a camera; you should have seen the look on his face when I answered, he looked stunned as if I'd just punched him in the stomach. I swear he stopped breathing. I thought I was going to have to give him the kiss of life!"

Lucy clapped her hand across her mouth trying to stem her laughter, as Rachel continue, "You could virtually see the cogs turning in his head as he worked out my age because he knows how old my children are. After a long awkward silence, barely able to disguise his shock/horror, he whispered, 'How old are you then?' I whispered back, 'How old do you want me to be?' He didn't say anything and looked aghast when I said 'I'm forty two.' He remained dumbstruck so I said, 'Nick, now is the time to say, "Well you don't look your age."' Predictably he never said a word. Honestly the way he reacted anyone would think I was Methuselah! Goodness knows how old he thought I was, but I do know one thing, he would not have asked me to work for him had he known I was in my forties. And there m'dear lies the reason we're uncomfortable with each other - good old fashioned ageism."

"Oh surely not," said Lucy. "Anyway, you can't discriminate about age can you?"

"It's not against the law yet, but being considered. Trust it to happen to me! All I want is someone who appreciates my work, is that too much to ask?"

Discovering Rachel was over forty had really shocked Nick, he knew her children's ages and wrongly assumed she had had them in her early twenties, making her a few years older than him. He was not at all happy that she was twelve years older; that was too big an age gap, she would have to go.

The decision was easy, the how was the hard part, particularly as she was a reliable worker and he would have Gillian on his back. Normally, when he wanted out of a relationship he would give the other person a wide berth, be too busy to talk, be indifferent or on rare occasions resort to downright ignorance. Unfortunately, this was not a normal relationship, they had barely spoken since she had started working for him, so ignoring her was pointless, and Gillian had already accused him of being indifferent. Also there was the question of who would be a suitable replacement.

Nick was still pondering the situation when he remembered, triumphantly, that Rachel would soon be on annual leave for a week, affording him the opportunity of asking Jennie Enderby to do his work without raising suspicion. *Perfect, just perfect,* Nick smiled to himself.

Understandably Jennie did not churn out the work as quickly as Rachel and struggled with some of the more complex documents and there was the added problem that other people were giving her work too. Nevertheless, Nick was able to assess she had potential and more importantly they had laughed with each other, despite Gillian's penetrating glare whenever Jennie came near him. He quickly made up his mind that Jennie would replace Rachel. It might take a while but he would find a way; he usually got what, or who, he wanted.

Let's Be Friends

Hayden took an instant dislike to Bev Jelf. For a start she was over 35 and obviously full of herself with her designer suits, dyed hair and painted nails. The way she strutted about the office in her stilettos made him want to throw something at her. Just because she worked for one of the group leaders did not make her any better than the other secretaries and certainly not as good as him. He had heard she spent a lot of her time making personal phone calls when Hunter was out of the office. She was obviously being carried and experience told him who was doing the carrying: her young assistant, Jennie. He loathed people who took advantage. He also hated the way she had helped the Incredible Bulk settle into the firm. He decided to befriend Jennie as much for her benefit as his; she would be a useful source of information, particularly with regard to Mrs Jelf.

"Hello Sweetheart, have you got much on?" Jennie looked bewildered at Hayden's question. "I mean photocopying to do. Silly me, you must have wondered what I meant." They both laughed. "Do you mind if I jump in front of you? No not literally, it's just that I only have one page to copy." Again they laughed as Jennie stepped back to make way for Hayden to use the photocopier. *Hmm that has broken the ice nicely* thought Hayden as he made his way back to his desk.

A few days later Hayden had a meeting with June, the personnel officer responsible for managing the pool secretaries.

"Peter Richardson has asked for you to work for him, how do you feel about that?"

Hayden was taken aback by this question and it took a few seconds to process the request. "Well I get the impression he seems like a nice bloke, who's in his team?"

"Simon Miller, Nick Turner, Margaret Rollaston, Ben Tucker, Rachel Dawes, Lucy Penikett, Grace Zeglinski and Gillian O'Dwyer whose position you would be covering while she helps set up the New York office. Peter is very sociable and into team building. I'm sure you'd enjoy working for him."

"Hmm a bit of a mixed bag, but I'll have them eating out of my hand before they know it. Yes, I'm happy to be Peter's assistant." *Yes the team seems okay apart from the obligatory old women, Rachel and Grace. The clients want to see the young glamorous girls, not old hags. I ought to do a stint in personnel; I'd tell them a thing or two!*

Paul was on his way out of the building intending to buy a sandwich for lunch, when he caught sight of Sarah; she was chatting animatedly to another girl with red hair who was facing the opposite direction, but he was fairly sure it was Gillian O'Dwyer. He felt compelled to follow them. They went to Coffee Republic. He fancied a coffee too so joined the end of the queue about three people down from Sarah. He looked out of the window as he did not want to catch Sarah's eye because he planned to sit as near as he could in order to eavesdrop on their conversation. Out of the corner of his eye he could see Sarah carrying the two coffees over to the table Gillian had selected by the far wall, and was delighted that there was an empty table just in front. He sat in a chair facing away from them. He pretended to read the free daily newspaper while listening intently.

"What's Hayden like to work with?" asked Gillian.

"Well, although he's a terrible gossip and says the most derogatory things about people, I find him really funny. I'm just careful not to join in with his bitching, I wouldn't want anything I said to be misconstrued. He's a good worker too. Why do you ask?" enquired Sarah.

"You know that the firm is opening a satellite office in New York the beginning of next year don't you?"

"I had heard some talk."

"I've been asked to work there from the beginning of January, to be present at the outset helping to set everything up, recruit and train the staff into Stepwells' way of working. It's an opportunity of a lifetime and I'd be a fool not to take it. The thing is Peter has asked for Hayden to work for him in the meantime, so I just wanted to know what he was like."

"Oh how marvellous for you. Go for it, I would if I were you and hadn't got a family to think about. Don't worry about Peter, I'm sure Hayden will do a good job for him, he'll look after him."

"Hmm, I thought that. Just as long as he realises that it is still my job," added Gillian. She was feeling somewhat insecure since Peter had been so obviously excited at the prospect of Hayden working for him, she would have felt less threatened by another woman as she would know how to deal with her. She was beginning to think Peter was hoping she would not return to work for him. Well if that was the case he had another thing coming, there was no way she was going to let go of him. She had devoted the best years of her life to him and he was far too important to give up. She belonged with Peter, they were two of a kind and one day, when his children were adults, she was sure they would be together.

So Hayden is going to join Peter's team, very interesting. I've got a few weeks to make my services to Peter's team invaluable, determined Paul.

He did not have long to wait. Simon Miller's secretary, Grace, was off unexpectedly with a family problem and he was asked to step in for the last few weeks of the year.

The Knife

On the last Saturday in November Piers agreed to go shopping with Faye and was horrified to find himself inside a jewellery shop while she looked at engagement rings! He felt sick, looked sick and told her he was sick then beat a hasty retreat to his apartment, saying he would call her the next day. Realising it was time to finish their relationship he arranged to meet her after work on the Monday evening in their favourite restaurant, The Copper Kettle, a place where they regularly dined, figuring it would be busy enough to prevent a scene.

Collar turned up on his black Crombie overcoat, head bowed and shoulders hunched against the bitterly cold night and heavy rain, he quickly made his way across town. Despite the depressing reason for his journey and the battering elements, the beauty of the rain lashed buildings, shimmering pavements and flickering street lights did not escape him. Subconsciously, he slowed to a snail's pace and for a few precious moments he was back in the museum where he had first encountered and been enthralled by the paintings of Camille Pissarro, the French impressionist artist, in particular his masterpiece, 'Boulevard Montmartre at Night'. His spirits were lifted by the sparkling scene. He took a deep breath, to inhale its beauty, just as an icy raindrop slid down the back of his neck sending a shiver down his spine, jolting him back to reality and the task in hand. He sprinted the last hundred yards to the brightly lit restaurant which offered a warm welcome.

Faye had arrived before him and was seated at a table in the centre of the room, bathed in the light emitted from the central chandelier, which left the other diners in the shade. She looked radiant in his favourite red dress and his heart sank, knowing what he had in store for her. She had taken the liberty of ordering their favourite meals, sea bass and salad for her and gammon with pineapple and vegetables for him and a glass of house white wine for each of them, which was already waiting for him.

The restaurant seemed noisier than normal; the harshness of the weather seemed to accentuate the hustle and bustle of the staff and the chattering of the customers. Piers kissed her on the cheek, draped his wet coat over the back of his chair, sat down and sipped his wine while they talked about their respective days. Within minutes a friendly waitress served them their meals.

After a while Faye realised she was doing most of the talking and said, "You're unusually quiet Piers, what's up?"

Piers pushed his food around his plate. "I've got something on my mind."

"Anything I can help you with?"

"Well actually yes." He took a deep breath; he hated breaking up but knew it had to be done. "Faye, I think you're a lovely girl." He swallowed and looked down at his plate. "We've had a great time these last few weeks but I've got to be honest with you, I'm just not ready to commit to you… or anyone else for that matter," he quickly added as an afterthought. His eyes met hers pleadingly as he continued, "It's not fair to you to let you think otherwise."

She did not say a word but he noticed the nape of her neck turn red and the colour quickly rising until her whole face was alight. She looked down and dropped her fork, which clattered on the plate, but she held on to her knife, her hand shaking.

"You've used me," she hissed through gritted teeth, "just like all the others," she continued, not looking at him but pointing the knife in his direction.

"No, no, it's not like that, Faye, I genuinely like you," Piers tried to reassure her, mesmerised by the knife. "The truth is I'm not good enough for you. I can't make you happy," he rambled on, becoming more and more desperate, his eyes fixed on the knife. "You deserve someone who can offer you the whole package, marriage, kids…" his voice trailed off, sensing he had already diluted his sincerity.

Time stood still for what seemed like an eternity.

Suddenly Faye turned the knife in her hand and with a clenched fist and a raised arm she swiftly lunged across the table and plunged it into his jacket potato, making him jump back in his seat, his arms across his chest protectively. She grabbed her coat and bag and pushed her chair over while dashing from the restaurant, leaving the silver knife reflecting the light like a sparkling centrepiece.

Piers was oblivious to the stares of his fellow diners and unaware of the silence that had descended around him. All he could hear was the deafening beat of his heart and felt a bead of sweat trickle down his face and drop off the end of his chin.

He made a mental note to never, ever, finish with a woman again while she was holding a knife!

I'll Have The Fish

The Flakes were enjoying one of their regular coffee get-togethers.

"How's work gang?" Lucy asked. "'Coz I'm really busy."

"The whole firm seems under pressure," moaned Bev, except Gillian, nothing gets in the way of her "working" lunches. She was gone two and a half hours yesterday. It's just not fair."

"Does Frank know?" asked Piers, as he joined them on the soft red sofas at the far side of the café.

"Well I did mention it, but he just shrugged his shoulders and gave me a bundle of documents to paginate!"

"WOW! That must be the nearest he's ever got to a sense of humour," Piers exclaimed. They all laughed.

"I've been working ridiculous hours too," Ben sighed. "In fact, 1.30 am, the day before yesterday, I was actually roaming around Breakwells' offices trying to get a contract signed!"

"Who signed it? Wee Willie Winkie?" said Piers, to more laughter.

Rachel handed Lucy her coffee, "Well, Lucy, I did as you suggested, I asked Nick to have coffee,

"Oh good; you know it makes sense. How did you get on?"

"We didn't."

"What do you mean?"

"I waited until he was in the office on his own and said, 'As we never find time to speak to each other would you like coffee one lunchtime so we can chat about your work and clients etc?' Well his jaw dropped, his chair fell back against the wall as if I'd socked him one and although his mouth was gaping open he never said a word. Not one word."

The group burst out laughing and Rachel could not help but laugh with them.

"I know it sounds funny now but it was sooo embarrassing. I can still feel my cheeks burning. So, although it was a good idea of yours Lucy, it was actually a total waste of time. I've never had that effect on anyone in my life. He made me feel like the Bride of Wildenstein." This comparison brought fresh peals of laughter.

"Oh Rachel, what are you going to do now?" enquired Bev.

"Find myself another boss as soon as I can."

The natural lull in the conversation was broken by Piers who announced, "Well the good news is I'm footloose and fancy free just in time for Christmas," He was surprised and relieved that he had not heard from Faye for a couple of weeks.

"I take it you've finished with Old Fayethful then?" queried Lucy.

"Hey, you shouldn't call her that; she's a nice girl really just too generous for her own good."

"Never mind your own good! You're such a tart Piers," Lucy countered. "Do tell us all."

"Nothing to tell really, I just told her I wasn't good enough for her and she deserved someone who could offer her the whole package, you know, marriage, kids etc."

"Apologies, you're not a tart, Piers, you're a bullshitting tart!" Lucy declared to everyone's peals of laughter.

"Okay, okay." Piers raised his hands in a gesture of surrender to Lucy's friendly verbal assault. "Anyway, I'm relieved to say she must have got the message because I've not heard from her since."

None of them noticed the woman in a beige coat with the hood pulled up over her head, standing in the shadows of the doorway on the opposite side of the road watching Piers and the others laughing and drinking their coffees.

Frank Hunter was highly intelligent, very focused and a workaholic. Although he kept his team extremely busy he also had a close eye on everything they did. He was not one to relinquish power to his team, unlike Richardson, who he considered naïve for allowing certain people, such as Miller and Turner, far too much leeway.

"If Richardson thinks his generosity is appreciated then he's a bigger fool than I thought!" he had said to Lynda, his much loved wife and trusted confidant over dinner one night. "He'll have no sympathy from me when his clients change their allegiance, as they undoubtedly will. You mark my words."

He was also aware that keeping such a tight rein on his team ran the risk of demoralising them, so he took pains, with the occasional prompting from Lynda, to keep the right balance and regularly instructed Bev to arrange, no expenses spared, team nights out, which was something she excelled at. For the latest outing she had arranged a night at the casino, which was a great success, leaving the whole team buzzing afterwards.

Piers had thoroughly enjoyed the casino night until it came to home time. He, and everyone else, congregated outside on the neon-lit, recently rain-soaked pavement, laughing and joking while waiting for the pre-booked minibus to take them back to Stepwells, when he suddenly became uneasy, feeling someone's eyes on him. He quickly turned to look across the road directly into Faye's intense, luminous green eyes, her beige duffle coat clearly visible in the darkness of the doorway where she was lurking. She faded back into the shadows when she realised he had noticed her, which unnerved him and had a very sobering effect, leaving all his senses on high alert.

During the minibus journey back to the office he did his best to push Faye to the back of his mind but failed, and went straight home in a taxi instead of carrying on to one of his colleagues' apartments along with some of the team. Alone in his apartment he made himself a hot chocolate, settled into his comfortable, black, leather armchair, switched on the television and caught the tail end of the film 'Where Eagles Dare' starring Richard Burton and Clint Eastwood. By the end of the film he felt relaxed and sleepy and decided to call it a night. He walked into his bedroom and over to the window to close the vertical blinds, automatically glancing across the street as he did so. Immediately the hairs stood up on the back of his neck as he caught a glimpse of someone in a beige coat in the entranceway to the apartment block opposite. He momentarily closed his eyes and shook his head. When he looked again the doorway appeared empty.

He did not sleep a wink all night.

Thursday lunchtime the telephone rang and Rachel was surprised to hear Nick's voice.

"Rachel, Nick here. I'm in the pub with Simon." *That figures,* thought Rachel.

"I was thinking, that drink you suggested a while back, what about if we have lunch with Simon and his secretary Grace instead?"

Rachel's heart sank. She knew Simon was listening so felt obliged to agree with the suggestion but knew it would defeat the whole purpose of a lunchtime meeting.

"Yes that's fine." She did not attempt to disguise the deflation in her voice.

They went to The Tome, a restaurant near to the main library. It was a large square building from the outside but had a clever circular interior design. The main area had a domed ceiling with a drinks bar at the back. There were two circular areas with slightly elevated floors, one to the left and one to the right of the main entrance. The walls were lined with floor to ceiling shelving displaying ancient leather-bound books of various sizes. Two rolling ladders, in reality solid fixtures, were in place, adding to its authenticity. Free standing bookcases, also housing ancient looking books, divided the three rooms into three private areas, some with tables and chairs, some with old leather settees or armchairs and low tables, and there were also some wing-backed chairs that had been randomly placed and a couple of rocking chairs. Rachel wondered if any of the books were real but figured they must be fake as anything that old would be worth a fortune. Nevertheless, they looked genuine and if an old-fashioned library was the desired effect then it had certainly been achieved.

Somehow Gillian had managed to invite herself along which further inhibited Rachel who regarded her as a spy for Richardson. Predictably, Simon hogged the conversation but he was charming and entertaining, with amusing anecdotes of his travels. Bizarrely, the only words Rachel said to Nick were, "I'll have the fish."

Reflection and Change

The Flakes were enjoying a meal at The Toby Jug to celebrate their second year at Stepwells. They were all making good progress and admitted it had been a very interesting time.

Lucy was universally known as 'Luce', she had Ben wrapped around her little finger and had won Maggie's begrudging respect. Rachel made the most of her job despite Nick's ongoing indifference and she became close friends with Bev. Bev in turn had settled back down to working for Frank, mainly with the help of Jennie. Piers flirted with them all outrageously; they adored him. Hayden and Grace had made it clear at the outset that they did not want to become part of 'The Flakes' group and no one tried to persuade them otherwise.

"So Piers, are you still being stalked by Old Fayethful?" Bev teased.

"Unfortunately! I wish she really was in Yellowstone Park keeping watch over her namesake," lamented Piers. "Ever wondered why stalkers are such control freaks?" he continued.

"No, go on, why?" Bev said, rolling her eyes.

"Because they're too friggin' crazy to keep anyone around otherwise!" Everyone groaned. "Seriously, she's doing my head in, everywhere I go she turns up. I ignore her but I can feel her psycho eyes on me. Be a sport Luce, fix her up with someone pleeeease," Piers begged.

"I'm not sure I'd want to inflict her on anyone else. Don't worry she'll soon get bored and move on."

"I hope so, she's beginning to scare me."

New York, New York

Gillian flew to New York at the beginning of January. On the flight she reflected on her relationship with Peter and realised the last time she had felt so excited was when she had flown to Valencia, Spain for the first time to join Peter for a four day conference; it was 4th July 1991, her Independence Day. Unbelievably, that was more than a decade ago.. Since then every year they had somehow managed to sneak several weekends and at least one week together. The fact that it generally involved the rest of the group, either on a team-building exercise, long weekend skiing with clients or some other junket was a small sacrifice to make, as long as they spent their nights making love.

She considered her relationship with Peter was preferable to that of his wife's as she spent every working day with him, shared his passion for his work, knew his clients, his plans and ambitions. He included her in everything, ran ideas past her, confided in her and made her feel important. He had already lined up several weekends over the next few months when he would be joining her in New York to, amongst other things, help drive the business forward.

She loved him so much that she was willing to share him with his wife and sacrifice her chance of motherhood, confident her patience would pay off in the end and that once his children were old enough he would leave his wife and be with her forever, which would not be too long as his eldest daughter, Helen, was 19 and in her second year at university. The middle daughter, Abigail, was 17, taking A levels and the baby of the family, Emma, was 14 going on 24 and planning to go into nursing. Another four years and he could leave his wife and then she would have him all to herself.

Prevention

A few of weeks after Hayden started to work for Richardson, Paul had his first review and was pleased to receive good feedback from all of the teams he had worked for, including Richardson's. He indicated he would like to work for Richardson's team again. The weeks went by and he became very concerned that each request to work for the team was rejected.

"Lucy, have you any idea why I'm not getting work from Richardson?"

"I haven't heard anything, but the secretary who works for the head of the team is the one who decides which secretary helps out, so it's my guess that Hayden has put the block on you helping out."

"Why would he do that? I've done nothing to him."

"Who knows what goes on his mind, he can be difficult to get along with. By all accounts he's targeting Rachel and Grace at the moment. In fact Grace has been off ill with stress again, rumour has it it's because of Hayden. You're best out of that team, things are going to kick off soon, I can feel it in my water," Lucy laughed.

It's one thing for Hayden to ignore my friendly overtures but something else if he's deliberately preventing me from working. Paul was deeply hurt, confused and starting to feel threatened. He did not know how to deal with the situation.

Later that night in his apartment he mulled things over, eventually deciding he needed to find out Hayden's mobile telephone number on the principle of know your enemy. He had already followed him home so knew where he lived and found his home telephone number from the online telephone directory, which was the easy part. Getting the mobile number was going to prove more difficult, or so he thought.

Most days he passed by Sarah's desk and made a point of saying hello to her. On this particular day he found she had taken an early lunch. He could not believe his luck when he noticed she had left her mobile phone on the corner of her desk. He glanced around; no one was nearby and he could not see anyone looking in his direction, so he surreptitiously slipped it into his pocket and casually headed off to the toilets. He accessed her contacts and found the number he was looking for – Hayden's. *Yes!* He retraced his steps and returned the phone to Sarah's desk, confident he had not been seen. *Perfect, no one will ever know I have his number.* He felt very clever, very smug now that he had secretly managed to obtain Hayden's home and mobile telephone numbers. He felt so powerful. With his newly found power came an element of calmness. He decided not to telephone Hayden – instead he was going to try once more to make friends.

Teamwork

Hayden had quickly got to grips with Richardson's work and the team dynamics. While Simon seemed a nice enough chap he was too pedantic for him. Hayden liked to use his initiative; as far as he was concerned lawyers should stick to the law and leave the personal assistants to get on with their own work. He had already heard Nick was a livewire, a good looking boy too, just how he liked them, he also noted he resented Simon, Margaret (he refused to call her Maggie) was a lightweight, Benny was a mommy's boy, and Rachel and Grace were old hags who had no place in the firm let alone the team. *Lucy is the one to watch, she can give as good as she gets, she's a tough cookie, but I'll make her crumble.*

In the first few days Peter could not keep him fully occupied; he repeatedly praised him for the quality of his work and was genuinely astonished at the speed and accuracy with which he completed everything. Within the first week Hayden made up his mind he wanted to work for him on a permanent basis; Gillian was a lazy cow and Peter was better off without her. He heard rumours that they had been having an affair for years and reckoned she had done all the chasing, it usually was the women even though the men thought they were the chasers, but the fact that Peter would not leave his wife and children after so long spoke volumes to Hayden. *If I know human nature, Peter doesn't know how to get out of the relationship and for the quiet life he carries on with his double life, but when it comes to decision time I think little Ms "Lazy Cow" O'Dwyer is in for a big surprise, which could have very interesting implications,* Hayden ruminated.

In keeping with the tradition of any excuse for a team night out, Richardson suggested a casino night at a new club called Diversity that had opened in the street next to the train station. He had not been there before but had heard good reviews and thought it would be a perfect welcome to Hayden for joining the team. The whole team was up for it and agreed to congregate in The Toby Jug for drinks and then make their way to the nightclub.

Diversity was deceptively large considering that the front of the building looked only slightly larger than a double-fronted terraced house. It was a very long room divided into three sections. At the front right hand side was a bar selling alcohol, soft drinks, coffee, tea and light snacks, to the left were comfortable chocolate brown leather bucket seats with dark wooden, low level round tables. The middle section had three roulette tables and the back room was treble the size of the front and middle sections, opening up to a dance floor with a small stage in the left hand corner for the DJ and his equipment. The kaleidoscope spike lighting gave the place a soft, sensuous ambience. Everyone was in good spirits and there was lots of raucous laughter. The resident DJ played a lively mix of music and clearly a good time was had by all.

Hayden spent most of the evening observing the team and towards the end of the evening sidled up to Nick. "Hi Nick, I've been meaning to ask you for a while now, how come you haven't got a young, leggy blonde for a secretary, instead of Rachel, an old woman?. In my opinion she's just not right for you. I mean, I know they say 'there's many a good tune played on an old fiddle' but really, who'd want to fiddle with an old woman, you'd have to be desperate. Please or offend but I can't stand old women, after thirty-five they're past it. Don't you agree?"

"Since you ask …" Nick thought about confiding in Hayden, then, throwing caution to the wind, continued. "I've wanted rid of her for ages, I've ignored her, overloaded her with work, hinted about Jennie working for me, but she just ignores me. I can't even bear to look at her now. Unfortunately Richardson thinks she's an asset to the team and sees it as a test for me to get on with her! The situation is driving me nuts!"

"Oh you poor lamb. The situation is much worse than I'd imagined! Never mind m'dear, Hayden to the rescue!" he said, placing his hand on Nick's arm; he felt Nick flinch but pretended not to notice. "Leave it to me, I'll sort the old cow out and while I'm at it I'll sort out that old bat Grace as well, more like Graceless, she's definitely had her day. Have you seen that wart on her chin! Hideous or what! I'd wear a bag over my head if I were her. Don't they ever look in the mirror?" he said as he walked off with a backward glance at Nick, satisfied he had made him laugh.

Oh yes I'll sort those two witches out and enjoy every minute. There's nothing I like more than witch baiting. That reminds me, I'd better ring mommy dearest, can't have her writing me out of her will.

Witch Baiting

Hayden had enjoyed his welcome night out and on the bus journey home began thinking about witch baiting sessions aimed at Rachel and Grace; he could not wait to start goading them. He got a kick out of winding people up; he was good at it and it made him feel superior. In fact he always seemed to have someone in his malicious sights, which was good practice, it kept him on the edge which he liked.

He was remembering the evening's sequence of events as he stepped off the bus outside his Uncle Rhys' house straight into a pile of dog mess which splattered his new wingtip shoes. He was furious and got straight on to the police to complain. The police officer advised him to ring the local authority, which he did as soon as he got into work the next morning. Complaints out of the way, his thoughts turned to the previous night's conversation with Nick.

"Morning Nicholas can I pinch you for two minutes?" Nick looked mildly affronted. "Don't worry, I don't mean literally, although if you're interested…" Hayden let his words trail off knowing that Nick certainly would not be interested but secretly wishing he would be. *Oh I could show him a thing or two, women offer a different kind of pleasure; I would give the word pleasure a whole new meaning.* Nick obediently followed Hayden into a nearby quiet room.

What's he up to? Rachel pondered. *I wouldn't trust that poisonous bastard as far as I could throw him.*

"I've given some thought to your little problem," announced Hayden.

"What's that?" Nick asked, alarmed, having totally forgotten the previous night's conversation. *What on earth is he talking about?*

"You remember... getting rid of Rachel, that's what!" exclaimed Hayden.

"Oh! Oh, I see. What have you got in mind?" asked Nick feeling very uneasy.

"Rachel is uptight about her age, so I'll wind her up accordingly. As far as Graceless is concerned she's a dried up old prune, not been laid for a hundred years, either gagging for it or frigid. I'll go for frigid and wind her up too. You just sit back and enjoy the show, sweetheart. We're gonna have some fun. Now about that two minutes of pinching..." Nick willed himself not to back away. "Don't worry, only teasing." At that they returned to their desks smiling in anticipation of their impending fun. Hayden noted the look of concern on Rachel's and Grace's faces, pointedly glared at each of them in turn then laughed out loud. *Round one to me.*

Halfway through the morning Hayden started his witch baiting.

"Oh Rachel I must say I like your nails, I wish I could grow my nails that long. Don't you find it difficult to type?" His tone was full of sarcasm and his face covered with scorn. "And heaven help you if you have an emergency dash to hmm, powder your nose!" As he let out a loud guffaw he turned just in time to catch the smirk on Nick's face.

"You get used to them." Rachel was reluctant to get drawn into a conversation with Hayden; he made her feel most uncomfortable. She had heard stories about his histrionic outbursts, bitchy comments and lurid tales of homosexual encounters and preferences. While she did not have a problem with homosexuals he gave them a bad name. She thought he was loathsome.

She, and Grace, had their first silent phone call later that afternoon.

"Hi Sarah, fancy going out for a coffee this lunchtime?" Paul asked.

"Oh that would be nice, I'm actually already booked up to see Hayden and Jennie so come and join us. I'm sure neither of them would mind, the more the merrier I'd say."

"Thanks, but if you already have plans perhaps we can meet up another day instead?"

"Now don't be silly, I insist you join us."

Sarah called around to Paul's desk on her way to lunch. "Switch your machine off, it's lunchtime," she announced and Paul did as he was told. They walked around the corner to the Green Door café. Paul spotted Hayden with Jennie and before Hayden could say anything Sarah said, "Hi you guys, Paul is joining us, I said you wouldn't mind."

Hayden's face was thunderous. He carried on his conversation with Jennie totally ignoring Sarah and Paul.

Stupid cow, fancy bringing the Incredible Bulk with her. I shall have to spell it out to her.

Although Hayden had pointedly ignored him, which hurt his feelings, Paul still felt positive because he had been able to study him at close range. He noticed the way he raised his eyebrows when trying to emphasise a point and admired how manicured his nails were; if pressed he would have said he was wearing clear nail vanish.

Back at the office Hayden was still angry and made several silent phone calls to Rachel and Grace. With each call and the frustration it caused the two "old hags" his anger gradually subsided.

"Nick, did you hear the one about the woman who was so fat she could not get out of bed?" Although he was speaking to Nick he was staring at Rachel. "She kept rocking herself to sleep." Nick laughed but Rachel did not because she knew Hayden was poking fun at her. The previous day he had asked her if she had lost weight, but knowing he was being sarcastic she told him it was probably an optical illusion and carried on working.

"How can you tell if a woman is really fat and ugly?" Hayden continued. Rachel sensed he was still looking at her. "A cannibal takes one look at her and orders a salad."

"Why do men fart more than old women?" Hayden turned to sneer at Grace as he told yet another joke. "Because old women won't shut up long enough to build up pressure."

Rachel loathed working alongside him and she knew he was behind the silent phone calls.

Grace saw Rachel head off towards the kitchen and followed her. "Rachel can I have a word please?"

"Yes of course, what's up?"

"I've been receiving silent phone calls and wondered if you had too."

"Yes most days. Do you know who is making them?"

"Husslebea. I've only been getting them since he joined the team and I've heard that Emma Rushmore and Max Johnson were plagued by silent calls when he was working in their team, but no one can prove it."

"I wouldn't put anything past him, he's loathsome and a bully."

"He's like ringworm, gets under the skin and irritates. He's a fungus rotting from the inside out and I hate him!" vented Grace.

Rachel was surprised at how venomous Grace was about Hayden but could empathise with her. "Try to ignore him, it's only a few weeks until Gillian returns. I must admit though, I never thought I would be counting the days to her return!"

"If it continues I'm going to complain to personnel, it's getting me down.

"Did you watch Coronation Street last night Rachel?" Hayden tried yet again to engage her in a pointless conversation. Her instinct cried out against any involvement with him, she knew he was trying to get an angle on her.

"No, I was doing my other job last night, you know, looking after my family. I've told you before I don't have time to watch television." Rachel ended the conversation before it could begin. She caught the sneering look Hayden shot over to Nick and was sure they were in cahoots to undermine her. She could not understand Nick; although they seldom spoke to one another she always thought he appreciated her work and that had been enough to keep her there, but now she was getting bad vibes and silent phone calls.

Rachel had taken a document to the photocopying department and was surprised to hear Grace call her then sidle up to her.

"Just thought I'd let you know I've been to personnel to complain about Husslebea making silent phone calls and leaving his disgusting male bondage magazines lying open near to my desk. He makes my skin crawl." Grace looked visibly upset.

"What did they say?" enquired Rachel.

"Oh that's the best part, June in personnel said unless my fee earner backed my complaints they wouldn't get involved. Can you believe it!"

"Have you spoken to Simon?"

"Yes, but he won't help. He just said to ignore him and he'll soon get bored and that he personally wouldn't want to get involved in secretarial spats. Frankly, it's making me ill."

"Aw, Grace, no job is worth getting so upset about." *Hark who's talking,* Rachel thought before carrying on. "If I were you I'd check out job vacancies within the firm. In fact I've heard on the grapevine that Max Johnson is in need of a good secretary as his present secretary is serving her notice and going into nursing. He's very handsome and by all accounts very much the gentleman. Check it out, you have nothing to lose now that Simon has shown his true colours."

"You know I just might do as you suggest. Yes, I will."

"Good for you."

"Thanks Rachel, thanks for being a friend."

"You're welcome, just keep me posted."

"I will, and you should start looking too. Nick's attitude will get worse, you mark my words."

"I know, I know. If only I would take my own advice. No doubt it will all work out in time."

Relief

Personnel arranged Grace's interview very quickly. Max Johnson was polite and charming and seemed rather vulnerable which Grace found very endearing. When he asked why she wanted to leave Richardson's team she decided to be upfront and told him she loathed working alongside Hayden Husslebea, who was bullying and harassing her, he was also plaguing her with silent phone calls but as no one would speak with him about it she felt it was time to move on. She was also at pains to point out she was not the only one being tormented by him and had heard other teams he had worked in had similar complaints. Max, who had been writing notes, looked her straight in the eye as she made her final comment. He did not say anything but she noted the knowing look in his eyes.

Half an hour later her phone rang, it was June saying she had got the job and could she see her after lunch.

Just before her meeting Hayden had a hissy fit in front of the whole group about the lunchtime rota. He screamed across the office at Grace saying she was on the rota to cover the late shift and in a threatening tone hissed, "Don't you ever dare try to take advantage of me again. Ever!" Although he was wrong in his accusation Grace just ignored him, closed her computer down, put her office papers in order, calmly collected her personal belongings in a fold-up shopping bag and without a word or backward glance, head held high, walked out of the office and straight to personnel.

"Congratulations Grace, I'm sure you'll enjoy working for Max, he's a very pleasant chap and he's keen for you to start as soon as possible," said June. Grace's face crumpled and she burst into tears, which took both June and herself by surprise. June handed her a tissue, Grace dabbed her eyes and blew her nose before regaining her composure, then she told June about being harassed and bullied by Husslebea, Simon's betrayal and Hayden's screaming hissy fit in front of everyone, including Richardson and Miller a few minutes ago. She asked if she could move straight over to working for Max because she could not face returning to the team. June got her a cup of tea, then excused herself saying she would see what she could do. She telephoned Richardson and asked him for a quick ten minute meeting. Husslebea's face flushed deep red when Richardson whispered to him that he had been summoned to personnel and asked Hayden if he had any idea why.

June explained about Grace's situation and asked about Husslebea's behaviour and his screaming outburst. Richardson said he was sorry Grace had felt obliged to move, he agreed that Husslebea could be difficult to get along with but that maybe people needed to grow a thicker skin. Nevertheless, he conceded his latest histrionics was totally unacceptable and he would speak with him immediately. He agreed Grace could move over straight away.

To say Grace was relieved was an understatement, she had started to feel ill and feared she was heading for a breakdown again. She had suffered one ten years previously and did not want to return to that desperate situation. She quickly settled into working for Max and was delighted to discover he shared her love of poetry. Although he was young and attractive he also seemed lonely and would often chat to her. She started to think of him as the son she had never had. For the first time in years she was truly happy.

Appraisal and The Font

The annual appraisals were held earlier than usual due to the opening of the New York branch at the start of the year. Most people felt anxious when it came to the appraisals but not Nick, he was looking forward to his. He had had a brilliant twelve months, was becoming known for his quick turnaround on deals and his total billing figure for the year had surpassed all but one of his contemporaries. He was well pleased with himself and openly confident that Richardson would put him forward for next year's round of partnership promotions.

Richardson began by congratulating Nick on his billing figures. He told Nick he was impressed with the number of deals he had handled with efficiency. He read out some excellent feedback from the clients and was at pains to compliment Nick on how much progress he had made since his last appraisal. He asked him what he attributed his success and progress to.

"I took on board the comments you made in my last appraisal and I've worked really hard this year. I've also brought in two new clients, 1931 Developments Limited and Larchwood. In fact I've had a brilliant year. My best year ever," stated Nick.

"And?" prompted Richardson.

"Not only have I met all the deadlines but I've put in extra hours and on quite a few occasions I've managed to finalise matters well within the timescale. Let's face it, time is money and money is what it's all about. I'm good with the clients too and I've organised nights out which they've really enjoyed. I know I am ready for partnership and would like to discuss this with you," continued Nick.

"And?" A sharp tone had crept into Richardson's normally, gentle voice.

"Oh I know some of the junior members of the team have worked hard too and helped me out drawing up the contracts etc. All praise to them. It's a good team. But the initial instructions through to the final negotiations have been down to me and me alone."

"And?"

"Peter you keep saying 'and'," said Nick, somewhat irritated. "What are you getting at?"

"And Mrs Dawes' role in all of this?"

"Rachel!" Nick exploded, surprised to hear her name mentioned. "She's just a secretary, what's she got to do with anything?"

"That is precisely what concerns me," countered Richardson. "Does she not deserve some of the credit?" Before Nick could respond Richardson continued, "To quote John Donne, 'No man is an island, entire of itself, every man is a piece of the continent, a part of the main'. In other words she is a very good worker, who quietly churns out *your* work and regularly puts in extra hours yet doesn't even warrant a mention from you! That bothers me. The way I see it her supporting role has been part of your success, and anyone worth his salt would openly recognise that fact."

"I know she's a good worker but I don't like her, she's too old, too miserable and too boring," Nick responded angrily to Richardson's criticism.

"In that case why did you ask her to work for you?"

"Christ knows, but I don't want her anymore. Look at her behaviour on the last night out, making a fool of herself on the dance floor. She's an embarrassment!"

"Pot/kettle comes to mind," Richardson said, fighting to keep the lid on his own rising anger. "You can hardly criticise others when your own behaviour is less than exemplary. In fact Grainger is refusing to go on another team night out with you after you shouted insults about his looks! Unbelievable behaviour! Do you honestly think that's the way a partner should behave?"

Nick coloured up then snarled through gritted teeth, "Well I don't want her to work for me anymore; I can't stand the sight of her!"

Nick was clearly seething and Richardson shook his head in disbelief. There was a long tense silence before, Richardson, raising his hands palms upwards in an attempt to be conciliatory, said, "Okay, okay, I'll speak with Rachel about moving to work for someone else, because I want to keep her in the team."

They continued to discuss Nick's suitability for partnership but Richardson could tell by Nick's   agitated demeanour that he was too furious to participate properly, and consequently ended the appraisal prematurely with the advice that if Nick was serious about becoming a partner he needed to show he had settled down. His parting comment, "By the way how *is* Penny?" was met with a scowl.

Nick scooped up his papers and stormed out of the meeting room. Richardson, with his head poking out of the doorway and concern etched across his face, watched Nick stomp away. He had a sinking feeling in the pit of his stomach and an ominous sense of foreboding. He knew instinctively his attempt to keep Nick in check had not only backfired horribly but had quite probably unleashed a powerful opponent, one who would be determined to crush him. Things had gone too far and there was nothing he could do.

Rachel was alarmed at Nick's furious expression as he headed down the aisle towards his desk. Their eyes met for only a fleeting moment but long enough for the thunderbolt of his anger to have a direct hit on her, causing a physical pain which took her breath away. He marched past her to his own desk, grabbed his personal belongings and disappeared off the radar.

She sat at her desk, stunned. Clearly Nick's appraisal had gone badly and for some reason he blamed her. The anger and hatred in his eyes made her feel sick, she could not understand what had prompted such an extreme reaction towards her. A silence descended on the team as if no one dared say a word and for once even Husslebea kept his mouth shut.

Despite her emotions being all over the place Rachel managed to get through the afternoon. During the walk to the bus station and the subsequent bus journey home she mulled over the day's events, then while gazing out of the bus window at nothing in particular she caught sight of the reflection of her sad face and suddenly the floodgates opened and her suppressed tears of misery silently rolled down her face. She knew she was losing a job she loved and there was nothing she could do.

Richardson's words had quite literally made Nick see red, a red mist to be more precise. He was in a blind fury, as he stomped out of Stepwells' building and stormed down the high street. His words, 'I want to keep *her* in the team,' hit him hard and he vowed to himself that one day he would make Richardson pay for those words. *How dare he place a higher value on that fucking old cow!! How dare he want to keep her in the team instead of me!!*

He continued power walking to nowhere in particular, fighting the urge to vent his frustrations out loud. He walked on and on. He did not know how far he would go, only that he had to carry on until the rage coursing through his body subsided.

Approximately three quarters of an hour later he suddenly became aware of a chill in the air which prompted him to look around. Across the road he saw an old fashioned pub called The Font. The soft glow of its lights through its frosted glass windows threw out a warm welcome and lured him in. He had never been in there before and was confident none of Stepwells' staff would be in there either; its working-class persona would have offended their sophisticated sensitivities, which, from Nick's perspective, added to its attraction.

The entrance was through a dark wooden corner door. Nick was surprised at how stiff the door was and had to give it a hefty shove, causing him to quite literally spring into the room, slightly embarrassed as he could feel the eyes of its occupants on him momentarily. He quickly surveyed the room. There appeared to be only one room with a central, highly polished, dark wooden, square bar, with bottles lining the wall at the back and various sized glasses hanging from ceiling racks. The bar was only big enough to accommodate one person behind it. The walls had dark wooden panelling on the lower half and old fashioned floral wallpaper on the top that had seen better days and, rather disconcertingly, reminded him of his grandmother's bedroom. A continuous wooden bench, with worn but comfortable, dark-red padded seating, skirted the room to the left, accompanied by wooden tables and stools. To the right of the bar there were five small, cast iron tables and chairs and a dartboard mounted on the wall. By all accounts it was a dingy, old-fashioned pub but there was something about the ambience that compelled Nick to walk up to the bar and order a pint of beer.

While his drink was being poured he continued sizing up the place. There were about a dozen men enjoying lively banter. He surmised they were the usual crowd, mostly dropping in for a few pints after work before heading off home. One slightly rotund chap, who looked to be in his late fifties, was sitting on his own in the corner reading a newspaper. Nick sat a few seats away from him, swallowed a big mouthful of drink and nodded to his neighbour before flicking open his mobile phone cover to check for messages. There were none. He closed the lid and took another gulp of beer. His intention was to quickly finish the drink and move on; the question being 'where to?' He felt too hyped up to go back to his apartment, he did not want to speak with anyone from work until he had sorted out his own thoughts and then there was Penny. Why did he not feel able to talk his feelings through with Penny? Deep down in his soul he knew the answer… she was not Andrea. He closed his eyes in acknowledgement of his feelings and pressed his lips together, willing his thoughts to move away from Andrea. He picked up his glass intending to drain it when the chap in the corner spoke. "Quite chilly out," he said without looking in Nick's direction. He took a long sip of his pint before continuing.

"It's a recommended practice of mine to have a quiet pint and reflect on the day's events before ambling off home to 'her indoors'. I suppose you could say it's 'my time' as these women's magazines invariably bang on about. Not that I read women's magazines, you understand," he glanced over at Nick, "except to see if they've printed my problems!" He chuckled, revealing deep dimples in his rosy apple cheeks; it was an infectious chuckle which Nick subconsciously echoed.

"Seriously, I pop in here most nights on my way home, it serves to create a natural barrier between the rigours of my working life and the demands of my private life… Erm, I might have got that back to front." This time they chuckled together. "I must admit, try as I might I can't always separate the two and unfortunately these days rigorous is more wishful thinking than reality." Another laugh. "What about you, what brings you to this neck of the woods? Oh by the way the name's Jack, Jack Dipnal." He reached across and they shook hands.

"Hello, I'm Nick, Nick Turner. Why am I here? You might well ask, Jack." Nick pressed his lips hard together causing his cheeks to puff out. He was quiet for a long moment weighing up matters then decided that this Jack Dipnal, a friendly stranger, who he would probably never see again, was just the person to confide in.

"I had a surprisingly disastrous appraisal today ending up with me storming out of the meeting room and walking out of the firm. I carried on walking and walking, waiting for my temper to subside, then I saw the lights on in here. And that, Jack, is why I find myself in this neck of the woods." Nick finished his drink. As he stood up to approach the bar he asked, "Fancy another?"

"Yes, yes why not, don't mind if I do. I can always tell the wife I was held up at work, which will please her, she'll think I've earned more money to add to her shoe collection. I didn't find out 'til after the wedding that her middle name was Imelda!" He chuckled again. "Just ask Pete the barman for a pint of my usual, thanks."

Nick found Jack easy to open up to and before he knew it he was telling him everything that had gone on since he started at Stepwells, how much he liked the firm and enjoyed the work, the friends he had made with colleagues and clients and his close friendship with Andrea. That the partner of the team, had advised him to choose an older secretary, one who would just get on with his work and not prove to be a distraction. Rachel appeared to fit the bill perfectly, or so he thought. She was certainly older, definitely not a distraction and more importantly just got on with his work, but they were uncomfortable with each other. She seemed to be on her guard and made him feel uneasy, yet she was friendly with others in the team. The more Richardson pressurised him about getting on with her the more tense things became between them. He felt as if he had been set an impossible task which his disastrous appraisal had confirmed. He finished by declaring, "I am beginning to loathe the sight of her."

Jack noted two things, firstly, the twinkle in Nick's eyes as he spoke about Andrea; unless he was very much mistaken Nick was in love with her. Secondly, he needed to ditch his secretary not because she was the problem, indeed more likely a victim, but they were clearly not good for each other and in his experience matters would only get worse. To Jack's mind the real problem was the Richardson guy, he felt threatened by Nick, saw him as the 'young pretender' and was trying to restrain him. Time and time again over the years Jack had witnessed these power struggles; good guys held back for selfish reasons. Indeed, truth be told, that is why he had started his own business when he was about Nick's age. He could see a lot of Nick in his younger self.

"What's with this Rachel woman? Is something going on between her and Richardson for him to favour her over you?" Jack questioned, a puzzled look on his face.

"Oh no, oh definitely not! No, never!" Nick laughed out loud at the suggestion. "No, she's far too old and ugly."

"Hmm I see. He sounds a right arsehole." As Jack sipped his drink, a grin spread across his face, then he confided, "I had a surprisingly disastrous appraisal a few years ago too. Like you, I'd had a really good year, brought in new clients along the way and fully expected a 'pat on the back'; I was absolutely astonished to get 'a kick in the teeth' instead! I was actually compared unfavourably to someone I'd bloody well recruited! I still bristle at the memory." He shook his head before delivering the punch line. "Anyway, we had a heated exchange, I lost it and ended the appraisal prematurely by walking out. My 'Dirty Harry' style parting shot, I'm almost ashamed to admit, was, 'The trouble with assholes is everyone's got one!'"

Nick roared with laughter, he thought it was hysterically funny. Jack joined in and before long they were both rolling around on their seats holding their bellies, tears streaming down their faces. It was a brilliant release for Nick's pent up emotions and took a while for them to regain their composure. Suddenly Jack exclaimed, "Oh hell, is that the time? I really must dash off or her indoors will be throwing her precious shoes at me and making me sleep in the stables, if we had any stables that is. Never mind it's been a very pleasant 'my time' thank you. You know where to find me if you need me, I'm in here most nights, on my way home."

"I'm ready for the off too. Where are your 'stables'?" asked Nick.

Jack chuckled, "About four miles down the road. I normally hop on the bus which drops me at the bottom of my road, why?"

"In that case you're welcome to share my taxi," offered Nick.

"Don't mind if I do. Don't mind if I do," said Jack, smiling.

After speaking with Jack in The Font, Nick felt calmer, ready to think things through and plan his next move. He suddenly felt hungry and after dropping Jack off asked the taxi driver to stop at the Green Leaf Cantonese restaurant. Normally he would not entertain dining alone but the Green Leaf had cosy corners where a lone diner could be comfortable and not feel conspicuous. While waiting for his food he received a text message from Andrea, it was a joke.

"If you think life is bad… how would you like to be an egg? You only get laid once. You only get eaten once. It takes 4 minutes to get hard. 2 minutes to get soft. You share your box with 11 other guys. Worst of all, the only chick that ever sat on your face was your mother. So cheer up… your life ain't that bad!"

He smiled at the joke and the aptness of the "your life ain't that bad" comment. Right now the only person in the world he wanted to hear from was Andrea and it was as if by magic she had gotten in touch. He would have preferred to see her but her text was still enough to comfort him. Significantly, Penny did not even enter his head.

He texted back, "LOL. How are you?"

"I'm good, just off to my mum's. Et tu?"

Her instant reply conjured up a warm family feeling and made him feel achingly lonely for the comfort of loved ones… for her. The waiter bringing his food made him jump. He closed his eyes willing himself to banish all thoughts of Andrea and concentrate on his next career move. He picked at his food, his appetite having deserted him.

During his meal he mulled over his years at Stepwells, how passionate he had felt about his career, how hardworking and loyal he had been to the firm. He reflected on the number of good colleagues who, in recent years, had felt obliged to move on in order to achieve their full potential. He had had mixed feelings at the time; on the one hand he was sad to see the good guys leave but on the other hand it increased his chances of partnership, something he felt was his destiny. How naïve he had been. He should have realised as soon as Miller was appointed his chance of partnership had been blown out of the window and he was just being strung along.

With a heavy heart he realised he too would have to leave Stepwells, something he would never have contemplated before his disastrous appraisal.

Thoughts of the appraisal caused a fresh surge of anger, but this time a controlled anger, an anger which fired up an intense determination to not only prove he was good enough to be a partner but that he was the best.

The decision having been made he decided he would call into The Font next week to talk things through with his newly found friend and confidant, Jack Dipnal.

Nick did not turn in for work the next day, Friday, and no one heard from him. As far as *bastard Richardson and his fucking team* were concerned he was incommunicado for the whole of the weekend.

Lovers' Tiff

Although her time setting up the New York office was due to end in a matter of weeks Gillian flew home for a long weekend. She was really looking forward to it because she was going to spend it with Peter which was a rare treat, and she attached a great deal of significance to the fact that she was due to arrive on St Valentine's Day. Charlotte, Peter's wife, had arranged to spend a few days with her sister who was distraught over her husband suddenly leaving her for his secretary; she had had absolutely no idea about the affair. Fortunately, Charlotte was not aware of the irony of her own situation but of course Peter was, and, not for the first time, was wracked with guilt. Once more he wrestled with his conscience and again resisted the urge to confess his affair with Gillian, partly because he knew how hurt his wife would be but mainly because the reality was he wanted to end things with Gillian, he just did not know how.

Peter believed in punctuality, if anything he was generally early and considered it to be the height of bad manners to be casual about lateness, which unfortunately seemed to be more and more *de rigueur* of the day, so when there was no sign of him Gillian was rather concerned. After waiting for half an hour she rang his mobile phone, the line was engaged. It crossed her mind he had forgotten about their rendezvous but she quickly dismissed the idea, she knew how much he wanted her.

He finally arrived just over an hour later. Her mix of concern and irritation was instantly replaced by alarm when she saw Peter's face, he looked knackered, which was not a word she would normally use but in this instant no other word seemed more befitting.

"What on earth has happened to you?" she enquired.

"Why, what's the matter?" His voice was unusually sharp.

"You're late and you're never late!" Her tone matched his.

"Well I'm here now."

"With an attitude problem by the sound of you; anyone would think I was the one keeping you waiting!"

"Oh for goodness' sake woman does everything have to revolve around you? I do have a life you know!"

"I see." She felt tears of anger and hurt sting her eyes. "Perhaps you'd better get on with your life then." She opened the door for him.

"Yes perhaps I'd better," snarled Peter as he grabbed the door and slammed it behind him.

She could not believe what had just happened. They never argued. She sat in her lounge in a state of shock. She could not focus her thoughts and agitatedly started pacing around the apartment. Just over half an hour later her telephone rang.

"Hello?"

"Gilly, Gilly, I'm so sorry." It was Peter. She did not respond. "Can I come round?" There was no response. "Please," pleaded Peter.

Again Gillian hesitated before quietly saying, "Not if you're going to snap and snarl at me," her hurt feelings evident in her voice.

"No I won't, please forgive me," Peter's voice was thick with emotion.

"Very well," Gillian answered tersely. She replaced the telephone and waited once more.

The doorbell rang ten minutes later, it was Peter almost hidden by a huge bouquet of flowers. She held the door open for him and he carefully laid the wonderfully fragrant flowers on the antique telephone table in the hall, then swiftly turned and swept Gillian up in his arms, holding her close, kissing the side of her neck repeating over and over how sorry he was.

Their lovemaking had more urgency about it, almost a feeling of desperation, leaving Gillian satisfied but perplexed. Afterwards, during their tuna pasta bake meal and favourite Fitou Bin wine, she tentatively broached their earlier argument.

"I'm glad you came back," she said, tenderly reaching across the table to hold Peter's hand.

"Thanks for taking me back," he responded softly. "I don't know what came over me."

"When I said, 'what has happened to you?' I was concerned because you looked... hmm... well absolutely knackered and I was concerned about YOU, not concerned about myself."

"I know, I know. Truth is I'm really anxious about Nick's disastrous appraisal." He took another sip of wine. "I've repeatedly tried to contact him to smooth things over but he's not answering my calls." He closed his eyes and rubbed the back of his neck before continuing. "I hate confrontation or upsetting people," he said dejectedly. He sighed deeply and looked tenderly at her. Any lingering resentment on her part immediately melted away. "Unfortunately, Nick completely misconstrued my attempt to offer sound advice and guidance and the whole meeting not only blew up in my face but I fear it's started a disastrous chain of events. You see, the reason I was late getting to you was because I rang Frank Hunter to discuss my concerns. In hindsight he was probably the worst person I could have called because he blew up at me too!"

"Why? What did *he* say?" asked Gillian, worry etched across her face.

"In actual fact he screamed down the phone, 'I knew it! I fucking knew it! I warned you about that cocky bastard when you took him on. I told you he was one to watch!' He then accused me of being incredibly naïve by giving Nick so much free rein with my clients, that it was a recipe for disaster, and I'd better contact all of my clients to strengthen their allegiance 'because Turner is a taker be under no illusion.' He said he might have more of a turnover in members of his team but at least he held on to his clients, because they were the ones that counted."

He sat in silence, his right elbow on the table, propping up his forehead with his hand and ran his fingers through his hair caressing his scalp. His despondency was almost palpable. For once Gillian did not know what to say to comfort him and they sat in silence, each lost in their own thoughts.

Happy Birthday

Bev arranged her Flakes birthday lunch at Per Tutti Café, Bar and Grill. She booked the table nearest to the window, her favourite, and had the foresight to get them all to select their meals so that she could pre-book, which was just as well because the place was heaving.

"Wow Bev, have you invited all these people to help you celebrate your birthday?" Piers joked as he surveyed the room before pecking her on the cheek and sitting down next to her. She laughed then waved to Lucy, Ben and Rachel as they walked past the window on their way into the restaurant. They took it in turns to give her a peck on the cheek and wish her happy birthday. Lucy handed her a card and present from the rest of the Flakes. From the outset the group had decided on a collective gift and card for birthdays, Christmas and other celebrations.

Their meals arrived within minutes of them settling down at the table and after a general catch up Rachel surprised them all by announcing she had applied for another job.

"Why? Where? When?" Lucy bombarded her.

"Well, the "why" is twofold, I'm really fed up with Husslebea and Nick's not right with me, so when my school friend Jan said she'd like me to join her firm I jumped at the opportunity. The 'where' is Baker & Khan which is a couple of streets away, so don't worry we'll still meet up regularly, I'll make sure of that, I love you guys. The 'when' is hopefully soon after my interview which is this Friday," Rachel revealed.

"But Husslebea's days working for Richardson are numbered," said Bev, puzzled.

"I know but the damage is done, Richardson knows Husslebea is a bully yet has done nothing about it, which is tantamount to condoning bullying, so I'm going to do something instead. Besides, 'a change is as good as a rest', as the saying goes."

Career Move

Making up his mind to move on had been an incredibly hard decision for Nick and undeniably painful. He was effectively kissing his dream goodbye, a dream he had hung on to and nurtured for years. He loved working at Stepwells and remembered how euphoric he felt when he was offered a job there. The thought of moving into unchartered territory at such a crucial time in his career was daunting to say the least. Fortunately, Penny had gone away for the weekend to Dublin for her friend's hen party which allowed him the rare luxury of a weekend alone, giving him valuable time to think and plan without distractions and added pressures.

He had a brainstorming session on the Saturday morning, jotting down his thoughts under the headings: Aims; Ambitions; Clients; Team; Law Firms; and Timescale. The first major decision he reached was that he would only move to another firm for a partnership; it was pointless moving for anything less. This made building up a client base his main priority. Experience alone would be insufficient to secure the coveted partnership.He looked for his appraisal folder, which he had screwed up and shoved in his pocket when storming out of Stepwells and which, on his return from The Green Leaf, he had angrily discarded into the spare room. He needed it now because his comprehensive list of clients and their contact details were in it. He scoffed to himself when remembering how he had thought it would come in handy for his appraisal. *Some appraisal!* he thought as he retrieved it from the folder. *Who would have thought this precious list would be the bedrock of my new career in a new firm.* He held the list in both hands and gave it a smacker of a kiss in appreciation and for good luck. Never, not even for a minuscule of a moment, did it cross his mind that the precious list was actually Rachel's unique creation as his personal *aide-mémoire.*

He divided the clients into three categories: Definite – the ones he was confident would move with him; Potentials – the ones he would have to persuade; and the No Goers – the ones who would not budge. He was pleasantly surprised at the number of names in the first two lists.

Back at work, although still angry about his appraisal, Nick felt strangely empowered, the master of his own destiny, a sense of freedom that soon he would no longer need to kowtow to Richardson. He decided to play his cards close to his chest and go along with Richardson's over the top friendliness, although it was becoming increasingly irritating.

After dealing with his work as quickly as possible he concentrated on contacting his clients to arrange meetings to assess their support and future work plans in the event of him moving firms. He arranged the meetings for the following week, significantly after Friday, when he was hoping to meet with Jack in The Font and discuss his plans. Jack was the ideal confidant as the rat-race took no prisoners.

With growing excitement tinged with anxiety he made his way to The Font and was relieved to see Jack sitting in the same corner, holding the newspaper up while reading. As he ordered a drink Jack clearly heard his voice as he deftly flipped the top half of his paper over and grinned at Nick, prompting him to order another pint.

"Hello Jack, I'm glad you're a creature of habit," greeted Nick as he straddled the stool opposite his newly found friend. "I was hoping to see you tonight as I could do with your take on some plans I have in mind."

"Cheers!" Jack said as he sipped his fresh pint. "Always ready to lend an ear and my years' of experience, some good and some not so." They both grinned.

"Cheers!" Nick savoured his first mouthful of refreshing ale, mentally rehearsing his opening sentence.

"I've decided it's time to move on." He breathed deeply to allow his statement maximum impact. "After last Friday's appraisal I'm clearly wasting my precious time hoping to make partnership at Stepwells and have come to the conclusion that a smaller firm would probably be better in the long run anyway, more chance of progressing."

Jack was unresponsive, except his jolly demeanour had vanished behind his serious business face.

"I realise the first thing I need to do is check which clients would move with me. I'm pretty confident of at least seven, some I knew from university, some I've met through football and others Richardson has introduced me to. I've made arrangements to meet them all over the next couple of weeks. Once I'm confident of my clientele and their projected workload I will discreetly approach a few local, medium sized firms. What I need is someone to 'bounce' ideas off and that's where you come in. Frankly, I can't think of a better person than you. Are you with me?" Nick waited but when there was no response from Jack he continued, "I realise it's a lot to ask and I would understand it if you preferred not to be involved but…" His voice trailed off as the realisation dawned on him that he had considered everything from all angles except one crucial factor: Jack may not want to be his confidant.

Jack took another sip of his drink while he mulled over the proposition. He had taken a liking to Nick, he could empathise with him. Normally he would have had time to think things through and weigh up all the pros and cons before making a commitment, but he realised he had to make a decision now and that the success of Nick's next career move could well depend on him. A big responsibility.

"What have you in mind?" Jack finally asked, a serious tone evident in his mild Yorkshire accent.

"Basically your time, experience and trust," was the instant response. Jack's cheeky grin reappeared. "Yes I realise it's a lot to ask, especially as you are virtually a complete stranger, but I need someone I can be open and honest with. Someone outside my normal circle of friends, family and contemporaries. Someone who will not only listen to me but point out any pitfalls, give me the benefit of his experience. In short, I need you!"

Jack looked slightly stunned but remained silent as Nick shifted uncomfortably on his stool.

"Wow, that's a pretty powerful proposal!" More silence, then a grinning Jack said, "How can a boy refuse!" Jack chuckled and Nick laughed with relief as they shook hands on their unlikely allegiance.

Nick returned with a round of celebratory drinks and to Jack's wise summary: "A bend in the road is not the end of the road, unless you fail to make the turn. So when you feel you have reached the end and you cannot go one step further, when life seems to be drained of all purpose, what a wonderful opportunity to start all over again, to turn over a new page. Here's to the next page." They clinked their raised glasses and laughed out loud.

Although The Font was a cosy little pub it was obviously limited when it came to fine-tuning such a crucial step in his career, but Nick was reluctant to ask Jack back to his place because he did not want Penny asking questions, as occasionally she would insist on joining him on a firm night out and he was concerned she would inadvertently "let the cat out of the bag". As if he had read his mind Jack surprised Nick by suggesting it would be more conducive to business if he came to Jack's house where he had an office at the bottom of the garden, significantly somewhere "her indoors" never ventured. Nick readily agreed and a meeting was arranged for the following Tuesday evening.

Nick arrived a little before their 7.00pm allotted time. The door was opened by "her indoors", Mary. Nick was immediately struck by how alike she and Jack looked, they could have passed for brother and sister. He was also aware of the wonderful smell of baking.

"Hello, Jack's wife I presume, I'm Nick Turner, I have a meeting with Jack. I'm afraid I'm a little early," Nick smiled.

"Oh hello, Jack told me he was expecting you, do come in." She opened the door further and Nick stepped into the spacious hall to be met by a grinning Jack coming down the stairs.

"Hello Nick, come on in, come on in. Have you eaten?" Before Nick had chance to answer Jack ushered him into the kitchen. He swiftly pulled out a chair at the large farmhouse table and said, "Even if you have, I'm sure you'll find room for some of Mary's homemade steak and ale pie. Sit yourself down." Although he had eaten already the smell of the food was so tempting Nick did not have the willpower or desire to refuse a serving.

The kitchen had light oak units, was bright and airy with French windows opening onto a patio and large garden with a bowling-green lawn edged with pretty flowers, shrubs and trees. Through a wooden archway covered in small white flowers Nick could see "The Shed" at the bottom of the garden, exactly how Jack had described it. They quickly devoured the delicious food and headed off for the first of many meetings in "The Shed".

A better description was The Log Cabin. It was nestled at the bottom of the garden surrounded by decking, edged with low level, picket wooden fencing. There was a weathered old rocking chair to the right of the entrance door and two large fluted silver tubs, each inhabited by a bluey-green spiky plant, positioned in both corners outside the front of the cabin. Nick followed Jack into his office and was pleasantly surprised by the deceptively large interior, smelling faintly of beeswax. And what an amazing bolthole it was, a very busy place but with a sense of order; Nick's eyes were everywhere in fascinated curiosity.

To the right were two battered brown leather easy chairs, behind which was a desk with drawers, computer and chair. At the back to the left was a small kitchen with two stools tucked underneath the overhang of the breakfast bar which sectioned off the room neatly. There was a door in the front left corner, which Nick guessed led to a washroom and toilet.

By far the main attraction for Nick was the floor to ceiling shelving adorning the windowless back wall. Like a moth to a flame he immediately made his way over there and began examining the many books, CDs, DVDs, cassette tapes, old records and an old cube television and radio, similar to one his dad used to own which played records and cassettes and had built-in speakers. There was also a mini compact disc player with two mini speakers, several carved wooden boxes and figures including a beautiful wooden carving of a man fishing. Numerous model airplanes, toy cars in boxes with clear panels and a collection of tools and other tranklements were strategically placed. The large window to the left of the entrance door displayed an intricate model of the Cutty Sark, the famous tea clipper built in the 1800s now moored at Greenwich. Nick had seen the real one during a recent weekend trip with Penny and her parents. His favourite discovery was a painting of an African sunset with the unmistakable black silhouette of a huge, forward facing, elephant against the backdrop of the setting sun; it was utterly mesmerising and captured the essence and spirit of the African savannah. He was like a child in a candy store.

Jack stood back, smiling, watching his new found friend explore his belongings and felt a sense of pride and joy in introducing someone to his 'man cave' who so obviously appreciated the things he had spent a lifetime accumulating and cherishing. Yes, these four walls were a testimony to Jack's many interests and 'magpie' tendencies.

"Sit yourself down and I'll make us a coffee," said Jack pointing to the leather seats while heading off to the studio kitchen. Nick did as he was told and was astonished to see that even the low level coffee table housed a collection of old foreign coins, foreign banknotes and medals, visible through an inlaid thick glass top. Nick was beginning to realise there was a hell of a lot more to Jack Dipnal than he realised.

Jack settled in the other seat and handed Nick his coffee. They sipped their drinks in unison, each deep in thought mulling over how to begin their meeting. The comfortable silence was broken by the cuckoo in the carved wooden clock which was hung on the front wall. Nick looked up in surprise and turning to a grinning Jack enquired, "Did that say what I thought it said?"

Jack burst out laughing. "Yes I'm afraid his 'cuckoo' does sound remarkably like 'fuck you'. Yet another reason to deter visitors, crucially cold callers!" They dissolved into a fit of giggles.

Once they had composed themselves, Jack started their meeting. "Would you class yourself as ambitious?"

"Yes, yes I would," Nick responded.

"To what extent?"

"I want to be an equity partner in one of the top 100 UK law firms. In fact I don't care how long it takes but I won't stop pushing until I get there. Frankly, I'm not prepared to settle for anything less, I know it is my destiny."

"What's your ideal firm?" enquired Jack.

"I remember my old law lecturer, Mr Bissell, saying how the law affected every aspect of our lives from the cradle to the coffin, before and beyond and everything in-between. Over the years I've come to appreciate the wisdom of his words. Nick ran his left hand through his thick, dark mop of hair, as he tended to do when thinking and continued, "A firm with a strong real estate arm is fine when the economy is booming but not in a recession so I'd also like to belong to a firm that offers a range of services.

"I can bear witness to that," interjected Jack. "I remember a recession in my younger days, one in which my father lost his job. He worked for a whisky distillery company, Coates, which, for a number of reasons, went bump in the 1970s, a recession being one of the reasons." Jack's voice softened and looking down into his cup he continued, "My dad never came to terms with how his life turned upside down overnight." He became quiet for a long moment, clearly back in time, before continuing. "Anyway, after school I joined a building company and five years later one of the other lads, Kenny Taylor, and I started our own business. We did really well for about fifteen years, but my dad kept urging me to learn another profession as a fall back, something he wished he'd have done, so I went to night school studying design and planning which was just as well because a couple of years later a recession hit and Kenny and I had to wind up the business.   Kenny went off to Spain to live, settled down with a pretty señorita and they run a restaurant just south of Barcelona. I was lucky enough to become an architect for the council, which is generally more recession proof than private, and has strong union representation. So you could say I've witnessed and felt the effect of the "boom and bust" economic cycle. That's my first-hand experience. Have you got a firm in mind?"

"I've got contacts in a few firms that I'm going to explore, they're people who used to work at Stepwells and have done well. Hopefully, one of them will give me an opportunity to make an equally successful transition," Nick explained.

"When are you seeing them?"

"During the course of the next few weeks, significantly after I've spoken to all of the clients I want to take with me. Oh incidentally, I've discovered another lawyer, David Evans, is moving to Macefields a month before me, he's in a different team at Stepwells but we've worked on a couple of developments and I'm impressed with his *modus operandi,* fast and efficient. A good man who has suggested we consider joining forces at Macefields, which is certainly worthy of some serious thought. Yes, it's going to be a very, very, busy time for me. But I'm ready for it. Oh yes, it's time."

"Right, now we've established you're definitely going for it, let's discuss the clients you wish to take with you and the work they can put your way please."

Their conversation continued until just after midnight.

Stirring

Traditionally Thursday was the night for the city office workers to have team building or general social nights out and Piers readily joined in. His routine was to go straight from work and by 6.30pm he would usually be found holding court in The Toby Jug surrounded by a group of young women. After a few drinks and plenty of laughs he would ask one, or two, to join him for a bite to eat in one of the many city centre restaurants. He rarely dined alone or, for that matter, spent Thursday night alone.

On this particular night a couple of 'new' girls had joined his little circle and he was at his gregarious best. He bought them each a drink, they laughed at his jokes and he was not surprised when they accepted his invitation for a curry at The China Cottage, strategically near to his apartment. He waited while they 'powdered their noses' and the rest of the group drifted off. He could not see the toilets from where he was standing or, more significantly, that Faye had followed the girls in.

Faye combed her hair and caught their eye in the mirror as they reapplied their lipstick.

"I couldn't help but notice you laughing with the short, curly haired chap." She took a deep breath before continuing, "I'm embarrassed to admit this to two complete strangers but I had a fling with him recently and have only just got the all clear. I thought you'd better know," she added as she quickly left the toilets, leaving them wide-eyed and open-mouthed. She returned to her seat in the dimly lit corner and waited. It was not long before she saw them sneaking out of the back entrance to the pub. *Yes! That has put paid to your plans for tonight Mr Smallman.* She felt jubilant as she too left by the back entrance and made her way to the bus terminal.

There must be quite a queue in the ladies, Piers thought as he checked his watch and calculated they had been gone for at least ten minutes. After waiting another ten minutes he reluctantly accepted his potential dates had disappeared and, somewhat bewildered, headed back to his apartment alone. *Hmm, I wonder what happened to those two, I could have sworn they were up for it.*

Not wanting to be too obvious Faye waited four weeks before going to The Toby Jug again. She was irritated, but not surprised, to see Piers holding court in his usual place surrounded by a gaggle of giggling girls. It was time to thwart his plans once more. She was wearing a long dark brown wig, black rimmed round glasses and was delighted with the results of her disguise. *Piers definitely won't recognise me.* She had settled down in the dimly lit corner and was waiting patiently when Gerry Catchpole staggered over to her. *Oh no, not that drunken prat.* She felt frustrated and her jaw tightened.

"Hello, don't I know you?" said the grinning Catchpole.

"No I don't think so." Faye's tone was sharp.

"Your voice sounds familiar, are you sure we've never met?"

Oh we've met alright you drunken idiot, you dumped me last February.

"No we have never met, I don't forget a face, especially one like yours." She could not disguise the contempt she felt for him.

"What do you mean 'one like yours'?" he demanded as he pulled a chair out from under the table and sat down heavily in front of her.

"Kindly leave me alone, I am waiting for someone," she snapped as she craned her neck to look past him and noticed Piers' group leaving the pub. She was just about to follow them when she spotted a petite blonde who had been in the group heading towards her. *Yes, that's the 'Chosen One' for tonight,* her instinct told her. She followed her into the ladies' toilets as, annoyingly, Catchpole shouted after her, "I'll get you a refill, don't be too long love."

The 'Chosen One' was ages in the cubicle; in fact she was in there so long Faye was beginning to wonder whether she actually was 'the one'. At last she emerged. Faye adopted the same approach as before and informed her she had just been given the all clear, but this time the girl rushed out before her shouting, "You dirty bitch!" at the top of her voice, attracting the attention of four women who had just walked in. They stopped dead and stared at Faye. Two of them were in the doorway which hindered Faye's intended quick exit as she jostled with them for space. She returned to the table at the same time as Catchpole with the drinks and within seconds Piers and the girl appeared at the far end of the bar.

"That's her, that's the dirty bitch!" the girl shouted, pointing at Faye.

The next few moments seemed to be in slow motion but somehow Faye managed to grab her coat and escape through the pub's back door, leaving behind Piers' baffled look, the girl's angry glare and Catchpole's gaping mouth.

"Who the hell was that dirty bitch with you Catchpole?" snarled Piers as he stood over him, his arms by his side, fists clenched.

"Dunno mate," Catchpole said apologetically, immediately sobering up. "Never seen her in my life before, honest. She's nothing to do with me, I swear to God."

"Hmmm," growled Piers as he turned his back on Catchpole and left by the front entrance, petite blonde in tow.

Foam

Bev was already perched on 'her' stool waiting for her friend to join her for their weekly 'chips and Coke' catch-up. Rachel practically sprinted over to her.

"I must tell you what's just happened," said Rachel, red-faced and breathless with excitement. "That gangly prat Catchpole was walking down the main corridor towards me, and, like the idiot he is, he leaped to the side in an exaggerated way to create the maximum passing space between us." She struggled to control the laughter bubbling up, then in a higher pitched voice continued, "Unfortunately, he accidentally leaped on to the fire extinguisher! When I looked back in his direction he was lying on his back, all arms and legs, doing the dying fly, wrestling with the extinguisher which was spraying foam up the walls, on the ceiling, carpets, everywhere!" Her voice thick with tears, she just managed to finish her story before roaring with laughter. Bev burst out laughing at the image created in her mind's eye. "It was the funniest thing ever, particularly when the senior partner came out of his office to see what the commotion was all about! The look on his face was priceless! I wish I'd got my camera. I haven't stopped laughing since." They sat rocking backwards and forwards, both beside themselves in hysterics.

Laughter and Tears

The Land Registration System had not been reviewed for over seventy years. A major overhaul was long overdue and change was inevitable, namely, all land in England and Wales was to be registered at the appropriate Land Registry offices. Advancement in technology made this a fairly straightforward transaction and Stepwells was keen to implement the practice guides as soon as possible, therefore it arranged for all property staff, in batches of twelve, to attend the Land Registry offices for training.

Piers was in the third batch of staff and was delighted to find the angelic Jennie Enderby there too. Although they were in the same practice group he had not had chance to get to know her because she kept herself very much to herself. In fact the only time he could recall seeing her socialising was at Browns nightclub the previous September, when he had hooked up with Faye. *Huh, Faye.* The thought of her depressed him.

A minibus had been laid on for the staff and Piers made sure he was seated next to Jennie. He introduced himself, enquired how long she had been working at Stepwells and when she had replied eighteen months he teased her by saying in his best Sean Connery voice, "Good grief Miss Moneypenny, where have you been hiding all that time? In the lift? They both laughed. Laughing was pretty much what they did for the rest of the afternoon.

Whenever Piers was in a training environment he invariably became the classroom clown and the Land Registry training session was no different. The trainer mentioned ownership of property and Piers was at his wisecracking best. Imitating Groucho Marx, using his black marker pen as his cigar prop he began joking, "Beware as stated in the film 'Fight Club', the things you own end up owning you. It's only after you lose everything that you're free to do anything. Bricks and mortar are a heavy chain around your neck. You have been warned!"

True to form his jokes made the training session more enjoyable. When the trainer got on to joint ownership Piers interrupted, "My girlfriend visited my apartment and asked…" in a high-pitched voice he said, "'Can I have a drink?' I said, 'Feel free, my apartment is yours.' Then she ordered me to get off her property!"

The rest of the session was interspersed with Piers' humorous take on things. He may not have been so jovial had he noticed Faye glaring from a window on the second floor of Stepwells as he boarded the minibus for the Land Registry training visit.

On the bus home Jennie reflected on the day. She smiled as she recalled Piers' joke about his girlfriend, and then felt sad because it made her think of Zac. She could not remember the last time they had laughed together, yet in the beginning they had giggled all the time. She could pinpoint the change in him to her first, and last, team night out at Browns when Zac had picked her up as agreed. He had clearly been spying on her. His dark mood then had frightened her so much that she had avoided socialising at work ever since, and did not even go to the office Christmas party for fear of upsetting him. It felt like she was permanently walking on eggshells around him. She wished he would not smoke what he referred to as his 'recreational drug' because his black moods were becoming more frequent and she suspected he took other drugs, although he had never done so in front of her. She was glad he had not pressurised her to take any more substances since the first and last time she had smoked a 'wacky backy' cigarette and had been so violently ill afterwards it had scared her, and him.

Jennie would not find out until she got home that evening that Zac had called at Stepwells unexpectedly to treat her to lunch. He was not at all pleased to find she was out of town on a course. *What else has she been keeping from me?* The more he wondered the angrier he became.

Preoccupied about what to cook for their evening meal, as she opened the kitchen door of their apartment Jennie physically jumped when she saw Zac sitting there, elbows on the table, hands joined in a fist with his chin resting on top. He was completely still, there was an ominous silence and her body shuddered. He slowly raised his eyes to meet hers and she felt the full fury of his glare. She did not know what she had done wrong, only that it must have been bad and the knot of fear tightened in her stomach.

"I went to your office today to surprise you and treat you to lunch," he said, his voice harsh. "Unfortunately, I had the surprise; you weren't there. Apparently you'd gone off on some training session in Hull." She felt herself wither under his penetrating stare. "Just when were you going to share this piece of information? Eh? Think you're being clever do you?" he yelled at her, throwing the table aside as he jumped up and grabbed her by the throat, pushing her up against the kitchen door. "What else are you keeping from me, ay?" he demanded as he tightened his grip. "Don't play games with me madam!" he warned. "Don't even think about it!" he snarled. After what seemed like an eternity he released his grip and wrenched the kitchen door open. She heard the front door slam and sank to the floor behind the door, stunned.

The tears would come later.

Piers was still buzzing from the day when the phone rang in his apartment as he was getting changed to join Nick for a few drinks, at the casino and probably Nymphs, knowing Nick.

"Hello, Piers speaking, what can I do you for?"

Faye's heart lurched at the sound of Piers' warm, sweet-toned, familiar voice. It had been two months since he was hers, but instead of dying down her longing for him seemed to increase with the passage of time; she missed him so much.

"It's me. Faye."

Piers' heart sank. *Oh no not Old Fayethful, not tonight.* "Oh hello," he said, the tone in his voice suddenly flat.

"I was wondering if you fancied coming out for a drink tonight?"

"Sorry but I've already got plans for tonight."

"What about tomorrow night then?" Faye persisted.

"Are you in some sort of trouble?"

"No, I just wanted to talk to you."

"What about?"

"I'll tell you when I see you."

"Can't you tell me over the phone?"

"No!" she snapped.

"I'm sorry but I don't think it would be a good idea for us to see each other again," said Piers, sounding sharper than he intended.

"Too busy seeing your little slut are you?" sneered Faye.

"I'm not seeing anyone," protested Piers.

"Don't lie to me!" Faye shouted. "I saw the two of you on the minibus laughing like stupid kids. You make me sick!" she screamed as she slammed the phone down.

Later that evening in The Toby Jug, Piers told Nick about the telephone call from Faye. "Well, well, well, sounds like you've got your very own bunny boiler, old boy," joked Nick, slapping Piers on the shoulder. "Just ignore the silly bitch; she'll soon latch on to someone else. Come on, drink up, we're wasting valuable gambling time, I feel lucky." With a gnawing sense of foreboding Piers did as he was told, drank up and followed Nick outside as he hailed a taxi to the casino.

Nick was indeed lucky, although he lost heavily to begin with he ended the night £200 up. Meanwhile, Piers was happy to have managed to break even. Upon leaving the casino Piers felt uneasy; it took him back to the recent team night out when he had seen Faye lurking in the shadows. He quickly scanned the doorways and area around him and felt relieved not to see her, then chastised himself for letting her get to him in that way. If he had raised his eyes to the third floor of the building opposite he would have seen the ghostly silhouette of a woman staring down from the unlit window of the stairwell.

Zac did not come home all night and Jennie had not slept. She stared out of the fourth floor apartment window at the miserable looking grey sky, with its heavy, slow moving, rain laden clouds. She was grateful it was such a cold drab day because she could wear a polo neck jumper to cover the bruises on her neck without looking out of place and attracting comments from the likes of the ever-watchful Gillian who was actually due back in the office that morning from her stint in New York, having flown back on Saturday. It took an age to get ready for work that morning, she had no energy through worrying all night and she was petrified of seeing Zac again.

The team had mixed feeling about Gillian's return, some preferring Hayden because he was a more efficient worker and at times highly amusing, while others, particularly Rachel and Grace, viewed Gillian as the lesser of two evils. Nevertheless, the general consensus of opinion was that Gillian was a spoilt madam not to be trusted, who had Richardson where she wanted him. She was obviously bright and intelligent, enjoyed playing mind games with members of the team and used her status as Richardson's personal assistant to get out of doing her fair share of the work. Her long 'working' lunch breaks were the subject of much speculation and annoyance, particularly with Bev who told all who cared to listen that she had been having an affair with Richardson for a number of years, but he refused to leave his wife because his children were too young.

On the face of it Gillian appeared to accept the status quo and was embarrassingly nice to his wife on the rare occasions she visited the office. At other times she was very petulant with him, picking an argument over the slightest thing. She had even been known to have what could only be described as a temper tantrum and rush out of the office. Shortly afterwards Richardson would also disappear leaving the team in no doubt that he was going to meet her and attempt to placate her. She was known as his albatross.

Much to Hayden's chagrin Richardson asked him to organise a team night out as a 'welcome back' to Gillian and a 'thank you' to him for his hard work. With great difficulty Hayden managed to keep the lid on his hurt feelings and disgust at being 'lumped together' with Madam and duly organised the get-together.

Midway through morning, out of the blue, Gillian asked, "Are you coming to Mr Gee's tonight Rachel?" "I suppose so. Are you?"

"But of course, I wouldn't miss it. See you there then."

These team nights out were becoming a bind to Rachel, she would rather be at home with her husband and kids but felt obliged to go to these boring dos where she had to make small talk with strangers. Her sixth sense warned her that her every word was being recorded and her every move monitored, particularly by Gillian, something she was also aware of in the office. The walls definitely had ears at Stepwells, in fact Lucy had been told that covert cameras had been installed throughout the building but obviously did not know where.

Nick had just completed negotiations on a difficult deal and was miffed he had not managed to get the price per square metre he had hoped for. With adrenalin still coursing through his veins he went for a walk outside. He had just stopped for a cigarette by the bus station, a couple of hundred yards from Stepwells' offices, when he spotted Jennie Enderby by the last bus shelter looking unbearably sad. He caught up with her and asked if she was okay. She turned towards him and her big blue eyes welled up with tears. Hand on her elbow he quickly steered her into the coffee house on the corner without giving her a chance to refuse. He seldom had the opportunity to mix with Jennie, partly because she did not attend the team nights out but mainly because Gillian's beady eyes restricted him during office hours.

He secured a table for them at the back of the room, tucked away around the corner. He handed her a tissue and fetched two coffees from the counter. She had more or less composed herself by the time he returned with the drinks. Between sips she told him she had had a row with her boyfriend the night before about not telling him she had gone on a Land Registry course, and unfortunately he had turned up to surprise her for lunch (instinct was warning her not to mention his violence or her fear).

Nick was very sympathetic, telling her about some of the furious rows he and his girlfriend Penny had had and he managed to bring a smile to her lips, if not to her eyes. He reassured her all couples argued, Zac was very lucky to have her for his girlfriend and if he knew anything about blokes, Zac would probably have a big bouquet of flowers waiting for her at home. They finished their coffees and within minutes Jennie's bus pulled up. Nick waited while she climbed on board then returned to the office to clear his work away so he could go to Mr Gee's afterwards. He was pleased he had had chance to speak with Jennie, she seemed so small and vulnerable. He felt protective towards her and hoped he had judged her boyfriend correctly.

Jennie had not noticed Zac watching from the opposite side of the road but he had noticed her and the *arrogant bastard* with her.

Mr Gee's place was a short walk from Stepwells. It was a converted warehouse with light oak coloured wooden floors and matching wooden wall panels. Dark brown tables, with comfortable round backed leather chairs, skirted the central dance floor and there was a bar at the back of the room. To the left of the bar was an archway leading to a more secluded area housing big soft caramel coloured suede sofas which were randomly arranged, the kind you sank into and fought to get out of. The lights were dim and soft music was playing in the background lending to an air of intimacy. Richardson and two of the other partners put their expense cards behind the bar and the drinks flowed.

Richardson and Gillian sat at a table to the far right of the bar with Lucy, Rachel, Ben, Maggie and Sarah. As usual Nick was late getting there. Gillian was holding court discussing the benefits of the psychometric tests she had carried out on various people in the firm. She explained, "Psychometrics is a series of questionnaires and tests relating to educational and psychological measurement of a person's abilities, attitudes and personality traits. There are three main categories: driver, expressive and amenable, although sometimes the categories do overlap. For instance," she said with a smug look on her face, "I have fallen into the expressive amenable category with Peter." She grinned while looking askance at Richardson.

Lucy whispered to Rachel, "That's not all she's fallen into with Richardson from what I've heard." Rachel stifled a giggle.

Gillian continued, "Nick and Max are drivers whereas Piers is an expressive and Grace and Jennie are amenables."

"What about Faye?" asked Lucy.

"Faye? Why, everyone knows Faye is a drunk," Gillian announced loudly followed by a false, high-pitched laugh as if she had passed an incredibly witty comment.

Lucy and Rachel had not been tested but Gillian guessed that Lucy was an expressive and Rachel an amenable. She said amenable as if it was a nasty taste in her mouth. Rachel had not actively joined in with the discussion because she had already had these tests at college and they had proved conclusively that she was a driver, but instinct warned her to keep quiet about it; the less Ms O'Dwyer knew about her the better.

Richardson went to order another round of drinks and Bev appeared from nowhere and flopped down in his seat while Sarah dragged another chair to the table. Gillian was just explaining the psychometric tests to Bev when Colin, Bev's husband, appeared and judging from the look on her face she was not expecting him, and from his expression she no doubt would rather he had not turned up; he was clearly annoyed and everyone soon found out why.

"Here's your Bacardi and Coke," he snapped, "AND, for the record, I've paid your card off AND retrieved it from behind the bar!"

Bev's chin sunk into her chest, her shoulders hunched up and she did not say a word.

"Oops," Lucy whispered to Rachel. "Who does she think she is leaving her card behind the bar? A partner?"

Nick followed Richardson back from the bar; both were carrying a tray of drinks.

"Oh, hi Nick, we were just wondering where you were," said Gillian. Before he had chance to speak she continued, "We thought perhaps you'd gone to Nymphs, we've heard you go so often you have your own table there!" She scanned the others to see if they were laughing at him; she was clearly out to rattle his cage but for once his face gave nothing away.

"I had some business to attend to," was all he proffered. *The bitch, it would really get her goat if she knew who I had just had a drink with. Jennie is everything she is not: younger, slimmer and doesn't think she's God's gift to men, unlike madam. That's one pussy I wouldn't touch with a barge pole! Poor Richardson, she really is his albatross.*

Rape and Remorse

Her hand shaking, Jennie pushed the key into the apartment front door lock and stood listening intently for any sound; all her senses were on high alert. The silence was deafening. She took a deep breath and entered the kitchen. Relieved to find Zac not there, she started preparing their evening meal.

Four hours later she sat bolt upright in her armchair alarmed at hearing a key turn in the lock. Jittery when Zac shouted her name, she opened the lounge door to find him the worse for drink. She helped him to the bedroom and he slumped down on the edge of the bed, head bowed. He looked like a giant puppet, all loose limbed. As Jennie undressed him he kept repeating "my Jennie, my Jennie," over and over. He flopped back on the bed and by the time she had made him comfortable he was snoring for England. For the first time in two days she began to relax and, overwhelmed with fatigue, climbed into bed beside him.

Zac liked a cooked breakfast so the next morning, while he was sleeping, Jennie, in the fluffy red polka dot housecoat he had bought for her birthday, decided to prepare one. She was frying the bacon and sausage when she suddenly sensed his presence behind her. As she turned to smile at him she felt a hard blow to the side of her head which sent her flying into the kitchen table. The frying pan fell noisily to the floor, the bacon and sausages flew in different directions across the room and hot fat splashed her right leg and the right side of her face. She tried to straighten up but Zac pulled her hair, yanking her head back sharply. He grabbed her throat with his right hand and squeezed hard, then turned her to face him.

"I warned you not to play games with me and you didn't listen did you? DID YOU?" he shouted yanking her hair again, pushing her up against the wall.

"You are mine, do you understand? DO YOU UNDERSTAND?" She was afraid to speak but nodded in agreement. He was breathing rapidly and getting more and more agitated. He tightened his grip on her hair and dragged her out of the kitchen and into the bedroom, bashing her shoulder very heavily against the door frame before throwing her on to the bed, pinning her down and tearing at the belt on her housecoat.

"I'll teach you not to play games with me!" he yelled, giving her a backhander hard across her face. The pain was so sharp it took her breath away, then her nose began pouring with blood causing her to gag and splutter as the warm liquid collected at the back of her throat. He aggressively pushed her legs apart and forced himself on to her. Each violent thrust was accompanied by, "You bitch! You slag! You fucking whore!" The verbal abuse continued, over and over and over until at last he was spent. Without another word he rolled off her and walked into the bathroom.

Jennie lay on the bed, curled up in the foetal position, sobbing softly, blood oozing from her nose and the water from the shower whirling in the background.

Intermittently during the morning, Nick scanned the department for a sign of Jennie and was disappointed not to see her. Then when he overheard Bev complaining to Gillian that Jennie had not turned in yet again, leaving her in a mess, his disappointment turned to concern. He wanted to find out more about Jennie's circumstances but was at a loss as to how without the ever watchful Gillian cottoning on.

The bedroom curtains remained closed and all sense of time was lost. Drifting between sleeping and crying Jennie felt drained of energy and had no idea how long she had been lying in bed, only a sensation of shrinking and the heavy quilt holding her prisoner, pushing her deeper and deeper into the mattress, threatening to swallow her; not that she cared, nothing mattered anymore.

The swirling mist of her mind dissipated long enough to reveal her father in a checked red and blue shirt and denim blue jeans, smiling and waving as he rode her white pony, Shooting Star, through sunny flower filled meadows, flanked by soft green hills towards the sparkling blue sea barely visible on the horizon. Shooting Star stopped and turned, calling to her, before disappearing from sight with her father. The mist returned and a fresh wave of tears rolled down her face. When it cleared again, the sun was shining and she was a little girl, playing in the park, sitting on a light blue and white striped blanket with her dolls, Rosie and Poppy, and a red polka dot tea set. Her mother was standing by her side, leaning on the handle of her brown buggy, talking to a young man with curly, white blond hair. He looked down at her and the question in his cornflower blue eyes was answered by the innocence in her identically coloured eyes. Suddenly dark purple clouds appeared and contorted faces loomed out at her, ugly and menacing; they were the faces of men she had seen her mother with and the faces of her sisters in the guise of evil grotesque looking wasps. They buzzed her head and stung her neck. She screwed up her eyes in terror, feeling powerless to move or make a sound. When she opened her eyes again, Miss Roundtree, a kindly teacher, with wavy brown hair and warm brown eyes, smiled and said her work was so good it deserved a gold star. The star was displayed in the centre of the teacher's forehead. Sleep beckoned once more and as she drifted off various people she had worked with took it in turns to say goodnight as she floated away from them on her bed and into a deep, peaceful sleep.

Mid-morning, three days after his vicious attack, Zac returned to the apartment and was horrified to discover Jennie in a blood splattered bed, sporting a black eye, a bloody swollen nose, angry looking blisters on her cheek and leg and bruising on her neck, shoulder and thighs, and more worryingly, delirious. Once over the initial shock of seeing her, the awful truth dawned on him; he was the one responsible for her injuries! Wracked with guilt and mortified that he had hurt Jennie in this way, the one he loved so much, he was also afraid. Afraid because Jennie was rambling and he thought she had lost her mind, afraid of the person he had become and afraid to take her to her doctor or hospital knowing questions would be asked. He rang a contact, briefly explained the situation and within half an hour a "no questions asked" doctor turned up at the apartment, diagnosed severe dehydration, ordered an ambulance and had Jennie admitted to hospital.

Zac travelled in the ambulance with Jennie. Although she was not fully conscious, in an effort to cover his back and hoping to influence her subconscious, he kept saying over and over, "Don't worry Jennie, I'll get whoever did this to you!"

He prowled around the waiting room while the doctors tended to Jennie, praying that she would not reveal how she had been injured. Before being allowed to see her, one of the doctors asked him some probing questions about where he had found her, if he knew how she had come by her injuries, if it had been reported to the police. He kept up the pretence that he had been away on business and returned to find Jennie in bed, bruised, battered and delirious and had no idea what had happened, that he had not called the police because her medical needs had taken priority. He suspected the doctor did not believe a word he had said but he was eventually allowed access to her and received another shock. She was at the far end of the ward, sedated and hooked up to a saline drip and urostomy bag. The translucency of her skin emphasised the bruising to her eye, nose and neck and the blisters on her face. She looked so small and vulnerable, he wanted to sink to his knees and beg her for forgiveness.

Jennie was discharged from hospital three days later. Zac had stayed with her the whole time, thinking things over; their past, their present and, more importantly, their future. He vowed to himself he would make it up to her. He had already phoned her firm to explain that her mother had been taken seriously ill, and Jennie had had to make an emergency dash to her hospital bedside and would need to take it as holiday.

Zac could not have been more attentive during the first couple of months Jennie was back in the apartment. The place had been cleaned from top to bottom and was overflowing with fresh flowers, the fridge was crammed with goodies, romantic meals were prepared and Zac was full of apologies and promises for their future. He explained that he needed a couple of months to put things in place and they would be set for life. She so wanted to believe him. When he was like this she needed no one else and remembered why she had first fallen in love with him. Life could be wonderful. She pushed the memory of the attack to the back of her mind and hope for their future began to bubble up inside her.

Work was fine, she had had to have a return to work interview because personnel were tightening up on absenteeism, but she had stuck to the story Zac had created and soon settled back into a routine.

Marriage and Move

"Piers have you got a minute?" Nick said while walking off towards one of the internal meeting rooms. It was more of a command than a request and without hesitation Piers followed.

"I'm visiting my folks this Easter weekend and I am thinking of proposing to Penny whilst we're there. It's time I got married," announced Nick. He did not wait for a response before finishing, "I just needed to tell someone."

Piers was both surprised and honoured to be privy to Nick's intentions but also lost for words. After an uncomfortable silence he said, "Well you've been seeing Penny long enough so I guess you're sure she's the one for you." Then he timidly asked, "Why did you say it's time?"

"Careerwise it would be a good move, it would show I'm ready for responsibility. Penny ticks the boxes, the bonus being she has a rich father."

"Put that way it sounds like you've hit the jackpot. What can I say but congratulations mate and good luck!"

"Thanks pal. You know, although I've been seeing Penny for years, I feel surprisingly nervous at the prospect of proposing to her; it's such a big step."

"But worth it," Piers said, hoping he sounded encouraging because he was really thinking *rather you than me mate, the state of matrimony does not appeal in the slightest and I cannot envisage a time when it ever will.*

"Hopefully," answered Nick. "Well, we best get back to work," he finished, leaving no room for further discussion. As he opened the door of the meeting room he turned towards

Piers. "Oh by the way, it goes without saying that what was said in this room stays in this room in the unlikely event that she turns me down!"

His attempt at humour fell flat and Piers' biblical response of, "Thy word I have hid in mine heart," momentarily stopped Nick in his tracks and Piers immediately regretted his reply as being completely over the top even by his standards.

"Hi Pen, would you and Nick like to come with Ashley and me to Freddie Beresford's party in Oxford next weekend?" asked Zara, Penny's younger sister.

"Oh Zee I would love to but we're visiting Nick's parents." Penny's disappointment was clearly evident from the tone of her voice. "In fairness we're long overdue a visit so I really can't complain or put it off unfortunately. I'd much rather go to a party and Freddie's fab; he is such a licentious bastard you can't help but like him. Please be sure to give him my love and tell him we'll definitely help him celebrate his next party!"

"Ahh that's a shame. Never mind, Freddie's bound to have another one soon, he throws parties at the drop of a hat. Anyway, I'll see you at Mummy's on Thursday. Must dash. Byeeeeeee." With that Zara finished the call.

"Oh I've just got to get my straighteners," Penny called over her shoulder as she sprinted up the stairs.

"Will you hurry up *please*!" Nick could not keep the irritation out of his voice. "I wanted to be on the way by now."

"Oh for God's sake it's not like we've booked for a show!" snapped Penny as she pushed past him towards the car, leaving him to lock up.

The silence was deafening during the journey. Nick was clearly preoccupied even when they pulled into the motorway services, as they normally did, to break up the four hour journey to Nick's family home in the Snowdonia National Park, North Wales. Penny's half-hearted attempt at conversation fell on deaf ears so she idly flicked through the pages of her magazine. *Some weekend this is going to be, I don't think!* She thought as she finished her coffee and headed off to the ladies before joining Nick at the car ready for the second leg of the journey.

"Oh hello Penny," Nick's elegant mother Glenda said, her cultured voice cold as she pecked Penny on the cheek. Although on the face of it the greeting was warm and welcoming Penny sensed the usual underlying disappointment. It was quite obvious Glenda did not think Penny was good enough for her precious son.

"Hello love," Glenda said, her face aglow and her voice filled with love as Nick gave her a bear hug. "Let me look at you. Oh you've had your hair cut shorter. You've lost some of your curls! Have you lost weight too?"

"No Mum, I'm working out at the gym more and yes I'm eating properly, Penny's looking after me very well, so you've no need to worry. Anyway, you're looking good. Where's Dad?"

"Hello son," Nick's dad, Don, said as he joined them in the brightly lit, square hallway, a stunning flower arrangement filling the air with its fresh fragrance. He embraced him warmly then turned to Penny and said, "Hello Penny love," as he gave her a gentle hug. Penny started to relax; she had a soft spot for Nick's cuddly dad and his soft Welsh accent.

Later on father and son popped out for their usual drink and caught up on family and friends and local news. They discussed Nick's career, put the world to rights and eventually got round to the conversation Nick always dreaded and one he knew had been prompted by his mother.

"Son, how long is it you've been seeing Penny now?" his father asked as he stared at his pint of beer.

Nick hated it when his father asked about Penny; he knew his parents were anxious to become grandparents and he felt under increasing pressure to settle down, not least to further his career. Penny did fit the criteria: late twenties, attractive, leggy blonde, rich daddy, but he loved women and the thought of commitment to one woman filled him with dread.

"She was 22 when we met."

He took a long sip of his drink before his father broke the heavy silence.

"Here's a thought, when I was your age you were eight and your sister was five."

"I know, I know what you're getting at, I just don't think I could be faithful to one woman. Were you never tempted?"

"Hand on heart, no. Don't get me wrong I enjoy the company of women; I've even been known to flirt once in a while but nothing serious. The fact is, as soon as I laid eyes on your mother I knew she was the one for me. She gave my life a sense of purpose. She made a man of me."

"I hear what you say, Dad. I hear what you say."

Although this would have been a perfect time for Nick to confide his plan to pop the question, he did not do so for two reasons: one, he was yet to decide on venue and two, more importantly, he was still undecided. After long awkward pause Nick said, "Anyway, better drink up, my stomach's telling me it's time for lunch. Mum will be wondering where we are." Having finished the conversation Nick also finished his drink and with an air of despondency quickly strode across the car park. His father had to rush to keep up with him.

"Did you speak with Nick about his plans?" Glenda asked Don later that night in bed.

"Yes, he said he didn't think he could be faithful to one woman, so don't go raising your hopes Mrs Turner. That lad of ours still wants to play the field and Janine's showing no signs of settling down either. Frankly, I can't see us ever becoming grandparents and if we do we'll be too old to enjoy them." With a heavy sigh he kissed his wife, switched off his bedside lamp, rolled on to his side and was soon quietly snoring, leaving his wife to mull over his words.

I'm sure if he met the right woman he would settle down. Penny has had years to tame him so she is obviously not the one, certainly not if Nick's cheating on her. Why on earth do some women put up with cheating men, have they no self-respect? Huh! She felt wide awake and went downstairs to make herself a hot, milky drink in the hope of dissipating her growing frustration and induce much needed sleep.

She sat at the kitchen table sipping her drink and looked out of the French doors at the inky black night. The stars were out in force and she could clearly make out the great bear constellation which took her right back to the time when she was ten. She had stared up in wonderment at the night sky as her beloved father pointed out the bear shape to her. Although he had been dead for twenty years she still missed him very much, particularly at times like this when she felt troubled. She could have discussed her inner most thoughts without compunction, knowing he would not judge her but merely offer words of wisdom. She said a silent prayer asking her father to be there for Nick. She shivered, drained the last of her drink, yawned and made her way upstairs to bed.

Nick had hardly slept, so as soon as it was light he went downstairs leaving Penny asleep. He made himself a coffee and headed out to the conservatory where he stood looking out across the green fields sweeping down to the trout lake with its mountainous backdrop. He was surprised at the height of the trees to the left of the lake and how thick their trunks were. It seemed like only yesterday he had planted them with his father and yet it was actually fifteen years ago. He shivered, suddenly feeling very old.

"Morning Nicki-noo." Nick visibly jumped as Janine, his freckle faced, younger sister jolted him out of his reverie and threw her arms around his neck.

"How are you? Have you brought your latest girlfriend with you for Mummy and Daddy to vet?" Janine adored Nick and although she teased him about his succession of girlfriends she loved the fact that he was popular with the girls; indeed, all of her friends had had, at one time or another, a crush on him.

"Morning Ninny." Nick gave Janine a hug and whispered, "Penny is with me, you know, the girl who has been living with me for the last twelve months. So keep your voice down, I don't want her to hear you asking about new girlfriends."

"Just testing. You here for the weekend?"

"Yes."

"What's up? You seem a bit down, is everything alright?"

Nick remained silent, contemplating. Janine waited, then, clearly having reached a decision Nick said, "Let's go and check on the horses." Without waiting for her response he strode towards the back door which led to the stables. Janine hurried after him but did not catch up with him until he had reached Tim, his horse. She watched Nick pat Tim's long neck and sweet-talk him.

"There's something I want to discuss with you."

After a long moment when nothing had been said she asked, "So what did you want to discuss?" Nick hesitated just long enough for Janine to guess what he was about to say.

"Oh my God, you're going to propose…"

"Shush," gestured Nick, waving his hands. "I don't want the whole world to know." Janine was not sure how to respond and the silence between them hung heavily. Eventually Nick enquired, "Well?"

"Well what?" countered Janine.

"Now Ninny don't be obtuse. What do you think of Penny for a sister-in-law?"

Janine's mind was a whirl as she processed this information and it was a while before she answered. "It doesn't matter what I think, it's what *you* think that counts."

"It *does* matter what you think, it matters very much."

"Well, you've been seeing Penny for years and lived together for the last twelve months, so you've had plenty of time to decide whether she's the one. I'm sorry big brother but it's not for me to pass comment, I can't make the decision for you. All I can say is whatever decision you make I will support you one hundred and ten percent."

"Thanks Nin, you're right as usual, it is down to me. If you don't mind I'm going for a walk."

He patted her on the arm and headed off towards the lake.

From the bedroom window Glenda had seen Janine follow Nick into the stables and wondered what they were talking about, particularly as Nick had been unusually quiet at dinner the previous evening. She could tell he was mulling over something and if anyone could get him to open up it would be

Janine. She had many things to be grateful for and one was that her children were so close.

She was still looking at the stables when she saw Nick leave them and stride off towards the pool while Janine stood in the doorway looking concerned. In that instant her motherly instinct told her that Nick was going to propose to Penny during the weekend visit, but instead of feeling delighted she too felt concerned, concerned that Penny might not be right for her son. She continued to watch Nick as he quickly made his way down to the large pool that he and his father had created. She marvelled at the beauty of him, the sunshine turning his unruly hair a warm brown with flecks of gold. His long limbs and proud posture reminded her of her father. She continued to watch him as he headed to the bench erected in her father's memory. She loved her son deeply and unconditionally and suddenly had an overwhelming sense of sadness that things were never going to be the same; she feared she was about to lose something very precious.

He would have preferred a quiet, intimate occasion, involving just the two of them. He pictured them strolling along the river to the bench where they had often sat and marvelled at the resident kingfisher on the opposite bank, darting in and out of the trees, skimming the top of the water in search of food for his family. He would start by saying he wondered how many baby kingfishers there might be that year and how he had been thinking of the future recently. Then on bended knee he would pour out his heart and make his promises to her. After she had said yes he would conjure up the bottle of champagne and glasses he had hidden in a hollow at the river's edge, the bottle submerged in the water to keep it ice cold so that they could have their own private celebration before everyone joined in. This would have been his choice except he knew Penny would expect a public declaration of his feelings.

He toyed with several other ideas, for instance, their favourite restaurant while out with friends; on top of Ben Nevis, as his friend had proposed to his girlfriend; or hiring a small plane to fly a banner saying, "Penny will you marry me?". The ideas were endless but nothing enthused him and he was becoming increasingly frustrated, when, out of the blue, his mother unwittingly provided the solution. At the end of a family meal she announced she had something to tell them.

"Cousin Billy is performing in my favourite play, South Pacific, at the Assembly Rooms over Easter and I've bought tickets for us all for Monday's matinee performance. It's only a couple of hours and it will be my Easter treat to you all. Afterwards we can have dinner at Hill House." She started humming the tune to "Younger than springtime," as she cleared away the plates.

Immediately, as if a lightbulb had been switched on, a plan started to form in Nick's mind.

Nick disappeared as soon as dinner was over. Penny assumed he had gone to their room and was irritated to find he was not there. Her annoyance increased when she discovered his car had gone too. "Oh Nick you can be so rude at times," she said out loud.

Little did she know, but he had driven over to see his cousin Billy to discuss his proposal plan.

Glenda adored the theatre, in fact she had played a few small parts before starting her family and had taken Nick and Janine to the theatre umpteen times during their childhood.

Unsurprisingly, Nick was familiar with the South Pacific storyline and was delighted to learn that Billy was playing the part of Emile de Becque, in which he was required to sing, 'Some Enchanted Evening'. The sentiments of the song perfectly reflected his and Penny's relationship, for as soon as he had laid eyes on her across a crowded football presentation room, he instinctively knew she was one to keep, even though in the early stages of their relationship he continued to 'play the field'. Significantly, he always went back to her.

Now pressure from family and work had helped him reach the decision, it was time to settle down and have a family of his own. Yet, if pressed, he would have admitted he did not really need to be married; he was perfectly happy looking after himself and keeping his freedom.

Billy loved the idea of being instrumental in the proposal and readily agreed to Nick joining him at the line, '*The sound of her laughter, will sing in your dreams…*' singing the rest of the song as a duet and then Nick continuing on with his proposal. He was sure the play's production team would be equally accommodating. In fact he persuaded Nick to let his close journalist friend, Teddy Edwards of the local Herald, report the story; he knew he could be trusted to keep the surprise. Nick would have preferred not to include the newspapers but agreed because he knew Penny would love the attention.

They practised their duet a few times before Nick returned home to an angry Penny who accused him of dumping her at his parents, "…while you were God knows where, probably with an old childhood slag!"

Barely civil with each other over the rest of the weekend, Penny was thoroughly fed up and bitterly regretted not accepting her sister's invitation to Freddie Beresford's party. She would have given the theatre trip a miss if she could.

The six of them squeezed into the taxi for the fifteen minute journey, Janine's on/off boyfriend, Giles, made up the number. The Assembly Rooms had two theatre layouts, the traditional stage with the audience in front and the Studio, a smaller and more intimate auditorium arrangement, with the stage in the centre surrounded by tiered seating for the audience. South Pacific was being performed in the Studio which suited Nick's plan perfectly. They were all seated along the sixth row and everyone was thoroughly enjoying the performance, except for Nick, who was fidgeting for England.

"For God's sake Nick, will you please sit still!" hissed Penny. Ten minutes later he was fidgeting again. Penny huffed and puffed. She glared at him and he got up, excusing himself, saying he needed the toilet.

Penny was enthralled by the performance and refused to allow Nick's prolonged absence to detract from her enjoyment. Fortunately, she was oblivious to the guy standing on his own at the side of the stage who kept glancing in her direction. Janine spotted him and noted that Nick had vanished. Her suspicions aroused, she loosely put two and two together and she could hardly contain her growing excitement when at the very end of the play the final song was changed from 'Dites-Moi' to Billy singing 'Some Enchanted Evening'. She knew something was about to happen and thought she was going to explode. Billy's melodious voice filled the room.

"Some enchanted evening,
You may see a stranger,
You may see a stranger,
Across a crowded room,
And somehow you'll know,

You'll know even then,
That somewhere you'll see her,
Again and again.
Some enchanted evening,
Someone may be laughin',
You may hear her laughin'
Across a crowded room,
And night after night,
As strange as it seems."

Another voice suddenly joined in from the side of the stage. The eyes of the audience looked across, except the guy standing on his own who was capturing Penny's reaction on his digital camera.

"Nick!" exclaimed Penny. "What the…?" Her jaw dropped and her mouth gaped open as he continued with the song putting his arm around Billy's shoulder.

"The sound of her laughter,
Will sing in your dreams.
Who can explain it?
Who can tell you why?
Fools give you reasons,
Wise men never try.
Some enchanted evening,
When you find your true love,
When you feel her call you,
Across a crowded room."

At this point in the song Nick quickly strode up the steps to Penny's side and on bended knee continued with the song.

"Then fly to her side,
And make her your own,
For all through your life you,
May dream all alone.
Once you have found her,
Never let her go.
Once you have found her,
Never let her go.

My Penny, my love, I have loved you since the first time I laid eyes on you across the dance hall. You are as precious to me as the blood coursing through my veins and the air filling my lungs. I want to share my life with you, and God willing raise a family with you. I promise to look after you, work hard and be a good provider. Please say you'll be mine." Then he presented her with a single stone diamond ring set in platinum gold. She recognised it as part of his inheritance from his late paternal grandmother, which he had caught her slyly trying on months before.

Penny was completely taken aback by Nick's proposal. Although all eyes were on her, all she could see was Nick's face. Everyone and everything else was a white cloudy blur. She tried to speak but no words came out. She started to shake and then tears of joy rolled down her face before she finally whispered, "Yes Nick. Oh yes."

He took her in his arms and tenderly kissed her, then jumped up, punched the air and shouted, "She said yes!" at the top of his voice.

The whole audience erupted, whooping and clapping in delight and Ted continued to capture the event on his camera. He also captured the anxious expression on Glenda's face, which was at odds with the faces of the rest of the audience.

While Penny was telephoning her family and friends to share the good news, Nick was arranging interviews with several firms as part of his career move. While Penny was asking people to help with her wedding plans, Nick was reaffirming his 'would be' clients' commitment.

Nick managed to secure interviews at three firms and these would be held over an eight day period. The first one was a large firm, similar to Stepwells. He was not expecting to be offered a position and if truth be told he was not particularly interested, he just wanted to get into the swing of things. The interview was quite relaxed and went surprisingly well, which gave his confidence a welcome boost.

He was definitely interested in the second firm, which was run on similar lines to Stepwells, albeit on a smaller scale. It was a tougher interview; he was 'grilled' rather than being part of a discussion. Nevertheless he was quietly confident he would be offered a position as Leonard "Lenny" Nurse, an old mentor of his, was a partner there and was sure to put a good word in for him.

The third firm was totally different to the others and unlike anywhere he had ever worked before. There was more of a family feel to it, similar, he imagined, to high street firms rather than the sophisticated, highly technical city firms he had worked at. Again, he thought he acquitted himself very well.

Predictably, he decided he would accept the second firm's offer.

A week after his third interview he received a letter from all three firms. He was surprised to receive an offer from the first and third firms but a rejection from the second firm, the one he was really interested in. He was baffled as to why he was rejected and contacted his old mentor. It was an awkward telephone conversation and from Lenny's comments about Nick being better suited to a different type of firm it was quite obvious that far from encouraging his appointment he had actually discouraged it. Nick abruptly terminated the conversation. *Bastard, I'll show him! I'll show them all! The bastards!!*

After careful consideration and, of course, talking it through with Jack, he decided to accept the offer of Senior Associate at Macefields, the third firm. Jack was instrumental in wording the proviso that he be made partner in six months, as Miller had done at Stepwells. At a further meeting, Macefields agreed to his partnership terms. He confirmed his acceptance of the position. His start date was 27th August 2002.

Meanwhile, Penny had arranged their wedding day for 10th August at 3.00 pm. As luck would have it a couple had cancelled their plans and she had asked for their allotted time, otherwise they would have had to wait several months longer. Nick was ecstatic; it was all falling into place and he could not wait to inform Richardson. *That'll teach the bastard!*

April Fool

On Monday 1st April at 7.30am, while Nick was planning his proposal, Peter flew first class by Virgin airline to New York. The fact that it was April Fools' Day had not escaped his team.

"No fool like an old fool," said Nick the following day. He was still bitter about his appraisal. "Off to meet the Albatross and he has the audacity to tell me to settle down!"

"She certainly has some sort of hold over him," Simon added.

"He's too afraid to finish with her if you ask me," said Maggie. "Who knows what damage she would do to his career and marriage! Yes, unfortunately for him she is not the sort to just fade away, so he's well and truly stuck."

Hayden did not join in with the sneering but noted it. *All criticisms gratefully received if it helps to get rid of Lazy Cow O'Dwyer and keeps me in situ, I just need to keep "nudging" Old Dawes out of the team and then everything will be perfect, just perfect.*

With Peter out of the way he stepped up his harassment campaign against Rachel, the remaining hag. He would pick on her, get her to boiling point and then leave her to cool down. He continued making silent phone calls to Rachel, and occasionally Grace. At other times he would have a histrionic outburst, openly suggesting Rachel was cherry-picking work. When she tried to protest her innocence he was either very dismissive or argumentative. He made her life a misery and she did not want to go to work. He was a bully.

Normally Peter used the flight time productively, either studying legal updates, business strategy or other firm related literature. However during this trip he felt restless and he could not concentrate because his thoughts kept drifting back to the morning and saying goodbye to Charlotte, his wife. She had looked anxious, almost tearful, which had bothered him. They had been married for 23 years in July and she had surprised him by saying she would like to celebrate their wedding anniversary by spending a week in New York. Not for the first time he wondered if she suspected his affair with Gillian and he felt terribly guilty at the pain this would cause her. She was a good soul, an excellent wife and mother and he truly did not deserve her.

He reflected on the last few months and how much time they had spent with each other now that their daughters were 'doing their own thing', and, more significantly, Gillian was not there to put pressure on him. He had really enjoyed his wife's company, her gentleness made him feel relaxed, he loved her familiar rose perfume, her easy smile and how her nose crinkled when she laughed; it was like old times before the children had come along. Suddenly he ached to be with his wife, to take her in his arms and hold her close.

Gillian was waiting for him at JFK International Airport in New York. The last three months, except for a long weekend, were the longest they had been apart and she was surprised at how much she had missed him. As soon as she spotted him she rushed over, and, in an uncharacteristic display of public affection, she flung her arms around his neck and smothered him with kisses. She caught him completely off balance which caused them both to topple over, landing in an untidy heap, much to the amusement of the other people at the terminal. Peter made light of their 'performance' but inwardly he was seething.

"Is Hayden looking after you properly?" Gillian enquired during dinner, secretly hoping he was not and that Peter would say he could not wait for her to return to Manchester. She was surprised when he started to laugh.

"Oh he's coping very well, very well indeed. We're having quite a laugh with him but the biggest laugh of all is that he has an admirer." Peter laughed..

"What? Who?" Gillian queried, intrigued.

"You remember the other male secretary, Paul Husslebea, you know the 'big honey monster'? Well, he's had Hayden's initials tattooed on the inside of his right wrist, no need to explain the significance of that!"

Gillian's eyes flew open wide. "No, you're joking!" she laughingly exclaimed.

"Nick found out from Jennie and roared with laughter when he told Hayden in front of the rest of the team. Hayden went puce with embarrassment, had one of his frequent outbursts and stormed off to personnel to complain. It was so funny you should have been there to witness the drama unfold. I can't wait for the next instalment."

"Well I never! That's incredible. What does he expect personnel to do about it?" laughed Gillian.

"Precisely! What can they do? Paul Husslebea could always say that the tattoo is in honour of our royal family. Frankly, I'm beginning to wonder about this Husslebea phenomena. Are their surnames really Husslebea or do they belong to some weird Husslebea cult?"

"There's nowt so queer as folk as my grandmother used to say," Gillian volunteered. "Mentioning Nick, what's the situation with him now?" Gillian enquired.

"Oh, Nick." Peter's laughter immediately subsided. "On the surface everything seems fine, but I've known him long enough to gauge when he's up to something. Time will tell, but it wouldn't surprise me if he's planning to jump ship."

"Seriously?"

"Afraid so. He wanted me to put him forward for partnership, but I genuinely don't think he's ready for partnership. He doesn't take responsibility seriously enough. That's not just my opinion."

"What do you mean?"

"Well for a start Ken Grainger said he couldn't back Nick's application because he considers him quite flippant and impetuous. Gillian, I have to agree, he's something of a loose cannon. Just look at how things got out of hand with Andrea, she might be a law unto herself but he needs to know how to control people like her, and then there's Rachel, at best he's indifferent towards her and at worst downright ignorant. He just can't seem to have a normal relationship with his secretary!"

The irony of the last criticism escaped him but it did not escape Gillian.

"I must admit I'm not keen on Rachel," continued Peter, "much too guarded to my mind. Why she stays with him God only knows, but she is a good worker and everyone knows the secret to success is having a good supporting team. When I mentioned Rachel's role in this year's success he blew up saying he could not stand her and did not want her to work for him anymore. We ended his appraisal with me offering to try and persuade her to work for Simon instead. We'll see."

"Well, as I've said before, he's 33 going on 13!" added Gillian. Secretly it irritated her that over the years every male in Peter's team, including some clients, had flirted with her, some had made a serious play for her but not Nick. Nick slept with any little scrubber who fluttered her eyelashes in his direction; yet not once had Nick shown a glimmer of interest in her. Not once. She was deeply offended.

Rachel's Notice

In January 2000, after Rachel's second interview at Stepwells, her father drove her home. He had always been a careful driver but his reactions were obviously too slow, almost causing an accident. Her beloved father was getting old. Worryingly over the next two years his health rapidly deteriorated. Initially her mother coped but then old age caught up with her and Rachel became increasingly concerned about them. The only solution was to reduce her working days so she could be more supportive.

Nick's attitude had always left a lot to be desired but had worsened since his appraisal. She did not know why but sensed it must have gone badly and he blamed her. When he gave his work to other secretaries she realised he was trying to force her out and would use a request to reduce her hours as an excuse. That fear, together with Husslebea's continuing hostility, made Rachel decide to move on and when her old school friend, Jan, suggested applying for a job at her firm, she did not hesitate. The interview went well and she was delighted to accept the job offer, which she received via a telephone call later that afternoon.

She was at work early the next morning to speak with Richardson before Nick arrived. They had a brief meeting in one of the small rooms, out of sight of their department. Rachel explained she had accepted a part-time job in another firm because she needed more time to support her parents and anticipated Nick would not want a part-time secretary. Richardson seemed genuinely sorry she had decided to leave and empathised with her as his mother had been in a similar situation with his grandparents. He thanked her for her valuable contribution to his team and wished her well. She went straight from their meeting to see the personnel officer, June Wentworth, a kindly down-to-earth person, who also seemed genuinely sorry she was going.

Richardson was sorry, angry and annoyed about Rachel leaving. Sorry because he recognised she was an asset to his team and always eager to please, angry because he knew Nick's attitude was the real reason she was going and annoyed with himself for having words with Nick over her, especially as she was now leaving! Although Nick was his usual jovial self, Richardson knew their heated exchange had not been forgotten. He was also appalled at Nick's reaction when he informed him Rachel was leaving. Nick roared with laughter and sneeringly threw his words back at him.

"Well one thing's for sure, you can't keep her in the team!" he sneered and then sauntered out of the department laughing and shaking his head.

Nick was already at his desk when Rachel returned to her seat and judging from the broad grin across his face he had obviously been told of her news. She walked over to the photocopier to collect a document and he followed her.

"I assume you've heard I'm leaving," she said quietly.

"Onwards and upwards," was his nonchalant reply as he walked off towards the coffee machine and she fought to hold back her tears.

Holiday entitlement reduced her notice to three dreadful weeks.

She thought Nick would be pleased she was leaving but instead he turned malicious. By all accounts, he badmouthed her, blamed her for not getting a partnership and he forbid the team from signing a leaving card or contributing to a collection for her. She later heard he had hidden piles of filing and urgent work until after she had left, to put her in as bad a light as possible. She was distraught.

Nick's Notice

His mind was racing and he had hardly slept. There was so much to think about, so much to do. He was itching to get started. While he was on the train travelling to work he mulled things over. Richardson's words kept going over and over in his mind. *Rachel is a very good worker… yet doesn't warrant a mention from you!* He was loath to admit it but Richardson was right. He could not believe she had been going for interviews at the same time as him and he had had no clue. *How ironic if we'd both been offered positions at the same firm!* he mused. Ironically, he had been far from amused when he had learned she was actually moving to Leonard Nurse's firm, just a couple of streets away. He wondered what her reaction would be if he asked her to work for him at Macefields. He quickly dismissed the idea and thought about the morning task of handing in his notice.

The euphoria he had felt accepting the new position had gone and he felt undeniably sad, for he had never envisaged leaving Stepwells. Even when his colleague friends had moved on he had still clung to the belief that he would make partnership. Now here he was leaving because Richardson had said he was not ready.

Over and over he had rehearsed what he was going to say: that it was wrong to deny him the coveted partnership because he was more than ready for it; he had worked his ass off, as last year's target ratings proved; he had brought in new clients and was popular with existing ones. It was unbelievable he had sided with an easily replaced typist rather than back him, a lawyer who had proved his worth time and time again. He would take great delight in informing him that he had negotiated the same deal as Miller, i.e. partner within twelve months. His parting shot would be that he would make sure he regretted forcing him out.

Richardson chose the same meeting room he had spoken to Rachel in only weeks before. He looked tired and anxious. Speaking first he said he had guessed Nick was going to hand in his notice, in which case he was very, very, sorry to lose him, not just because he was an excellent worker, as the latest target statistics had proved, or that he had attracted new clients and was popular, but, he had grown very fond of him over the years. He finished by asking if there was anything he could do to change his mind.

Opening their meeting in that way had completely taken the wind out of Nick's sails. He was not sure what to expect but he certainly did not envisage Richardson looking so dejected. He considered what had just been said, then, with a heavy heart, shook his head to indicate nothing would stop him moving on. He did not rub salt into the wound by mentioning the deal he had brokered or vowing to make him regret not backing his application because he sensed he was already remorseful.

Three months' notice, less holiday entitlement, meant his leaving day was Friday 2nd August, perfect timing for his wedding. Richardson congratulated him on his forthcoming marriage and wished him well for the future. They shook hands at the end of their meeting, knowing their lives had changed dramatically; both were apprehensive about what their future held.

Later that afternoon Nick overheard Gillian in the kitchen. He could not see her or who she was talking to but realised she was discussing his imminent wedding, sneeringly giving it two years. He certainly had no regrets about moving away from 'the Albatross'.

Ping

Rachel's mobile telephone pinged, it was a text message from Bev.

"Newsflash, my contact in Human Resources has just told me Nick Turner has handed his notice in this morning. He's going to Macefields." Rachel could hardly believe her eyes and the news stirred up very mixed feelings in her. She felt sad for Nick for she knew how much he loved working at Stepwells; guilty because she suspected her moving firms had gone against him; regret for how badly things had ended between them and how she had personally handled the situation; and, finally, a real sense of loss of a job she had thoroughly enjoyed, been good at and more importantly had owned.

Leaving Do

Bev organised Rachel's evening leaving do, drinks and nibbles, predictably at Jugs. The Flakes, some of Richardson's team, Rachel's friend Jan from her new firm and a few others also joined them. Significantly, there was no sign of Nick, Richardson, Gillian or Husslebea, which was a relief because Rachel was feeling very emotional. Her head said it was right to move but her heart ached over leaving. Indeed, so much so that she could not bring herself to discuss Nick's surprise notice that morning.

She put on a brave face and pretended to enjoy herself but all she wanted to do was to go home. She could not believe that they had both been going for interviews at the same time and might even have ended up at the same firm! *What on earth is that all about?* Rachel asked herself, struggling to get her head around recent events.

Warning and then Stabbed

Like many young people Zac thought he was invincible and able to cope with anything that life threw at him, but it was almost inevitable that his halcyon lifestyle would lure him into a world of risk and temptation. His easy smile and air of confidence, coupled with money in his pocket, was a powerful combination and the girls flocked to him. He loved them all and flirted indiscriminately. In fact he was so popular that if his friends were throwing a party it was left to him to supply the girls. He never disappointed.

He smoked cannabis at parties and on rare occasions popped pills but considered pills to be for losers and would not allow them to take a hold of him, he was too smart, or so he thought. Unfortunately, temptation has many guises and it was not long before Zac's reputation for supplying girls became known to people in the drugs trade, who were always looking for an opportunity to expand their business by recruiting dealers, who invariably brought their own clientele.

At first Luke, Zac's dealer, casually mentioned he made a good living out of supplying cannabis, it was easy money and if he was ever interested just to let him know. The next time a deal was struck he asked Zac if he had given his proposal any thought, but Zac turned him down flat. Nevertheless, Luke continued to encourage him, so much so that by the time Jennie came into his world the thought of easy money proved irresistible. They developed a routine of meeting up on Wednesday nights at the gym, Luke supplied Zac with the drugs and Zac sold them to his increasing clientele. Soon the money came rolling in and more and more people started approaching Zac.

The arrangement continued uneventfully for a few years until one cold, damp night, a short walk from the gym, a dark-skinned lad approached him for drugs. Zac could not tell his nationality but guessed he was in his early 20s. His gut instinct warned him the lad was dangerous and so he denied being a supplier. The lad became aggressive, squaring up to him and pushing his face towards him he barked, "I know you're a dealer, because it takes one to recognise one, *pal*." As he walked away, in an act of aggression he brushed shoulders with Zac and through gritted teeth snarled, "Keep to your own territory! You have been warned."

Zac felt his anger rise but kept calm as he watched the lad cross the road and walk down to a parked black BMW with its engine ticking over, parked under a streetlamp. The window at the driver's side slowly opened and the lad spoke to the driver. He then looked back in Zac's direction before walking off around the corner. The driver, also dark-skinned, glared menacingly at Zac, who could make out one other man in the vehicle but suspected more. As the car was slowly driven off the driver poked two fingers through the window and then quickly raised them to simulate firing a gun at Zac. His stomach dropped, a feeling that took him right back to when he was expecting his father to return home and fearing the unknown.

The brief encounter with the man in the car pretending to shoot him unsettled Zac more than he cared to admit. It had brought it home to him just how dangerous his world was and that there was no future in this line of illegal work. For a couple of weeks afterwards he was very much on edge, constantly looking over his shoulder, scanning the streets for anyone suspicious looking. Yet, despite his concerns, he carried on supplying as normal. Meanwhile, a loose plan began to form in his mind about getting a large sum of money together to set Jennie and himself up, so that they could move away and have a fresh beginning, get married and start a family and, ultimately, he could find a legal way of earning a decent wage.

He rang Luke to discuss his options and meet Mr Baxter, also known as 'The Boss'.

One stormy, rain-lashed night, before Luke got back to Zac about meeting Mr Baxter, a regular customer beckoned Zac from an alleyway. Thinking it was to shelter from the weather he crossed over the road to join him in the dark, narrow alley. Big mistake! The regular vanished but three strange men suddenly appeared, one from a doorway a few yards further into the alley and the other two from behind Zac. He recognised the one in front as the man who had pretended to shoot him.

"It seems the verbal warning went unheeded," the front man growled, as he moved towards Zac. Although he did not turn around Zac sensed the men behind him had moved nearer. Adrenalin shot through his body, he instinctively tensed his muscles and all his senses were on high alert as he clenched his fists and assumed a boxing stance in readiness for the first move. Predictably, the man in front lashed out first, he aimed his right fist at Zac's nose but Zac ducked and caught him with a well-aimed blow to the left side of his ribcage, winding him. At the same time Zac spun around and landed a blow to the nose of one of the men behind him. He heard his nose crack, saw blood and mucus spurt out and the man fell to his knees and clutched his face. *One down two to go.* A blow landed on Zac's left cheek but not before he had punched the third man in the gut, followed by a swift uppercut to his chin, sending him sprawling on the ground. *One to go.* He quickly turned and saw the glint of a knife as the first attacker lunged at him again. He deftly moved to one side and the knife sliced his jacket, as he karate-chopped the back of the attacker's neck causing him to drop to his knees. The assailant whose nose was broken grabbed him in a neck lock from behind but Zac forcefully jerked his head back, bashing the bridge of his nose again, forcing him to release him. The man with the knife then lunged at him once more.

"A disturbance has been reported by Betty Eustace at number 117, Willingsworth Way, could you check it out please?" Sid Stringer's Black Country voice commanded from the radio in the police patrol car.

"On our way," was the automatic response from PC Bellingham.

"Oh no, not old Mrs Eustace again. This must be the third time this month. Boy crying wolf comes to mind," moaned WPC Ward.

"I know, I know, it will probably be a complete waste of our time again. She's just another lonely old soul, but it's sod's law, if we don't check things out then something is bound to have happened and we'll end up being, at the very least, disciplined about not responding. So buckle up and let's get over there post haste," countered her colleague.

It had been an uneventful shift, the highlight being the instructions to call on Mrs Eustace again following her telephone call to the station. PC Bob Bellingham drove the police car slowly across the entrance to Willingsworth Way, WPC Sarah Ward was sat by his side. Both of them were lost in their own private thoughts. Bob was thinking about how long it was until the end of his shift, when he could go home to Jean, his wife, and Andrew and Stephen, their two lads, particularly as he was keen to find out how their sports events had gone, whereas Sarah was making a mental list of the groceries she needed for her weekly shop. They both noticed the commotion in the alley at the same time and witnessed Zac get stabbed in the stomach and drop to his knees. The attacker raised his arm to lunge at him again just as Bob switched on the car's siren which served to distract him, and all three assailants ran off. Sarah instinctively ran a short way down the alley shouting after them but her effort proved futile as they sprinted off in different directions. Meanwhile Bob radioed for an ambulance and also radioed the station to give a brief description of the men and their escape routes, simultaneously grabbing the first aid kit from the car.

Zac was writhing on the dirty, wet flagstones of the alley. Blood was pouring from his stomach wound. Sarah, satisfied there was no danger of further attack, knelt down beside him, explained who she and Bob were, asked him his name and advised him to be still. Bob handed her a pair of protective gloves while putting on a pair himself. He moved Zac on to his back, positioned himself by Zac's head and checked there was no obstruction to his airway. He gently opened his jacket and shirt to identify the precise location of the stab wound. It was about an inch above his belly button. He applied pressure to the wound with a clean and absorbent cloth from his first aid kit in an effort to slow down the rate of bleeding. The cloth quickly became soaked with blood so Bob added more cloth on top. Sarah tried to reassure Zac that he would be okay and the ambulance was on its way. She wrapped a blanket around his shoulders as Bob continued to monitor his airway, breathing and circulation.

Zac remained conscious during the short time it took for the ambulance to reach them and subsequently whisk him off to hospital. Sarah accompanied him in the vehicle. During the journey she reflected on what had just happened. It never ceased to amaze her how cool, calm and collected they both were while dealing with such incidents. She was under no illusion, it was definitely Bob's matter-of-fact manner that had been a huge influence on her, for which she was very grateful.

Bob sat in the police car and watched the ambulance speed away, its siren brightening up the dismal night, alerting pedestrians and motorists of its presence. He searched the pockets of Zac's black leather jacket, which the paramedics had removed and had handed to him. It smelt of nicotine. There was a black leather wallet with £80 in £10 notes in, a mixture of loose change, a packet of cigarettes, a cigarette lighter and a large white handkerchief in the pockets, but there were no bank cards and no mobile telephone, nothing to confirm his identification which was puzzling.

Before going back to the police station he called on Mrs Eustace, a tiny, bright-eyed, 85-year-old widow. Her home was cosy, inviting and smelt of lavender. Soft music was quietly playing, Bob recognised it as one of his favourite melodies 'Somewhere in Time', written by John Barry, which was very apt because Mrs Eustace's home, with its dark wooden furniture and floral wallpaper was like stepping back in time. China tea cups, a milk jug and a sugar pot were laid out in anticipation on a silver tray. The tray was set on top of a circular white lace doily on her beautiful antique mahogany occasional table.

When she said, "Officer you will stay for a cup of tea won't you?" he had not the heart to refuse.

"Yes of course, but it must be a quick cup because I need to be back at the station."

She was very quick, he surmised she must have put the kettle on when the ambulance sped off. Between sips of tea he took her statement about the disturbance. She was surprisingly observant, describing each assailant and what they were wearing. Fifteen minutes later he waved goodbye to a happy old lady, knowing he had helped to brighten up her day.

He took Zac's jacket back to the police station as evidence of the attack and informed the duty officer of what had happened and that WPC Ward had gone to the hospital to take a statement from the victim.

"It's unusual not to have anything of a personal nature in a jacket," Bob observed. "My instinct tells me the absence of personal data is deliberate. I couldn't smell drugs but I'd bet my badge he's a dealer." The duty officer pursed his lips and nodded in agreement.

Zac was fortunate on several counts: he had remained alert during and after the attack, he had no drugs on him, having sold his last packet less than half an hour before the attack, he was astute enough to give the WPC a false name, address and date of birth (he had given a combination of two school friends' details, David Williams, 12th December 1978) and he was seen by a doctor as soon as he arrived at the hospital.

Being tended to so quickly was a relief because in the ambulance on his way to hospital his mind was in overdrive, so much so that by the time he had been wheeled in, checked over by the doctor, had six stitches inserted into his wound and bandaged up, he had fine-tuned a long-term plan of action. He and Jennie would start afresh in Leeds. He had still got Archie Fieldhouse's number stored on his private mobile telephone and, although they had not been in contact for a while, he was confident his friend, who had been living in Leeds for a few years, would help him set up. He would still carry on working for Mr Baxter, as it did not matter where he lived because he and Luke had only ever dealt with each other by phone and he had a separate mobile for that purpose. For now he needed to focus on his present priority which was to get out of hospital before being interviewed.

Zac was aware of the WPC waiting to take his statement so he pretended to be asleep until an opportunity to escape presented itself. As luck would have it he did not need to wait long. A commotion occurred at the end of his row of five beds at the one nearest to the windows, which proved to be the perfect distraction. A visitor suddenly began shouting and swearing and attacked a patient. The victim, an elderly man, slid out of bed and fell onto a mattress which had been laid out for the patient in the next bed who was at risk of falling out of bed. He lay helpless on the floor as his visitor stood astride him and started raining blows down on him.

Everyone's attention was drawn to the incident, including Sarah's. She had been standing by the nurses' information desk while waiting for Zac to rouse and instinctively dashed over to pull the attacker off, as did the nurses. It was not easy because the attacker was like a raging grizzly bear and very strong, growling and throwing everyone off him.

In the ensuing pandemonium Zac seized his opportunity, grabbed his bag of clothes from the bedside cabinet, casually picked up someone's overcoat draped over one of the chairs and made his way to the toilets which were just out of sight of the fracas. He quickly dressed in the toilet. The dark grey coat was a size too big, which was fine, the pair of glasses in one pocket and the scarf in the other were a useful disguise, and the twenty pound note in the wallet would pay for the taxi. He checked the coast was clear and swiftly left the ward. It had only taken him a couple of minutes. A taxi was just dropping off a group of visitors as he reached the hospital's main entrance. He jumped in the taxi, gave the name of the next street to his, sat back and marvelled at how his escape could not have turned out better if he had planned it.

Meanwhile, Sarah, despite feeling that she had been thrown around like a ragdoll and being elbowed in the eye by the violent visitor, managed to restrain him with a little help from one of the nurses and a visitor. She cuffed and cautioned him and was well pleased with the outcome until, that is, she noticed Zac's empty bed. Elation was soon replaced by deflation because she knew it would reflect badly on her, even though she felt she could not have done things differently. To top it all her eye was throbbing and beginning to swell.

The Boss

Zac did not mention the attack to anyone, his instinct warned him not to. Instead he asked Luke about expanding to another area. A knowing smile transformed Luke's normally deadpan expression; he did not ask why, he just said he would see what he could do.

The following week Luke said he had spoken with 'the powers that be' who had decided it was time for Zac to make the acquaintance of The Boss. They agreed to meet the following night at Echoes, a nightclub in the city centre.

Luke was obviously waiting because as soon as Zac approached the pretty red-haired girl in the kiosk to pay his entrance fee, he appeared from nowhere and quickly ushered him through the back door into a secluded car park. Without speaking he pointed to a red Ford Fiesta and they quickly sped off to an underground car park belonging to an apartment block on the outskirts of the city. Once there they swapped cars for a black BMW with blacked out windows. Zac sat in the back as instructed and he felt his stomach muscles tighten as suddenly two strangers flanked him. Luke spoke for the first time.

"These are two other employees, who, for security reasons, will now blindfold you, as much for your protection as our employer's." Zac flinched as the man sitting to his left swiftly wrapped a thick, dark coloured length of material around his eyes, tying it tightly behind his head. It had the same earthy smell of his picnic blanket and completely blocked out his vision. The swiftness of the blindfolding action took Zac by surprise; his immediate reaction was to reach up to remove the blindfold, but the firm hand of the man to his right resting on his arm prevented him and strangely calmed him. He took a deep breath. Luke continued. "This way if you decide not to join our organisation then the less you know the better for all concerned. So relax and enjoy the ride." Without further explanation he drove out of the car park.

With his vision gone his other senses were heightened. He noted the car stopping, he assumed at several sets of traffic lights, or slowing down while driving around islands. He was also aware of the initial traffic noise gradually reducing, then the picking up of speed as the car reached, he assumed, the open road of the countryside rather than a motorway because it was quiet. He also estimated they had been driving for about 45 minutes when the car slowed to a halt and he felt a blast of cold air as the automatic window was opened. He heard Luke speak into an intercom.

"Luke Lewis and three others, we're expected."

There was a faint whirring sound, Zac guessed it was electronic gates swinging open and the car was driven for a few more minutes before slowly scrunching to a halt on gravel. Zac was ushered out of the car and as his blindfold was untied he heard the eerie hoot of an owl in the distance and smelt the distinctive pine and grassy aroma of the night, which momentarily transported him back to his one and only camping trip as a child.

It took a second before his eyes were able to focus on the expansive rolling lawns leading to dense forests on the horizon, lit up by the full moon. The night was still and there was a cold dampness in the air. One of the men who had sat by him indicated with the sweep of his arm to walk up the steps to the huge wooden door of the Georgian mansion. The door was opened by a tall, well-groomed gentleman with white hair, a slight stoop and a surprisingly deep voice. Zac presumed he was the modern equivalent of an old fashioned butler.

"Good evening gentlemen, follow me please."

They obediently followed along an oak panelled corridor to a comfortably furnished sitting room. They sat down on a dark chocolate brown leather Chesterfield settee and two chairs. The smell of beeswax and tobacco filled the air. The butler poured them each a glass of brandy and offered cigars around. Zac was impressed with the ornate blue and gold shield and helmet of the Baxter coat of arms hung above the fireplace, revealing the family motto 'Vincit Veritas' – truth conquers all things.

"I'll inform Mr Baxter that you are here."

Zac watched the butler leave and then scrutinised the room. Warm brown wooden panels covered the lower half of the walls. The upper part was painted a dull red, where four elaborate gold framed oil paintings were mounted, depicting gentlemen in formal dress. Zac surmised they were generations of the same family judging by the fashion of the clothes and, although obviously different men, the family resemblance was clearly evident by their narrow, piercing steel blue eyes.

Being blindfolded, the butler, the house with its old fashioned style all gave the evening a surreal quality and it felt like he was in another time zone.

Mr Baxter joined them about twenty minutes later. Zac recognised him from one of the portraits. He was dark-haired, not quite as tall as Zac, with the outline of a beard emphasising his square shaped jaw. His suit was clearly expensive and Zac put him in his mid-forties. He epitomised sophistication but it was his intense steel blue eyes that held everyone's attention; they were eyes that missed nothing and spared no one. He was not a man to cross.

"Luke tells me you are a regular client of his," Baxter said as he poured himself a glass of brandy. His voice was cultured, he was obviously well educated. "I gather you're a bit of a party animal too." He picked up a cigar and sniffed it appreciatively, closing his eyes momentarily, then, fixing his beady eyes on Zac, he continued his cross examination. "In fact, whether a party is successful or not hinges on you and your ready supply of... hmm... female companions."

The mere hint of a self-satisfied grin flickered across Zac's face, nevertheless it was enough to be noticed by Baxter.

"I understand you're interested in increasing your earning capacity?" he asked without looking directly at Zac.

Zac cleared his throat. "Yes, yes I am interested."

"Do you mind me asking why?" the question was more of a demand.

"No, no, not at all. It's just that I need a new place."

"Why?"

"Well, I've met a girl."

A big grin lit up Baxter's face and he laughed out loud. Looking at Zac he said, "I might have known. There's usually some woman calling the shots."

"No, no, she's not like that," Zac protested. "She doesn't even know I'm planning to get a better apartment. It's a surprise for her. She's the least demanding girl ever."

"Yeah, I bet," Baxter replied knowingly, smirking at the rest of the ensemble who all mirrored his grin.

Zac felt his face flush bright red, then suddenly Baxter stopped his kidding, the tone of his voice taking on a sudden harshness as he loomed over Zac, a hand on each arm of his chair, noses almost touching. Zac shrank back into the chair, feeling intimidated.

"Actually I couldn't give a *shit* why you need to make money, we're all driven by different needs but I am interested in commitment, loyalty and a code of honour to my organisation, and to me. At times the risks may be high but the rewards are even higher and definitely worth it." He stood up straight, picked up his brandy glass and, holding his cigar between the fingers of the same hand, moved his hand around indicating various aspects of the expensively furnished and decorated room as if to prove his point that the risks had been worth it. He continued, "If I allow you to join my organisation I demand total commitment and will accept nothing less. Be under no illusion, I make a very good employer but an extremely bitter enemy with an exceptionally long memory. There is a lot at stake and I do not suffer fools. Do I make myself clear?"

Zac momentarily bridled at the sharpness of his voice and felt self-conscious as all eyes in the room were on him, waiting for his response. All remnants of bravado instantly deserted him. He cleared his throat before nodding his understanding then added, "Yes, yes, I understand and if you take me on I promise total commitment."

Baxter glared at him for a long moment as if weighing things up in his mind then said in a loud voice for everyone's benefit, "Good, we understand one another. Luke will show you the ropes to begin with. Come gentlemen, I believe dinner is about to be served." He walked over to the far wall and to Zac's astonishment he slid open two of the wooden panels which revealed a large dining room.

It was an absolutely stunning room. Its high ceiling was adorned with biblical murals, enhanced by two large crystal chandeliers, and the walls were covered with ornately framed mirrors and oil paintings. One wall had floor to ceiling French doors, opening out onto beautifully manicured lawns and landscaped gardens, illuminated by soft lighting strategically position to maximise their beauty . The highly polished Italian dining table, with marquetry work of floral motifs and arabesques, complemented by twelve intricately carved chairs, was fit for a king and queen. Zac had never been in such an opulent room let alone dined in one. Again, it all seemed so surreal.

Dinner was served by two small middle-aged waitresses with blonde shoulder length hair who were clearly identical twins. The wine glasses were continually topped up imperceptibly by the elderly butler. The conversation flowed easily, interspersed with the occasional roar of collective laughter. Zac hardly spoke, he was too busy observing and absorbing his new world.

After a superb five course meal, the best one Zac had ever had, Luke led him to a small, sparsely furnished sitting room with a large window looking out across the rolling lawns and trees on the horizon. They sat opposite each other at a square pine table. Luke produced a little black book from his pocket and flicked it open at a page listing various points. He then started to explain the ins and outs of Nexus, the name of the organisation run by Mr Baxter. It was like being back at college as student and lecturer.

Zac listened intently as Luke went into great detail about the part of the organisation he was involved in, its members, its history, the work involved, the rewards on offer, the why, when, where and how of the business. At every opportunity he reiterated how total loyalty and commitment were expected. He was at pains to mention he had only known of one person, in the eight years he had been with the organisation, who had tried to double-cross them and he was sent abroad on an assignment where he vanished without trace. The story was he had been executed and fed to pigs.

Luke quizzed him about Jennie, his life and background including any brushes with the law, of which there were none. He seemed pleased to learn Zac had not had any contact with his family since leaving home five years ago, after his mother had moved yet another violent man into their home and that he had no desire to go back.

Two things were apparent to Zac. Firstly, there was a lot riding on his success, Luke had put his neck on the line; Zac was clearly his responsibility and if he messed up Luke would be cut loose too. Secondly, Mr Baxter was the brains behind a complex warren of businesses, with many side roads and an escape route to each. He had the ideas, provided the funds, took his cut but nothing could be traced back to him. He was a highly intelligent and ruthless man, a man who commanded respect, who gave Zac confidence in the organisation, so much so that when Luke asked if he was in, Zac said yes without hesitation. Luke could not disguise his relief. He explained there would be an initiation ceremony after breakfast the following morning and that immediately beforehand he would recap on what he had just told him. He then led him to his overnight accommodation. It was just after 1.00am.

The room smelt of fresh linen, it had a double bed, was decorated in neutral colours and had a picture of several white horses galloping across the sea shore hung on the wall at the foot of the bed. Zac used a new toothbrush he found in an unopened packet in the ensuite and quickly stripped to his boxer shorts for bed. He was asleep within minutes.

He slept surprisingly well considering the excitement of the evening and was showered, dressed and waiting for Luke's knock on the door by 8.00am. Everyone had a full English breakfast in the same room as the previous evening's meal. Afterwards, Luke briefly went through the details of the organisation and the oath Zac was to pledge, then it was time for the initiation ceremony.

The group moved to the drawing room. Luke ushered Zac to a small table at the far end of the room, he guessed it was the pine table he and Luke had sat at the previous evening. There was a red tablecloth runner draped across it and a big leather bound book placed in the centre, with the Nexus symbol, which consisted of a series of triangles, stars and circles, inlaid in the leather. Luke formally introduced Zac to the group, he said he was putting him forward for membership, that he had explained the history and organisation of Nexus and was personally satisfied Zac genuinely wished to become a member and could be trusted to respect, honour and obey its members and rules. He asked if anyone had any objection to the proposal, waited for a short while to allow for any response, not really expecting one as existing members would have been fully briefed about Zac already. Luke then pricked Zac's left index finger and smeared a droplet of blood on a card sporting the Nexus symbol. The card was passed to each member of the group while Zac read the typewritten oath handed to him by Luke.

"I, Zachary Thomas Owen, will be an honourable member of the organisation of Nexus. I will help and assist other members wherever possible. I will be loyal and respectful towards other members. I will not interfere with other members' interests. I will not inform on other members. My blood has been shed and passed to each of you in acknowledgement that I am now a member of the family of Nexus."

Baxter announced, "Zac that concludes your initiation. Welcome to Nexus. As explained in the ceremony, you are now expected to make advancement on behalf of Nexus. To help you to do this, we have asked Luke to act as your guide and mentor." He shook hands with Zac and Luke and then likewise all the other members shook their hands also.

Zac was very impressed with the solemnity of the ceremony and felt honoured to be a part of Nexus. The fact that he would be involved in making money on the backs of people's abject misery could not have been further from his mind; it was a world away from what had just happened.

The following week Zac attended a meeting hosted by Luke in the musty smelling, dingy back room of The Cottage, Luke's local pub, as he was well in with the manager and trusted him implicitly. There were six of them: Big Dave, Jacko, Mava and Pitty, collectively known as "the LTs" (Luke's Team). Like Zac they were fit and strong, with ages ranging from the mid-twenties to the mid-forties, all dealt in drugs and worked in the building trade. They sat at a large, solid, round oak table with heavy, high backed wooden chairs. Big Dave quipped it all seemed rather Arthurian as in Knights of the Round Table, which prompted a collective chuckle.

Luke was clearly excited as he began to explain their new assignment and they were his captive audience, particularly when he mentioned the sum of £2.5 million as a starting point. Basically, they were going to cut out the middleman from abroad and cultivate their own cannabis plants in England on a grand scale. Luke had a contact who owned a great swathe of land in Norfolk, running a legitimate farming business that had been in his family for generations. He was looking to make some serious money quickly for his retirement. Luke added they could all retire if everything panned out as planned.

The contact, Andrew Kettle, had several large warehouses on his farm and the idea was to create a huge cellar underneath each barn for the cultivation process. They would have their own generators, independent of the National Grid, unlike other would-be cultivators, which had proved to be their downfall.

The farm grew wheat, barley, vegetables and fruit, reared free range pigs and chickens, ran a farm shop and sold wholesale fresh flowers imported to Great Yarmouth from Europe. Before dawn each day a small army of white vans would roll up to collect the fresh flowers for various florist businesses. Their plan was to weld a false floor to a couple of the vans in which to transport the drugs. The main part of the van would be for the transportation of the fresh flowers; their fragrances would mask the smell of drugs. They would each have a role to play, the operation would take about twelve months, they would make their money then close it down and the warehouses would revert back to farm produce only. A few questions were asked, then one by one they all indicated they were in.

The next nine months was a hive of activity, with regular meetings and trips to the Norfolk warehouses. Things were progressing nicely and on schedule.

Marriage

Nick left the wedding arrangements to Penny and her team, which mainly consisted of her mother, Lillian, and sister Zara, while he concentrated on building his career.

Although traditionally the father of the bride paid for his daughter's wedding, Nick's father insisted on paying half of the bill and paying for the dark grey wedding suits and pewter coloured waistcoats for Nick, himself and Daniel, the best man. Glenda's 'Mother of the Groom' outfit, was a fitted navy blue dress, navy and cream shoes with matching accessories, including a cream feathered fascinator which pick up the blonde highlights in her medium brown hair. She ordered the flowers from her lifelong friend Annette who owned a florist shop called 'Forget-Me-Not'.

Lillian and Zara enjoyed a hedonistic few weekends helping Penny shop for her wedding dress, taking full advantage of the personal assistant service on offer and the complimentary glasses of champagne. Lillian had chosen her 'Mother of the Bride' outfit quite quickly: a tiered two piece, a subtle blend of blues with threads of gold woven through, a flimsy, pale pink hat with matching clutch bag and high heeled shoes, at least half an inch higher than she would normally wear but, "What the heck, it is my daughter's wedding". Maid of honour, Zara, and bridesmaids Janine, (Nick's sister) and Penny's cousin Julia all had matching slimline, three quarter length pale grey dresses with matching high heeled shoes.

Penny had set her heart on a lacy 'princess dress' and had tried on dozens in different shops and various towns, but could not find 'The One'. She was becoming very despondent. Then her mother almost dragged her into a tiny 'blink and you would miss it' shop tucked away in a back street.

The shop was originally an old cottage. Its small frontage belied its size, because the building opened up at the back into a large, gown lined room with a spiral staircase leading to a tastefully decorated upstairs fitting room hosting a central, small circular stage allowing the bride-to-be to do a twirl for her helpers to view the dress in its entirety.

Penny half-heartedly selected six dresses and was quite irritated when the mousy little shop assistant suggested a plain fitted dress, with a fine corset back and slight fishtail would suit her figure. With gentle encouragement from her mother she relented and agreed to try on the dress... last. Predictably, none of the lacy numbers had the 'Wow' factor. Fed up and fighting back tears of frustration she pulled the assistant's choice on. Not bothering to look in the mirror she walked, unsmiling, straight through the dressing area curtain to where her mother and sister were waiting.

"Oh wow! You look absolutely stunning!" they both exclaimed.

"That dress looks tailor-made for you. Just perfect," added Lillian, her eyes becoming moist.

Penny turned to view herself and her jaw dropped in astonishment. For the first time in her life she felt truly beautiful. Her tearful smile of gratitude met with a beaming smile of delight from the mousy little assistant.

Before they knew it the wedding day was upon them and they could not have wished for better weather. It was a perfect summer's day, warm with a Mediterranean blue sky and a smattering of light fluffy clouds. The path leading to the 12th century village church shimmered in the sunlight and the stained glass windows threw out a kaleidoscope of colourful rays as Penny made her way under the arched gateway to the church entrance on the arm of her proud father, Eric. The beribboned, standard rose bushes lining the way, supplied by a contact of Annette's from Forget-Me-Not, filled the air with their heady perfume. It was a pretty church and something of a tradition because it was the same church that Penny's parents and maternal grandparents had been married in.

The service ran smoothly, their vows were expressed before God, family and friends, and hymns were enthusiastically sung. Nick gently teased the wedding ring onto Penny's third finger and as the immortal words, 'You may now kiss the bride' were spoken Penny's school friend, Debbie, sang a crystal clear, classical version, of My Prayer by the Platters, (Eric's favourite song), to an enthralled congregation as the beaming newlyweds made their way down the aisle and out of the church to the waiting photographer.

The reception was held in a marquee erected in the grounds of The George Inn, a village pub which was originally a manor house and conveniently situated within walking distance of the church. Eric's 'father of the bride' speech was a wonderful tribute to Penny and a warm welcome to their new son-in-law, Nick. Towards the end of his speech his emotions almost got the better of him, causing most of the congregation's eyes to well up too. Then David's 'best man' speech brought the house down causing widespread tears of laughter. Fantastic!

The meal was delicious, the drinks flowed and the local Take That tribute band was superb. Laughter filled the air and Penny and Nick could not have been happier.

Their happiness continued all through their fortnight's honeymoon in Protaras, Cyprus. Fraternal twins, a daughter and a son, born on 16th December 2003, completed their family. Life was so good it scared Penny.

Nick at Macefields

Nick felt good on so many levels. He was settled with Penny, they had both thoroughly enjoyed their wedding day and relaxing honeymoon. He had a sense of freedom from the restrictions of Stepwells as he no longer felt obliged to curry favour with certain individuals for the sake of his career and, more importantly, he instinctively knew he had made the right decision by joining Macefields. Energy was coursing through his body, he was raring to make his mark and show Richardson, Stepwells and all its Doubting Thomases just what a valuable asset they had lost! *Yes I'm ready to show them, the whole bloody lot of them. Bring it on!*

For his first day he wore a new navy-blue pinstriped suit, a white shirt and a pale blue tie with tiny Welsh dragon motifs and matching dragon cufflinks that Penny had bought him for good luck.

As he stepped through the sliding glass doors into Macefields' spacious reception he took a deep breath then nodded and smiled at the two attractive female receptionists. He walked past them along the short corridor to the lifts. One of the guys in his new team joined him at the lifts and by the time they had reached the third floor they were enjoying a laugh about a comedy programme shown on television the previous evening. A perfect start to his first day, chasing away any lingering reservations he had about his move.

Short, stocky, fair-haired, David Evans, who had joined Macefields the month before Nick, had arrived early, as he tended to do, in accordance with his 'early bird' philosophy. Upon seeing Nick he walked over to his desk to greet him. Immediately they both burst out laughing because, bizarrely, their suits and shirts were almost identical; even David's tie was the same shade of pale blue except it had a small fleur-de-lys pattern, which his wife Jane had also bought him for good luck when he had started. Fortunately, they did not look alike, that would have been far too weird. Dark-haired Lisa, Nick's new secretary, who had worked at Macefields for a couple of years, brought him a mug of coffee.

Lisa was a few years younger than Nick, attractive, quite plump with big blue eyes and a wide smile. He had met her a few times for coffee while serving his notice at Stepwells. He liked her and, more importantly, they were comfortable with each other.

For a few minutes, he quietly sat at his desk and sipped his coffee whilst getting a feel for his new office. He liked the glass partitioned lawyers' pods, set around the edge of the offices, which cleverly provided an element of privacy without detracting from the fashionable open-plan trend. His quiet moment finished as he drank the last of his coffee. He grabbed the notepad and pen Lisa had thoughtfully placed on his desk and headed off to his first one-to-one training session. He was now a man on a mission to take his career to new heights.

Surveillance

Zac and the other members of Luke's team made regular trips to Norfolk, at least once a week. Usually it would involve just one team member at a time, either driving one of the specially adapted flower vans or checking on the cannabis plants. Things were progressing nicely, very nicely indeed. They had already successfully cultivated, processed and distributed three crops and the final crop was almost ready. Then one day three of them broke with protocol and decided to meet up for breakfast at a roadside café.

By pure chance PC Bellingham had called into the café for breakfast ten minutes earlier than the trio. He was off duty on his way to visit an elderly relative in Norwich. He recognised Zac instantly; he recalled the stabbing incident almost twelve months before. Zac and the others sat at the table behind him, in fact the back of Zac's chair touched his. He had already selected a free newspaper from the wall mounted newspaper rack and pretended to read it while listening intently to Zac and his companions' conversation. He managed to catch enough snippets of information to arouse his suspicions, so much so that, although he was off duty, he decided to follow Zac, relieved that he had filled the fuel tank before stopping at the café. Unfortunately for Zac it was his turn to attend the warehouses in Norfolk. The others went their separate ways, but not before Bellingham had noted their registration numbers and a brief description of them.

During the ninety minute journey to the warehouses Bellingham managed to keep Zac's car in sight, staying either one or two cars behind, and he even managed to catch up with him after being caught by traffic lights a couple of times.

Luckily, when Zac turned into the farm's entrance he was able to pull into a nearby layby which gave clear views of the farm and its warehouses. The land was skirted by a low lying grey stone wall, the gate was inset a couple of cars' length into the entrance, the drive to the farmhouse was about a hundred and fifty metres and the land was flat with a backdrop of trees.

One of Bellingham's hobbies was ornithology and consequently he was in the habit of taking his high powered camera with him on his days out, just on the off chance a bird watching opportunity presented itself. From the lay-by he zoomed in on Zac's meeting with the farmer and took numerous quick-fire photographs of the two talking and entering the warehouses. They spent approximately twenty minutes in each, which aroused Bellingham's suspicions that they were tending to something and his gut instinct said drugs. Finally Zac followed the farmer into the farmhouse; he was in there another twenty minutes. This time Bellingham guessed for coffee and negotiations. He patiently waited until Zac emerged. He witnessed him shake hands with the farmer and drive out of the farm entrance, turning back in the direction he had come from. Bellingham had a map spread across the steering wheel and pretended to study it as Zac drove past. He had already made the decision not to follow; he reasoned that he had enough information to be going on with and did not want to risk Zac suspecting he was being tailed. From the layby he telephoned the head of his section, Detective Inspector Gallagher. He gave him all the details then carried on to see his Aunt Charlotte as planned.

DI Gallagher sensed Bellingham had picked up on something big and quickly put the wheels in motion, setting up a covert operation, aptly named 'Operation Barn Owl'. He liaised with his contemporary, DI Holmes, at the Norfolk Police Headquarters, who arranged surveillance in his area and likewise Gallagher set up his own local surveillance team. Six weeks into 'Operation Barn Owl', the final crop of cannabis was processed and ready to be dispatched to various venues in Greater Manchester. Gallagher gave the go-ahead for a dawn raid on Friday 20th June at each of the premises.

Zac had felt uneasy for a couple of weeks, he could not say what had spooked him; the team was on schedule and things were running smoothly. Perhaps it was just that: things were going too smoothly and it was making him hypersensitive. They were so close to having it all, so near, yet everything seemed in slow motion and the mounting tension made him feel like a coiled spring. He decided he needed an early night, because the weekend was going to be very intense but once the weekend was over, the job was done and they could wrap it up and all begin a new life. A brand new start, fantastic!!

As he parked his silver Volkswagen Polo car in one of the parking bays at the front of their apartment, he checked his watch, it was 8.30pm. *Jennie will be home soon* he thought. As he opened his car door he casually glanced at the black Ford Focus car parked a little way up the road on the opposite side. Although it was quite dark he caught the eye of its male occupant who quickly looked down, too quickly. The hairs stood up on the back of Zac's neck and a tingling sensation swept through his body. Nevertheless, he forced himself to act naturally by slowly climbing out of his car and strolling to the entrance of the apartment block, but all the time his heart and mind were racing.

Through the side of the vertical blind he slyly looked out of their second floor apartment window and saw the man in the car speaking into his mobile telephone while looking at the entrance, then he looked up at Zac's window. Alarmed, Zac stepped back. He moved to the other side of the window and looked in the opposite direction down the street. He spied a man lurking on the corner as if waiting for something. He also thought the net curtain of the house over the road was twitching but he could not be certain. He sensed danger. Pacing the lounge, turning things over and over in his mind, considering the options, he finally accepted he had no choice, he had to stop the operation and get away. Future plans to move to Leeds would now be started immediately, he would have to abandon his car and not tell anyone. Concerned his telephone calls were being monitored he decided to liaise with the team by Jennie's telephone once he and Jennie were safely away.

Where the bloody hell are you Jennie?

There was an important housing project at work and a huge backlog of documents to be typed. Zac agreed to Jennie working overtime until 9.00pm, so long as the firm provided a lift or a taxi to ensure she reached home safely.

It was 10.00pm and Jennie had just been dropped off after the evening shift. In the lift and along the short corridor to their apartment she wondered what sort of mood Zac would be in. His mood swings and angry outbursts were getting worse. Everything she did or did not do, said or did not say, seemed to irritate him and the ever present knot in her stomach turned a notch. She lived in fear of him and longed for those carefree days when she was a child living in the country, riding her pony, her daddy walking alongside. She had felt safe then. With a heavy heart she put the key in the lock, took a deep breath and as she turned it she forced a smile as she opened the door.

"Pack your bags, we're out of here!" Zac barked at her. Her smile vanished, instantly replaced by a look of bewilderment as she tried to take in what he had said. She stood transfixed, watching him dash from the bedroom to the bathroom throwing things into a holdall.

"Get a bloody move on you dumb bitch!" he yelled. "Our ride is on its way!" The look she gave him was akin to a rabbit startled by headlights and he flew at her, grabbed a handful of her hair and pulled her towards him. He felt her shrink away from him and saw her eyes screw up in fear which made him want to smash her face in.

"Get a fucking move on," he hissed menacingly, "we're leaving for Leeds because I've got to lay low for a while. Now move it!" He pushed her forcefully towards the bedroom. Her whole body jittered and she started shaking but she did as she was ordered to. He had already thrown most of her shoes and clothes into a holdall. She managed to cram her knitting bag, toiletries and straighteners in and finally put her jewellery box and make-up bag in a plastic foldup bag, just as Zac took a call on one of his mobile phones. She never understood why it was necessary for him to have two mobile phones.

"Okay Joe, we're taking the lift to the basement now, you know where to go, it's dark, the lights were smashed two nights ago, probably kids, well they've done us a favour. Anyway, we'll hide in the back of your car as discussed. Just make sure we're not followed mate. I'm relying on you."

Zac was very agitated in the lift, pacing like a caged tiger. Jennie shrank into the corner. The lift seemed to take an age to reach the basement and she wondered why they had gone there instead of the first floor as usual. The doors had barely opened when Zac shot out of them and grabbed both of their holdalls; she carried her handbag and foldup bag. He tentatively opened the door to the passageway housing the communal bins and peered out. The driver spotted him and beckoned him over. Zac threw their things onto the back seat, climbed in after Jennie and crouched down on the floor with her. Joe, the driver, was someone who owed him a favour. Zac told him again to make sure they were not followed. Fortunately he knew the area like the back of his hand and a few twists and turns on the estate reassured Zac they were not being followed.

Tom Drake, a police officer in plain clothes, sat in an unmarked police car waiting for Zac's return. He watched Zac pull in to a parking bay at the front of the building and open the car door to get out. In doing so he glanced up the road, unfortunately straight into Drake's eyes. Although their eyes were locked for only a split second before Drake looked down, he felt deflated because he knew instinctively his cover was blown. He waited until Zac had entered his apartment block before telephoning the station to report his concerns. While waiting for a call back with further instructions he remained stationary, observing. He saw the chap who had been hanging around down the road wave at a white car before getting into it and being whisked away. His mobile phone buzzed, it was Sergeant Jones. She instructed him to return to the station and explained that PCs Bates and Davies would continue to cover from the upstairs room in the house opposite the apartment block. Frustrated, Drake did as he was ordered.

Davies spotted a taxi pull up outside the apartments and watched a blonde woman get out. He recognised her as Zac's girlfriend and updated Sergeant Jones by phone. A few minutes later she rang back to instruct them to check out the rear of the premises again. Bates, in plain clothes, left the house by the back gate. He turned right which took him around the back of the row of terraced houses into a side street, another right turn brought him into the road in front of the apartments where he turned left and walked a short distance down the road before crossing over to the side of the block as if going to the local Spar shop. At the back of the premises was an outbuilding housing the apartment block's rubbish bins. Just as Bates rounded the back of the premises he caught sight of the tail lights of a car driving off. He had not noticed the car on his inspection twenty minutes previously and the fact that the registration number was obscured made him suspicious. He immediately reported back to Sergeant Jones who in turn spoke to Detective Inspector Gallagher. Ten minutes later Bates and Davies entered Zac and Jennie's apartment, dismayed to find it empty of personal effects and clothes. Clearly they had managed to slip away.

Leaving the apartment lights on, abandoning their car and laying low in the back of his contact's car was a stroke of genius by Zac, fooling the men observing, meaning they left unhindered.

The silence between them was deafening during the ten minute ride to the train station. Events seemed to be in slow motion to Jennie as she was swept along by Zac, but she was shocked back to reality when she heard him ask the ticket office attendant for two one way tickets to Leeds. Suddenly the frightening implications of their flight became apparent and a wave of nausea washed over her. Once again she was plunged into a world of insecurity and fear.

They were fortunate on three counts: the train was not packed, they were able to get a seat in the corner and no one sat beside either of them. Zac sat facing down the carriage so he could gauge if anyone was listening to the mobile phone calls he needed to make and Jennie sat opposite him, staring out of the window.

As a precaution Zac used Jennie's phone. His first call was to his old school friend Archie, one of the few people he trusted. He told him he was on his way to Leeds and needed somewhere to stay until he could sort something out and that he would explain when they met up. Archie said he would get back to him as soon as possible.

His second call was to Luke. Right at the outset of the operation it was agreed between the team that if things went 'tits up', as Luke had so eloquently put it, without hesitation the priority was to get away and call in immediately so everyone else could do likewise. Zac explained his suspicions that he was being watched and his decision to 'leg it' to a safe place. Instinct told him to say he was going to stay with a friend in Coventry and lay low until the dust had settled. He said he would get back in touch in a couple of days.

While waiting for the return call from Archie he ruminated on how easily he could deceive people. He marvelled at how, over the years, he had created an alias with a web of lies backed up by false documentation i.e. driving licence, bank account, etc, well before getting involved with Luke. It had started out as a bit of a joke when he had first hit the party scene. For a laugh or to impress the girls he would give a false name, address or job as part of his chat-up routine. Occasionally he would throw in a foreign accent; that was until the time he was caught out by a girl who spoke fluent Italian. He still felt his cheeks burn with embarrassment when he recalled his humiliation. Nevertheless he'd learned a valuable lesson, 'Freedom is knowing your own limitations' as his old English teacher, Mr Heath, once said. He had not really understood what he had meant until his 'Italian fiasco' brought it home to him. Nevertheless, what started out as a bit of fun soon became the norm once he realised the benefits.

"Shit, shit, SHIT!" Luke punched the door in frustration. His fist shattered the top panel of the white door. "Oh shit!" he yelled again, this time in agony, vigorously shaking his hand to diminish the pain. He telephoned the other members of his team.

"Dave, Luke here, bad news I'm afraid. Zac's convinced he's being watched and, as per group agreement, has done a runner to stay with a mate in Coventry and lay low until the dust settles. You do the same," Luke commanded.

"B-b-but we're so close to the finish," Dave protested.

"No arguments, it's too risky and you know the rules. You ring Jacko and Mava and I'll ring Pitty and Kettle." As an afterthought he added in a softer tone, "Good luck." Then he had the same conversation with Kettle. Unfortunately, despite persistently ringing Pitty's mobile, he could not contact him and with each attempt his feeling of foreboding increased.

Unluckily for Luke's team DI Gallagher was quicker off the mark and had instructed his officers to round up the suspects. Dave was arrested in his apartment, Mava while running back from the local Indian restaurant where he had been enjoying a meal with a group of workmates from the building site and Jacko was picked up as he left a 'gentleman's club'. The reason Luke was unable to contact Pitty was because he was already driving his white flower van with a false floor, housing drugs with a street value of £200,000 and was out of range of a mobile phone signal. Just as the police ordered him to pull over Pitty's phone finally rang. He automatically pressed receive.

"Pitty, Luke here, we may have been rumbled, lay low as discussed and I'll be in touch."

"Too late mate." Resignation was evident in Pitty's voice. "The police have already pulled me over." Before he could terminate the call his phone was snatched out of its hands-free holder. At the same time there was a loud banging on Luke's front door.

"Police, open up, we have a search warrant." Within seconds the front door of his house was smashed in. Luke tried to leave via the rear door but the police were waiting. Luke's farmer contact, Andrew Kettle, and one of his workers, Gary Starkey, were also arrested.

The only one to evade detection was Zac. Much to PC Bellingham's annoyance neither the LTs, Kettle or Starkey would admit that there was another person involved.

Zac had escaped again.

Leeds

Zac did not speak to Jennie at all during the two hour train journey, indeed he spent most of the time on his mobile phone speaking in hushed tones, while she stared out of the window. Her mind was blank, oblivious to the buildings and countryside whizzing past which were shrouded in darkness. She did not attempt to speak with him because she was too afraid.

At Leeds station he ordered a taxi and within minutes they were dropped off outside a row of old, three storey terraced houses, their height accentuated by four worn steps leading up to the entrance doors. Light from a nearby lamppost illuminated tiny overgrown gardens edged by a two foot high black brick wall which marked the properties' boundaries. The buildings had clearly seen better days judging by the window frames with their dirty white paint flaking off.

Archie was waiting to meet them. He was stocky, about her height, 5'7", bald, with smiling blue eyes and a generous mouth. He and Zac touched hands in a high five, they hugged each other affectionately then Zac introduced him to Jennie. Archie grinned broadly as they shook hands. He had a happy face.

Their house was the second from the left, the one with the door painted bottle green, its thick paint indicating several layers. Archie lead the way into the house. The hall and stairs were dark and dingy with part of the faded floral wallpaper coming away from the top, but the first thing Jennie noticed was the strong smell of urine by the entrance. Fearing Zac's reaction she resisted the urge to cover her nose and mouth to mask the stench. The house had been turned into three apartments, one on each floor; they had the second floor one.

She was relieved to find that shutting the door to the apartment kept the pungent smell at bay and was pleasantly surprised at how spacious it was, although it was not anywhere near as good as the one in Manchester. Tears threatened as she thought of the Manchester apartment; she had not realised how much it had felt like home, despite Zac and his awful outbursts.

The two friends disappeared into the kitchen, speaking very quietly, leaving Jennie sitting on a worn red leather settee, which was surprisingly comfortable. After a short while Archie waved goodbye and left. As if sensing her turmoil Zac took her in his arms. His voice was warm and tender as he tried to reassure her.

"Look babe, everything's gonna work out just fine, don't worry." She put her head on his shoulder and he stroked her hair. "I know you liked living in Manchester but I need to lay low for a while, trust me babe, you know everything I do is with you in mind." He lifted her chin and kissed her gently on the mouth. His tenderness triggered the release of her tears which rolled down her cheeks. He used his thumbs to wipe them away softly saying, "I love you with all my heart, Jen, you're so precious to me." He kissed her again and a groan escaped from deep within him. "I need you," he whispered and the passion in his voice and his kiss overwhelmed her. He carried her into the bedroom and gently laid her on the bed. He quickly undressed himself and lay down beside her, slowly undressing her, making love to her tenderly until her passion matched his and she begged him to take her.

Afterwards, their bodies spent, they lay on the bed side by side in naked splendour, at peace in the stillness of the moment. The darkness of the night was intermittently sliced by moonbeams thrown out by the scudding clouds, reaching through the curtainless window, gently caressing the contours of their bodies. Neither of them wanted to bring an end to their intimacy.

The persistent ringing of Zac's mobile phone in the next room broke the spell and caused him to groan in frustration as he rolled off the bed to answer it. She watched him sprint into the next room and marvelled at his beauty, his broad shoulders, long back leading to slender hips and long sturdy legs. His body was lean, tanned and smooth.

Suddenly the room felt cold and she shivered on hearing the harsh tone of his voice.

"I said I'd be there and I will be there; just give me twenty minutes, okay. I'll be there!" The heavenly bliss of a moment ago completely evaporated. He came back into the room and without saying a word quickly dressed, grabbing his wallet and mobile phone. As he left the apartment, as an afterthought he said over his shoulder, "I'll be back later. Don't leave the apartment." She knew better than to protest.

Fear of abandonment reared its ugly head again as she found herself alone in the sparsely furnished apartment. Every reminder of their earlier shared passion had disappeared, as if an invisible force had yanked it through the door as Zac closed it. Tears welled up but she suppressed them, unable to let herself go in this impersonal, unfamiliar place. She dressed and sat on the edge of the bed staring out at the starless night sky, trying to gather her thoughts and make sense of the last few hours. After a while she felt hungry and thirsty and made her way to the kitchen only to discover the tired looking cupboards were completely bare; there was nothing, not even a spoon. She was afraid to leave the apartment in case she lost her way and, more significantly, in case Zac returned to find her gone when he had specifically ordered her to stay. She returned to the bedroom and sat in the same place on the bed looking out at the stars, feeling invisible, a non-person, as if the darkness of the room had absorbed her.

A large, dusty white moth, looking for a night-time resting place, fluttered its wings for a few moments before settling on the window pane, its wings partially outstretched to the elements, its fat grub body pressed against the window, its eyes red pinpricks, glowing. Another vulnerable, lonely heartbeat to share the empty night. Eventually she fell asleep thoroughly exhausted.

Sunlight streaming through the window woke her. The strange surroundings made her feel disorientated at first then the memories of the previous evening came flooding back along with feelings of anxiety, this time emphasised by pangs of hunger and thirst and the fact that she was alone. Zac had been out all night.

There were no cups or glasses so she had to cup her hands together under the tap for a drink of water. After freshening up in the bathroom she started to unpack the suitcases but as there were no coat hangers she laid their clothes in various piles on the floor. She found a flapjack cake in her handbag that she had forgotten she had bought Zac on the way home from work. Work! The word sent her mind reeling, she needed to let them know she was not going to be in. What could she tell them, that she was never ever going to see them again? She sat down on the edge of the bed in despair staring out of the window once more; she could not get her head around all that had happened and what the future had in store.

She had been sitting there for a while, drained of energy, when the sound of the key turning in the lock of the door made her heart lurch, causing her to bring her left hand up to her throat in a subconscious act of defence. She was relieved to see Zac walk through the door. He was carrying a brown paper bag displaying the McDonald's logo: 'M I'm loving it'.

"Here babe do something with this!" he said, tossing the food bag over to her. "I figured you'd be hungry, I know I am." He grinned at her and she felt light-hearted with relief as she caught the bag and made her way into the kitchen. There were no crocks or cutlery so she improvised by tearing the bag in half creating a paper plate each and, although they sucked their Coca-Cola drinks through straws it was one of the best meals she had ever had.

While eating Zac decided Jennie should phone work to resign, saying her mother had been taken seriously ill again and that she had had to rush up to see her in Blackpool and did not know when she would be back. She hated lying but it had to be done.

The following morning Zac was up with the dawn chorus and said he had just got to collect something and that she had exactly one hour to get ready; he was grinning and excited. An hour later he bounced into the living room.

"Jennie babe are you ready? I've got something to show you!" He grabbed her hand and she had to sprint to keep up with him as they raced down the dingy stairs. When they emerged onto the street Zac put his hands over her eyes saying, "Close your eyes and hold your hand out." Jennie excitedly complied and felt something small and cold placed in the palm of her hand; her fingers traced the outline of a key. Zac removed his hands from her eyes and pointed to the opposite side of the road. Jennie looked at him, puzzled.

"There she is, the black BMW convertible, it's ours! Come on girl let's go for a spin." Again he grabbed her hand pulling her across the road around to the passenger side. He opened the door, bowing in an exaggerated manner as she sat in the front seat and swung her legs as elegantly as she could into the car.

They drove into the countryside. The sun was shining, Zac lowered the roof, the wind blew through their hair and they were two young lovers without a care in the world. In all the excitement they had forgotten to eat, so when hunger pangs kicked in they stopped off at a Morrison's supermarket, enjoyed a big breakfast and a leisurely stroll around the store, filling their trolley with anything and everything that took their fancy.

Jennie pushed her suspicions about the wad of money Zac was carrying to the back of her mind; for the moment she did not want to know where he had got it from and more importantly did not want to spoil their fun.

Unexpected Departure

"So what's the truth behind Jennie's sudden departure to Leeds?" Bev asked the rest of the Flakes as they tucked into lunch at Bella Italia.

"I know, it was a shock. Something's not right there," said Rachel.

"Hmm, I know what you mean. She keeps herself very much to herself, almost as though she's afraid," added Ben.

"It's obviously to do with that boyfriend of hers, Zac, he's a surly looking bloke. I've always thought there's something dodgy about him," Lucy declared. "He's probably a control freak too."

"Yeah, talking about control freaks," said Piers, "three men in a bar, two are bragging and laughing about how they control their wives. The third one says nothing. Eventually they turn to him and ask 'What kind of control do you have over your wife?'

He sighs and says, 'Well the other day I had my wife on her knees.'

'Wow! What happened next?' they ask excitedly.

He takes a long, slow swig of his beer, before continuing, 'She started screaming, *Get out from under that bloody bed and fight like a man!*'"

Everyone laughed.

After a pause Bev asked, "What's going on with Yasmin Saunders?"

"Dunno, why'd you ask?" queried Ben.

"It's just the last few times I've seen her she's looked awful, really scruffy, holes in her tights, hem hanging down, greasy hair, hardly the way you'd expect a barrister to dress for work. Frankly, she looks like she's on something," continued Bev.

"I've always thought she was quite attractive in a waifish sort of way," said Rachel.

"Waifish? I'd say more like a posh speaking scrubber! In fact she could do with a good wash and scrub," Lucy scathed.

"Wow, who's rattled your cage?" asked Ben.

"Uh, no one, it's just that she gets on my nerves the way she looks down her long pointed nose."

"You're looking rather sheepish Piers," observed Bev.

Piers gave her a cheeky grin.

"Oh no, you haven't have you?" Bev responded.

"In fairness, it was a while ago, when I first started at Stepwells," protested Piers.

"Oh honestly, is no female safe from you?"

"What can I say? I can't help being charming and irresistible to the female sex!"

Change

Zac and Jennie's new found sense of euphoria continued for a couple of weeks. Each morning over breakfast they would plan the day's adventures. They loved, laughed and lived just like when they had first moved in together. Jennie's usual state of anxiety had all but dissipated, along with her pangs of homesickness when thinking of their apartment in Manchester. She even started to believe fleeing to Leeds might prove to be a good move after all because the Zac she had fallen in love with had returned to her.

Ever practical, she realised she needed to find work and, although disappointed, she was not surprised when on the Thursday of their third week Zac bought a newspaper. They circled various jobs for her to apply for and agencies to register with. Zac found casual work on a building site and the following week Jennie's time was taken up with interviews at five agencies, one a day, undergoing their various tests. She wrote off for three advertised jobs, enclosed her curriculum vitae and also telephoned a call centre in response to their "immediate start" advert. After conducting an initial telephone interview they invited her to the call centre for a face-to-face interview the following day, Friday. The interview went well and she was not surprised to be offered a job, just sorry to start on Monday, coincidentally the same day as Zac was starting his new job. She had hoped for a few more days together enjoying their blissful happiness.

The job in the call centre was within walking distance of where they lived. Although it was work she had never done before and quite boring, her team of six was fun to work with and they had plenty of laughs. Zac seemed happy to be back in the building trade. Oh life was good and remained so for the next seven months.

If pressed, Jennie would have said Zac started to gradually change approximately six months after their flight to Leeds. At first his mind was obviously elsewhere, he would be silently preoccupied or moody. Then he began disappearing for the occasional 'no questions asked' weekend. She was afraid to question his moves fearing his reaction and the reason. After each disappearance he would return and be on a high for a few days before he began drinking and chain smoking, and, more worryingly, taking cannabis in the apartment.

Christmas

Jennie loved Christmas and was determined they would celebrate their first Christmas in Leeds in style.

Even though it was just the two of them, they bought a six foot high artificial Christmas tree, which Jennie decorated mainly with red and gold baubles and ornaments. For presents she bought Zac a dark blue jumper from Next; it was a perfect match to the colour of his eyes, Levi jeans, Nike trainers, a book about Bruce Lee, his favourite film being Enter the Dragon, a Monopoly set, a bottle of Jack Daniels whisky and both of them a selection box and an advent calendar offering a daily chocolate surprise. Jennie was delighted with her gifts from Zac, which were a cornflower blue cashmere poncho by Catherine Robinson the same colour as her eyes, a book about the zodiac, a bottle of perfume – Flower by Kenzo, a set of Lush bath bombs and a box of Thornton chocolates. She was amazed he had bought her an easel, paints, canvas and an artist instruction book because it had been months since she had said she would love to paint some pictures for their apartment and at the time she thought her idea had fallen on deaf ears. Obviously not.

She cooked a turkey crown, a small joint of pork, sage and onion stuffing, fresh vegetables, including sprouts with roast chestnuts, (Zac's favourite vegetable combination), Christmas pudding and brandy sauce. She was desperate to make this a magical few days because it was a poignant time for both of them. She knew Zac's memories of Christmas were tainted by the drunken violence of his father, a stark contrast to the happy Christmases of her childhood, which she missed terribly, but for now she suppressed her nostalgia to concentrate on the present and was secretly impressed and excited with how well she had organised everything and hoped Zac enjoyed the fruits of her labour.

Zac thoroughly enjoyed Christmas, it was his best ever and all thanks to Jennie. He loved her so much it hurt and he was so relieved that he had not lost her a while back when drugs had taken hold of him and he had hurt her.

Once they had cleared everything away after their meal they settled down to watch the film Titanic. At the end of the film, in front of the twinkling Christmas tree, Zac knelt on one knee and said, "Jennie I love you with all of my heart, my mind and my soul. I fell in love with you the night we met and I bought you a hot chocolate. My love has continued to grow. I want to share the rest of my life with you, to look after you, plan for our future. I will do whatever I can to give you the best in life, because you are the best in my life." He took a deep breath then softly sang the last verse of the Titanic's theme song,

> *"You're here,*
> *There's nothing I fear,*
> *And I know that my heart will go on,*
> *We'll stay forever this way,*
> *You are safe in my heart,*
> *And my heart will go on and on."*

Then he presented her with a little black box. He flicked open the top to reveal a sparkling diamond ring set in white gold and said, "Jennie, will you marry me?" Jennie burst into tears, threw her arms around his neck and agreed to be his wife.

The next few weeks were full of love, laughter and growing excitement as they traded ideas about marrying and their honeymoon. Life was good and offered a promising future.

Mêlée and Court Case

On the fourth Saturday in January George Gains, the proprietor of the building company, had organised a night out in Leeds city centre as a Christmas treat for the men. Eight of them were able to make it, including Zac and Mr Gains. They started off with a delicious Indian meal accompanied by lively banter. The high spirits carried on during their subsequent visit to a nearby casino where, surprisingly, they were all lucky enough to enjoy modest wins and ended their gambling session slightly better off than when they started. Just before midnight, Gains and two of the older men decided to call it a night while the rest went on to a nightclub.

There was a great party atmosphere in the club. The lads had a couple of drinks each while eyeing the girls dancing, then they began dancing too. At first they were just mucking about on the floor, dancing with each other, then fair-haired, cheeky-faced Billy started flirting with a trio of girls dancing together. Before long he had clearly singled out a pretty dark-haired girl by positioning himself between her and her friends and when a slow record was played he made his move and gently, but firmly, pulled her towards him. His mates nudged each other, grinning at his technique. Unfortunately, the girl's boyfriend was not grinning. He pushed his way onto the dance floor and roughly grabbed her bare arm. Billy squared up to him and within seconds they began fighting.

Zac waded into the mêlée to try to break it up but several of the other chap's mates decided to get a piece of the action.. What followed next was like something out of a Wild West movie. Men and women were jumping on each other's backs, throwing glasses, smashing tables, ripping clothes, and in no time the brawl was completely out of control. The nightclub bouncers called the police.

Three squad cars and twelve police officers later, Zac, his friends, the three girls and several others ended up at the local police station being interviewed and fingerprinted. One by one all were processed and, when necessary, treated by the police doctor. They were then bailed to attend the police station at a designated date and time in order for further investigations to be carried out. All, that is, with the exception of Zac, who remained incarcerated in a cell for another couple of hours.

He sat on the metal bench which was securely bolted to the wall and floor. The grubby cell walls needed a lick of paint and its high narrow window only permitted a sliver of light into the room. The metal reinforced security door had a small viewing hatch towards the top of it to enable the duty officer to periodically check on the prisoners in his care.

Zac leaned his back against the wall and stared at nothing in particular, just waiting and thinking. He recapped on the events of the evening and how, in the blink of an eye, the mood of the group had changed from one of joie de vivre to one of violence. His left eye was swollen and throbbing and his shirt sleeve had been ripped off. Then his thoughts turned to Jennie and how upset she would be when he told her he had been arrested.

Eventually he was taken to an interview room by the cell duty officer.

Although Zac was unaware he had been locked up longer than the other people he had been arrested with, he nevertheless had a sinking feeling in the pit of his stomach and his instinct was things were about to take a turn for the worse. His instinct was right.

The duty officer pushed the door open and moved back to allow Zac to enter the dimly lit interview room. As Zac stepped past him he was shocked to recognise one of the interviewing officers as the one who had tended to him when he was stabbed in Manchester. A feeling of dread overwhelmed him as he sat down at the table because he knew the 'game was up', and that his fingerprints had linked him to the warehouses. His future looked bleak, very bleak indeed, and so did Jennie's. The thought of hurting Jennie again made him feel nauseous and tearful.

Throughout the Norfolk drugs cultivation case DI Gallagher's team was very efficient. All the evidence had been quickly collated and double, triple and quadruple checked before being handed over to the Crown Prosecution Service. He had made sure prosecutor Warren Bassett, a thick-set, affable chap, took the case. He had worked with him on numerous cases and considered him to be the best prosecutor by a mile. Warren was meticulous and methodical, rather how he was inclined to view himself. The only 'thing' missing was the person PC Bellingham had recognised but whom none of the defendants would acknowledge. The case against those arrested under Operation Barn Owl had already been referred to the Crown Court by the Manchester Magistrates' Court when the 'thing' dropped into the prosecution's lap. Bellingham could not believe his ears when he heard Zac had been arrested over a nightclub brawl and his fingerprints had implicated him in the drugs case.

"I knew it, I just knew he was involved in drugs," he had said to WPC Ward when discussing the latest development.

Before being interviewed Zac was given the opportunity of legal representation. He rang the solicitor Luke had recommended earlier on, Harry Rochester, who advised him to ask for the duty solicitor initially but to tell him he would be representing him thereafter. While waiting for the duty solicitor to arrive Zac was allowed to telephone Jennie. He picked up the phone, dialled her number and his hand began to shake while waiting for her to answer. His voice thick with emotion, caught in his throat, and turned into a whisper.

"Jennie love, I'm in the police station. There was a fight at the nightclub. I'm not hurt but I'm in trouble, big trouble." His voice tailed off breaking up as tears threatened. "I'm in court tomorrow morning, can you come to the court please?" he sobbed. She made a teary promise that she would be there for him.

He did not sleep that night, and neither did Jennie.

At 8.00am the next morning a bleary-eyed Zac was escorted to the court holding cells where he was met by the stunning Rameena Khan, the duty solicitor from the previous night. She again went through what would happen and agreed to speak with Jennie and explain his situation to her.

His legs were wobbly and he thought they would give way as he climbed the steps leading into the court. In the dock he was flanked by two officers, they were tall, like him, but not as well-built. In different circumstances he could easily have taken them on. There was a smell of beeswax and stale sweat in the light oak panelled courtroom and there were lots of people milling about.

Three magistrates sat in an elevated position at the back of the courtroom under the crest, "Mon Dieu et Mon Droit". On the next level down an attractive female court clerk, her blonde hair tied up in a French roll, sat in front of them with a bundle of documents in front of her. The silver-haired prosecutor sat to her right at the lowest level; he had a corresponding bundle of documents. Behind him numerous lawyers and their assistants sat, spread across the seven rows that made up the well of the court. Members of the press and probation service sat on the opposite side of the court to Jennie. She was sitting to Zac's right on the second of five graduated rows of benches. A dozen or so other people were scattered over those rows. She had dark circles under her eyes and looked worn out and scared. They locked eyes for a long moment, a moment filled with every emotion they were feeling, then he had to tear his eyes away to confirm his name, address and date of birth. He heard the prosecutor outline the offences against him and ask for a remand in custody for two reasons: the severity of the charges, one charge being an alleged violent assault in a nightclub, and the likelihood he would abscond as they had proof he had used at least one alias and left a hospital ward before being discharged knowing an officer was waiting to interview him.

Ms Khan did her best to make a case for bail, although the odds were very much stacked against such. She argued that Zac had not been violent but had merely tried to break up the nightclub fight, and that he was unlikely to abscond as he was working. He had left the hospital as soon as he could because he had a fear of hospitals. He had not appreciated an officer was waiting to interview him and he was confused when he gave false details at the scene of the stabbing. Predictably, Zac was remanded in custody.

He mouthed, "I love you," to Jennie across the courtroom as he was led away, and she reciprocated. He had never felt so low or such a failure in his life. Meanwhile Jennie was in a daze, she had no one to turn to and Ms Khan had left the court without even a backward glance in her direction. How she got back to their apartment was a mystery to her and she fell into bed and slept like a log.

Zac had a fitful night's sleep, tossing and turning in-between nightmares, dreaming his father was chasing him upstairs and he just managed to lock himself in the bathroom before he caught him. Then his father hammered on the door shouting threats. Sadly, a real life occurrence from his childhood.Zac appeared in court for a further three consecutive weeks, where he was again remanded in custody while police enquiries were continuing and committal papers prepared. Each time the court duty solicitor represented him. The remand hearings took only minutes but waiting in the holding cells beneath the court for his case to be called was frustrating as the time varied between minutes to hours. Knowing Jennie was waiting patiently added to his anxiety and guilt at the misery he had caused her.

Zac's fifth court appearance was for committal proceedings. This time the portly, rosy-cheeked Harry Rochester attended, with Jennie; who looked more ashen and haggard with each week's passing. Mr Rochester told Zac that the committal hearing was really just a formality, that there was a prima facie case against him, which, in lay terms, meant the prosecution evidence was strong enough to bring charges and the case had to go to Crown Court to be linked up with the other defendants involved with the manufacturing and distribution of cannabis. He said he was fairly confident the assault charge would be dropped and confirmed he had explained everything to Jennie and reassured him she would visit him as often as she was allowed to.

The hearing took approximately fifteen minutes, and Zac was remanded in custody pending trial at Crown Court.

Two months later there was a pre-trial hearing at Crown Court as one of the co-accused, Gary Starkey, had changed his plea, as advised by his solicitor, to one of 'not guilty' which meant further delayed proceedings despite the fact that Zac's case had been fully processed and he had been slotted in with his co-defendants' case. By this time Zac's remand hearings were dealt with in his absence, along with those of the others involved.

Zac could not believe how slow the whole court process was and complained to his solicitor. Mr Rochester reassured him this was normal and any time spent on remand would, in all likelihood, be deducted from the sentence of imprisonment which would inevitably be imposed.

Behind the scenes discussions took place between Mr Bassett and Mr Rochester so that the next time Zac and his cohorts were brought before the court two months later, it was to plead guilty. As predicted by Mr Rochester the assault charge against Zac was dropped.

When they realised the strength of the prosecution evidence and on the advice of their barrister, Timothy Cahill, they all, including Starkey, pleaded guilty to their involvement in the production, distribution and supply of cannabis. The case was adjourned for a further twenty-eight days while pre-sentence reports were compiled. By the time sentence was given, nearly eight months had passed since Zac's arrest at the nightclub.

Shortly after the case was finalised DI Gallagher gave a statement to the press.

"Following a four month investigation, uncovering a complex organisation involving huge barns at a farm in Norwich, several men were arrested for their involvement in the large-scale production, distribution and supply of cannabis.

The barns had undergone extensive and costly adaptation by installing generators, fans, lighting, ventilation, preparation, equipment and cannabis plants with a potential annual cannabis yield worth around £3 million.

This enterprise was thwarted in its early stages thanks to excellent work by the dedicated and outstanding team of officers from our Serious and Organised Crime Unit, supported by our colleagues in Norfolk.

The following sentences were passed:

Andrew Kettle, *farm-owner, aged 54, was jailed for seven years after admitting conspiracy to produce and supply cannabis.*

Luke Lewis *aged 36, a labourer, was jailed for six years after admitting conspiracy to produce and supply cannabis.*

David Michael Mitchell, *aged 41, a crane-driver, was jailed for four years after admitting conspiracy to supply and produce cannabis.*

Graeme Pitt, *aged 38, a driver, was jailed for four years after admitting conspiracy to supply and produce cannabis.*

Iain Maverick, *aged 31, a bricklayer, was jailed for four years after admitting conspiracy to supply and produce cannabis.*

Frank Jackman, *aged 29, an electrician, was jailed for four years after admitting conspiracy to supply and produce cannabis.*

Zachary Thomas Owen, *aged 26, a bricklayer, was jailed for four years after admitting conspiracy to supply and produce cannabis.*

Gary Starkey, *aged 34, a farmhand, was jailed for six years after being found guilty of conspiracy to produce and supply cannabis.*

These men were part of an organised crime group, with criminal links nationwide, who set up one of the country's biggest cannabis factories. Several of them met up in a roadside café where one of my dedicated officers, who was off-duty, recognised one of the men, followed him and as a result Operation Barn Owl was set up and is still continuing to bring drug dealers to justice across the county.

Today's sentences send a clear message to people who are thinking of producing or dealing in drugs: they will be caught and brought to justice.

There is no doubt that several of these offenders were living lavish lifestyles funded by drug crime. Significant amounts of cash were seized during the arrest operation and the Proceeds of Crime Act will be used to strip them of their assets."

Significantly Mr Baxter was not implicated. In any event he was well away, sunning himself on the Grand Cayman Islands.

Sentence and Jennie Leaving

Throughout the eight months of his remand in custody pending his trial, and for the first month of his subsequent four year prison sentence, Jennie visited Zac at Leeds Prison once a week. She hated it. The perpetual tension building up to each visit and the short-lived relief immediately afterwards was making her ill. Lack of sleep and loss of appetite meant her weight plummeted. Even on a sunny day the sight of the unforgiving granite stone of the prison walls sent a shiver down her spine. Its fortress design was the stuff of nightmares and appeared to loom over her, making her shrink under its judgmental gaze. A murder of crows "caw, caw, cawing" as they circled above their roof top nests added to its eeriness, as did the hollow crunch of gravel under her feet as she walked to the entrance door which was set in huge, arched, wooden gates, painted dark green. Once through the door the stale and dank smell of the prison filled the air and clung to her clothing. She knew it would take days to shake off the feeling of desolation and then the depressing cycle would begin again.

Initially Zac had been frightened and tearful, telling her over and over how much he loved and missed her. He begged her forgiveness. Gradually he became more positive in his outlook. He decided he was going to appeal his sentence but in the meantime he was going to take advantage of the various rehabilitation courses on offer in the prison so that upon release he would be able to get a decent job, buy a house for them and they could start the family they had always planned.

Once upon a time this would have been Jennie's dream but living apart from Zac made her realise just what a stranglehold he had had over her. Managing on her own gave her confidence and made her think about her future... alone.

As soon as Zac had fully adjusted to his new life behind bars he became increasingly angry about the police, the courts, the prison, the whole establishment and his so-called friends and family who had betrayed him. More worryingly he was still trying to control Jennie, demanding that she give notice to quit their flat and rent somewhere nearer to the prison so she could visit him more often and he could continue to 'look after her'. She did as he ordered and gave notice to quit, except instead of renting somewhere nearer, she decided it was time to escape Zac's clutches for good and make a new life for herself by moving back to Manchester. She was unsure about how best to break the news to Zac and resolved to face the problem after she had found somewhere to work and live.

Zac ultimately made the decision for her because the last few times she visited him he became increasingly agitated and menacing. She suspected he was taking drugs again. Then her final visit was cut short because for no apparent reason he threatened to kill her, in fact the guards had had to overpower him and drag him away while he continued to scream threats and hurl abuse at her. She had never heard him use such foul language before and was in a state of shock on leaving the prison.

Somehow she managed to keep her emotions in check as she waited in the drizzling rain for the return bus. After settling into her seat she was relieved that the space next to her remained empty.

A large woman in a drab brown coat wearing a paisley patterned headscarf sat on the opposite side of the bus, a few rows nearer to the front. She was hunched up, her shoulders jerking as she quietly wept, which struck a chord with Jennie who could no longer suppress her tears as feelings of complete and utter despair washed over her. She wept about the day's events, the loss of her love for Zac, a love once so full of promise and hoped that that would be the last time she ever saw him, which would put an end to her nightmare. She also wept about her uncertain future and the loss of her father.

After her tears had subsided her thoughts turned to the future. Fortunately, since being forced to move to Leeds she had had the foresight to start secretly stashing money away, mainly in the lining of her large red and white polka dot sewing box, a gift she had chosen and Zac had bought her one Christmas. She also hid money in a rolled up pair of grey leg warmers in the bottom drawer of her dressing table, managing to save just over eight hundred pounds; a fortune considering Zac had complete control over her money, insisting that her wages were paid into his account and he in turn doled out pocket money to her each day. She had managed to save most of the money by going without lunch, having to force herself to smile when Zac marvelled at how she managed to keep her trim figure! In hindsight she realised any love for him had long since died; her life was a nightmare but not anymore. For the first time she felt free and nervously excited about her future.

She went to the library to use the free internet service and check out jobs and apartments to rent near to Manchester city centre. Luckily the letting agent she rang, a Mr Rich, said he might have the ideal apartment which had only recently come on to the market. He also had a couple of other places on his books she might like to see. She arranged a morning viewing date and then rang Phil Allen at ASPECT recruitment agency. She was surprised to learn he remembered her. She explained she had recently split up from her partner and was planning to return to Manchester and start afresh. She also mentioned the date she was viewing accommodation. He asked if she could give him a couple of hours as he needed to make a few phone calls. Ninety minutes later she was delighted to hear he had lined her up for three interviews in the afternoon of the same day she was viewing the apartments.

During the rain-lashed train journey from Leeds to Manchester Jennie's head was spinning with all the things she needed to do. She felt totally overwhelmed, which was hardly surprising because it was, after all, her first big step towards independence. She made a to do list, starting with job, accommodation, new bank account, buying cheap suitcases to pack her things, giving away as much as she could to charity, settling outstanding bills with her current landlord, making sure she did not leave a forwarding address instead saying she was going to live with her mother in Blackpool. The list seemed endless and of course there was the dreaded task of packing Zac's things, arranging storage at the prison and dealing with the inevitable emotional turmoil. She refused to dwell on Zac, instead taking the positive view that at least having so much to think about took her mind off how tragic her situation was.

She was glad she had worn her favourite navy blue, pin-striped suit and white blouse for the interviews and viewings; she felt good in the outfit, applying just a hint of make-up, or war paint as her daddy used to say when her mother put make-up on. She quickly pushed the memory of her father to the back of her mind in fear of becoming pessimistic.

She viewed the three apartments. The first one was fairly spacious but she was not keen on the outlook from the lounge window, it looked straight into another apartment block. The second one was equally spacious but there was a damp, musty smell which was off-putting. Mr Rich had obviously saved the best apartment until last for as soon as he held open the lounge door for her she was bathed in a ray of sunlight and it felt like home. Sliding doors opened on to a small balcony. As she stepped out she was enthralled by the view across a section of the city and along the road leading to an old church with trees and benches in its grounds, its stained glass windows clearly visible. Even though she had not yet found a job she knew she just had to have the apartment. Mr Rich, or rather Malcolm, as he insisted she call him, agreed to hold the apartment for her for 48 hours to give her a chance to find employment.

The three interviews were very different; two in the city centre and the other a short walk away but nearer to her apartment block. The first one was in two parts. An attractive fair-haired woman in her mid-fifties with soft blue caring eyes explained the job, gave her a simple typing test then took her to meet the person she would be working for. He too was in his mid-fifties. Unfortunately Jennie felt uncomfortable with him and found him rather leering. The second interview consisted of an astonishing eight tests! The usual exercises in timed speed typing, audio typing and spelling were no surprise; the word selection, grammar, punctuation and presentation tests would normally have been incorporated into the other tests rather than dealt with separately, but what really took her by surprise was the mathematical questions, including multiple fractions, logarithms and currency conversions! She wondered if she had been put forward for something other than a legal secretary. Nevertheless she completed the tests in the time allotted and the personnel lady said they would telephone her soon. She was beginning to feel despondent and quite anxious about what the next one had in store.

The final interview was at an office a short walk from the city centre, downhill in one of the back streets. The offices certainly were not as prestigious as the previous offices but the elderly chap on reception was jolly, the leather chairs were soft and comfortable and Jennie's first impression was that it was a pleasant firm. A small woman with short, brassy blonde hair and a Liverpudlian accent greeted her and gave her a typing test. Afterwards she was taken to meet the man she would be working for. She was immediately struck by his beautiful humorous smoky-grey eyes framed by long dark lashes and laughter lines. He was a large man, probably old enough to be her father, who immediately made her feel at ease and more importantly safe. It seemed that Phil Allen had also saved the best one until last and shortly afterwards she accepted the job working for Gordon Humphrys, a solicitor at Denbighs.

At last things appeared to be falling into place and she was delighted to be able to move into her apartment a week before starting her new job.

Was It?

Ben was on his way to an early Monday morning meeting at Walkers, a firm of architects just outside the city centre. He was rehearsing what he was going to say in the meeting and not particularly paying attention to the crowds of people mostly heading in the opposite direction towards the centre, he assumed for work. Then, out the corner of his eye, he thought he saw Jennie Enderby in the distance, disappearing around a corner and out of sight. It had been a couple of years since he had seen her and was not sure it was her. The following Thursday night the Flakes met up at Jugs for a quick drink.

"Does anyone still keep in touch with Jennie Enderby?" Ben enquired.

Judging from the blank look on each of their faces the answer must have been no. Then Lucy said, "I haven't heard from her since she suddenly left Stepwells. I'm not aware of anyone else being in contact with her either. Why do you ask?"

"I thought I saw her on Monday morning, when I was on my way to Walkers, that's all," answered Ben.

"Ooh I liked Jennie," said Piers.

"Piers is there any woman you don't like?" reprimanded Rachel to group laughter.

George and Joan

George and Joan Finch were childhood sweethearts and soulmates. Over the years they had grown to look like one another; George slightly taller and Joan slightly rounder. More often than not, whether deliberately or subconsciously, they wore colour co-ordinated clothes. Their once brown hair had turned to an attractive snowy white and the onset of arthritis in the hips had given both of them a rolling gait, which to onlookers looked quite comical especially when their lopsided walks were synchronised. They led a quiet life, utterly devoted to each other, hiding their heartache behind jolly demeanours.

After several miscarriages Joan had finally given birth to the very much adored David, a healthy boy. Unfortunately, when he was thirteen David developed leukaemia and lost his life after a horrendous four year battle, leaving them devastated. Joan became suicidal and George was so concerned about her he gave up working at the firm he had joined as an apprentice and where he had risen through the ranks to the position of managing director.

That was seven years ago and neither of them had worked since; instead they had sold their large four bedroomed detached house in Alderley Edge, Manchester, a much sought after area, and bought a top floor penthouse apartment near to Manchester city centre. Moving to the apartment was necessary not merely from a financial perspective, but for emotional reasons too; they needed to get away from everyone who knew of their loss. Well intentioned people would say "time will heal" and such like, which made Joan want to scream that that might apply to most situations but never for the loss of a beloved child. That pain was raw and would remain so forever. She could not cope with the thoughtless comments and people's obvious discomfort when they saw her, so in the end they felt it best to make a new life elsewhere. At first it was very difficult for both of them but eventually they developed a routine and learned to cope... most of the time.

There were only two apartments on the top floor. The two lower floors had three apartments and were obviously much smaller. The one immediately below theirs had been empty for four weeks and Joan was becoming anxious about it.

"What if squatters break in there? Or someone noisy moves in? Or a drug addict or a prostitute?" Joan mithered, wringing her hands.

George lowered his newspaper and gave her what he hoped was a reassuring smile. His voice was soft as he said, "Now, now Joan, try not to fret love, there's a coded security lock on the entrance to the apartments and we can always report noise, drugs or other problems to the service manager. After all, that's one of the things he's paid to deal with." He hoped he had managed to placate her.

Despite George's reassurances Joan still kept vigil; she could see the paved area leading to the entrance to the complex from their balcony and as a result noticed Jennie the day the letting agent called to show her the apartment.

Initially Joan was suspicious of a pretty young girl apparently living on her own, so she kept her distance for the first few weeks, just observing her routine. When she was satisfied that the new occupant did indeed live alone and nothing untoward was going on, she decided it was time to break the ice and 'accidentally' bumped into her one evening at the entrance to the apartments, as Jennie was returning from work.

"Hello my dear, you must be the young lady who is living in the apartment below mine. I'm Joan Finch and my husband is George," she smiled, holding out her hand. Without hesitation Jennie returned her smile and shook her hand. That was the start of a bond between three lonely souls.

Jennie was born the same year as David and became the daughter Joan and George never had and they became the parents she had only dreamt of and very much needed, particularly as, for self-preservation, she had severed all ties with everyone from her past, including her mother. Sometimes it bothered her that she did not miss her mother, because children were supposed to be close to their mothers, who in turn was supposed to be warm and nurturing, kind and caring. Unfortunately Jennie shuddered at the thought of hers, with her permanent state of tension, always on the defensive ready for verbal altercation; unhappiness courted her mother and others by association. Frankly, meeting Joan and George could not have come at a better time in her life. She quickly fell into the routine of most evenings, straight after work, calling in for a cup of tea and a catch up, shopping with them on weekends and she almost always had her Sunday lunch with them.

Tsunami

Lucy loved everything about Christmas: the excitement, the planning and organisation, decorating the Christmas tree the first day of December, buying and wrapping presents, card writing and posting, the numerous get-togethers, in fact the whole 'kit-and-caboodle' as her grandmother used to say.

This year was no exception. Christmas Eve, in keeping with her family tradition, was spent at the Christingle event at the local church and Christmas Day was a 'stay in and chill out' day. Perfect.

Boxing Day they had planned to go for their usual walk around the local park, but switching on the television changed everything as they sat transfixed while the horrors of the Indian Ocean earthquake and subsequent tsunami unfolded before their eyes. In the afternoon Lucy texted the Flakes about the awful disaster and asked if they knew anyone who was affected. They texted their own shock and horror and fortunately did not know anyone out there, but all agreed the tragedy highlighted how precarious and precious life is and not to take anything for granted.

Humpy Dumpty

Jennie's ethereal beauty and sweet nature took Gordon's breath away and although he was pretty sure she would accept his job offer, he still felt euphoric when Phil Allen rang to confirm her acceptance.

She was a stark contrast to his previous secretary, who he had inherited and detested on sight. Some might have said it was because she was too much like him, old and fat, but he would not have agreed for he saw himself as a young stud. Indeed, as if to endorse the stud factor he had hung a couple of attractive photographs of himself on his office wall, which, under normal circumstances would not have warranted comment, except in this case the pictures were obviously taken when he was in his 20s, over 20 years ago and now bore so little resemblance to him that he felt obliged to point out, to anyone who showed any interest, that it was actually him in the photographs. The fact he had been married for years, had a grown up son, Anthony, and a 'princess' of a daughter, Jordan, who was on the brink of womanhood, did not feature in his fantasy world either, nor did he consider the twenty year age gap with Jennie to be a problem; he would merely give her the benefit of his life experience.

Before she had walked into his life he had been in a rut. He was not aware of it at the time but with hindsight he realised he had been waiting for someone like Jennie to come along and "relight his fire", and that is exactly what she had managed to do. He felt alive, excited, young and carefree while at work. Although it was difficult to carry on as normal at home he was confident he had managed to do so and fool his wife into the bargain. Of course he loved his wife, but he was not in love with her anymore and had not been for a long,

long time. They were just used to each other and life had been boringly routine for too long. However, that was all about to change, for he had been given a chance to recapture his youth!

Jennie found Gordon easy to work for. She loved listening to him wax lyrically about the big cases he had won over the years, the celebrities he had acted for and the famous judges and barristers he had rubbed shoulders with; he had led such a glamorous life.. She did not care that the other staff, behind his back, called him Humpty Humphrys because he was bald and rotund like the nursery rhyme character. Instead she thought of him as cuddly, like a giant teddy bear. She saw his kind eyes and easy smile and he made her feel safe. As far as she was concerned Mr Humphrys was the perfect gentleman.

To lure Jennie into his world needed careful planning because he did not want to frighten her away, far from it, he wanted to cherish her. He decided to win her over by involving her, as much as he could, in his work, briefing her on each case he was dealing with, asking for her input, including her in meetings, taking her to court with him, introducing her to clients and contacts as his personal assistant. He did everything within his power to make her feel valued and important at work.

That was step one.

For her two months' review, instead of carrying out the process in an office meeting room, which was normal practice, he took her to lunch at Il Forno, a top class Italian restaurant. The delicious food and good wine made her relax and she opened up in a way she had not felt able to since returning to Manchester. The story of her life just came tumbling out, unstoppable, her earliest memories, her parents' divorce, meeting Zac, being happy for the first two years with him but then how he had changed and become threatening, their moonlight flit to Leeds to escape his enemies, his arrest, trial and subsequent imprisonment and her eventual freedom. She looked physically drained when she had finished and near to tears. Gordon's heart ached for her and he longed to take her in his arms and hold her close, but it was too soon. He leaned across the table, gently took both of her hands in his, looked deep into her eyes and said the words she had longed for someone to say to her. "Don't worry Jennie, you're in safe hands now."

That was step two.

He was at a loss as to how to execute his next move when, a few months later, Mother Nature unexpectedly provided the solution. It had been hot and muggy all afternoon and just as the staff were leaving for the day, streaks of lightening zapped across the angry deep purple clouds and dark grey sky, followed by booming thunderclaps directly overhead which shook the building. Jennie had already begun her usual brisk walk home and Gordon had jumped into his old dark green Ford Focus estate car, parked at the rear of the office, just as the heavens opened and released a deluge of torrential rain. His first thought was of Jennie caught up in the storm. He shot out of the car park to find her and offer her a lift home. He spotted her sheltering in a doorway a short distance from the office and pulled up.

"Get in, I'll give you a lift," he shouted through the open front passenger window while reaching across and pushing the door open. She jumped in the car and he roared with laughter. She looked at him perplexed. Without a word he pulled down the passenger sun visor revealing a vanity mirror showing her bedraggled hair and black mascara running down her cheeks, making her look like Pagliacci, the sad clown. She burst out laughing too.

He drove to her apartment. He did not have to ask where it was, he had checked shortly after she had begun working for him and she did not attempt to direct him. He parked near to the entrance and hesitated just long enough for her to invite him in for a coffee. *Perfect,* he thought as he accepted.

His heart began beating faster as she fumbled with the key in the lock to the door of her apartment. He took a deep breath as the door opened and he stepped into her hallway. Her coat was soaked through and she rushed straight to the bathroom to hang it over the bath to drip dry. Gordon seized his opportunity, grabbed a towel and began drying her hair. The intimacy of this seemingly innocent act hit both of them at the same time. Their eyes locked and suddenly they were in each other's arms, kissing passionately. He scooped her up and she pointed the way to her bedroom.

That was the final stage… and the start.

Gordon's imagination had run riot when fantasising about making love to Jennie, the places varied and the times differed, but he was always in control and he impressed her with his stamina and lovemaking prowess. He was her knight in shining armour and she was a sweet innocent maiden unable to resist his manly charms, swept off her feet and overwhelmed by his sheer masculinity, begging him for more. The reality was the opposite.

Her bedroom curtains were open from the morning, the inner net curtain, while ensuring privacy, allowed just enough light from the street lamp on the opposite side of the road to softly illuminate her room, lending an air of intimacy. Their lingering, probing, kiss finished and Gordon set her down, feet on the soft carpeted floor. He moved his hands to the buttons on the front of her blouse but instead of deftly undressing her as he had imagined he would, his fingers morphed into thumbs and his hands trembled uncontrollably, so much so that she had to take control. She put her hands on his shoulders and gently pushed down. He obligingly sat on the edge of her bed. The only sound he could hear was his rapid breathing interspersed with his occasional passionate sob as she undressed herself, slowly, provocatively, her naked beauty bathed in the subdued light adding to her allure. Her body slowly moved to silent music, her eyes burning into his, which rendered him powerless. She could feel his eyes devouring her nakedness and her body tingled in anticipation.

She began to undress him, caressing him, savouring the moment, enjoying her power over him as he relished his passive role. When all of his clothing had been removed she again gently pressed down on his shoulders and he obediently lay down on the bed while she ran her soft hands over his dark-haired chest. He marvelled at the beauty of her creamy white skin, her swan like neck, pert breasts, the slight mound of her stomach leading to her dark-blonde pubic hair. Her sweet, natural musky smell was intoxicating. She was an angel, a vision of loveliness. The passion between them increased and she swiftly and smoothly straddled him. A surge of lust coursed through his body and he lifted her up to claim her and surrender to her.

He stayed until just after midnight.

Gordon had been bowled over by Jennie and was determined to make her his. After pondering the situation for a while he decided to join the Committee for the Homeless, for although he had a social conscience about those sleeping rough and had been approached before about becoming involved with its charity work, his real reason for joining now and attending Friday night meetings was that committee work would be the perfect cover under which to conduct an affair. For good measure he told his wife it would further increase his chances of becoming a partner, which he knew would please her. It worked out better than he had dared hoped; he was actually able to take Jennie away for the occasional long weekend under the guise of committee work, which left him certain that his wife would never suspect a thing.

Working together made it easy to conduct an affair, for apart from seeing Jennie throughout the day they also spent their lunchtimes together, often taking extended lunch breaks using the excuse of unexpected delays at court, and they would also pretend to work over on various cases. Sometimes he would surprise her by visiting her before work and it was part of their routine that most Friday evenings he would go to her apartment for a meal. They would make love before, sometimes during and always after their meal. He would stay until the early hours then go home for the weekend to play happy families with his wife and children.

He had found it surprisingly easy to take Jennie away for the occasional weekend, because although his wife, Diane, did not actually go to work, she did lead a very busy life, running around after their children and looking after her elderly mother and his elderly father. To assuage his conscience he reasoned with himself that he was doing Diane a favour by keeping out of her way during those precious weekends. The only problem he encountered was financial. Stolen weekends away obviously put a considerable strain on the family finances. He racked his brains about how to earn more money. Overtime was hard to justify and detracted from his time with Jennie, and while he could claim some expenses for his day job and charity work it certainly did not stretch to financing weekends away. The only thing he could think of to ease his financial burden was to encourage his wife to return to work, which was not going to be easy because she had been a full-time mother for nearly twenty years.

He started putting pressure on Diane by asking what she planned to do when their daughter finished school. She said she had not thought about it.

That was step one.

He did not mention the matter again for a few weeks then casually dropped it out in general conversation that she would probably be bored when Jordan left school. She had said she was sure she would find plenty to keep herself occupied, sarcastically adding, "For example looking after elderly parents!"

That was step two.

A few weeks later, in passing, he mentioned that a colleague's wife had gone to college to train to be a hairdresser and had said she wished she had thought about it years before. His wife had not verbally responded but merely glared over the top of her glasses at him and he assumed she had dismissed this piece of information too, but a couple of days later he noticed a college prospectus on the dining room table amongst some of Diane's paperwork.

That was step three, and hopefully the final step.

Diane's first reaction to Gordon's *loud* hints about her returning to work was one of anger. Reading between the lines she felt he was criticising how she spent her days and that she was not making a proper contribution to their lives. *How dare he criticise me when I do so much tearing around after **his** children, not to mention **his** cantankerous father*.

Once her anger had subsided she sat down and considered the wisdom of his words, particularly about what she would do when Jordan left school. She was also mindful that she was hurtling towards the big five-0 and concerned her employment opportunities would be seriously depleted once she reached that depressing milestone. She considered her options and decided to enrol at college to train as a medical secretary. She had always had an interest in medicine, which was hardly surprising considering the number of times she had ferried the children and elderly parents to various doctors, dentists and hospitals over the last twenty years. She decided not to tell Gordon of her plan, instead she preferred to surprise him when she got a new job.

Time Out

For their first weekend away Gordon whisked Jennie to Rome, the eternal city. It was perfect. The hotel was luxurious, the weather hot and sunny and there was something of historical significance around every corner. They had a guided tour around the Colosseum and although Jennie thought it was amazing, it had a sobering effect on her when she imagined the trauma of those sentenced to be executed *ad bestias:* death by wild animals.

Afterwards, as Jennie and Gordon were making their way to the Pantheon, two men dressed as gladiators took them by surprise, snatching Jennie's camera. One of them quickly draped a toga costume around Gordon, completing the image by thrusting a helmet on his head, a shield on his arm and a sword in his hand. Simultaneously the other one wrapped a cape around Jennie's shoulders finishing off by popping a plastic green laurel wreath on her head. They were obviously experienced in this tourist sideshow judging by the speed with which they dressed their victims.

Although Jennie was amused by the attention, alarm bells were ringing in Gordon's head with just cause. One posed with the couple as the other took their photograph with Jennie's camera, of course for a price. The subtle implication being if refused he might *accidentally* drop the camera. As it turned out the only thing that dropped was Gordon's jaw over the ridiculous number of Euros for their *services*. Although miffed, Gordon did not want to spoil things for Jennie by arguing so he reluctantly paid up, making a mental note to inform everyone he knew to beware of the scam.

They also visited the magnificent Vatican Square, watching the Pope's sermon on huge video screens, along with a milling crowd of thousands. They were both unexpectedly emotional and awestruck by the significance of the occasion.

By far Jennie's favourite attraction was the romantic Trevi fountain; they visited it during the evening when it was floodlit. She was mesmerised by its impressive beauty, sparkling cascading water and was completely taken aback when Gordon dropped down on one knee and delivered a speech, smattered with Shakespearian quotes, ending with a heartfelt marriage proposal. Caught up in the moment she accepted, to the delight of a growing crowd. The fact that he was already married was conveniently forgotten.

A few weeks later they managed another weekend trip to Prague. The hotel was not as luxurious as the one in Rome, but comfortable. It rained for most of the three days but the weather did not deter them from sightseeing and walking over the famous Charles Bridge with its thought-provoking statues. The only upset was when two girls appeared from nowhere and surrounded Jennie as she was about to board a bus going to Prague Castle. Gordon realised immediately that they were pickpockets and shouted while pushing them out of the way. The incident was over within seconds but nevertheless Jennie was quite shaken up. Fortunately, after they had climbed the steps leading to castle square, the sun shone long enough for them to witness three wedding photo shoots, which took Jennie's mind off the earlier incident.

In the evening they dined at a restaurant in the Old Town Square with its beautiful turreted buildings enhanced by soft pastel coloured lighting. Their restaurant overlooked the world famous Astronomical Clock. Although the weekend break was different from the one in Rome because there was not so much to see and it rained, Jennie enjoyed it just as much, Gordon was wonderful company and she felt so at ease.

Their third trip was to Lloret de Mar in Spain. Gordon was surprised to find such a cheap holiday in a four star hotel. The flight was comfortable and the coach journey to the hotel took just over half an hour. The hotel foyer was very opulent, marble floors and walls, big soft beige leather settees, soft lighting and eye catching oil paintings of Spanish haciendas with trailing bougainvillea in full bloom. Their spacious bedroom was equally impressive, with plush carpet, solid wooden furniture, a double shower and a balcony affording breathtaking sea views. Unfortunately the clientele was not as impressive, in fact quite the opposite.

They knew they were 'in trouble' as soon as they went to the poolside bar and their feet stuck to the beer sodden floor. They looked at each other aghast before bursting out laughing. Jennie went back into the sunshine to look for a table while Gordon queued for their drinks. She chose a table as far away as possible from the rest of the holidaymakers. Gordon eventually joined her, complaining he could not believe how many drinks people were ordering in one go, concluding he supposed it was to be expected with cheap, all-inclusive packages. He apologised for organising a weekend with society's dregs. She laughed off his apology and they lapped up the sunshine fascinated by the drunken antics of 'the dregs' sitting on the opposite side of the pool.

A skirmish developed between two of the men; one of them tried to throw a baby strapped in a buggy into the pool. He was restrained and left the area shouting abuse. Then an elegantly dressed woman walked towards the hotel, obviously the worse for drink as she was concentrating so hard on walking in a straight line that she failed to notice the patio doors were closed and bashed straight into them, landing with a loud plop on her ample backside. It was hilarious. Gordon and Jennie, unable to contain their laughter, hastily left the poolside intending to go to their room but bumped into the man who had been restrained earlier. He had packed a brown suitcase and was striding around the foyer talking to himself, reminding Gordon of Yosser Hughes from an old television drama series Boys from the Blackstuff. In a strong Liverpudlian accent he asked,"Did yer see where me missis went mate?"

"Sorry sir, I don't know who your wife is," replied Gordon using his best posh voice; Jennie struggled to keep a straight face.

"Yer know, she was sittin' opposite like, she's got long blonde 'air, it's dyed like, yer know, not natural."

"Sorry, can't help friend; good luck with your search." Gordon did not wait for a response but grabbed Jennie's elbow and steered her towards the lift which fortunately opened as they reached it. As soon as the doors closed they collapsed against each other crying with laughter.

Despite 'Yosser' continually roaming around, the dregs and pigswill food, which forced them to eat away from the hotel, they had a wonderful time. Jennie was completely happy, not a care in the world. Gordon was happy too, but not entirely carefree.

How the hell am I going to explain away my sunburn? he quizzed his image in the bathroom mirror, appalled he had not been more careful in the sun.

He worried about his sunburn throughout the return journey and was almost home when he finally thought of the solution. After he had seen Jennie safely back to her apartment he called into a chemist and bought some fake tanning cream. Relieved Diane was not at home, he was able to apply generous amounts to his reddish/brown bits and then wait for the cream to take effect.

"What on earth have you done to your face?" exclaimed Diane, on her return home later that evening.

"Why, what's the matter?" Gordon feigned innocence.

"Have a look in the mirror."

"Oh my God, what are all those brown streaks?" he picked up the fake tanning bottle. "I thought it was moisturiser, not fake tan!" he exclaimed, indignantly. Diane doubled up in laughter and did not stop. Every time she looked at Gordon it brought fresh peals of laughter. She thought it was one of the funniest things ever. Later that evening she threw Gordon a bottle of Cif scouring cream.

"Here, you'd better see if you can reduce the streaks, otherwise you'll be even more of a laughing stock at work."

Gordon breathed a sigh of relief that she had bought his excuse for his tan and set about scrubbing his skin. *Eight lives left!* he cautioned his reflection.

The next day at work Jennie too laughed at his streaky face, which had faded somewhat after his intensive scrubbing session. They arranged to meet for lunch as usual, but as Jennie sat at her desk she mulled over Gordon's explanation about the fake tan, more importantly the reason behind applying it and for the first time, instead of pushing Gordon's other life to the back of her mind, pretending it did not exist, Jennie questioned the state of his marriage and his insistence that they led separate lives, that they were only together for the sake of the children, because if that really was the case why did he have to go to such extreme measures to hide his tan? His action raised serious doubts in her mind, finally forcing her to consider how she would feel if she was Diane and discovered her husband and children's father was having an affair and sneaking off for weekends.

The image of her mother and father quarrelling came to mind, her mother's tearstained face as she implored her father to stay and the pain in his eyes as he took a last lingering look at Jennie before walking through the door and out of her young life. She felt a sharp pang of conscience which left her feeling sick to her stomach.

The seed of doubt had been firmly sowed and shortly afterwards Jennie reached the decision that their affair must end. She was very sad. Truth be told the passion had fizzled out almost as soon as it had started for her but he was a tender and considerate lover, he made her feel safe and cherished, he called her Princess and treated her like one. Frankly after the abuse of Zac he was what she had needed then, but not any longer.

She had known all along that she was not in love with him, just very fond of him, but now she wanted more than a father figure. The sneaking around and stolen moments were taking its toll on them both, particularly Gordon. His efforts to convince her, and himself, that everything was wonderful were beginning to look pathetic. At times, when he did not think she was looking, he would let down his guard and the strain would be etched all over his face. She knew she had to be the one to finish the affair soon, which she dreaded, knowing it would break his heart, but at least his wife need never know.

Who's for Coffee

"So what's everyone's news?" asked Lucy as she placed a tray of steaming drinks on the table.

Rachel had a sip of her drink before saying, "Well folks, I'm planning to jump ship again, this time working nearer to home. I've got an interview lined up next Wednesday. Fingers crossed."

There was a collective, "It makes sense. We'll miss you. Good for you. Best of luck."

"Ooh keep me posted," requested Bev.

"Of course, we'll all still meet up too."

They sipped their beverages then Piers volunteered, "I've got an announcement of my own to make. I did my first stand-up comedy shot at my local football club on Saturday night."

"Wow!" exclaimed Ben. "How did you get on?"

"I just walked up the steps at the side of the stage."

"What? You idiot, you know I mean, how did your first gig go?"

"To be honest it wasn't planned. The entertainer, a singer, cried off and the club proprietor asked if anyone could fill in. Suddenly my mate Dave volunteered me and before I knew it he and the rest of the members were shouting, 'ON! ON! ON!' clapping their hands and stamping their feet. Then a couple of burly blokes practically hurled me on to the stage. It was surreal. Fortunately, a football joke immediately came to mind, the adrenaline kicked in and I have never felt so alive."

"What was your opening joke?" asked Bev.

"You've heard it before, it's a tame one about monks." In an Irish accent Piers continued, "An amateur team in the west of Ireland played a match against a team from the local monastery. Just before the kick-off the visiting team, all of whom were monks, knelt down solemnly on the pitch, put their hands together and indulged in five minutes of silent prayer. The monastery then proceeded to trounce their hosts 9-0. After the match the home team captain said, 'Well boys, we've been out-played before but this is the first time we've ever been out-prayed!'"

Everyone groaned.

"Well I did tell you it was tame, and, in my defence, my jokes improved greatly as the night progressed."

"Good for you," said Lucy. "I predict you'll soon become a much sought after comedian. After all, you've been entertaining us for years!"

"Let's hope you're right, Lucy," said Piers. "I'm certainly going to give it my best shot."

"Changing the subject," said Ben, "remember a while back I thought I'd seen Jennie Enderby? Well it was her, she's working at Denbighs, I bumped into her the other day."

"Hmm that's interesting," smirked Piers.

Motherly Advice

By chance Jennie bumped into Rachel one lunchtime, a few days after Ben had seen her. She had coffee with her at Starbucks. After a general catch up, Rachel asked if she was seeing anyone. Jennie lowered her eyes, looking into her coffee as she slowly stirred it. She pursed her lips then confirmed she had been seeing someone for six months. Her sad expression compelled Rachel to question her further. When she confided he was unhappily married and only stayed with his wife for the sake of their children, Rachel's expression turned to one of sadness, prompting Jennie to quickly protest that he treated her very well, like a princess. Jennie's use of the word "princess" added to her vulnerability bringing out Rachel's motherly instinct. Her face softened, as did her voice.

"Aw Jennie love you're young and lovely, you could have it all, don't sell yourself short. I'm saying this out of concern for you. The longer your affair continues the less likely he is to leave his wife and children. Even if he did, if he's as nice as you say he is, then he'll never be able to completely walk away from them. You deserve someone just for you."

Jennie did not respond, there was nothing *to* say; she knew in her heart of hearts that Rachel was right, she had more or less made up her mind to finish with him already. Rachel's comments merely endorsed her decision.

After an awkward silence Rachel explained she was leaving the city to work at a firm which was nearer to her home. Neither of them said so, but both thought they would probably never see each other again. They finished their drinks, hugged, said goodbye and wished each other all the best.

Jennie walked slowly back to work mulling over how to finish things with Gordon, and by the time she had reached the office she had decided to end their affair when he visited her, as usual, on Friday night.

Categories

Some say a man falls into three categories: ladies' man, man's man or own man. Nick was a combination of all three. An air of excitement, mercurial wit and good humour drew people to him. That and his wild side were guaranteed to entertain. He was charming and magnanimous with a strong sense of self-belief, confident of his ability to get what he wanted through sheer tenacity, regardless of any difficulties or obstacles. Love and admiration was his for the asking and he was not afraid to ask. He loved life, lived it to the full, refused to compromise and all was fair in love and war.

He was easy to love.

Life was near perfect. He was happily married to Penny who was a wonderful mother to their 18 month old twins, a daughter and a son, and he was their proud, doting father. Workwise he had a good team and his career was soaring. Oh yes, life was sweet.

It was a warm July day, the sun was shining brightly and scattered fluffy white clouds were slowly drifting along as Nick made his way to a meeting at another city centre law firm. The journey took him past the coffee shop where he had once bought Jennie Enderby a coffee, when they were still employed by Stepwells. Over the years he had often thought about what had happened to her, particularly when he heard on the grapevine of her sudden departure from Stepwells because she had brought out his protective instinct and he felt he had somehow let her down, which was totally irrational as he had already moved firms the previous year. Nevertheless, it was a feeling he could not quite shake off. For a while her disappearance haunted him. Seeing the shop now evoked memories of that day and he was lost in thought as he continued his route across 'The Square', a large pedestrianised area, with benches and imaginative gardening displays, edged by eclectically designed tower blocks.

Although only paying scant attention to his surroundings and the milling crowds he was suddenly snatched back to the present, stunned to see Jennie coming towards him, as though he had somehow conjured her up out of thin air. She looked absolutely stunning: blonde hair flowing, her slate grey suit hugging her slender figure, her radiant smile creating a brilliant aura around her and everyone and everything else appeared washed out and distant. She greeted him warmly. He felt his face flush and he stammered while responding, which embarrassed him, causing him to hurriedly move on, but not before discovering she worked at Denbighs.

After a few steps he turned to look back in her direction just as she turned to look back at him. They both laughed loudly at being caught out then waved each other on.

Their impromptu meeting stirred something within Nick, something which had lain dormant for a few years, in fact since deciding Penny was the one. He recognised what it was, it was the hunting instinct and Jennie was firmly in his sights.

Later that day Nick did some research and discovered Gerry Catchpole had had recent dealings with Denbighs.

"Gerry what do you know about Denbighs?" Nick enquired.

"Why who wants to know?" was Catchpole's irritating response. He never failed to irritate Nick, who was seething when Catchpole joined Macefields shortly after he had, and was rumoured to have made a big thing in his interview about them working together at Stepwells! Working in the general group but separate teams could hardly be classed as "together". Nick was astonished to learn that Husslebea had accepted Catchpole's request to move with him because he had been pretty scathing about working for Catchpole when at Stepwells. "I do. I'm just curious," was Nick's casual response, without actually looking at him.

"Well it's not so much what, but who," Catchpole said smugly, disdainfully looking at his fingernails. "I happen to know the senior partner, Jim Godwin, we go way back. As a matter of fact I'm seeing him for lunch tomorrow, for a general catch up."

"Hmm that's interesting, I'd like to meet with him soon. I'll leave you to arrange it please," Nick commanded, simultaneously looking at his watch. "Anyway must dash, I have a meeting." He did not have a meeting but could not bear to prolong their conversation.

Catchpole did as he was asked by Nick and arranged a meeting with Jim Godwin for the following Thursday afternoon. Nick, who would have preferred a meeting between the two of them but could not shake Catchpole off, immediately warmed to the well-groomed Godwin and was secretly impressed at how, within minutes, he had politely, but firmly, put Catchpole in his place. From then on it might as well have been a meeting between just the two of them. He understood why Godwin was referred to as 'The Silver Fox'; his thick hair was silver and there was a keen intelligence evident in his small brown eyes and the sobriquet suited his lean physique.

Over the next fortnight Nick met up with Godwin several times, alone, and within weeks a merger of the two firms was signed, sealed and delivered; Jennie was to be his secret bonus.

Caught

It was Thursday, the day before Jennie planned to break up with Gordon. They had attended an employment tribunal and he had won his client's case of constructive dismissal, bullying and harassment. His client was a mature lady, nearing retirement, who had been manipulated into moving teams only to find within days she was subjected to bullying and harassment. Basically a younger woman wanted her job. She was so traumatised it had caused her to have a breakdown and give up work. Gordon secured a significant award for her by citing Johnson v Unisys 2001, where for the first time a judgment indicated unfair dismissal claimants might be compensated at tribunal for injury to feelings, and if 'someone had been through a dismissal that was so traumatic it brought on a stress-related illness… they could get a very significant award.'

With an order for all the legal costs to be paid by the company, Gordon felt exuberant and took Jennie to lunch to celebrate his success. Whether it was due to the outcome of the hearing, or because Jennie had finally made a decision about them and did not want to spoil his victory, or a combination of both, they were both very relaxed. They really enjoyed their lunch and if truth be told they were a bit tipsy.

It had been raining during their meal but as they left the restaurant the sun was shining and a rainbow appeared, adding to the joy of their day. As they walked back to the office they held hands, which is something they never did, but somehow a public display of affection seemed in keeping with the moment.

Gordon's wife, Diane, had popped into the city unexpectedly to do some shopping and saw them. She stood rooted to the pavement, transfixed as they crossed the road a little way in front of her, completely oblivious to the fact that she was there. Her eyes followed them as they walked hand-in-hand down the hill, talking and laughing together for the entire world to witness them as the couple they undoubtedly were. As they turned right towards his office, they exchanged a quick passionate kiss and then disappeared from view. The full force of what she had seen hit her like a lead balloon. Her stomach flipped somersaults, causing her to feel nauseous. She managed to stop herself from vomiting by staggering into a nearby office side-exit, leaning on the wall and taking deep breaths. She remained there for ages, collecting her thoughts as so many pieces of the puzzle which had been gathering over the months fell into place. She then began shaking uncontrollably as her whole world collapsed right there and then in a dusty street doorway.

Diane could not remember anything about her journey home but by the time it was over she had worked out the affair must have started before she had felt obliged to return to work to boost the family's coffers. The idea she had somehow helped to finance their sordid affair left her incandescent with rage. She had never felt so angry in her life, angry enough to do him physical harm, and his slut.

She recalled the heart-wrenching guilt she had felt at leaving her daughter in the care of a childminder, instead of being there for her as she had been for her son. (She could not bear to think of the children as *theirs*). Oh how her daughter had loathed being at the childminder's and how they had argued over the necessity of it. They had never argued before. She had felt incredibly stressed out with juggling work and family life but consoled herself that it was for the benefit of them all. What a fool she had been and what a selfish, heartless bastard he had been, and was.

She had the house to herself; the children had their own plans for the evening and *God only knows where the lying, cheating, conniving bastard of a husband is.* She sat in the conservatory in the dark with the blinds open to the night sky contemplating her future and how she was going to deal with her discovery. The conservatory was her favourite room in the house, its wicker furniture had well-padded floral-patterned cushions that embraced whoever sat on them. There were several small ornamental birds that her beloved father had bought her over the years, displayed on the high shelf on the side wall. Somehow they added to the room's innate calmness. She missed her father, all the more so in times of trouble. After a while her red-hot anger subsided and was replaced by a steely determination to handle the situation in a cool, calm and collected way instead of her usual all guns blazing manner.

Darkness had fallen by the time her plan had been fine-tuned. She gazed up at the full moon, captivated by its beauty and could not remember a clearer or starrier night. She watched a shooting star travelling from one side of the universe to the other and felt strangely comforted by its lone journey, seeing it as a sign that her decision to go it alone was the right one.

A few miles away Jennie sat in her lounge curled up in an armchair, reflecting on the day, the successful outcome of Gordon's court case, their extended lunch break and spontaneous laughter and how happy he was. It had been a while since she had felt so at ease with him and for a moment she questioned if her decision to finish their affair was right. As she turned things over in her mind she stepped onto the balcony and looked out across the city lights. It was a beautiful night, a warm breeze caressed her, gently brushing her hair off her face while softly blowing her long, pale green, silk dressing gown. The moon was big and luminous, a lover's moon and her aching soul cried out across the twinkling skyline to her soulmate, whoever and wherever he was. As if in answer to her heartfelt yearning, a shooting star glided effortlessly across the heavens, lifting her soul and filling it with hope for her future.

Bad to Worse

Gordon carried on celebrating his court victory with a few of the chaps after work, grateful he had had the foresight to get a lift to work. It had been ages since he had felt so jubilant and it was midnight before he found his way home by taxi. Diane had waited up for him, intending to confront him, but changed her mind when she saw the state he was in; she wanted him fully *compos mentis* when she told him what she intended to do. Her well-rehearsed speech would have to wait, so she retired for the night. She lay in bed, heart racing, listening for the familiar creaking of the stairs indicating he would be joining her, but she heard nothing. It was 2.00am the last time she checked the bedside clock and, exhausted, she finally fell asleep.

The alarm sounding at 7.00am woke her. She felt drained but relieved he had not slept beside her. She dragged herself out of bed and into the shower. Half an hour later she was dressed and ready for breakfast. She found him asleep in the reclining chair in the lounge, an empty whisky bottle and tumbler on the table. She was disgusted with this bloated blob of a man who had destroyed her life, and her children's lives. She gently closed the lounge door, anxious not to disturb him, packed her lunchbox and drove to work leaving him sleeping. On her journey to work she decided to visit her friend Anita for a few days, to discuss her situation before confronting her errant husband.

Gordon woke up with a start, it took a while for it to register where he was. His watch read 9.30am. *Oh fuck, fuck, fuck!!! I'm late for work!* His head was pounding, he felt awful and the mirror made him feel worse. A shower and two cups of black coffee later did not help either. Diane had obviously gone to work and deliberately left him asleep. "Oh bugger, you must have really upset her this time," he said to his reflection in the mirror.

Although he was well over the legal drink drive limit, he took a chance and drove to work, fortunately, without incident. He snuck into his office, hoping no one would notice he was late, and nearly jumped out of his skin when he closed his office door and encountered John Bentley, who was standing in the corner of the room, sort of wedged at the side of the tall, grey, filing cabinet. His long thin frame and gangly limbs reminded Gordon of a giant praying mantis, his reddish brown jumper adding to the illusion.

"Good God man you nearly gave me a heart attack hiding in the corner like that!" barked Gordon.

"Thought you might appreciate this," said John, handing him a cup of black coffee from the top of the cabinet. "It was a great night but boy does my head hurt this morning. You had your fair share too if my memory serves me well, I'm surprised you drove in. I caught a taxi. Knowing my luck the police would be waiting around the corner for me."

"Oh thanks pal, much appreciated." Gordon took a sip of the coffee, surprised at John's friendliness; he had also been surprised he had turned up for the drinks the previous night. "It *was* a good night, and yes my head hurts, but it was worth it. I don't mind telling you now, I could do with a few more cases like that, it's been a bit of a lean time for me these last two years. Hopefully this is the turning point to better things."

"Yes, hopefully," John echoed, but his bombshell of a parting shot as he left Gordon's office, dashed all hope. "Oh, I thought you might be interested to know, Godwin has been in talks with Turner from 'Macies' about our firm merging with theirs, so hang on to your hat old boy, that usually means redundancies."

Gordon flopped back in his chair, gobsmacked at this revelation. Macefields had a reputation for being an aggressive firm, which pulled no punches and took no prisoners; he knew he would have a battle for survival on his hands. The pounding in his head intensified.

The day dragged on into eternity. The only light at the end of the tunnel was the thought of seeing Jennie for their usual Friday evening tryst. He had not seen her all day – Godwin, the senior partner, was without a secretary, his own having called in sick and Jennie had been commandeered to work for him. It crossed his mind he should give Diane a call but he could not face her wrath, or the prospect of being in the dog house for the weekend. The day seemed to be going from bad to worse.

Jennie was cold and unresponsive when he took her in his arms as she closed the door to her apartment. He thought perhaps she was annoyed he was still hung-over; God knows he was annoyed with himself, all he wanted to do was crawl into bed and sleep!

He sat in the lounge, exhausted, trying to concentrate on the evening news as Jennie was busy making them coffee. He made a silent vow to never drink so much again. After a while it dawned on him that Jennie had been gone ages and he wondered what she was doing. Rather than call to her, for fear of aggravating his headache, he dragged himself out of the chair and into the kitchen. His whole body ached. She was standing at the sink, facing the window, which was black against the night. Something about her stance stopped him in his tracks.

"What's wrong Jen?" he asked softly.

She slowly turned and he could tell by the sadness in her eyes and the tightness of her jaw that she was going to finish with him. He had known this day would come, he had thought about it often, particularly when overwhelmed with guilt; guilt at betraying his wife and children and guilt because he knew the longer their affair continued the longer he was denying her the chance to meet someone who could offer her the kind of future she deserved. He knew it was selfish to go on seeing her, but he could not bring himself to end it, she was his drug, his fix and he had become dependent on her. Now that dreaded day was here and the pain in his heart overshadowed the pain in his head and was a million times worse than anything he had ever experienced before.

The tears were streaming down her face as she told him she would always love him but could not go on living a lie. She wanted someone to share her life with, honestly and openly, someone she could build a home and raise a family with.

His legs suddenly felt weak and he slumped onto the pine chair at the matching oval kitchen table, his head in his hands. She sat beside him. He looked up at the kitchen window, the darkness of its pane matching the black void that had opened up in his heart and his eyes brimmed with tears as he fought to control his emotions. She tenderly placed her hands on his. Time stood still and neither of them spoke. He turned to face her, the pain in his eyes reaching out to hers in need. She broke the silence by whispering words of sorrow. When she had finished, somehow he found the strength to stand and walk out of her apartment… and out of her life.

He drove around aimlessly in the dark for miles, eventually ending up in the office car park. He had no idea how he got there or what to do next, so sat in the car in a daze, forehead leaning against the steering wheel, mind blank. He visibly jumped when he heard a tap on the window; it was a police officer who asked him if he was okay. He just stared at him. The officer asked him his name but he could not remember it.

The police car arrived within minutes.

The officer suspected Gordon had been drinking and asked him to provide a specimen of breath. To make matters worse Gordon's leg had gone to sleep while sitting in his car, so when he started to walk towards the police car in order to be breathalysed, his leg buckled and he rolled along like a drunken sailor, to the muffled laughter of the officers. Dutifully he followed instructions for blowing into the breathalyser tube, an act which brought him back to his senses. He was relieved (and secretly astonished) to be told it was a negative test and that he was free to go. He felt obliged to explain he had had some shocking news which was why he was where he was and behaving as he had been. The officers accepted his explanation and asked where he was going. He said home and, satisfied with his answer, the officers drove off leaving him in the car park, alone again. He climbed into his car and headed home with a heavy heart. It was just before midnight of what felt like the longest day of his life.

It was not over yet.

A raging thirst sent him into the kitchen for a glass of water. He was puzzled to find the blinds open and instinctively looked out of the window. At that exact moment the clouds parted, enabling a shaft of moonlight to escape and pierce the darkness of the conservatory, bathing Diane in its silvery beam, giving her a ghostly quality. The shock of seeing his wife startled him, sending him reeling backwards.

"What the fuck!" he exclaimed, then walked through the dining room and opened the sliding patio door to the conservatory. "Are you alright love?" he asked, his voice full of concern.

The moon had vanished behind the clouds again, plunging the conservatory into darkness. When his eyes became adjusted he could see the outline of her suitcase and handbag by the side of her chair. She continued to stare, unseeing, towards the garden for a while, then without looking at him announced, "I'm going away for a few days to think about my future."

"B-b-but where? And why?" he stammered.

"The where you don't need to know, and the why, huh, I suggest you ask your slut!"

He was speechless. She picked up her suitcase and handbag, strode past him, careful not to touch him, opened the front door, climbed into her car and drove away without a backward glance.

How many more shocks can a man take? he asked himself.

He spent the weekend with his mind in a fog. He had tried telephoning his wife but she had switched her phone off. Their son, Anthony, had gone to a concert in London for the weekend and their daughter, Jordan, was staying with her friend, and, as tempted as he was, he did not contact Jennie.

Two things threw his world into further turmoil. Firstly at work on Monday morning he discovered that Jennie had moved to another branch of the firm, which twisted the knife in his heart and hurt like hell, and secondly the merger negotiations with Macefields were further advanced than he had anticipated; the move was scheduled to happen at the end of the year and he knew he would soon be fighting for his professional life.

That night he did something he had not done in years – he got down on his knees and prayed.

Anita

Diane and Anita met at secondary school when they were 13 years old. Although in different school houses and classes, people often mistook Diane for Anita and vice versa because they were both above average height at 5'8" tall, slim, with waist-length, thick blonde hair. Nevertheless, they did not actually speak to each other until Diane went to the cinema to see the film 'Bonnie and Clyde' and sought Anita out the following day at school to tell her she reminded her of Fay Dunaway, the film's leading female. It turned out that Anita had also seen the film and thought Diane looked just like Bonnie too. That was the start of a lifelong friendship. Although nowadays Diane jokingly bemoaned the fact that Anita had hardly changed over the years, whereas she had changed out of all proportion, the word proportion being very apt considering she had gained about four stone in weight since their school days.

In her mid-twenties Anita married Jean-Pierre Sireau and moved to his small family château just outside Dijon in France. The two school friends remained in contact, regularly spoke on the telephone and in alternate years would meet up for a week or so. Anita was the sister Diane had never had and now it seemed only natural that she should fly down to stay with her friend at this crucial time in her life.

Anita was waiting for Diane in her old fashioned red Citroën C1 car at the airport de Dijon-Bourgogne as arranged. It was a 40 minute drive to the chateau, which had its own vineyard producing Château burgundy pinot noir. Normally during the journey they would chatter away twenty to the dozen, eager to update each other on their respective news, but this time they hardly spoke. Anita sensed the emotional turmoil that her much loved friend was going through and thought it wise to let her take the lead in any talks.

The day was beautiful. Although the sun was shining it was a fresh day rather than hot. The drive took them through fields of sunflowers which never failed to lift Diane's spirits, and at long last she began to unwind and relax.

As they drove slowly through the gates into the lovely south facing walled garden, Diane felt a pang of envy at the elegant beauty of Château Sireau, with its pale stone exterior and grey slate roof tiles complemented by the pale blue shutters flanking its windows. It was a small five bedroom family château, with outbuildings on the right-hand side, a covered terraced area opposite and a smaller guest house containing four compact apartments to the middle left-hand side, which created a private courtyard in the centre. Bougainvillea, wisteria and clematis intertwined and competed to cover the surrounding six foot high stone walls. There was a rose garden in front of the guest house and a vegetable and herb garden to the left of the château. Everything about it was picture-postcard pretty, peaceful and inviting.

Jean-Pierre and their children, Claudette, Brianna and David, were sitting around the old wooden table in the terraced area. It was obvious from the empty plates and glasses and the almost empty carafe of red wine that they had enjoyed a leisurely meal, which was just one of the many things Diane loved about the French way of living, a stark contrast to the rat race Britain was renowned for. As the car came to a dusty halt near to the steps leading to the front door, Bailey, their larger than average, rust coloured Irish red-terrier, ran to Diane, barking his usual greeting. She flung her arms around his neck.

"Hello Bailey, good boy, good boy, it's soooo good to see you too," Diane said and in keeping with their ritual she rubbed him behind the ears. In response he curled back his top lip giving her a shy smile, revealing a row of small, neat, front teeth, which always made her chuckle. She remembered the day Anita told her about Bailey's smile and her cynical reply. "Yeah right, I've heard it all now. Okay you're kidding me; everyone knows dogs don't smile."

"I'm telling you Bailey smiles," said Anita, and, of course, she was right. Diane grinned at the memory.

The rest of the family embraced her, kissing her on both cheeks, another wonderful French tradition. She took her bags up to her usual room in the château where the Sireau family resided. The guest house was a purely commercial bed and breakfast venture, fully occupied throughout most of the year, providing a steady income and, not surprisingly, attracting the same visitors time and time again.

In the room she dropped her bags on the floor and flopped down on the edge of the bed, catching sight of her sad, worn looking face in the narrow, full-length mirror on the yew wardrobe at the foot of the bed and wanted to cry but it was too much of an effort. She was emotionally drained. *Pull yourself together gal, get washed and changed and join the family, it's the least you can do,* she urged her reflection.

Fifteen minutes later she was enjoying a glass of Château Sirett wine and generally catching up with Anita and Jean-Pierre. They sat in their impressive exposed stone wall dining room at a large wooden table with seating for twelve on exquisitely carved chairs. A tall corner unit displayed crockery and glasses, a tapestry depicting a hunting scene hung on one wall and glass patio doors looked out onto lavender fields and woodland.

After a while Jean-Pierre excused himself as he sensed the girls needed to speak confidentially, and it was also time for him to prepare the evening meal. He was a superb cook. It had gone a little chilly so he lit the fire in the lounge.

Diane sat in a soft leather, high wing-backed chair by the open fire. The fire was framed by a stone mantle shelf displaying a trio of candles in a pewter holder in its centre. Her legs were outstretched, crossed at the ankles. She was lost in thought staring into the fire, mesmerized by its dancing flames. Anita sat on the opposite side of the hearth in a matching burgundy coloured chair, patiently waiting for Diane to open up.

"I popped into Manchester city centre last Thursday lunchtime, to look for a new outfit for Mr and Mrs Dalley's grandson's wedding. You remember my neighbours, the Dalleys, don't you?" she looked over to Anita, who nodded that she remembered the family. Her gaze flitting between Anita and her glass, she continued. "As it was a last minute decision, I didn't think to mention it to anyone."

Anita could tell by the way Diane was chewing on her bottom lip that she was fighting to keep her composure, so waited patiently for her friend to carry on.

"While walking along I was making a mental list of different stores to check out and wasn't paying particular attention to the other pedestrians, when suddenly a familiar, hearty laugh broke my concentration, causing me to look around. I couldn't believe my eyes! There he was, bold as brass, on the opposite side of the road, hand-in-hand with this young blonde woman, young enough to be his daughter! From the way they were laughing and joking it was quite obvious they were more than just friends!" She caught her breath as a stabbing pain cut through her chest.

"I couldn't take my eyes off them!" she whispered, her voice thick with emotion. She took a deep breath before continuing. "I watched them cross the road and head down the hill, hand-in-hand, in the direction of his office. Just before they turned the corner I witnessed them... kissing," she hissed, then looked over towards Anita. "I couldn't believe my eyes. It was as if I was invisible. My heart was pounding so loudly I couldn't think straight. I stood in an office doorway for ages, willing myself not to vomit." She suppressed a sob. "The next thing I remember I was sitting on the top deck of a bus, at the front, thinking. The more I thought, the more the pieces of the puzzle fell into place. Nita," she implored, "they must have been seeing each other for about twelve months, since he *supposedly* started doing charity work for the homeless. He was doing something alright but there was nothing charitable about it! How could he? The bastard! All the late night working, the early morning starts, the weekends away. The lies he must have told me. What a gullible fool I've been. What a stupid, idiotic fool!" Her face crumpled, her shoulders sagged and she quietly sobbed, tears cascading down her face.

Anita went to her friend, knelt down by the side of her chair, handed her a box of tissues and put her arm around her shoulders in comfort. Diane wiped her eyes and blew her nose. Anita handed her a glass of water from a bottle on a small table nearby. She drank it before continuing.

"Do you want to hear something really bloody funny?" She forced a strangled laugh but did not wait for a response. "Unbelievably, I actually helped fund the sordid affair!"

Anita looked perplexed.

"Yes, I paid for his little slut! You see I'm married to a devious, conniving, lying bastard!" She paused before elaborating. "Over a number of months he put pressure on me to return to work. Subtle hints, you know, making out work would be good for me once Jordan had left school. Then there were the guilt trips, saying his overtime payments had been stopped yet he was expected to cope with the same workload. How he was worried our finances would suffer. Like a prize idiot I took the bait and found myself a part-time job at the surgery, thinking my earnings would go into the family coffers to help with the finances. Oops, did I say finances, I meant slut!" She almost spat the last word out.

She sobbed again and continued to do so, intermittently, throughout the rest of the evening. Anita hardly said a word, deciding it was best for her friend to let the tears flow. There would be plenty of time for discussions tomorrow.

"Morning love," Anita greeted Diane, her smile captured in her voice. "Coffee?" Diane nodded in response and sat down at the large farmhouse table with chunky legs and scrubbed surface. "How are you feeling today?" Anita asked as she handed her friend a mug of steaming coffee.

Diane took a sip. "I slept surprisingly well, thanks." She had another sip of her coffee before continuing. "To be honest I was dreading going to bed, afraid that when I closed my eyes I would be plagued by images of..." her voice dropped to a mere whisper, "them. I thought I wouldn't be able to sleep, but thank goodness it was nightmare free and my mind feels clearer; which is just as well because I need to make decisions and that, my dear friend, is where you come in."

"Just let me know what you need from me and I'll do my best," said Anita.

"Well, it's a lovely day so after breakfast would you mind if we walked to the village?"

"Yes of course. What do you want from the village?"

"Nothing, it's just that I think clearer when I go for a walk."

Just over an hour later the two friends were walking in the sunshine towards the village. The path ran alongside a field of sunflowers with brown faces framed by yellow petal fringes, bobbing and swaying to the rhythm of nature's gentle breeze. Bailey was a little way ahead weaving in and out of the field, sniffing anything remotely interesting, occasionally turning his head in order to check the girls were still following behind. A rabbit suddenly popped out in front of him. He barked and half-heartedly gave chase but quickly returned to the dust path the girls were treading.

A pleasant sight to an onlooker, except Diane felt anything but pleasant. She was consumed with anger and repeated again her sighting of the 'lovebirds' as she had sneeringly labelled them.

"I could throttle the little slut for destroying my marriage. Men do the chasing but it's the women who give the go-ahead." Her face contorted and hands claw-like she continued, "Yes, I could quite easily put my hands around her skinny little neck and wring the life out of her!"

After her ranting had subsided followed by a long silence she turned to Anita. "Apologies about my outburst but I do feel so much better now. I'd intended to use you as a sounding board for my decision, not to vent my anger, sorry." They both laughed. "Anyway," she continued, "I have decided to leave Gordon." She paused to gauge the effect her announcement had had, but when Anita did not respond she carried on. "I'm not going to leave him immediately, certainly not until Jordan has finished her exams, which will be next June, then I'll review the situation but I will leave him, it's just a matter of when. I plan to keep up the charade of happy families until then. But, in the meantime, suddenly my husband's snoring has become so unbearable he'll have to sleep in another bedroom."

They continued to walk in silence for a few minutes before Anita spoke.

"I can understand how angry and hurt you are Di, but you've been together for such a long time. Are you sure your marriage can't survive? What about a session with someone at Relate?"

"No, I've made my mind up. You see for me it's all about trust. How can I have a worthwhile relationship with someone I don't trust?"

"Oh Di," Anita sighed, "please don't do or say anything until you've considered all the options."

"Nita I know where you're coming from love, but put it this way, if he'd gone to a conference somewhere and had had too much to drink and woken up the following morning next to some little scrubber, I'd be angry and hurt, probably demand that he have a thorough health check and he'd have to worm his way back into my good books, but I could get past it, because it was a one off, unplanned encounter. What I can't get past, and never will be able to come to terms with, is the deliberate deception, compounded by months and months of lies; his audacity in encouraging me to return to work to help ease his financial burden, a burden increased by the cost of conducting an affair! I feel utterly humiliated, and a fool. My self-esteem, what's left of it, will not permit me to just carry on as if it doesn't matter. It hurts like hell and matters hugely." Her voice faltered and her eyes began to sting as tears threatened. She took a deep breath, blinking the tears away then continued, her voice quavering with emotion. "It goes to the very core of me, our marriage, our children's lives, our history and our memories. In fact it's undermined our whole way of life, past, present and future, all… tainted. My chance sighting of them in Manchester has changed everything… forever."

Anita did not respond immediately, she gave her friend time to rein in her emotions which also allowed her a moment to carefully consider her next question before voicing it. Her voice soft, almost a whisper, she asked, "Can you be absolutely sure that they have been seeing each other for a long time? Could there be an innocent explanation?"

Diane waited a few seconds before replying, "Nice try love but no. I know my husband well enough to interpret the way he looked at her. Also what if there have been others? How long before he strays again? Obviously there is something lacking in me which has caused him to look elsewhere in the first place," Her bottom lip quivered at this assumption.

"Oh no, I can't accept that," protested Anita. "You have been a first rate, wonderful wife and mother. Not to mention caring daughter and daughter-in-law. If anyone is lacking in something, it's Gordon. He is an idiot of the first waters to jeopardise the family life you have both worked so hard to achieve. No, you must not reproach yourself in any way whatsoever."

The rest of their walk to the village was in silence as each thought about the situation.

Anita bought them a coffee and a piece of chocolate gateau in the local supermarket. Diane produced a notebook and pen saying, "I want you to help me draw up a list of things that I need to do, for example, one of the first things I need to do is sort out my financial security. Get the house valued. See if I can increase my hours at work etc."

"Well, I'll be honest, I hope you and Gordon can work things out between you but if it helps you feel more in control of things then… Hmm, let me think." After some thought, Anita said, "First and foremost you need to look after yourself, think about the care you provide for your mum and

Gordon's dad. I've thought for a while that their needs were becoming too much for you. Contact Social Services about care support for them, also ring Age Concern to see if they can offer advice and help. Assess what you do for the children, encourage them to become more independent, you know, do their own washing and ironing, hone their culinary skills. You need to lighten your existing workload before increasing your working hours. I suppose what I am trying to say is, you need to plan ahead and put things in place if you're serious about going it alone."

Two coffees later, a more positive Diane was armed with a list of things to do and anxious to start the ball rolling. Having exhausted discussions, they walked back to the château reminiscing and laughing about their school days. Nita's two eldest children had returned to their own homes, and David, her youngest child, was staying at his friend's parents' house, so just the three of them enjoyed a pleasant evening meal, leaving Diane relaxed and able to enjoy another good night's sleep before catching her return flight the next day, heralding the start of her new, independent life.

Confrontation

Diane arrived home at 5.00pm to an empty house. The house had not been the same since her son had gone to Leeds University, two years previously to study engineering. She missed him terribly and hated the silence he had left behind. That night the usual empty feeling had been replaced by a soul destroying cold void filling the rooms and clinging to the surrounding four walls, four walls that had once meant so much to her. She remembered the excitement when they first moved in, buzzing with ideas of how to decorate and furnish the rooms and landscape the gardens. How they had made love in every room, including the garden. Their joy when she found out she was pregnant. Love and laughter aplenty back then. And now? She could not see a future.

Jordan had telephoned her just as she had opened the front door and asked if she could stay another night with her friend. Diane had agreed, not letting on that it suited her for Jordan not to be around when she spoke to her *husband*. Even in her mind the word was difficult to form let alone say out loud.

She prepared the evening meal, stew, because it was quick and she wanted to eat by herself. She was sitting in the lounge staring at the television, not actually watching it, when Gordon let himself in. She heard him go into the kitchen, as was his usual routine, to hang his coat in the cloakroom adjoining the downstairs toilet and to put his bag by the table in the corner. She heard him kick off his shoes and guessed he had put on his slippers, slippers she had bought him. She heard the door to the dining area at the back of the room open and sensed him peering around it.

"Hello love, are you okay?" His voice was soft and full of concern.

She felt sick to her stomach and did not answer. He quietly walked over and sat on the arm of the settee opposite and waited for her to speak. Without looking at him, her voice harsh and cutting, she said, "Your dinner is in the microwave, it just needs heating up. After you have eaten I need to talk to you."

"W-w-what about? Can't we talk now?" he asked pleadingly.

Still without looking at him, she said, "I need to tell you my plans for MY future. It is not open to discussion, I just need to tell you what I am going to do."

"B-b-but…"

She raised her right hand, palm outwards, in an authoritative way to silence him.

"I said it is not up for discussion! I know all about your sordid affair." Only moments before he had arrived she had decided to make believe she knew much more than she actually did.

"I know how long it's been going on. I know that you have lied about starting work early and finishing late. I know about the weekends away, when and where you've been and the cost. I have my sources and have checked."

"I-I-I don't know what you are talking about…"

"Don't insult my intelligence any further," her voice firm and full of anger. "I have seen you together… kissing!" she almost gagged as she said the last word.

He fought to maintain a blank, innocent expression.

"Out of love for Jordan I have decided to stay here until she has completed her exams next June. I DO NOT, I repeat DO NOT want anything to jeopardise her crucial exams. Do I make myself clear?"

He nodded his understanding.

"Good. When she has completed her exams I will move to my mother's house until this house is sold." She took a deep breath to allow the significance of her words to sink in. "If, in the meantime, you carry on living here, there will be three major changes. Firstly, I will be starting full-time work on Monday. Secondly, you will sleep in the spare bedroom from now on. You are no longer welcome in my bed. By way of explanation to Jordan, it will be because your snoring is disturbing my sleep and now that I am working full-time and learning a difficult job, I cannot afford to go without sleep. We're used to you hardly ever being here anyway so I'm not expecting her to notice any changes, certainly not initially. Thirdly, I will no longer look after your father. Too much like father, like son. He cheated on your mother throughout their married life and I suspect that is the reason for her untimely death eight years ago. Well I am NOT your mother and you will NOT bring me down. I'm 49 and as such still young enough to forge a new life for myself! And by God I will!" She stopped and looked directly at him, her face hard, her eyes blazing with a mixture of hatred and disgust and he knew better than to remonstrate with her. Instead he slunk away and made himself scarce.

The atmosphere at home was unbearable; although Gordon and Diane were trying to be civil with each other it was obvious there were problems. Jordan was certainly not fooled by their pretence, indeed she took advantage of the situation by asking if she could study for her exams at her friend Amy's house for a change. Normally Diane would have insisted Amy came to their house, so that she could ensure the girls actually did study, for Jordan was more rebellious than Anthony had been, which Diane attributed to her being looked after by a childminder another thing she could blame her *bastard husband* for. But in the present situation she was relieved that Jordan had somewhere else to go, because it meant she could escape to her mother's.

Fearful of the future, in both his personal and professional life and aware that Jennie was deliberately avoiding him, Gordon hit an all-time low and the bottle. His wife was as cold as ice towards him and consequently he spent most nights getting drunk and sleeping in the armchair. His despondency was further compounded by being assigned to Gerald Catchpole's litigation team and inheriting Hayden Husslebea as a secretary. He had yet to meet them but had heard of Catchpole's reputation for being a prize prat and a gut feeling told him Husslebea could be as bad, if not worse.

Once the merger with Denbighs was common knowledge, Hayden made it his business to uncover the lowdown on its staff. Luckily one of his many acquaintances worked in Denbighs' post room and proved to be a mine of interesting gossip. He was delighted to learn that Jennie Enderby was there but taken aback to discover she had been having an affair with one of the lawyers, who was married. By all accounts she had been distraught when he had recently finished with her. Consequently, Hayden instantly hated Gordon Humphrys, even though they had yet to meet. Oh and he would make sure they met. *Poor Jennie, poor sweet, innocent Jennie, being taken advantage of by a married man. If only I'd been there to protect her, I'd have soon scared him off, huh!*

He found it highly amusing that, unbeknown to Humphrys, the staff referred to him as Humpty Humphrys. He was sure the information would prove useful.

Mr Whittington

They managed to secure a table at the back of a newly revamped coffee shop, just around the corner from Stepwells' offices.

"So come on everyone, what's the view on the merger between Macefields and Denbighs?" Bev questioned the rest of the Flakes before taking a sip of her coffee.

"Merger my arse, it's a takeover," announced Lucy.

"Why do you say that?" asked Ben.

"Denbighs is full of deadbeat lawyers, should be renamed Deadbeats!" laughed Lucy.

"Oh why so?" asked Rachel.

"I know someone who started working there recently. She's not impressed, says the firm is made up of odd personalities. She recently had a run in with one of the female partners, who public lambasted her for not doing some task on time but who had actually forgotten to ask her to do it! She's seething and looking to move."

"Tell her to apply for my job," offered Piers.

"Er?" queried Bev.

"I've handed my notice in and leave for London in three months, the beginning of December."

"London? What are you up too now?" demanded Ben.

"Well just call me Dick Whittington and get me a cat."

"Piers have you forgotten to take your tablets today or have you taken something else?" questioned Rachel.

"No, I can assure you all I am fully compos mentis, but, for some time the bells of London have been calling me. I might as well tell you all now, after three months of working part-time on the local comedy circuit, I've decided to spread my wings and move to London and give stand-up comedy my best shot. By leaving now I'll be there in time for the festive season. Indeed, I've already got a couple of gigs lined up."

"Oh Wow! Good for you! I would love to live in London and let's face it, you can always return to the legal profession if things don't pan out as you hope." Lucy enthused.

"So Bev, can I leave you to organise my Flakes leaving meal on the Friday before?"

"Of course," agreed Bev.

"Good for you and remember it's better to say 'I wish I hadn't' rather than, 'I wish I had', so go for it," added Rachel.

"You've certainly got the talent, your timing is superb and you know how to work an audience, you regularly have us in hysterics. If anyone can make it, it's you," encouraged Bev.

Ben sat there in silence, processing Piers' news.

Merger Day

Knowing he was fighting for his professional life, Gordon managed to abstain from alcohol for the whole week prior to starting at Macefields, resorting to the occasional sleeping tablet to ensure he had sufficient beauty sleep in order to be as fighting fit as possible. On merger day he wore his best suit, black with narrow, light grey pinstripes, a new white shirt and a dark grey tie.

Originally he had selected the grey tie with a delicate purple fleur-de-lys design that Jennie had chosen for him on their first foreign trip together. The tie with its poignant memories caught him off guard for he was suddenly transported back to the Galleria Alberto Sordi, the Art Nouveau style shopping mall in Rome, with its magnificent glass roof, where Jennie decided to buy him a tie as a holiday memento. What fun they had had choosing the most outrageous designs. In his mind's eye he could see her beaming smile as she finally settled for the tie he was now wearing, and how later that night in their hotel room she had giggled uncontrollably when he wore the tie and nothing else as they made love.

He suddenly felt achingly lonely, an almost unbearable sense of loss. He longed to take Jennie in his arms, hold her close, smell her familiar vanilla aroma, feel the warmth of her soft skin and never let her go. He swayed and screwed his eyes up tightly as a wave of pain swept through his body, it was all he could do to stop shouting "God help me" out loud as he roughly removed the memorable tie and threw it over the back of a chair.

It took a few minutes for the intensity of his feelings to subside and he had to psych himself up again to being upbeat and humorous for his first meeting with Catchpole, a meeting he dreaded. He secretly considered it very bad management that they had not had the opportunity to meet before the merger day but suspected it was a psychological ploy to undermine people's confidence.

Macefields had organised a breakfast event in the main boardroom as a welcome for the Denbigh newcomers. There was a buzz of excitement and jovial banter amongst the attendees which, under normal circumstances, Gordon would have readily joined in with, as he was gregarious by nature. Unfortunately though, he had felt compelled to scan the room in search of Jennie. Within seconds he had spotted her across the room. She had her back towards him and was wearing his favourite dark blue pinstriped suit. She was chatting to a small group of people, significantly nearer to her own age. The sight of her caused his heart to lurch and a fresh wave of pain swept over him. He shivered and suddenly felt very old; the last thing he wanted to do was socialise and the thought of eating made him feel nauseous. Lost in his own misery he had not noticed the tall gangly man bending forward talking to a slightly shorter, frizzy-haired chap, who was pointing in his direction. A few moments later someone slapped him on the shoulder and shook hands with him. The handshake was so limp that their hands barely touched.

"Hello, I'm Gerry Catchpole, pleased to meet you."

"Oh hello, Gordon Humphrys, pleased to meet you too," said Gordon, taken by surprise.

"Help yourself to a drink and something to eat and I'll see you in the office afterwards," said Catchpole over his shoulder as he made his way over to a group of men who had just entered the room. Gordon watched him greet the group and whisper something to them prompting loud guffawing. Puzzled and rather miffed by Catchpole's obvious indifference towards him he looked around the room searching for his Denbigh colleagues, when his casual gaze caught the eye of the frizzy-haired man. The sheer hostility of his penetrating stare sent a shiver of foreboding through his already emotionally beleaguered mind; he did not understand the bad vibes he was receiving but what he did know was he needed a drink… desperately.

He spotted John Bentley and queued with him for breakfast, half listening to him waxing lyrically about a caravanning rally he had been to that weekend. He nodded occasionally in an effort to feign interest but his mind was unsettled by the indifference and hostility he had just encountered and the knowledge that Jennie was near. She sat at a table over the far side of the room with the crowd she had been talking to. He saw her glance in his direction but quickly turn away before he could acknowledge he had seen her.

When most people had finished their breakfast, John Clark, the Chairman of Macefields, a short barrel of a man with dyed black hair, which disguised the grey but not his mid-fifties age, gave a short, matter of fact 'Welcome to Macefields' speech, which, to Gordon's amusement, had the effect of clearing the boardroom. Gordon followed Bentley to the lift, irritated to hear him still droning on about his wonderful weekend. As the lift doors opened on the third floor an attractive young Asian girl asked them their names and showed them to their workstations. Gordon was relieved to find Bentley's office was out of sight of his but was horrified to find he shared an office with Catchpole, who sat at the back of the room facing towards the glass door looking out at the rest of the office, whereas Gordon's desk was on the left hand side of the office, with the door opening on to it; his desk seemed to have been shoehorned into the gap.

He had just sat down when Catchpole flung the door open causing it to slam into Gordon's desk. Although he must have heard the bang he chose to ignore it. Instead he turned and looked back out of the door and ordered someone to get him a coffee. Gordon thought Catchpole's behaviour bizarre and wondered if it was some sort of show for his benefit. Minutes later the frizzy-haired chap appeared with a cup of coffee, blanking Gordon completely until Catchpole said, "Hayden Husslebea meet Gordon Humphrys, you'll be working for him too." Husslebea looked Gordon up and down in an exaggerated way, sniffed and walked out of the office, no hello, no greeting, no nothing. Gordon could not believe how rude they both were.

Their offensive attitude continued and it was obvious, for reasons known only to Husselbea, that he hated Gordon on sight, who in turn considered him to be the most irritating person he had ever had the misfortune of working with, not least because of his weird penchant for telling Humpty Dumpty jokes, to no one in particular, then laughing hysterically.

"Two cows were standing in a field. First cow says to the other, 'So are you worried about this Mad Cow Disease going around?'

Second cow replies, 'No, why should I be? I'm Humpty Dumpty!'"

Hayden burst out laughing just as Gordon walked by on the way to his office and smirked as he watched him angrily tug at the knot of his tie in order to loosen it. *Yes! I'm already beginning to rattle Humpty's cage.* To keep the momentum going, halfway through the afternoon Hayden made his first of many silent phone calls to Gordon.

Sexual Tension

For various reasons the merger of the two firms pleased Jennie. Macefields was a much bigger firm and, she hoped, would afford her more opportunities to avoid Gordon. She had not seen him since his last visit to her apartment and knew he was deliberately keeping away from her too; he always was sensitive to her needs. She trusted he was okay and getting on with his marriage and was grateful he had respected her decision to break up. It was not a decision she had taken lightly, as he had made her feel safe.

She was pleased to learn several colleagues from Stepwells had already moved over to Macefields. There was Sarah Price with her unmistakeable Cleopatra hairstyle, she liked Sarah, Gerry Catchpole who she found comical and the two Husslebeas. Secretly she was amused that they still pointedly ignored one another while knowing each other's every move. Just like cats where one has strayed into its rival's territory, neither acknowledging the other's presence but their senses on high alert psyching each other out, just waiting for one false move and an excuse to pounce! Then last, but certainly not least, Nick Turner. The memory of their coffee time sprang to mind, as it had numerous times since. She had found him surprisingly sympathetic and easy to talk to. She also found him dangerously attractive.

Throughout her first morning, one-by-one, her old colleagues made a point of walking over to her desk to welcome her, all except Nick. What she could not and should not know was how excited Nick was at the prospect of her working in his department, that he had thought of little else since bumping into her and had not slept a wink the previous night; how he had pressurised the other partners into agreeing the merger was a sound financial risk, thereby putting his own reputation on the line, and, more importantly, how he could barely wait to be on his own with her. He had not felt this excited for years, not since Andrea had been assigned to do some legal work for him, which was precisely why he chose to play it cool now and keep away from Jennie, at least initially, for he was desperate to avoid the humiliation he had experienced over Andrea. Gillian's snide comments to Richardson echoed down the corridors of his memory, making him cringe with embarrassment. "Oh Peter you should see how Nick's behaving, he's like a dog on heat around Andrea, so juvenile, like a 13 year old! It would be laughable if it wasn't so tragic!" Gillian's witchlike cackle rang in his ears. That was just one of many times he had wanted to throttle her.

Private Detective

When Jennie stopped visiting him in prison Zac was devastated, he felt suicidal and became increasingly dependent on drugs. As the weeks turned into months his devastation turned into bitterness and he blamed Jennie one hundred percent for his predicament. It incensed him that she had dumped him so callously after all that he had done for her. He had rescued her from the gutter, financed her career, given her a home, a life, and, more importantly his heart. He had even risked his life for her and this is how she repaid him! And not knowing where she was or who she was with was driving him insane!

Within days of being incarcerated he was befriended by a fellow prisoner, David Maroni, a short stocky man, with dark hair and olive skin. Zac found him sympathetic and confided how hurt and angry he was about Jennie cutting him loose. Maroni listened intently as his friend vented, pacing up and down the changing room in the prison gym. After Zac had finished speaking Maroni quietly said, "I might be able to help."

Zac immediately stopped pacing and looked at his friend, puzzled surprise etched over his face. "What? How can you help?" he asked.

"I'm due to be released in six weeks' time, I'll try and find her. I know what it's like to be betrayed."

"What will you do?"

"A mate of mine is a private detective and owes me a couple of favours. Just write down as much information as you can about Jennie, her family, where she's lived, worked etc and the latest photograph of her. That type of thing. I'll look him up as soon as I'm released and let you know how it goes."

Zac was lost for words. Tears welled up as he hugged his friend in gratitude. Eventually he managed to say, "Thanks mate, you have no idea how much your offer means to me, Jennie was everything to me, it's eating away at me to think she might be with someone else."

Maroni's offer of help lifted Zac's mood and galvanised him into preparing to confront Jennie. It was the turning point, something to focus on. He wanted to be at his best when he saw Jennie again and realised he needed to wean himself off drugs, so decided to go 'cold turkey' that evening. It was harder than he thought.

Mid-afternoon he had flu-like symptoms, shivering, runny eyes and nose and a bout of sneezing. He could not face food but craved drugs. He felt wound up and anxious that he would not be able to stop his dependency. He lay awake that night, sweating, mind racing, leaving him lethargic the next day. By the third day he had sickness and diarrhoea. Maroni was a tower of strength, reassuring and encouraging Zac.

"Man, this is normal, hang on in there, it's worth it. Trust me, I'm speaking from experience. I'd been a drug abuser for years but being sent down for four years got me away from my dealer and gave me the kick up the backside I needed. Don't get me wrong, it's hard and will get harder and it doesn't help that drugs are rife in here. You've gotta be strong and stick to your plan. You can do it."

"I know, I know," Zac agreed. "I just need something to take my mind off drugs."

"Promise you won't laugh," said Maroni, "but I found reading the bible helped me."

Zac could not laugh he was too taken aback by this revelation.

"I'm telling you man, the book makes sense. You can borrow mine."

So it was that Zac turned to the bible and the more agony he felt the more he read. He also continued working out in the gym and developed an exercise routine in his cell at night to combat insomnia and ease the stiffness and pins and needles in his joints which were withdrawal symptoms. Lack of appetite was hard-going, at first he literally had to force food down and fight the urge to throw up, but he managed. By the time Maroni was released Zac was over the worst and looking healthier.

"I'm gonna miss you man," Zac said as he hugged Maroni and then slapped him on the back wishing him good luck.

"I'm proud of you, stay clean, stay focused and I'll be in touch," Maroni said in farewell.

Initially Zac felt lost without his friend, scared he would succumb to the temptation of drugs, but reading the bible really was his salvation, certainly while waiting for news. Yet, conversely, the bible did not diminish his desire to confront Jennie.

Although it was two months before he heard from Maroni, he never lost faith that his friend would come through for him. His patience paid off with a message from another prisoner's brother. After visiting hours Broadbent, a fellow prisoner, told Zac that Maroni knew of Jennie's whereabouts, would keep watch and see him on his release. Zac was jubilant.

Redundancies

Within weeks of the Macefields and Denbighs merger and after numerous meetings, rumours and vicious betrayals, certain members of staff were sent 'at risk of redundancy' letters. Nick made sure Gordon was one of the unfortunate ones. He found it totally unbelievable that he had had an affair with Jennie; he definitely had to go.

Gordon was not surprised to receive a letter, he had been expecting one ever since John Bentley had begged him not to let on that they had been out for the occasional coffee. As was often the case in redundancy situations, the one going was the last one to know and obviously Bentley was aware Gordon had been selected and was concerned he would be tarred with the same redundancy brush. Although Gordon had never really rated Bentley it still hurt that he viewed him as some sort of leper. Nevertheless, he nodded his agreement to keep their tête-à-tête coffee sessions quiet and followed with a snort of derision which was totally lost on the relieved Bentley. *One more nail in my coffin.*

Interviews were conducted, followed by a point selection process and 95% of those at risk were offered generous Compromise Agreements. Most of those affected accepted their fate with dignity, albeit reluctantly, including Gordon. He was particularly upset by the cavalier way in which Catchpole had greeted him on the fateful morning. "Morning Humphrys, it's pointless you being here, I'll let Hayden explain," he had said over his shoulder as he carried on walking into their office, slamming the door behind him. Seeing Hayden turn bright red and visibly squirm in his seat afforded Gordon a modicum of satisfaction and for once Hayden did not say a word, not even a Humpty Dumpty joke.

In fact the only person who did not accept a Compromise Agreement was John Bentley, who had been incredulous at receiving a letter in the first place. With each day's passing he became angrier and angrier, until eventually the firm had felt obliged to put him on 'garden leave' and immediately escort him off the premises, after, bizarrely, he had been overheard threatening to set fire to the curtains in the main boardroom!

It was an awful time for everyone, particularly for Gordon, who was utterly devastated and on the edge of a breakdown. His life was in turmoil, his mistress had dumped him, he and his wife were living separate lives and their kids hated him, his career was in tatters and his excuse of a secretary was sending him crazy with stupid jokes and silent phone calls, though unfortunately he could not prove he was responsible for the calls.

"Humpty Dumpty sat on a wall,
Humpty Dumpty had a great fall,
All the King's horses,
And all the King's men, said,
Fuck him! He's only an egg!"

Although Gordon loathed employment agencies, he reluctantly registered with several, because his contacts had either said there was nothing about, painted a deeper picture of doom and gloom, or had not even bothered to return his calls. After one particularly harrowing registration appointment, where he had had to sit a number of aptitude tests, including a horrendous maths test, he decided to call into The Chapel Arms, a nearby pub, to drown his sorrows. He was both amazed and delighted to bump into Dean Freer, someone he had known for years but had not seen for ages. Although they had often found themselves on opposite sides of cases, they had had a good rapport and mutual respect.

Over lunch, laughing and reminiscing about old cases and generally catching up, Dean was very sympathetic to Gordon's current dilemma and threw him a lifeline of a possible job at his firm, Freer & Son. He fished in his inside jacket pocket for a business card and handed it to Gordon, who started to thank him but was interrupted by a call on his mobile phone. He noted it said 'number unknown' and excitedly hoped it was one of the agencies, which would have created the impression that he was in demand.

"Hello, Gordon Humphrys speaking." There was no reply. "Hello? Hello? Who's calling please?" Still no reply.

Gordon ended the call, made light of it and thanked Dean, saying he would be in touch. They shook hands on the pavement outside the pub and as they turned to head off in opposite directions Gordon's phone rang again but this time he cringed because he just knew it would be another of Husslebea's silent calls. He had guessed correctly.

New Boss

She answered on the third ring of the phone, "Hello?"

"Hi Bev, Rachel here. You're not going to believe what's happened. Remember me telling you the chap I was working for had left?"

"Yes?"

"The main boss called me into the office to reassure me my job was okay because he'd got a replacement for me to work for."

"Ah ha?"

"It's Gordon Humphrys!"

"What! Well I never! Does he know you?"

"He's never actually seen me. Though he almost saw me when I was with you."

"What do you mean?"

"You and I were on our way to Jugs when we saw Jennie with Gordon, he had his back to us while speaking on his mobile. Jennie told us he'd received a call about his father who was ill, so we carried on to Jugs and he never actually saw me. Do you remember?"

"Vaguely."

"Well it's rather awkward for me because I know about his affair with Jennie. I'm obviously going to have to play things by ear. Watch this space."

Jordan

Jordan loved her mother and brother but adored her father. He was such fun to be with, always saying and doing silly things to make her laugh. If she had a problem he was the one she would run to, confident he would know just what to do because he seemed to know everything, he was so clever. They had a special bond, not least because there was no mistaking she was his daughter; she had the same mischievous smoky-grey eyes, framed by long dark lashes. She loved the fact that he chose her name because it sounded very similar to his and remembered, when she was very young, collapsing in a fit of giggles whenever he pretended to be tongue-tied trying to say, "I know a little girl called Jordan with a daddy called Gordon, so really Jordan's Gordon's Jordan."

Now she could see through his smile, which could not hide the desperate unhappiness in his eyes. She did not know why he was so sad or why her mother seemed angry all the time, but sensed it must be serious because she could never recall such a lingering tension in her home before. She was also aware that her father had begun drinking heavily. At first she had laughed about it with Amy, but as the weeks went by she became increasingly concerned about him.

She had completed her exams, so there was no reason to go to Amy's, and was sitting watching the Simpsons on the lounge television waiting for her father to come home from work. Her mother had disappeared to her nan's house an hour earlier leaving a beef bourguignon cooking in the slow cooker for dinner. Jordan had decided to wait for her father to come in from work so that the two of them could enjoy their evening meal together for a change. She was alarmed to witness him walk straight to the drinks cabinet and pour himself a large brandy, before taking his coat off. He downed his drink in one and poured himself another. She did not comment and instead busied herself laying the table and dishing up the food.

"Dinner is served, your honour," she announced pompously, in a vain attempt at humour. "Sorry love," he said, ignoring her humorous offering, "I'm just not hungry."

"Aw come on Daddy, I deliberately waited so that we could eat together. We haven't eaten together for ages, come on, for me. Please."

Her plea touched a nerve and he joined her at the table. She made small talk as he moved his food around the plate. Eventually she decided to confront him.

"Daddy, what's wrong?" She waited for a response but he did not even look up at her so she continued. "You seem so sad all the time and Mummy seems permanently angry. In fact I hardly see either of you at all. I can't remember the last time I saw you together. You're always late home and Mummy's always over at Nana's house, in fact she's there so much she might as well move in with her!" She saw her father flinch at her last throwaway comment and was horrified to think she may have stumbled across what was happening.

"Is that it? Is Mum leaving us?" she whispered.

There was a deafening silence before her father, still looking down at his plate, quietly said, "I don't know." Another pause and then he added, "I honestly don't know what she's planning to do." He looked at her, his eyes full of sorrow, his words throwing her mind in a whirl.

They sat in silence eating their meals, neither knowing what to say. Jordan cleared the table. When she returned to collect the condiments set she saw that Gordon had poured himself yet another drink.

"Oh Daddy not more alcohol, you're going to make yourself ill!" she protested, tears threatening. "I'm really concerned about you, I've noticed you're drinking more and more and I know that you often spend the night asleep in the armchair. You really need to sort things out with Mum." Her voice cracking with emotion she yelled in frustration, "Tell her it's upsetting me too!" She flounced out of the room, running upstairs to her bedroom, leaving him to think about what she had said.

Gordon sat in the armchair, switched the television off leaving just the soft glow from the standard lamp in the corner to light the room. He swirled his drink around the brandy glass, mesmerised as the warm, inviting liquid balanced itself, slowing to a halt, glistening in the light, tantalising, beckoning to him; he was tempted, oh so tempted. Then a voice of reason inside his head gave him the strength to resist the temptation while thinking things through. Although full of dread he decided he must speak with Diane as soon as she came back from her mother's and rehearsed in his mind what to say. He rewarded himself by finishing his drink, again in one, then sat back and waited.

Two hours later her key turning in the front door woke him up. She walked straight into the lounge. He suspected she had assumed he had gone to bed as there was no sound from the television, and although he felt groggy from sleep he seized the opportunity to try and open up discussions.

"Jordan was upset tonight." Diane visibly jumped at the unexpected sound of his voice.

"Why, what have you done to her?" she accused.

"I've done nothing to her," Gordon protested, trying to keep the irritation from his voice. "She is upset because of how things are between us." His voice softened and he continued, almost pleading, "If only for her sake we need to speak to each other."

Diane waited, tight-lipped.

"Please sit down; I can't talk to you properly when you're standing up as if you're going to walk out of the room," he implored.

She looked as if she was going to say something but obviously thought better of it and sat down on the edge of the chair, looking most uncomfortable.

"I'm sorry." Gordon's apology was barely audible as he sat looking down at his hands, which were clenched together on his lap. He waited a few seconds before continuing. "Please believe me when I say I'm so sorry I've hurt you." He looked up at Diane who was staring towards the front of the room at nothing in particular. "I'm sorry I've hurt the children. I wish with all my heart I could turn the clock back and we could be the happy family we once were. I've been a fool, an idiot to jeopardise everything that we have worked so hard to achieve, and have achieved." He sighed, hoping for a response; again he was disappointed and continued, his voice breaking. "You and the children are everything to me." His voice dropped to barely a whisper. "I've never stopped loving you Di and need you now more than ever, you are my world, without you my life is nothing, it's meaningless. The thought of losing you tears me apart. If there is anything I can do to make it up to you, please let me know. I'll do anything, anything you ask." He buried his head in his hands, unable to stop tears streaming down his face.

Diane remained silent and still, cold and unemotional. He would have preferred her to throw something at him, hit him or swear at him, anything was preferable to this hard faced woman he no longer recognised.

"I'm begging you for another chance, please," his voice cracking as he pleaded.

After what seemed like an eternity, she finally spoke, her voice full of contempt. "You bloody fool!" she hissed. "What do you think you were doing?" She didn't wait for a response. "Your sordid affair has undermined and tainted our marriage, our lives, our children's lives, our past, our present and our future." She threw her arms up in the air in exasperation then slammed her fists down on to her lap. "You even pressurised me to return to work, saying they'd stopped paying you for overtime!!" She glared and he saw her jaw tighten. "Like a fool I believed you and thought I was helping the family, never suspecting that you'd stopped doing overtime so that you could be with your… your slut and I was making up the shortfall!!! How could you do that to me? How could you do that to Jordan? Because I felt obliged to return to work she was forced to go to a childminder, which she hated and hated me for making her go!" she yelled, then stood up and paced like a caged tiger before walking to the back of the room, where she stood looking into the conservatory, her arms wrapped around herself in a comforting way.

After a few moments thought she marched back to where he was sitting. Standing over him she snarled, "How could you treat me with such contempt? What a despicable way to treat the mother of your children!" she exclaimed, then waited to let her words sink in. "I've given you the best years of my life and I don't deserve to be humiliated like that. I have never done anything to warrant such appalling behaviour, never! Well I hope your young slut is worth it, because it will cost you big time." She opened the door leading to the kitchen but before walking though it she turned and said, "Oh, and for the record, you look ridiculous together, she's clearly young enough to be your daughter. If you imagine yourself as Michelangelo's David, look again buster, because to the rest of the world you look more like Humpty Dumpty!"

She saw his eyes shoot wide open; her words had definitely struck a chord. *Good*, she thought to herself, *the penny has dropped!* Oh the penny had dropped alright, but not about their marital predicament, it was because he suddenly realised what was behind the Humpty Dumpty jokes.

"*Humpty Dumpty said:*
'Roses are red, violets are blue,
Sugar is sweet, and so are you.'
The Princess replied,
'The sugar bowl's empty, and you make me sick.
The flowers are wilting, and so is your dick!'"

Cross-Stitch

Cross-stitch was Joan's creative passion. Most days, after completing her morning chores and routine shopping excursions with George, she would sit in her comfortable high-backed chair by the glass balcony doors with her wooden seat stand, working on her latest masterpiece, as George liked to call them. They ranged from simple yet appealing cards for church fund-raising events to her most intricate work, a wedding scene depicting a tall, dark and handsome groom and his beautiful bride with tumbling blonde curls and flowers in her hair to match those in her bouquet. Her slimline ivory dress had a lace bodice and a long train, held up by two page boys, followed by two bridesmaids, carrying flower ball pomanders. As a finishing touch Joan had sewn lots of minute beads into the bodice of the bride's dress and train, which caught the light and drew gasps of appreciation from all who beheld it. The local art and craft store, which supplied the materials, had commissioned her to create it and had hung it, pride of place, in their shop, and, much to Joan's surprise had insured it for £500! She had never considered insuring her work before and was very flattered that someone should value her work so highly.

Working by the window had its obvious advantages in terms of natural light but Joan also liked sitting there with a view of the streets around the apartment, so she could enjoy one of her other favourite pastimes: people watching. Folks never ceased to amaze her, particularly the inappropriate way they dressed irrespective of the weather conditions. She would often draw George's attention to people in the street and they would chuckle about them being wrapped up and wearing boots on a hot sunny day or a T-shirt and shorts on a freezing cold day. George had a unique talent for choosing silly names for the different people they spied and this became a game they would play each day, the sillier the nickname the better, often leaving them helpless with laughter.

"There goes 'Raggedy-Anne' on her way to sign on," Joan called out to George about a teenage girl wearing a flowing skirt, beads and bangles. She routinely passed by Tuesdays and Fridays; they surmised Tuesdays she probably had to sign on and Fridays she went shopping and socialising because unlike Tuesdays they never saw her return later in the afternoon.

"Oh quick come here dear, quick!" Joan commanded. "'Skimpy Knickers' is late and running up the road." They both laughed as a middle-aged woman, with dyed curly blonde hair, in a short tight skirt with matching white high heels, half ran and half tottered up the road towards the church. She had been given the amusing sobriquet after Joan had pointed out to George that her skirt was so tight the outline of her hipster knickers could clearly be seen despite the distance between their apartment and the street below. They decided she prepared sandwiches for a local pub and worked behind a bar during the day.

Another character they named 'Mr Routine Man' on account of the fact that each week day at precisely 7.45am, as they were drinking their first cup of tea of the day, the bald and rather chubby, well-dressed middle-aged man would park his car and call into the newsagents on the far side of the church. The shop doorway was just about visible to their apartment; the rest of the building was hidden by the church. He would buy a daily newspaper and sit on a bench to the side of the church. First of all he would scan the buildings and streets and Joan observed that he spent slightly longer looking at their block before holding up his open newspaper in such a way that it hid his face. He would lower his paper just as

Jennie cut through the middle of the Swan Rise apartments on her way to work. He would watch her disappear then carefully fold his newspaper and walk off in the same direction. Joan was convinced he was stalking Jennie and said as much to George. After observing him a few times George declared him harmless and did not show any further interest. Joan could not be so dismissive, she had an uneasy feeling and continued with her daily observation, deciding to jot down dates and times and anything else she thought relevant 'just in case'. She was not sure why her notes might be useful, only that it was prudent to make them

Macefields

Macefields' offices were in a red-brick Victorian building; the interior had been gutted and refashioned in an ultra-modern style, in contrast to the outside of the building, which had been restored to its former glory as a textile warehouse. There were five floors and each floor was divided into quarters. Glass partitioned offices for the senior staff edged the walls and the secretaries and administration clerks worked in the central, open plan area, their desks attached in a cross formation.

Jennie was on the third floor. Her desk was on the far side of the room directly across from Nick's office. He continued to keep his distance. At first she was hurt he had not spoken to her, he only nodded hello if he had happened to pass her workstation on his way to speak with one of his contemporaries. She reasoned he was far too busy to speak with the likes of her and so concentrated on learning Macefields' way of working, soon settling into a routine. Nevertheless, occasionally she could feel Nick's eyes on her and a corresponding excitement zapped through her body. Once or twice she had looked up quickly, straight into his eyes, before he had had chance to avert his gaze and thought she had seen something there. She could not say what: a mixture of excitement, desire, fear, effectively a mirror of her own feelings. She knew she wanted him more than she had ever wanted anyone.

Generally everyone was more than happy to help her settle in, all except Nick's secretary, Lisa, who was cool towards her. Cool was not exactly how Lisa would have described her feelings towards Jennie, more like a steaming hot geyser of jealousy. Nick did not know it, but she was in love with him, had been from the moment he had interviewed her, he made her feel needed and important. Nothing was too much trouble for him, early starts, late finishing. He made her want to be the best she could be. She had even sacrificed her relationship with Dave, her childhood sweetheart; they had broken up because of her devotion to Nick. Now this insipid flake of a girl was threatening her place in his life. She felt helpless, threatened and prayed with all her heart, night after night, that Jennie would go away.

Nick was thrilled with how well Macefields was doing since the redundancy victims had gone and the firm had settled down. One of the firm's major clients was holding a charity social evening and Nick saw it as the perfect opportunity to make his move on Jennie.

For the umpteenth time Jennie scrutinised her appearance in the hall mirror and was still pleased with what she saw. The previous day's pampering had certainly paid off; her newly shaped eyebrows, straightened hair and French polished false nails all added to an air of sophistication. Her calf length dress with its heart shaped neckline and short capped sleeves fitted her slender figure like a glove and matched her cornflower blue eyes perfectly. She wore her sale bargain Jimmy Choo blue striped shoes with matching handbag and imagined she was a star. She hoped Nick would be pleased too, she wanted to please him more than anything in the world.

She was excited and full of nervous tension, unable to settle. She prowled the apartment, fluffing the pillows on the settee, checking the windows were locked, the lights, radio and television were switched off, her purse, keys, makeup, perfume etc were in her handbag. She sprayed some perfume in her hair, it was Irresistible by Givenchy. She hoped Nick would find her irresistible. She checked her wristwatch yet again. Time was dragging. Once more her mind went over his surprise invitation to the charity client night out. She was so excited to be one of the few girls chosen and thrilled when he offered to drive her and Lisa there and back. She was pleased he was picking her up first because it meant he would drop her off last and she would have precious time on her own with him.

The doorbell buzzed. She checked herself in the mirror again, smoothed her dress once more, licked her lips, took a deep breath and with a trembling hand opened the door.

Nick caught his breath and his eyes opened wide in wonderment as he gazed upon the vision of beauty standing in the doorway before him. She looked so different, he was speechless. Neither of them moved, both were transfixed for what seemed like an age but in reality was only seconds. Then his mobile telephone rang, breaking the spell. He let out an involuntary groan as he reached into his suit jacket pocket to answer the call. "Hello?"

"Hi, how long you going to be? We're all ready to rock and roll." It was Catchpole.

"I'll be about 15 minutes, I've got to pick up Lisa."

"Just checking. Get your skates on man you're holding up the proceedings."

He replaced his phone, she closed her front door and they walked towards the lift.

"You look beautiful, so sophisticated." His voice was soft. She could feel his breath on the back of her neck as he stood very closely behind without actually touching her. She could hear his fast, shallow breathing, which made her back tingle. She thanked him and felt self-conscious when she realised she too was breathing quickly.

The lift doors opened and George and Joan Finch from the apartment above hers smiled at her. She was relieved they were in the lift; things were moving too quickly. She was shocked at the intensity of her feelings and Nick's reaction to her. Although she was not looking at him all her senses were in overdrive and George and Joan could well have evaporated; Nick's powerful presence had blocked out all other thoughts and her knees felt weak.

His car was parked in the nearby multi-storey car park. As they walked towards the parking bay he guided her to his car by casually putting his arm across her back, sending shivers down her spine. . He opened the passenger door for her and she could feel his eyes caressing her legs as she settled into the seat as elegantly as she could. From the corner of her eye she watched as he twisted in his seat in order to reverse, his arm resting on the back of her chair, his shirt pulled tightly against his muscular chest. His nearness made her body tense and her nipples tingle. The silence between them was deafening during the short drive to Lisa's home.

Lisa had obviously been keeping a lookout for the car because she was already leaving the house as he beeped the horn. Jennie noted that Nick had not opened the car door for Lisa.

"Hi Jen, hi Nick, how are you two? I'm so excited about tonight and hope we don't have to wait long for the food because I'm so hungry I could eat a horse. I've been so busy today, had to go into town to buy some shoes, and you know what it's like when you want to buy something you can never find what you're looking for…" Lisa's endless prattling dissipated the sexual tension between Nick and Jennie and Jennie began to relax.

Catchpole was standing in the doorway at the restaurant as Nick and the girls walked up the steps. "Ah, at last," he said, slapping Nick on the back. "Hi Lisa, and who have we got here?" He turned to Jennie, grabbed her hand and led her into the restaurant. To the entire world it looked as if she was with him. His hand was pressing on the small of her back with his fingers straying a little too low for comfort, hinting at a non-existent intimacy. He firmly guided her towards the bar and ordered her a drink. Instead of a general introduction to the crowd he chose to introduce Jennie to everyone individually, compounding the impression that she was with him and predictably managed to secure a seat for her between him and Simon Miller from Stepwells.

Jennie was completely overwhelmed by Catchpole. When she eventually scanned the room looking for Nick he was nowhere to be seen. There was about a twenty minute delay before the first course and as the waitresses began serving, as if he had planned it that way, Nick returned. Although he hid his annoyance at being outmanoeuvred by the hapless Catchpole he could not quite bring himself to look at Jennie, let alone speak to her. Instead he made a fuss of Lisa and at the end of the evening Jennie watched the two of them heading off in the direction of the car park. She was flabbergasted that Nick had left without checking to see how she was getting home. Catchpole came to her rescue and ordered a taxi for them both. In the taxi he tried to kiss her and invited himself back to her place but she managed to get out of the taxi without him and escape.

Distraught at how the night had turned out and hurt at Nick's abandonment of her, as she entered her apartment she burst into tears and sobbed like a baby at the kitchen table. After her tears subsided, she washed her make-up streaked face. While waiting for the kettle to boil for her soothing night time milk drink the doorbell rang. Alarmed at who would be calling at this time of night, concerned it might be Catchpole, she crept up to the door and looked through its spyhole. She let out a gasp when she saw Nick, his head bowed. He suddenly looked up, as if he had heard her. She waited a few seconds, trying to compose herself before opening the door the width of its chain.

"Jennie I had to see you, to apologise for my behaviour tonight." Her heart skipped a beat and his pleading tone took her breath away.

"I'm so sorry, please forgive me, I was jealous seeing you with Catchpole." He inhaled deeply. "I saw you get in a taxi with him and followed. I was scared you were going to invite him in. I can't bear the thought of you with him, or anyone else. I want you Jennie. I need you," he whispered. "Please can I come in?"

It took her three attempts to uncouple the door chain and one second for Nick to take her in his arms.

"Oh Jennie, Jennie, Jennie. I'm so so sorry," he murmured while kissing her neck. She closed her eyes, lost in pleasure. His hand at the back of her head turned her slightly so that he could move his lips onto hers. He let out a groan of pleasure as she opened her lips in response and as his tongue explored her mouth, she moaned deep within and instinctively her tongue engaged with his. Passion overwhelmed her. His hands moved confidently over her body and her knees gave way as he unzipped her dress. It fell to the floor and then suddenly they were tearing at each other's clothing until they were both naked, panting with desire. Her back against the wall, he picked her up and she wrapped her trembling legs around his body, groaning loudly as he entered her, each thrust accompanied by another groan and another and another, until the violent shudder of his body triggered off a huge explosion in her own. He scooped her up in his arms and carried her into the bedroom, gently laid her on the bed and lay down next to her, softly kissing her lips, her chin, the nape of her neck, running his tongue over the mound of her left breast, fastening on to her nipple, gentle flicking his tongue over its centre, whilst caressing her other breast. Waves of desire crashed over her, becoming more intense, as his mouth and hands continued to explore her body, possessing her, owning her, rendering her helpless and she willingly surrendered herself body, heart and soul to him.

They made love all night long.

The following morning he was the first to rouse. Sunlight was streaming through a small gap between the curtains lending a soft glow to her face as she slept. He leaned on his elbow and gazed down at her. She was so beautiful, his tender heart surged with love and he wanted to hold on to this moment for all eternity. His mind wandered down the years to her first day at Stepwells and his instant attraction to her, then buying her coffee and his concern when shortly afterwards she had suddenly left the city, then more recently their chance meeting leaving him tongue-tied and now… Although they had only spent one night together he knew his life had changed forever. He could never let her go.

She stirred, moving towards him. Her eyes flickered open meeting his loving gaze and her slow smile aroused his desire. He kissed her tenderly and she responded eagerly, wrapping her arms around his neck as she moved to accommodate him and surrender once more. It felt so right.

They caught a taxi to the office. During the short journey Nick's mind was in overdrive thinking of ways to see Jennie while keeping their relationship under wraps as he dealt with his responsibilities at work and, more importantly, managed Penny and the children. He asked the driver to drop him off at the next street down from Macefields. He swiftly kissed

Jennie, explaining he had got to see someone. He would text her about meeting up after work and asked her to keep quiet about the two of them until they could work things out.

She could barely contain her excitement over what had happened since yesterday evening. Her body was still tingling, her head was all over the place, she could not concentrate, there were butterflies in her stomach and each time someone spoke to her she physically jumped.

Nick was nowhere to be seen. Unbeknown to anyone he was spending the day with his wife.

It was late afternoon before Jennie received a text saying he would be at her apartment at 6.30pm. As soon as she finished work she raced back to her apartment to arrive half an hour before Nick was due.

She had just inserted her key in the lock when suddenly strong arms swept her off her feet, pushed the door open, carried her over the threshold, straight to her bedroom and onto her bed. It was Nick. Frantically they tore at each other's clothes while hands, lips and tongues explored, roughly, voraciously, both desperate to satisfy their primal lust. Although frenetic they were in perfect intimate rhythm and quickly climaxed together. Afterwards they lay side-by-side, naked and clammy, waiting for their heartbeats to slow to normal.

Nick's stomach rumbling very loudly prompted their shared laughter. He rolled off the bed saying, "I'd better order some food. Care to join me for a pizza young lady?" Smiling, Jennie nodded her agreement.

In the short time it took for the food to be delivered both were showered and dressed. They quickly polished off the delicious pizza then Jennie, sensing Nick's more sombre mood, made them a coffee and sat down at the table to listen to his plan.

He reached out and held her hands. His thumbs gently stroked the back of them. His face very serious he explained, "Jennie, I will always be honest with you and want you to trust me." Looking down at her hands he cleared his throat before continuing. "As you know I'm married with two young children. Well, I love my wife, as the mother of my children and will always look after her, but sadly we are no longer 'in love'. We're together for the sake of our children, whom I adore." he swallowed then continued.

"The first time I saw you, the day you started at Stepwells, I was instantly attracted to you, then when you were upset waiting for a bus and I persuaded you to let me buy you a coffee you seemed so young and vulnerable, something stirred deep within me, you brought out my protective instinct and after you suddenly left Manchester I couldn't stop worrying about you. Over the years you've crossed my mind countless times. Recently seeing you walking towards me, across the square, I was completely thrown and tongue-tied because it was as if I'd conjured you up out of thin air. I'd just walked past the coffee shop and wondered how life was treating you and suddenly there you were! Now spending only one night with you has changed my life forever, it has made me realise I've been lonely for a long time, too long."

Jennie's heart lurched as he looked up into her eyes and in little more than a whisper he said, "I need you." He looked down again and she waited with baited breath for him to continue. She sensed his turmoil, he seemed surprisingly vulnerable.

"I need you Jennie, I want you as I've never wanted anyone in my life. If you give me time to work things out, I promise I'll do all in my power to give you everything you want, and more. Please Jennie, please give me a chance," he pleaded, his eyes full of anxiety.

Without a word she walked around the table and stood in front of him, putting her hands out for his. He held her hands and followed her into the bedroom. Her agreement to his plan was sealed with a sweet, lingering kiss. She placed her hands on his shoulders gently encouraging him to sit on the edge of the bed. This time she took the lead in their lovemaking, lightly running her fingers over his face, tracing his lips and the line of his jaw, slowly unbuttoning his shirt, gently caressing his neck and chest. He lay back on the bed and she slowly removed the remainder of his clothing while continuing to run her fingers all over him. Her touch was like a feather and her breath ticklishly exquisite. He felt himself growing hard and groaned in ecstasy when her mouth moved to pleasure him.

Afterwards she lay naked in his arms and told him her story, of a happy childhood in the country until her parents divorced, then living with her mother after discovering her real father was a man who had worked in the village for a few days and who had not been seen again. Overcome with emotion she stopped speaking. He felt her tears roll down his chest and held her close as his own eyes welled up. He stayed until midnight.

She knew he was married, she knew he had children, she knew their relationship was wrong and she knew she was powerless to resist him. Her body craved his touch, her mind was filled with his words, her soul cried out for more and her heart ached when they were apart.

Being with Nick was incredibly exciting. Each day he would make sure they spent time together. Whether it was a quick passionate embrace or an all-night session she was on a permanent sexual high. She never knew what to expect sexually except he liked to push the boundaries. Sometimes he was like a sex starved beast and she his prey; he would see an opportunity and devour her in a sexual frenzy. At other times he would be so gentle and tender, whispering sweet nothings and setting her heart on fire. Whatever his preference, sex was exciting and fun and she would always accommodate him. Some days he would surprise her with an early morning visit to her apartment, other mornings he would send her a text telling her to book the afternoon off as holiday or an emergency dental/doctor appointment then rearrange his work schedule so that they could spend the afternoon together. If he had to travel to another city for a meeting he would book a hotel for the night and take her with him. Inevitably there were times when work or family commitments prevented them from being with each other, then he would bombard her with texts and phone calls. He never let her forget he had staked his claim and she was his.

Murder Reunion

Beware

Joan had been making a daily note for over a month of Mr Routine Man following Jennie and was becoming increasingly concerned about his odd behaviour, so, despite George's view that he was harmless and Jennie would be upset if told about him, nevertheless she decided to have a word with her the next time she popped in for a cup of tea, which happened to be the next evening.

The smell of homemade apple pie sprinkled with cinnamon baking in the oven filled the air as they sat in the sunlit kitchen at the small pine table on matching country farmhouse chairs, sipping their tea and catching up on general chitchat as George watched the news on the television in the lounge. As Joan poured them a second drink she casually mentioned, "I read an article in the local paper yesterday about stalking and assaults being on the increase in the city. Have you seen or heard of anyone being stalked or assaulted?"

Shocked, Jennie shook her head to indicate she had not heard anything, her face full of concern.

"Well my dear I don't want to alarm you but please bear in mind cities are a magnet for unsavoury characters and you are a very attractive young woman. I'm just asking that you please be extra careful when you're out and about."

Having said her piece Joan changed the subject by showing Jennie her latest cross-stitch work. It was a picture of a white stone cottage nestled in the mountains near Barmouth in

Wales. While out walking with George, many years before, they had come across the cottage with a lake at the bottom of its garden surrounded by a small stone wall and thought it was idyllic and photographed it. She remembered George saying he would like to live somewhere like it, so when she recently saw the photograph while clearing out a sideboard, she decided to capture it in cross-stitch.

Unease

Although Joan had said she did not want to cause alarm that is exactly what happened, because Jennie had a fitful night's sleep, rolling around in her bed, mixed-up dreams invading her mind. In one, a crowd of masked people followed her into a dead-end, looming over her shouting threats. She woke up with a jolt, feeling cold and clammy. After calming down she eventually went back to sleep straight into another frightening dream, one in which Zac, her sisters, Gordon and his blank-faced wife were being chased towards her by Nick. Again she woke with a start. It was 3am in the morning. She lay there, her head and heart pounding, her mind racing before eventually drifting off to sleep, this time into oblivion. Unfortunately the seed of fear had been sewn.

The next few days were hectic at work. Nick had gone to London for a conference and Jennie felt shattered after work. Consequently she slept like a log and was too tired to give further thought to Joan's warning. Then things calmed down at work, Nick was still in London and Jennie started feeling uneasy again, as though her sixth sense was trying to warn her of danger. A couple of times when walking to work she thought she was being followed, but on looking back there was no one there. She chastised herself for being silly, questioning who would want to follow her. Zac was still in prison and did not know where she was. She had had no contact with Gordon since their relationship finished and was unlikely to as he had been made redundant, and anyway, she assumed he was still with his wife and she was not aware of anyone who disliked her, certainly not enough to follow her. She wished Nick was back, he made her feel safe.

Nick was back but spent the night at home with Penny and the children. He left the following morning at 6.00am saying he had a breakfast meeting to attend. There was no breakfast meeting. By 6.30am he had let himself into Jennie's apartment, climbed into her bed and was making urgent love to her. Afterwards he watched her cook breakfast and thought she seemed tense. She said she was okay and he assumed she was upset because he had been away.

Jennie was so relieved Nick was back in Manchester and more importantly with her. She needed him close and felt terribly insecure when he was away. She wished he would leave his wife and be with her exclusively, but knew he was trying to find the right moment to minimise the hurt he would cause his wife and his adored children.

Zac Released

Zac stepped through the gates and took a deep breath. He looked to the heavens and savoured a lingering moment of freedom. He could not have wished for a better release day, it was warm and sunny with a caressing breeze, the kind that made you feel good to be alive. The air smelt fresh and there was a brightness to the surrounding colours. He mentally rehearsed his plan once more while waiting for the bus to Leeds city centre. As he boarded the bus he showed his paper, revealing the probation office address to the driver and asked to be dropped off at the nearest stop. The bus journey was fifteen minutes followed by a five minute walk.

His probation officer was a middle-aged, squat woman, with spiky dyed red hair, huge gold earrings and thick purple rimmed glasses. Her voice was loud and clipped as she quickly went through the paperwork with him, including details of the bedsit he would be staying at and a letter for a local building firm where she had arranged for him to work.

The bedsit was better than he expected. Although it was small, it was bigger than his cell and he did not have to share it. It had everything he needed and the piece de resistance was the wet room at the back with a power shower, a toilet and a wash basin. It was an excellent use of a small space and home for the foreseeable future.

He showered and changed clothes before going to find the building firm and, more importantly, to telephone his Italian friend, David Maroni. They arranged to meet at 6.30pm at Wetherspoons in the city centre.

Zac was sitting at the table perusing the menu when David arrived.

"Aw man, it's good to see you," said David, patting Zac on the back followed by a high five and a hug.

"Good to see you too, you're looking well."

"You too. Tell me, did you manage to stay focused?" David asked as he sat down at the table.

"Sure did with the help of your good book. It was hard going but I did it! I'm in a bedsit on the city outskirts and start work tomorrow, so it's all go." Zac cleared his throat before asking, "Have you got any information for me?"

David handed him a folded piece of paper. He hesitated before unfolding it, suddenly afraid of what he might learn, not knowing how he would react. He could feel David's eyes on him as he nervously opened it. At first he could not focus, the words seemed blurred, then he read the address where Jennie was living and the firm where she worked. The next words caused him to have a sharp intake of breath for they confirmed his worst fears, she was seeing someone. Suddenly his determination to confront her became a matter of urgency. He closed his eyes and willed his racing heart to slow down.

He had wanted to catch the train to Manchester straightaway when he discovered Jennie's whereabouts but knew it would be madness because he would be arrested for not reporting to his probation officer and ultimately sent back to prison. The phrase 'patience is a virtue' gave him the strength to bide his time and knuckle down to working hard for the building firm. In the meantime Maroni's friend, Bob Jones, continued to keep watch and report back.

Zac was desperate to get to Manchester but did not know how, then, as if by divine intervention, an opportunity to work there for his firm presented itself. His probation officer transferred him to her colleague covering the area and accommodation was arranged.

Working for the building trade meant starting and finishing early. Consequently Zac spoke with Jones and took over monitoring Jennie in the evening. He borrowed his car and parked in the road at the side of the church.

At precisely 5.45pm, as Jones had said, he saw Jennie, in a light grey suit, quickly walking down the road opposite from where he was parked. His heart lurched at the sight of her and he automatically sat bolt upright in his chair. Fortunately, she was looking at her mobile phone and did not see him. She looked lovely, even better than he remembered. His heart ached with longing for her, his chest tightened and tears threatened as he watched her carry on down the road to her apartment block. He continued to watch, while the memories queued.

At 6.15pm, again as Jones had said, he watched a tall, dark-haired man, in an expensive looking charcoal suit, follow the same route as Jennie. He was talking on his mobile telephone too. Although Zac never moved, the man looked straight into his eyes, a lingering, probing look, which Zac returned, and held until the man turned the corner towards Jennie's apartment then anger coursed through Zac's body.

The following week Zac had a few days off work in lieu of working Saturdays and kept watch early mornings as well. After several mornings it dawned on him that someone else was watching Jennie too. *Who the hell is he? What's he got to do with Jennie?*

Tension

A consequence of the earlier London conference was that Nick had to go to a series of business meetings in London, which resulted in Jennie becoming increasingly tense and Penny became increasingly suspicious.

Joan's warning had had a profound effect on Jennie's peace of mind. She started missing breakfast as it felt like her stomach was being twisted in a vice. She dreaded her daily journey because as soon as she stepped out into the street it was as if an invisible cloak had been thrown around her, bearing down and weighing heavily across her shoulders. She could not shake off the feeling she was being followed, although she had no proof. She thought about mentioning her concerns to Nick but decided against it as he had enough on his plate with his demanding career and family commitments, without worrying about her. She wanted their stolen moments to be loving, happy and carefree. She told herself it was probably her mind playing tricks. She wished there was a different route to work but unfortunately there was not and ordering a taxi was too costly.

Cheating

"How can you be sure Nick's cheating?" asked Zara.

"I know Nick, I can read him like a book." The tears rolled down Penny's face.

"But have you any proof?"

"You mean apart from regularly coming home late, smelling of cheap perfume and the four day 'business trip' in Dubai and other weekends yes, I have proof!" She waited for the all too familiar waive of anxiety to subside. "Do you remember me telling you of his fetish for collecting bows from my underwear?" Zara nodded her head in response. "Well he hides them all in a wooden box his grandfather made when he was a prisoner of war. He keeps the box on top of the wardrobe. I looked in the box and the evidence was there staring me in the face, brazenly twinkling up at me – a bright blue bow with diamante insert. No way would I buy that colour, it's the colour for a cheap slag. There were others too. I hate him!" She broke down in tears again.

Zara was three years younger than Penny and although she loved her sister deeply she had spent most of her life feeling jealous of her, jealous because she was slimmer and prettier, every success seemed effortless, she sailed through her exams, passed her driving test first time, excelled at ballet, her skin would tan and she was never short of admirers, whereas Zara had to battle for everything, she was on a permanent diet and she secretly adored Nick. He was the reason her relationships fizzled out because none of her boyfriends measured up to him. Over the years she had prayed her sister and Nick would split up and that after the lapse of a respectful period of time he would be hers, and now her prayers seemed as if they were about to be answered. Ironically, she was afraid she might lose him altogether and she could not bear the thought. She realised she wanted him in her life forever even if only as a brother-in-law and she found herself being more supportive than she would ever have thought possible. She called round to see Penny the next day.

"You told Mother! What on earth possessed you to do that? You know she can't be trusted to keep things to herself!" exclaimed Zara, incredulous that her sister had confided in their mother.

"I didn't intend telling her but she visited unexpectedly and could tell straightaway things weren't right with me. When I told her of my suspicions she was surprisingly comforting."

"Oh yeah, and how would that be?" Zara said scornfully. She was still smarting over their mother informing the whole family that her boyfriend Michael had dumped her last year.

"She told me it isn't the end of the world if a husband has a fling, that some men are weak willed but it doesn't necessarily mean they don't love their wife and children. She advised me to consider the trade-off: I have the status of being married to a successful man who earns good money, treats me and our children very well and I have a lovely home. She said as long as Nick is discreet then not to make waves, these flings, for want of a better word, soon fizzle out and life returns to normal. She said that if I found her take on things too hurtful to contemplate then I should consider the alternative. Divorce is ugly, I'd lose my home and worse the effect on the children would be devastating and they have to be my main concern. Her 'take' on the situation sounded very much like the voice of experience. Do you think Daddy has cheated on Mummy?"

"No! No. He wouldn't. Would he?"

Penny desperately wanted to follow her mother's advice, be strong for the sake of her children and carry on as if nothing was wrong between her and Nick. She tried to suppress the jealousy raging through her mind but failed miserably. Her permanent nausea had destroyed her appetite and she was losing weight she could ill afford to lose because running around after two small children kept the pounds off as it was, but the thing that distressed her the most were the sleepless nights. She feared going to bed because she knew in the dead of night she would find herself wide awake, her mind in turmoil and all she had to look forward to was another day feeling utterly exhausted.

Although she would not normally advise medication, Penny's mother could see that her daughter was struggling and suggested she should book an appointment and talk things through with "that nice Dr Bolderston and perhaps he could prescribe something to help her sleep" and so it was Penny found herself sitting in the waiting room.

"Hello love, sit yourself down, what can I do for you?" The doctor's soft, soothing voice was just the trigger needed to open the floodgates.

"My marriage is falling apart and I can't cope." Penny's words were barely audible as she fought to maintain her composure. Her eyes welled up, a lump formed in her throat and tears started to roll slowly down her cheeks. She made no effort to stem their flow as she gave way to feelings of utter despair. Her pain was mirrored in the doctor's warm, brown eyes. He handed her a tissue and waited patiently. Despite his years of ministering he had not become hard-hearted, unlike a lot of other doctors, and hoped he never would.

"We were together for years before we married," Penny sniffed. "It's destroying me that he's cheating, I thought we were very happy together. Our children are so young, they need their father, and I need him. How could he do this to us, how could he…" her words trailed off. The doctor handed her another tissue and she wiped her eyes then blew her nose. He waited for her to calm down sufficiently before asking a few pertinent questions including establishing that her sister was being supportive and helping with the children. He knew how jealous Zara had been at times about her sister and found it heart-warming that she was there when needed. Nevertheless, he prescribed a course of anti-depressants, handed her a leaflet from the Mediation Service, suggesting she might benefit from a visit and not to mention anything to her husband until the counsellor advised her to.

After visiting the doctor Penny called in on her mother. She told her the doctor had advised counselling and was surprised when her mother snatched the leaflet off her and immediately rang the telephone number. "Might as well start the ball rolling. The quicker you see the counsellor, the quicker you'll take control." The speed of her mother's response again made Penny think she had been down a similar route. The first session was fixed for the following week.

On the day of the appointment at the Mediation Service Penny was nervous and, irrationally, felt guilty and disloyal in not telling Nick about the appointment. She was undecided about going for counselling right up to her hesitant ringing of the doorbell. Indeed during the few seconds it took for the door to be opened she still toyed with the idea of running away, and the sight that greeted her very nearly made her do just that!

The door was opened by a very tall, very large young woman dressed all in black with long black hair, enormous green eyes enhanced by thick black eyeliner. She could not take her eyes off the woman nor could she make up her mind whether she was ugly or attractive. Striking she certainly was. In an unusually loud voice she demanded Penny's name and ordered her to take a seat. She even made the offer of a drink sound compulsory. Penny meekly obliged.

The building was an old, midterrace house converted into offices. Penny sat in one of the surprisingly comfortable chairs in the bay window, surprising because the cluttered office and mismatched furniture seemed anything but comfortable. Middle of the road pop music was being transmitted from an old ghetto blaster on top of a cupboard to her right. There were three women in the office: the striking woman, who Penny guessed was in her late 20s, was on reception and two older women, again Penny guessed in their 50s, worked at the back of the room which was sectioned off by cabinets with shelving on top. All three of them were constantly taking telephone calls and quickly moving from desk to cabinet to photocopier. Amazingly, against all the odds, Penny found the chaotic informality strangely comforting and, started to relax, her gut feeling was that she had made the right decision to seek counselling.

A tall, thin, middle-aged man with a mop of wild grey hair, in a light brown crumpled suit and a deep red bow-tie greeted her. "Hi I'm Jeremy Hall." Although he had the stubble of a beard it added to his friendly face. Evidence of his comedic personality soon became apparent when he glanced down and swiftly covered the front of his trousers with his papers.

"Oh my word, I am so sorry, I find myself in an apparent state of undress!" He grinned inanely and swiftly retreated backwards through the same door, only to reappear within seconds, his state of undress having been rectified. Penny struggled to stifle a fit of giggles as her grandfather's apt saying 'like Fred Karno's Circus' came to mind. She followed Mr Hall up the steep stairs to the cluttered meeting room.

"Do please take a seat," Mr Hall said to Penny, his open hand indicating the seats across the table to his. "Initially, I'm going to ask you for your personal details, name, address etc, then explain what the Mediation Service offers. Is that okay?"

"Yes," said Penny.

He went through the list of routine questions before explaining the Family Mediation Service deals with all relationship breakdowns, financial arrangements and anything to do with children. Penny nodded her understanding. He continued to explain that the service helps couples (whether married or unmarried) and other family members, such as grandparents, to discuss and resolve any issue due to separation or divorce in a sensitive, thoughtful and co-operative way.

At his use of the word 'divorce' Penny gasped. He asked if she was okay and rushed to pour her a glass of water from the dispenser in the corner of the room. She took a few sips before saying she was fine.

Mr Hall noticeably softened the tone of his voice and explained separation and divorce is usually a painful experience for all involved, particularly children. Research had shown that children suffer less harm and cope better if parents are able to resolve conflict over arrangements for their children, finances, the family home and other matters reasonably quickly, which is where mediation is of benefit. The parties needed to consider what issues they wanted to discuss. At first each party is seen individually and then, if they agree, they are seen together. The mediator helps them negotiate and reach agreement on the issues. After which the parties would see their solicitors to formalise and implement any agreements reached.

"What issues would you like to discuss?" he asked.

Penny mulled things over again. Mr Hall sensed she needed time alone and asked if she wanted tea or coffee. She said coffee. He left the room but when he returned she was still undecided and near to tears.

"Would it help if you told me what prompted your doctor to recommend mediation?" he gently pressed in an effort to open up their discussion.

The concern in his voice and his sad facial expression was all the encouragement Penny needed. She told him all about her relationship with Nick, how they met, that he was popular with the girls and she was just one of several girlfriends, but once they married and the twins came along he had settled down and they were very happy, that was until a few months ago when she detected a change in him. Suddenly he started coming home late, sometimes not at all, and he kept having business weekends away. Finally, finding the evidence in his grandfather's box proved what she had suspected, that he was having an affair. Penny sobbed and said she knew this was a serious threat to her marriage.

Mr Hall waited until she had composed herself. He explained that if her suspicions were correct no wonder she felt so distressed because her husband had, effectively, broken a fundamental agreement between them. He established she had not confronted Nick and advised it was best, for herself and the children, to speak with him as soon as possible but not in front of the children, and then to have a further mediation appointment with him.

"I know, I know I need to speak with him. I thought if I ignored the situation it would just fizzle out, but in my heart I know it won't and it's eating away at me and making me ill. I'll be in touch," she said as she shook hands with Mr Hall.

"Good luck," he said with a sad smile.

Incensed

Diane was devastated over the disintegration of her marriage. Yet, having gone through the range of negative emotions, had somehow found the strength to build a new life and, thankfully, was enjoying her job. Nevertheless, she remained terribly sad at how things had turned out and, although she was loathe to admit it, still cared about Gordon and missed him. In fact she was actually beginning to think along the lines of whether a reconciliation was possible.

By chance Caroline, a friend of Diane's, lived in an apartment near to Jennie. Neither of them was aware of Jennie but Caroline had noticed Gordon hanging around her local church each morning and made a point of letting Diane know. Diane was perplexed at her husband's odd routine and decided to drive past the church to see for herself. She parked in a side road with a good view of the church, but behind another car for anonymity, and waited. Before long Gordon's car appeared. He parked in another side road, then crossed over the road to the newsagents. Within minutes he emerged carrying a newspaper. Puzzled, she watched him sit on a church bench reading the newspaper. She continued to observe him for a good 15 minutes. Then she saw the reason behind his bizarre behaviour. "The slut!"

Jennie was walking very briskly down the road towards her. Just before reaching the church she turned into a street opposite it. Gordon lowered his paper as she turned. He waited a few seconds, folded his paper and then followed her. Diane could hardly believe her eyes.

"He's stalking the little bitch!!" she shouted out loud as white hot anger surged through her being. "Unbelievable!!"

she exclaimed, slamming her hands down hard on the steering wheel. "His obsession is still ongoing!" She sat in silence, her head pounding, unable to process what she had just witnessed.

For the rest of the day Diane was deep in thought, reliving the initial moment she saw her husband and 'that' girl, their shared public kiss, how the pieces of the puzzle in her marriage suddenly fell into place, her flight to France, then confronting her husband and eventually moving in with her mother. Now, just when she was beginning to think there was a chance of a reconciliation, she discovered her husband was stalking 'that' girl! *Reconciliation? Who am I kidding? While she's still around there's no chance! While she is still around?* Diane repeated the words out loud as she tried to think of a way to make sure the 'the slut' was no longer around. *I should have confronted them when I first saw them. Maybe it's time I did.*

Turmoil

He was a lost soul, lonely and still reeling from all that had happened to him in such a short space of time. He sat on 'his' bench, in dappled sunlight which was shining through the overhead branches of an ancient yew tree. He pretended to read the newspaper while waiting for Jennie so that he could follow her. For the umpteenth time he ruminated over the stress of the last 19 months, starting with his affair, the breakup of his marriage, his guilt at hurting Diane and their children, his firm merging, the reptilian, repugnant Husslebea harassing him, being made redundant and caring for his incontinent father who, on moving into a care home, had become a serial groper! But, more importantly, he was struggling to accept Jennie had ended their relationship. In fact he could not get her out of his mind.

He planned to follow Jennie to her office, as he normally did, then continue walking around in a big loop back to his car, before driving on to his new firm, Freers, based outside the city centre. He was not sure what he was hoping to achieve by following her, if anything it compounded his sense of sadness and loss. He just could not pick himself up; nothing really mattered anymore. He was amazed she had not spotted him following her.

This morning things changed. He had driven to the church and settled down on the bench with a newspaper, waiting. Jennie walked by and he followed until her office block was in sight. The regular routine, except today he recognised Nick Turner walking towards her, smiling. Gordon watched, mesmerized, as Nick grabbed her hand and pulled her into a doorway where they shared a hungry, lingering kiss. Gordon's heartbeat pounded in his ears. He felt lightheaded and his jaw hung loose. He could not tear his eyes away. Eventually, Jennie and Nick came up for air and walked off into their office building, laughing. Gordon followed them with his eyes, his face burning and his mind in a frenzy. He needed to sit down and wished 'his bench' was near. He made his way to a nearby café and by the time he had drunk two cups of coffee his air of despondency had been replaced by angry indignation.

Of all the men she could have become involved with she chooses the one who made me redundant! How could she betray me in this way? How could she rub salt into my wounds? Does she think so little of me? Does she think of me at all? Clearly not! When I get the chance, and I'll make sure I do, then I will tell her, in no uncertain terms, exactly what I think. Oh yes, I'll make damn sure I get the opportunity to tell her; in fact, I may make a surprise visit to her apartment. Hmm, yes, the more I think of it the more tempted I am.

Terror

It was a glorious September day with hardly a cloud in the pale blue sky. The sun was warm on her skin as she walked briskly through the crowds of ambling shoppers to her apartment, a short distance from the office. She had a feeling of butterflies in her stomach and was smiling like a Cheshire cat as she thought about her secret tryst with 'him' last Tuesday lunchtime. She wanted to skip and twirl around and tell the whole wide world that she was in love and was going to spend the afternoon loving and being loved, that no one else mattered except the two of them.

Shivers of delight ran up and down her spine as in her mind's eye she could see him naked, smiling, as he pranced past the bottom of the bed disappearing through the door to the en-suite, leaving her trembling with satisfaction, too weak to move, wanting the moment to last forever. She felt heady as she recalled the power of the water surging through the shower and his rich baritone voice filling her ears as he sang loudly, "All I need is the air that I breathe just to love youuuuuu…"

She hummed the song all the way to the third floor and although the sound was amplified in the lift it did not inhibit her, it just merely enhanced her growing excitement.

While opening the door to her apartment her mobile phone bleeped, indicating a text message. Distracted, instead of securing the door as she normally would have done, she rummaged around in her handbag to retrieve her phone. She read the message while walking towards the lounge. It was from him.

"Stuck in London, train delayed, bad reception, ring u l8r soz Luv u xxx"

Her heart sank and her eyes stung with tears of disappointment and the pain of longing. She closed her eyes as she fought to control her emotions.

Suddenly the hall became cold and dark. She sensed danger and shuddered as a feeling of terror engulfed her, making the hairs on the back of her neck stand up. Fear coursed through her body. She slowly turned and saw a dark silhouette filling the doorway. There was no escape. She looked up and their eyes locked for what seemed like an eternity, but really only a few seconds. Not a word was spoken. Then the figure lunged at her, powerful like a panther, hands clasped around her throat, pressing on her windpipe. She landed heavily on the floor and her assailant landed on top of her with a thud, forcing all of the air from her lungs. Everything was in slow motion. She could not catch her breath. 'I CAN'T BREATHE' she wanted to scream out, but the words would not come.

A voice hissed, "You little bitch, where is he?" Eyes bored into hers and hands tightened around her throat. "WHERE IS HE?" The demand was accompanied by her head being banged hard on to the linoleum covered concrete floor. Her life flashed before her. "WHERE IS HE? WHERE IS HE! WHERE IS HE…" She was questioned over and over and all the time her head was being smashed on to the floor.

Suddenly aware of being drained of energy and emotion the assailant slowly stood up, smoothing clothing while looking down on Jennie's lifeless body, feeling oddly detached from her as if she was a complete stranger. Jennie's eyes were wide open, staring lifelessly up at the ceiling and blood trickled from her nose and mouth. The sunlight streaming through the open lounge door gave a glow to her long blonde hair which was splayed out like a golden fan around her head.

Her assailant picked up her mobile phone, scanned the hallway, eyes fastening on the picture of a shooting star which hung above the kitchen door then turned away, noiselessly pulling the door to.

PART IV – MURDER ENQUIRY

Florida

It was a 'Florida Day' as George would say, in memory of the many times they had visited the sunshine state before his wife's panic attacks had put paid to flying. Joan sat gazing out of the window, working on a picture of a houseboat, reflecting on her past creations particularly the wedding scene and how much the bride resembled Jennie, marvelling that it was created before they had met. She noticed Jennie walking down the road heading towards their apartment block. Her hair was glowing in the sunlight, there was a distinct skip in her walk, she was smiling and looked so happy, a breathtaking picture of beauty, one Joan wished she could capture in cross-stitch. She wondered if Jennie's young man, Nick, would be joining her. She had only seen him once in the lift but he seemed very nice and quite a handsome chap. When Jennie had mentioned she was seeing someone at work and was clearly falling in love Joan had been relieved to learn he was nearer to Jennie's age. She did not know he was married. Jennie had been careful not to mention that fact, sensing Joan would not approve. She had already made the mistake of mentioning that Gordon was an unhappily married older man, which clearly concerned Joan. Consequently, Jennie had made sure Joan and Gordon never met.

Oh how Joan would like to have given Gordon a piece of her mind, followed by his marching orders! Fortunately, George had managed to talk her out of it, for which she was grateful, because Jennie had eventually come to her senses by herself. *All's well that ends well* she said to herself and continued her work.

Although she kept looking out of her window, in between stitches, she did not see Nick but she did see another man enter the apartment block shortly before Jennie. He was tall, broad shouldered and wearing a smart suit. She wondered who he had come to see. She was still wondering when she saw him leave the building about half an hour later and disappear around the corner. She stood up to get a better view out of the window and within minutes he pulled up in a shiny black BMW. He halted at the entrance to the apartment block, looked up at Jennie's window, then, as if he was aware Joan was watching him, he looked straight into her eyes. The strength of pure hatred emanating from his intense dark eyes felt like a body blow which caused Joan to stumble backwards into her chair. She sat in shock; she had never experienced anything like it before. It was a few moments before she composed herself and then a feeling of dread overwhelmed her as instinct warned her that their paths would cross again, and soon, and more significantly he was something to do with Jennie. A sharp stab of fear sliced into the very core of her.

Throughout the afternoon a cloud of foreboding hovered over Joan. She felt increasingly anxious because she had not seen Jennie leave after lunch, or return from work. She had tried her mobile phone a couple of times but there was no reply, which was most unusual.

"George I'm concerned about our Jennie, she's not answering her phone and I didn't see her leave to go back to work. She's not popped in for a cup of tea either. It's not right, I tell you, something's not right." She was standing in the kitchen wringing her hands, which she was apt to do when agitated, then continued. "That awful man with such an evil look has got something to do with our Jennie, I'm

350

convinced." At that she grabbed Jennie's spare key, hidden behind the tea caddie, announcing, "I'm going to check on her apartment. Don't try to stop me."

George had no intention of stopping her because he was just as concerned but as usual kept his anxiety to himself. With fear in his heart and mobile phone in his hand, he followed his wife into the lift, to the floor below.

The door to Jennie's apartment was not quite shut and as Joan tentatively pushed it open she called, "Jennie, Jennie, are you there…" Her sentence finished midflow with a heart stopping scream. "AHHH OH NO, NO, DEAR GOD PLEASE NO…" she pleaded as she saw Jennie lying on the floor, obviously dead. George reached out trying to stop her touching Jennie, in case she destroyed crucial evidence, but he was too late. Joan dropped to the floor and instinctively cradled Jennie's head in her arms, rocking backwards and forwards, while sobbing, "Jennie, oh no, no, not Jennie, not our lass, not again, please Dear Lord not again, I can't bear it, I just can't bear it." George, his voice choking with emotion, telephoned the police.

Announcement

Detective Chief Inspector Sean Gallagher was in charge of the investigation. He was well respected for his no-nonsense, tough talking approach, which, together with his six foot seven inch lean, muscular frame, crew cut grey hair and chiselled features, was a force to be reckoned with. He had assigned Sergeant June Jones to assist him with the investigation. He had time for Jones, she was a good officer, hardworking and reliable. A handsome woman, just under six feet tall, she wore her thick black hair in a short feathery style, which emphasised her dark violet blue eyes and high cheekbones. She had a strong face and mind to match and had been with the police for about twelve years, six of them in his team and, like him, she believed in the police and had risen above the cynicism that was rife in the force.

Gallagher arrived within thirty minutes of George Finch's telephone call. He was the officer in charge of the investigation into Jennie's death and experience had taught him quick actions often brought swift results. He was pleased to find the first officers on the scene, PC Clark and PC Wistow had acted as efficiently as they had by immediately sealing off the apartment with yellow crime scene tickertape and alerting the doctor and forensic team who were already at work when he arrived. He nodded his acknowledgment to the two police officers who had posted themselves outside the apartment for security measures. He established from PC Clark that neighbours from the floor above, Joan and George Finch, had discovered the body and Mr Finch had made the emergency call.

He spoke briefly to Mr and Mrs Finch, established the time they found the body and that they enjoyed a close relationship with the deceased. They informed him she was working at Macefields and had worked at Denbighs and Stepwells in the past. He asked Jones to take a more detailed statement while he made a few phone calls, including one to Blake Bytheway who was the senior partner at Stepwells. He met Bytheway through charity work and they shared a mutual respect for one another, he trusted him to be discreet. Bytheway gave permission for a room at Stepwells to be used to conduct the interviews of Jennie's colleagues, from Stepwells, Denbighs and Macefields. They arranged to meet later that day to discuss the announcement Bytheway would make the following morning about the investigation.

Gallagher instructed his officers that only brief details were to be given to the press and confirmed with Jones that she had also instructed the Finchs not to discuss the matter with the press. He preferred the need to know approach.

Notwithstanding that this was a murder enquiry, Gallagher was looking forward to the interviews. He had a healthy dislike of lawyers, having witnessed all too often some of his hardworking officers being undermined and ridiculed in court. He had felt powerless as evil criminals walked free because some smart arse lawyer had twisted the meaning of the law, thinking he was clever, yet conversely at the first sign of trouble their immediate reaction was to ring 999. A hard day's work would kill the majority of them. Most of the lowlifes he dealt with were there because of circumstances, poverty, abuse, poor education, etc and although his job was to enforce the law, he understood how they ended up on the wrong side and did not take pleasure in outsmarting them. They might be lowlifes but there was a code of honour most of them adhered to, which is more than could be said of the dog-eat-dog fat cat lawyers.

The interview room was unusually windowless, with light beige walls and a dark beige carpet. It was very plain except for an abstract skyscraper painting hung on the wall to his right. The room housed an oblong table with eight dark brown leather high-backed chairs. There was a small cabinet at the back of the room displaying pots of pens and pencils, various note pads and a tray on which stood glasses and bottles of still and sparkling water.

Gallagher sat at the top of the table. He had asked Sergeant Jones to sit at the side of the table on his left so that questions fired at the interviewees would come from different angles. He also deliberately kept them waiting for ten minutes or more. Having studied psychology at Lancaster University he knew these practices would make the interviewee feel ill-at-ease and, more importantly, make it clear who was in charge.

"I've had Jennie's emails checked, including the double-deleted ones. She was one popular young lady. Here's a list of people to start with." Jones handed the list to Gallagher.

"Thanks Sergeant," Gallagher said as he scanned the list of mainly male names.

A fatality on the main London to Manchester train line had caused horrendous delays, so much so that by the time Nick reached Manchester he was tired and grumpy. The delay had put paid to a stolen afternoon with Jennie. He was irritated not only because he would not be able to see her but he could not contact her either; she was not answering her mobile phone. He had tried her again the following morning but she still was not answering her calls and by then his irritation had turned to concern, which intensified when she did not arrive at work that morning. His instinct was to immediately visit her apartment to check she was okay, but an emergency meeting called at 10.00am prevented him from doing so.

Nick always knew he would make it career wise, despite the Doubting Thomases of Stepwells. Even he, though, was surprised at how his career had soared since jumping ship. Nevertheless, it still rankled with him that he had had to move to Macefields to prove himself so when he and his colleagues received a request from Blake Bytheway of Stepwells to attend an important meeting, although he was annoyed and would like to have refused, curiosity had gotten the better of him, all the more so because not even his spies at Stepwells could throw any light on the purpose of the meeting. He resolved to call around to Jennie's as soon as the 'important' meeting was over.

Gillian was sat at her workstation. She had just read the firm-wide email from Bytheway and leaning to her right towards Peter, who was sat at his desk, she said, "By the way what do you reckon Bytheway wants us for?" She never could resist the tired play on words. "I assume you've read his email."

"I'm as much in the dark as you," said Peter. "I only hope we won't be long though because we've got to get that contract sent to Brewsters by midday."

Rachel was bewildered to receive a telephone call to attend a meeting at Stepwells. She went early to catch up with Lucy to find out what was going on and was told by a colleague she was in the basement floor toilets. She tapped on the door of a cubicle after hearing muffled sobs from behind it. "Lucy? Lucy, are you in there?" She heard a sniff. "Come on Luce, come on out, let's talk."

Lucy opened the door. Her eyes were red and her face was streaked black with mascara and swollen from prolonged sobbing.

"Oh you poor lamb come here." Rachel pulled Lucy to her in a comforting hug.

"H-h-he w-w-was restless last night," Lucy sobbed, "and kept dis-dis-disturbing me. I asked him w-w-what was bothering him. As I said the w-w-words my stomach churned – I knew he was going to s-s-say something bad. I don't know what I was expecting but it was such a shock w-w-when he said he had feelings for a girl he had met at the gym ." She took a deep sob-racked breath. "I n-n-never expected that. We've been together six years and planning to get married next year. How c-c-could he? How could he?"

Rachel waited for Lucy's sobbing to subside and offered to get her a cup of water. When she returned Lucy had washed her face, the mascara streaks were gone but her puffy eyes would take a while to deflate.

"Come on, let's go for a walk outside and have a coffee. I'll ring Ben and let him know, he can cover for you," said Rachel.

They went to 'Serendipity' a café by the bus station. It was a cheap and cheerful place for ordinary workers. Rachel sometimes went there if she had time to kill or wanted to be on her own. She had never seen anyone from Stepwells there; it was not quite the place to be seen. Lucy poured her heart out to Rachel. After they had finished their coffees she seemed calmer and they made their way back to the office.

Ben was waiting for them in the foyer.

"Thank goodness you're both back, the senior partner has called an emergency meeting of the entire staff. He's going to make some sort of announcement. It's taken everyone by surprise; people from Macefields and elsewhere are attending too! Come on, it's in the main hall." The three of them dashed up the stairs, managing to sneak in at the back of the room just as the office manager was closing the door.

"I've called you all to a meeting this morning to give you some very sad news about one of our ex-employees who recently moved to Macefields. Representatives of Macefields have kindly attended this meeting too."

Silent tension swept through the room as minds recalled the list of those who had moved firms.

"The police have informed me that Jennifer Enderby was found dead yesterday afternoon."

There was a collective gasp of breath as Bytheway paused to let his announcement register before continuing.

"Her death is the subject of a police enquiry. We have agreed the initial investigation can be conducted in our offices. Those employees who knew Miss Enderby may be required to answer questions. If you knew Miss Enderby or if you have any information relating to her then please remain in this room and speak to one of the two police officers at the back of the room or contact me by telephone or email. I have assured the police of our full cooperation." His voice softened, "I appreciate that this is a tremendous shock to you all. Jane Bingham from Human Resources has organised two counsellors to be available. If you feel the need to talk things through with them then again please stay behind after this meeting or contact Jane by email or telephone. The police, and of course, the partners of this firm, would very much appreciate it if you did not discuss what has been said here in this meeting, or elsewhere, particularly with any members of the press. Thank you for your cooperation. We will keep you all informed of any further developments."

Nick's face turned ashen. He suddenly felt drained of energy, weak and dizzy. He slumped onto a nearby chair. His hand automatically covered his mouth in an effort to contain a gut wrenching scream, which was gaining momentum in his soul and threatening to burst forth. The words *It isn't true, it can't be true,* reverberated in his mind. His throat tightened, he could not catch his breath. *I CAN'T BREATHE* he wanted to shriek and holler, but the words would not come. He loosened his tie. *I've got to get out of here! I'm going to pass out.*

Someone pressed a plastic cup of water into his hand which he downed in one before struggling to his feet. *I've got to get out of this room.* He stumbled to the toilets and locked himself in the disabled cubicle, which was separate from the general toilets. He was no longer able to contain the bile from the depths of his being and retched until his body ached and there was nothing left to expend. He started to gather his wits and realised he was in dire straits. The police were bound to link him to Jennie and discover they were having an affair, and it was inevitable that Penny would find out. *She'll stop me seeing the kids! Oh no! What a mess! Oh Jennie, Jennie, Jennie.* He buried his head in his hands and sobbed.

Extraordinary Coffee Break

Straight after work the Flakes met at Serendipity and settled for a table at the rear of the café. They chose the venue because it was out of the way and unlikely to attract their colleagues, present or past. All were subdued, stunned by the announcement of Jennie's murder and unusually quiet, staring into their coffee cups, lost in thought. Then Bev broke the silence.

"I'm so shocked by what's happened, especially as the last time I saw her was Monday lunchtime when I was dashing out of WH Smith, heading back to work. She had such a worried look on her face I said, 'Cheer up Jen it might never happen.' She didn't say anything just gave me a sad smile and because I was running late I carried on, making a mental note to drop her an email. I wish now I'd stopped and spoken to her and tried to find out what was wrong. It's unbelievable that, 'it might never happen,' were my last words to her."

The rest of the group remained silent, looking at Bev, as her words sank in.

Interrogations

"Sir, I thought you might be interested in this." Sergeant Jones handed a criminal record sheet to DCI Gallagher and waited for his right eyebrow to rise in surprise as it normally did when something grabbed his attention. She was not disappointed.

"So Jennie's good friend Hayden Rhys Husslebea uses an alias, his birth name is actually plain Barry Jones with a criminal record for harassment. Do we have the details?"

"Yes Sir, I anticipated you'd want a fuller picture and requested the original files. He was charged with harassment and sending obscene articles in the post to three women he worked with, they were in their late 40s to early 50s. Apparently he'd been making silent nuisance phone calls at work for a number of months and then started calling their homes, progressing to sending them obscene literature and articles in the post. He was given three months imprisonment on all six charges, to run concurrently, suspended for two years and was ordered to pay the three victims £300 each in compensation. His excuse was that they reminded him of his mother!"

"Hmm, so we have a misogynist amongst our suspects, that's interesting. We'll keep quiet about his past and his current alias for the time being. Let's see what the majestic HRH has to say for himself first."

June picked up the telephone and said, "We'd like to interview Hayden Husslebea next please."

Gillian immediately went over to Husslebea and whispered in his ear, "The police would like to interview you next, follow me please."

She did not wait for a reply but continued walking towards the lifts. Hayden automatically followed her, his face unusually flushed.

"Wait here please," Gillian commanded, pointing towards the three chairs outside the waiting room. She knocked and opened the interview room door.

"Hayden Husslebea is waiting outside for you," she announced then closed the door and walked off down the corridor, totally ignoring Hayden who was sitting staring at the opposite wall.

Gallagher had said "Thank you" without looking up from the papers he was reading about Husslebea's convictions. He made a few notes on his legal pad, checked the time and started talking about holidays to June. He told her of his first camping venture into France and how at the picnic area they had found, just south of Paris, they had stopped to make a cup of tea and afterwards he drove straight over the portable gas stove and kettle, which made her laugh out loud. She was still chuckling as she stood up to walk to the door to call Husslebea in.

Hayden, who had heard the laughter, looked at his watch for the third time and started to fidget. *What on earth can be taking so long? It isn't like I've got nothing to do.* He wished he had gone to the toilet before being called for an interview and resolved to ask to be excused when they finally summoned him into the interview room. *They've kept me waiting so I'll keep them waiting.*

The sergeant poked her head around the door and asked him to come into the room. She returned to her seat before he had had chance to speak.

"Shut the door behind you Mr Husslebea and take a seat please," ordered Gallagher.

Hayden did as he was ordered; he noted the stern look on Gallagher's face and thought better of asking to be excused for the toilet.

"I am Detective Chief Inspector Gallagher and this is Sergeant Jones." Gallagher turned towards June and inclined his head almost indiscernibly, a move she copied while engaging eye contact with Hayden.

"I am assuming you were present during Mr Bytheway's announcement this morning?" Gallagher turned his piercing pale blue eyes on to Hayden, who confirmed he was at the meeting.

"We are interviewing everyone who knew Miss Enderby. Initially the interviews will be on an informal basis. Now then, I understand you were good friends with Miss Enderby, is that correct?"

Hayden was annoyed because his throat had suddenly gone dry. He coughed in an attempt to clear it before answering.

"Yes, hmm," he swallowed, "she was a friend of mine." His voice sounded crackly.

"How long had you known each other?"

"Hmm eh hmm about six years." He coughed again and glanced over to the bottles of water.

"How did you meet?"

"At Stepwells, she came to work in the same group as me." He could feel the sergeant's eyes boring into the side of his face and the colour spreading from his neck upwards as she continued to scrutinise him. *There's nothing worse than a police woman except an old police woman* he thought as familiar feelings of hatred coursed through his veins.

"In what way were you friends?" asked the sergeant.

Hayden turned towards her with an expression of scorn on his face. "Well it certainly wasn't sexual," he sneered. "We were colleagues who occasionally met up for a coffee in our lunch break, that's all."

"I see," said the sergeant. "So, if, as you say, you weren't in a sexual relationship with Miss Enderby do you know who was?"

"I don't know, we didn't discuss our sex lives. All I know is that she had a boyfriend who used to beat her up but he was locked up a couple of years ago for drugs offences, and as far as I am aware he's still incarcerated."

"Thank you Mr Husslebea, that's very interesting." Gallagher took over the questioning.

"When did you start working at Stepwells?"

"January 10th, 2000."

"When did you move to Macefields, and why?"

"October 21st, 2002.   I was headhunted."

"By Macefields?"

"Sort of. Gerry Catchpole asked me to move with him."

"Do you live near to the office?"

"A 15 minute bus journey away."

"Do you live alone?"

"I live with my uncle, if you must know."

"How long have you lived with your uncle?"

"Since starting work at Stepwells." Hayden sighed and without thinking said, "What's the point in questions about where I live, I mean it's hardly relevant…"

Before he had time to finish Gallagher pounced, the tone of his voice menacing. "I'll determine what questions are relevant Mr Husslebea," his eyes flashed, "you just answer the questions." He waited while his words sank in. "Where did you live before moving in with your uncle?" Gallagher lowered his eyes to the paper in front of him and Hayden's stomach turned. His gut instinct was that they already knew the answers to the questions they were asking, in fact they already knew everything about him, including what his real name was and his record.

The atmosphere on the fourth floor could have been cut with a knife. The usual hustle and bustle and peals of laughter had vanished. Apart from the occasional whispered telephone call and tapping of keyboards, silence was the unspoken rule. Grace could feel the tension building, so much so that when she spotted Gillian O'Dwyer, appointed as the police gopher, walking towards her she shot up from her desk and announced in a loud voice, "I am not going to be interviewed, I have nothing to say."

She grabbed her bag, planning to march out of the office, but unfortunately its strap caught on the back of her chair and, as if in slow motion, sprang from her grasp. It flew through the air and emptied its entire contents on the floor at Gillian's feet. Gillian automatically knelt down to retrieve the scattered objects but recoiled in horror when she saw three wax effigies mixed in with the rest of Grace's seemingly normal items.

"Are those what I think they are?" accused Gillian, her mind racing. One had strands of black hair, another strands of blonde hair and another frizzy grey coloured hair, which looked suspiciously like Hayden Husslebea's hair. All had pins strategically inserted into them. Grace said nothing, she just looked at Gillian, eyes wide open, owl-like.

Grace had been fascinated by Voodoo since working at another law firm a few years prior to joining Stepwells. The supervisor had been picking on her friend, so in revenge they would stick pins into a wax effigy they had made in her likeness and laugh hysterically. They even managed to attach some strands of her hair and a button belonging to her. What started out as a bit of silliness soon became an obsession with Grace, she read every book she could find on the subject. She noted with particular interest that the Voodoo Society believed there was no such thing as an accident, nothing had a life of its own and that the universe is all one and everything affects something else; scientists, spiritualists and nature agreed with this. In other words "what you do unto another, you do unto yourself because you ARE the other. Voodoo means view (voo) you (doo)".

"Thanks for seeing me so quickly June, I can imagine how busy everyone in the personnel department must be with the murder investigation but something happened in the office this morning and I needed to bring it to your attention." Gillian paused. "It is concerning Grace Zeglinski."

"Oh, okay," said June, a puzzled look on her face.

"As you know I have been chosen to liaise between the police and staff." She took a deep breath before continuing. "Sergeant Jones had telephoned me to escort Ben Tranter to the interview room and I was walking towards his desk when Grace Zeglinski suddenly shot up in front of me, frightening the life out of me. She shouted that she wasn't going to be interviewed and that she had nothing to say. She then grabbed her bag and unfortunately, or perhaps fortunately for the firm, it caught on the back of her chair, flew into the air and emptied itself practically on my feet. I automatically stooped to help pick things up and noticed three wax effigies with hair and bits of cloth attached and pins sticking out of them."

"Wax effigies!" exclaimed June.

"Yes, wax effigies. One with blonde hair, which could belong to any number of people, including Jennie, one with grey coloured frizzy hair, the same colour as Hayden Husslebea's and one with black hair, that could have been mine, which doesn't bear thinking about. Anyway, as you can imagine, I recoiled when I saw them saying something like, 'Are those what I think they are?' There was a hushed silence as a crowd gathered, then quick as a flash Grace scooped everything up in her bag and rushed out of the office down the front stairs and she hasn't been seen since!" She waited for a response from June, who was checking through the notes she had taken while she assimilated what she had just been told and if any questions came to mind.

"I wasn't sure what to make of the effigies, or if they are significant, but I thought it best to inform you."

"Thanks Gillian, I'm not sure of their significance either, but it all seems rather sinister and not to be tolerated. I'm glad you brought it to my attention; I shall discuss it with my colleagues in personnel to see what the best course of action should be. I'll keep you posted. Thank you for the information."

Four days later Gillian was invited to a meeting with Jane Bingham in Human Resources.

"Hi Gillian, thanks for coming to see me. Do take a seat please. Would you like a drink? Tea, coffee, water?" asked Jane.

"Still water please."

While pouring their drinks Jane said, "Following on from your meeting with June the other day I thought I'd give you an update on Grace Zeglinski. I was in the throes of organising a meeting with my colleagues in personnel to discuss, amongst other things, the wax effigies situation, when I received a surprise telephone call from the police seeking confirmation that Grace worked here."

"Oh!" Gillian responded in shock.

Jane continued, "Apparently after she dashed out of the office she went home, grabbed her and her mother's Post Office books and rushed down to the local Post Office. She managed to draw the maximum money out of her own account but when the cashier wouldn't allow her to draw the maximum amount out of her mother's account without authorisation Grace went berserk. She shouted, swore, threw things and pushed over several wooden display shelves. She then forced her way behind the counter and used the shelves as barricades!" Gillian's jaw dropped as she sat goggle-eyed listening to Jane. "Obviously the police were called, she was swiftly removed from the Post Office and arrested. A doctor examined her at the police station and sectioned her under the Mental Health Act. She is now in the care of Social Services."

"Oh my God!" exclaimed Gillian. "The poor woman and her poor mum! What a sad situation. Do you know what will happen now?"

"Your guess is as good as mine," said Jane. "Frankly I'd be surprised if we see her again. The officer suggested I box up her personal effects, let him know and he'll collect them and pass them on to Social Services."

Weeks later the officer in the case informed Jane that both Grace and her mother had been diagnosed with dementia and moved into a rest home, together. Jane was indeed correct – no one from the firm ever saw or heard from Grace again. Very sad.

Nick's face was a picture of mixed emotions, fear and anxiety, the dark circles under his eyes indicated a lack of sleep and he could not sit still. After his usual introduction DCI Gallagher launched straight into his questioning.

"What was your relationship with the deceased, Jennifer Alexandra Enderby?" The word deceased made Nick's head jerk back as if he had been struck.

"W-w-we worked at the same firm," he stammered.

"I'm well aware that you worked at the same firm," Gallagher said sarcastically, "I actually asked about your relationship with the deceased." He deliberately said deceased again to see what Turner's reaction was, and he was not disappointed because there it was again, an involuntary jerk. "I don't know what you mean?" Nick said playing for time.

"Don't play games Mr Turner, you and I both know that you and Miss Enderby enjoyed more than a working relationship." Nick sat bolt upright at the abruptness of the questioning. He had expected a more general interview but this was straight to the point and he realised, with fear in his heart that any thoughts of being economical with the truth had been blown out of the window.

"We have a copy of an email sent by Miss Enderby to you on 2nd September at 4.30pm saying, and I quote, "See you at my place tonight, don't be late, I have something special for you." Nick closed his eyes reeling at the memory, which was so vivid and real. Tears threatened. "What was special?" pressed Gallagher.

After a tense silence, in which Nick fought to hang on to his composure, he said in a barely audible voice, "She'd bought a new set of lingerie she wanted me to see."

"I'm sorry, I didn't catch what you said, could you repeat that please?" asked Sergeant Jones, pen poised to make a note. Nick repeated his last sentence.

Then as if to twist the knife Gallagher asked what colour the lingerie was. Nick squirmed before answering, "Blue. Cornflower blue." Nick was totally dejected.

"Can you tell us where you were on the afternoon of Tuesday 19th September please?" Jones asked.

"Stuck in London," Nick said, rubbing his hands through his hair, before putting his elbows on the table and resting his forehead on his joined hands. He looked up at Gallagher, emotional turmoil and pain visible in his eyes and in a sob-stifled voice said, "I should have been with her, I should have been there to protect her." No longer able to contain his anguish he hid his face in his hands and sobbed.

DCI Gallagher and Sergeant Jones had interviewed nine of Jennie's colleagues and Gordon Humphrys was the last one. Their records showed that Humphrys was 49 years old, married with two children, a boy at university and a teenage daughter at college. He had worked at various law firms in the city centre, curiously moving to a different company every couple of years, which begged the question how many times was he encouraged to move on. More significantly they discovered he had had a six month affair with Jennie, which ended just before Denbighs merged with Macefields.

"She must have been looking for a father figure in this relationship," said Sergeant Jones, looking at his photograph as she read Humphrys' details, "because according to our records he could hardly afford to be a "sugar daddy". In fact it would appear that around about the start of their affair his wife returned to work after over twenty years as a full-time mother. Was it a coincidence or some strange arrangement between Mr and Mrs, I wonder?"

"Who knows, people never cease to amaze me. Ask Ms O'Dwyer to call Humphrys in please," Gallagher instructed. Jones did as she was asked and a few seconds later Gillian poked her head around the door and announced, "Mr Humphrys is sitting in the corridor," closing the door quietly after her.

Before making a career in law Gordon had designs on becoming an actor, it is a well-known view that all lawyers are at some level really failed actors with a need to command a stage. Unfortunately, Gordon's acting ambitions were quashed when he needed to support his family, which meant a legal career with its steady income was more sensible. Nevertheless, his love of an audience prompted a lifelong involvement with the local amateur dramatics society and he desperately hoped his acting ability would get him thorough this interview, leaving his reputation intact.

When the attractive female officer opened the door to the interview room and invited him, Gordon could not help but give her a cheeky grin. Her wide-eyed response prompted an inner smugness and boosted his confidence, so much so that instead of sitting on the chair nearest to the door, in keeping with the previous interviewees, Gordon confidently strode to the top of the table and took the two officers completely by surprise by shaking hands with them. Gallagher instantly regained his composure and with a stern look on his face gestured, with a dismissive wave of his hand, for Gordon to sit at the other end of the table.

Gallagher opened the interview in the usual way, by introducing himself and his colleague, explaining the purpose of the interview and asking Gordon to clarify his personal details: address, status, children and work etc then he quickly drew the focus back to the interview by asking Gordon, "What was your relationship with the deceased, Jennifer Alexandra Enderby?"

Gordon visibly started at the directness of the questioning. "We both worked at Denbigh Solicitors for approximately twelve months before the firm merged with Macefields twelve months ago."

"In what capacity did you both work at Denbighs?" asked Gallagher.

"Actually she worked as my assistant."

"For how long?"

"During the time she worked there."

"The whole time?"

"Yes."

"Are you sure?"

Gordon started to feel uncomfortable, sensing Gallagher knew more than he was letting on, but attempted to disguise his feelings and flippantly replied, "More or less."

"What does that mean?" A sharp tone had crept into Gallagher's voice.

"Well the month before Denbighs merged with Macefields she was commandeered by Denbighs' senior partner, Mr Godwin, to work for him because his own secretary was convalescing from an operation," condescendingly adding "for women's trouble I believe."

Gallagher saw the look of derision in Jones' eyes and with a very slight roll of his own he indicated to her that she could take over the questioning.

"So, 'women's trouble', as you so eloquently put it, took your assistant away from you. How did you feel about that?"

Humphrys bridled at the mixture of sarcasm and contempt in Jones' voice. He sniffed loudly before replying, aware he had already put his foot in it.

"Inconvenienced."

"In what way?"

"A recent case I'd been working on for nearly two years had been successfully concluded and there was a lot of urgent administrative work to do."

"Such as?"

"Trial bundles to be prepared and sent to the costs draftsman, correspondence, filing, archiving etc. Without Je... er Miss Enderby to help me with that, and, of course, my other work, it was an extremely inconvenient time for me to be without my own secretarial support, notably as the firm was merging."

"Was Miss Enderby told to work for Mr Godwin?" Sergeant Jones waited before continuing, "or did she volunteer to move away from you for more personal reasons?"

"I-I-I don't know what you mean!" Gordon responded indignantly.

"We have reason to believe that you and Miss Enderby enjoyed more than a professional working relationship for a number of months, in fact for practically the whole time she worked with you! More or less."

Gordon could feel his confidence ebbing away, replaced by a jittery stomach and hot flushes. The game was clearly up and he realised it was pointless trying to deny his relationship with Jennie, in fact if he did it would most probably make things worse, much worse. He made a split second decision to be honest and open and in a faraway voice he could hear himself revealing everything about their relationship, from the day she had attended the interview, their love affair, stolen weekends, how he felt about her and how heartbroken he had been when she had finished with him, to his shock and devastation about her murder. The floodgates had opened and he was unstoppable. He felt a huge sense of relief that he was finally able to talk about Jennie. When he had finished he felt so utterly drained that not even tears presented themselves.

The officers did not attempt to stop the outpourings and they waited for Gordon to finish his glass of water before Gallagher asked, "Could you tell us about your early morning workday routine please?"

The odd question immediately snapped Gordon out of his reverie and with a puzzled look on his face he replied, "I leave the house at 7.30am and drive to the office."

"Directly to the office?"

"More or less." A look of irritation crossed both officers' faces.

"Could you elaborate please?"

"I stop and get a daily newspaper on the way."

"On the way? Are you sure about that?"

Gordon's started to feel uncomfortable again, fearful of where this line of questioning was leading. "Well…" he paused, unsure, then decided honesty was still the best policy. "Because I get into the city with time to spare I usually go for a brisk walk to a newsagents just outside the city centre, it's good exercise for me and then I head on to the office."

"The name of the newsagents and location please?"

Gordon's screwed his eyes tight shut for a second, realising they already knew and like a lamb to the slaughter he had followed their lead. "Argent News, near St Mark's church."

"Then what do you do?"

"I return to my car and drive to work."

"Immediately?"

"Yes."

"That's not entirely correct, is it?" said Gallagher. "We have witnesses who will swear that each morning you would buy a newspaper and sit on a bench in St Mark's church grounds reading it until Miss Enderby had walked down the road and cut between the apartment blocks opposite, heading up the road leading to the city centre. You would wait until she was almost out of sight then follow. Is that correct?" Gallagher demanded.

"Yes." Gordon's whispered response was hardly discernible. The realisation of how things must seem sent him plunging further down into the black hole of despair he had been trying to claw his way out of since Jennie had finished with him. His hands started shaking again.

After Humphrys had left the room, Sergeant Jones rolled her head around to loosen her neck muscles and was in the throes of stretching her arms when a surprise yawn caused her to bring her right hand up to her mouth in an effort to stifle it. As she did so she realised DCI Gallagher was looking at her and they both laughed in unison, which banished the seriousness of the long day.

They had a brief discussion about the people they had interviewed, gathered up their papers and notebooks and headed back to the office which was a brisk ten minute walk away. As soon as they entered police headquarters PC Wistow called out to Gallagher, "Sir could I have an urgent word please?"

"Of course, what is it?" Gallagher walked over to the young officer.

"I've received an urgent call from Sergeant Bellingham to inform you that Jennie Enderby's ex-boyfriend Zac Owen has been arrested in Norfolk."

"Norfolk?" Gallagher said more to himself than anything.

Wistow interrupted his flow of thoughts. "I understand he was one of a group of men imprisoned for cultivating and supplying cannabis. Owen was sentenced to four years but released earlier because of time on remand being taken into account and, eh, good behaviour. Enquiries reveal that just prior to his release Owen asked a former inmate to locate Jennie Enderby for him.

"Thanks Wistow, and you say the officer in charge is Sergeant Bellingham?"

"Yes Sir, Sergeant Bellingham." He handed Gallagher a piece of paper. "This is his telephone number."

"Thanks Officer Wistow, good work," Gallagher said, patting the officer on the shoulder.

Norfolk

Bellingham was promoted to sergeant shortly after the conclusion of Operation Barn Owl. Obviously, passing the sergeant exams was a crucial requirement in gaining rank, but his tenacity in recognising Owen from when he was stabbed, following him and discovering his involvement in an elaborate scheme to cultivate and supply drugs had no doubt helped him secure the position of sergeant.

When Zac Owen and his cohorts were sentenced to varying terms of imprisonment his gut instinct was that he would re-offend once released, and consequently he kept in regular touch with the prison to check when his release date was. This proved to be very prudent as although he had been sentenced to four years he was actually released after two years, July 2006, because the eight months on remand were taken into account and also his subsequent good behaviour.

The news of Jennie Enderby's murder instantly conjured up the image of Owen at the Norfolk farm where he had taken several photographs of him. He remembered that at the time Jennie was Owen's girlfriend and now she had been murdered three months after his release; it was too much of a coincidence. His contact at the prison told him Jennie had stopped visiting Owen shortly after he began his sentence which further aroused Bellingham's suspicions.

Although Kettle, the farmer, was still serving his sentence, Bellingham's hunch was that it was possible Owen had gone to ground at or near to the farm. He decided a trip to see his Aunt Charlotte was due and as luck would have it he was off duty for a few days. He regularly visited his aunt and since Operation Barn Owl he had been in the habit of stopping off in the village nearest to Kettle's farm for a bite to eat in the pub before continuing on and spending a few hours with her. He had built up a good rapport with Jim Wall, the jovial public house manager over the years and when he showed him a photograph of Owen he was both amazed and excited to learn he had seen him recently at the local church.

Bellingham immediately made two telephone calls, the first one to DI Holmes at the Norfolk police station. He told him what he had discovered and he in turn quickly dispatched a team of officers to the village where Bellingham was. Their enquiries revealed Owen was staying in a bed and breakfast guest house almost opposite the church. Within the hour he was arrested. The second call was to DI Gallagher at the Manchester police station, who unfortunately was in an interview so he left a detailed message with one of his team, PC Wistow, stressing the message was extremely urgent. Consequently, first thing the following morning, Gallagher and Jones drove to Norfolk police station to interview Owen.

"Good morning DI Gallagher and Sergeant Jones, we meet again," Zac said in an exaggerated friendly tone, before either of them had chance to speak. Gallagher noted the bible with a silver crucifix indentation in its dark blue cover that Zac was holding. His ice blue eyes pierced Zac's fierce sapphire blue eyes. Neither of them flinched.

"For the record," Gallagher said, switching on the tape recorder. He went through the formalities of introducing himself and Sergeant Jones and their reason for the interview, and he gave the standard caution, "You do not have to say anything, but it may harm your defence if you do not mention when questioned something which you later rely on in court. Anything you do say may be given in evidence. Do you understand?"

"Yes," said Zac.

Gallagher also advised him to consider independent legal representation. Again Zac acknowledged he understood and waived his right to a legal representative. The interview commenced.

"What was your relationship with the deceased, Jennifer Alexandra Enderby?"

Zac continued to hold Gallagher's glare for a few seconds before stating in a quiet, matter of fact voice, "She was my girlfriend. We met when she was 15. At 16 she moved in with me. I loved her, she was my world, my reason to live and ultimately my downfall."

"What do you mean by downfall?" Gallagher seized on the point.

"You will know from my records that I have been in prison for drugs related offences. I wanted to give Jennie the best in life." He held his bible aloft before continuing, "But those who desire to be rich fall into temptation, into a snare, into many senseless and harmful desires that plunge people into ruin and destruction. Timothy 6:9-1."

Gallagher exchanged a look of astonishment with WPC Jones before indicating with a slight nod of his head for her to take over questioning.

"To summarise, is it correct to record that you turned to the crimes of cultivating and selling drugs to provide Jennie with the best in life and as a consequence you served a term of imprisonment?"

"Yes. If we confess our sins, he is faithful and just and will forgive us our sins and purify us from all unrighteousness. John 1."

Gallagher and Jones mirrored each other's sceptical expressions. Jones continued with her questioning. "When did you last see Jennifer Enderby?"

Zac hesitated for a few seconds before saying, "I see her all the time, in my dreams, in the church, in the streets, she is in my thoughts and in my heart."

"Mr Owen," Jones said, irritation creeping into her voice, "when did you actually last see Jennifer Enderby in the flesh?"

"Hmm, I can't remember the exact date."

"Where were you on the 19th September 2006?"

"I'm not sure."

"We have a witness who will swear you were at Swan Court on the afternoon of Tuesday 19th September 2006. That you were driving a black BMW which had been parked near to the apartment block where Miss Enderby was found murdered."

"And the truth shall set you free!" Zac suddenly announced. "I would now like to speak with a solicitor please." He refused to answer any further questions despite Gallagher and Jones's best endeavours. The interview was terminated and Owen's chosen solicitor, Mr Rochester, was contacted.

Harry Rochester was not surprised to receive a call to be Owen's legal representative. He had been notified of his client's release and when he read of Jennie's murder only weeks later he knew it was only a matter of time before Owen was picked up for it. His heart sank for she was a lovely young woman, sweet natured, unassuming, with her whole life before her.

On the drive to Norwich police station he reflected on his legal career spanning almost 40 years, from the young man with a burning ambition, working long hours to help make the world a better place, to the people he had represented, the cases he had won, the press coverage and last but not least his family's pride in his achievements. Fortunately, he had had very few lows, too few to contemplate. He had been lucky, very lucky indeed. Now, as he was nearing retirement, finishing with a murder case should have been the icing on the cake except he felt terribly sad about the fate of these two young, basically decent, people. He had gotten to know both of them when Zac was arrested for the drugs case and he had visited him several times while he was serving his sentence. Such a waste of two lives, a tragic waste.

"Hello Mr Rochester," Zac said, his pleasure at seeing him evident.

"Hello Zac," Harry replied, his mellifluous voice soft and comforting. Harry took his coat off, placed his notebook and pen on the table and sat down on the wooden chair. He noted the bible on the table but did not pass comment. After a long moment he looked Zac straight in the eyes and asked him to tell him everything that had happened, from him being released to their current meeting. He did not attempt to mask the sorrowful tone in his voice.

Zac took a deep breath. Hearing the sorrow in his lawyer friend's voice had a profound effect on him. Up until then, in his own mind, he had justified his crime, convincing himself he was the real victim. Now suddenly the realisation of the terrible thing he had done hit him and he unburdened his conscience to Harry, telling him everything, significantly confessing his guilt.

Harry proceeded to, in essence, cross-examine Zac, to make sure he was telling the truth, then discussed at length the ramifications of what he had said and the probable consequence being a lengthy prison sentence or quite possibly a life sentence. At the conclusion of their meeting Zac sat with his head bowed as Harry packed his legal notepad and custody papers into his briefcase and put his coat on. He did not even look up when Harry said he would see him in court the following day.

His case was called first the following morning. He was surprised at how crowded the courtroom was. He was flanked by two burley duty officers, one standing in the dock with him and the other outside near to the waist high dock gate. His handcuffs were removed temporarily while he confirmed his name, age, his legal representative, etc. He heard the prosecutor give a brief outline of the charge against him and the reasons why he should be remanded in custody. He heard Mr Rochester say there was no application for bail, (he had already explained to Zac that such an application would be futile given his situation). Predictably, he was remanded in custody pending evidence being collated for eventual committal to the Crown Court.

Zac was remanded in custody twice more before the prosecution committal papers were ready. The actual committal proceedings in the Magistrates' Court were a mere formality because, as Mr Rochester advised, there was a prima facia case against him. And so it came to pass on Friday 8th December 2006 he was duly committed to Manchester Crown Court in custody, just in time for Christmas.

Life Imprisonment

Throughout Zac's remand in custody Harry Rochester liaised with the Crown Prosecutor, Warren Bassett, the same prosecutor who had dealt with the drugs case. There was a mutual respect and a straightforward honesty between the two lawyers. From the outset Harry had been transparent about advising his client to plead guilty to murder.

Zac looked upon Mr Rochester as a friendly father figure, rather than his legal representative. He wished his father had been more like him: kind, caring and approachable. Indeed if he had been Zac was sure he would not be in the trouble he was.

For two reasons the case was brought before the Crown Court very quickly: one he was in custody and two he was pleading guilty. His plea was accepted and the case was further adjourned for social enquiry reports to be compiled, which was a standard requirement. This was basically to ensure all aspects of the defendant's personal circumstances and appropriate sentencing had been considered. Sentence was finally passed on Wednesday 7th March 2007. The judge summed up the case against Zac.

"Jennifer Alexandra Enderby died from strangulation in her own home. Zachery Thomas Owen, you have pleaded guilty to her murder three months after being released from a jail sentence. You were in a relationship with each other for a number of years but shortly after your sentence you became verbally abusive and threatening to her and she decided to end the relationship by moving to another city and starting a new life.

"There is medical evidence that you abused her prior to your imprisonment. While serving your sentence you arranged for her to be located and her routine monitored, your intention to resume contact. Unfortunately for Miss Enderby you discovered she was in a relationship with another man, so you watched and waited for an opportunity to confront her, which resulted in her murder.

"Zachary Thomas Owen this was a premeditated crime, therefore I sentence you to life imprisonment with the proviso you serve a minimum of 15 years before being considered for release."

The court case, numerous remands, the subsequent sentence returning him to Leeds prison, in fact everything since his release from the drugs sentence had happened so quickly Zac had hardly had time to take it all in. He again turned to the bible and as if in answer to his prayers a few weeks later he was astonished and secretly delighted to greet his little Italian friend, David Marconi, who had been given a five year term of imprisonment for burglary and handling stolen goods. This time they sought biblical solace together.

Life Is Too Short

"Let's hope the bastard actually serves a life sentence," exclaimed Ben as he placed the tray of drinks on the table. "I don't hold with this nonsense of being allowed out early for good behaviour."

"Well he played the religious card so perhaps the 'an eye for an eye' principle should apply in his case, maybe one of his fellow inmates will do us all a favour and strangle him," suggested Piers.

Doing a fingertip drum roll, Lucy announced, "Listen up everyone, I've got some news," grinning conspiratorially at Ben, who blushed and looked down at his coffee. Everyone waited with baited breath for her to elaborate. "As you know Ben has not been offered a training contract with Stepwells, well," she coughed, in an exaggerated way, she so loved to tease, "he's moving to a job in London and guess what?" She did not wait for a response. "I'm going with him!"

"I knew it, I knew things were kicking off with you two!" exclaimed Rachel. "I've noted your furtive glances and how you always managed to sit by each other. Congratulations, how long have you been an item then?"

"When I found out I was not going to be offered a training contract, my first thought was to confide in Lucy," explained Ben. He took her hand in his, looked tenderly into her eyes and continued, in barely a whisper, as Lucy blushed bright red, "The way she reacted to my news, with such a sad little face and tears in her eyes, my heart melted and I knew we felt the same way about each other."

There was a collective "Ahh."

PART V – AFTERMATH

Gordon's early morning battle getting his father ready, struggling to come to terms with the ending of his relationship with Jennie and the guilt of hurting Diane and their children left him incredibly stressed.

To make matters worse his father began soiling himself, then fell and broke his hip. While in hospital he suffered a series of mini strokes leaving him with vascular dementia. The medical team decided he was no longer fit to live alone and Gordon spent six weeks checking out care homes and liaising with social workers. Eventually he chose Green Fields Rest Home. Surprisingly, the move from hospital to the care home went smoothly and his father settled in very quickly.

Meanwhile Diane spent most of her time living at her mother's, Jordan spent weekends at her friends, Anthony was at university and Gordon was left feeling isolated, lonely and fearful for the future. Nevertheless, he applied for Lasting Power of Attorney to sell his father's home to fund his care. Filling in the numerous pages of the Power of Attorney forms provided by the Office of Public Guardian was a massive headache for Gordon, exacerbated by his father's reluctance to agree. In the end he only agreed after one of the pretty female carers explained if he refused he would have to leave Green Fields. *It's amazing what a pretty face can achieve,* Gordon said to himself after his father meekly signed the forms in the presence of his solicitor, who then certified that his client, Gordon's father, fully understood the implications.

The nightmare was over but it had taken its toll on Gordon's health. He had lost his appetite and three stone in weight, leaving him looking old and haggard.

Then Jennie was murdered.

Somehow Gordon found the strength to deal with the police interrogation and subsequent trial. Then his internal 'coiled spring' rapidly unravelled and he had a mental breakdown, could not stop crying and was off work for several weeks, during which time divorce papers were served and he learned from Anthony, that Diane was seeing one of her colleagues. He completed and returned the papers and seriously contemplated suicide, indeed, he had actually written suicide notes to his wife, children and father. Fortunately, he could not go through with his planned death because of his children, he could not hurt them any more than he had already done and found an inner steel to carry on. Jordan was a tower of strength and regular visits to see his father were actually uplifting because he became friends with the staff and in time learned to laugh again through their friendly banter.

It was the last Saturday in November and freezing. He had been feeling the cold for a while and popped into the city centre to buy himself a hat. He chose a dark brown, fur-lined trapper's hat because the flaps would keep his ears warm. As Christmas was looming he continued shopping in the department store for presents for the children. At lunchtime he decided to have a sandwich and a drink in the store's very busy restaurant and was pleased to find an empty table in the corner. He was wearing his new hat sitting with his back to the self-service till, compiling a 'to do list'.

"Excuse me please, are all of these seats taken?"

"Eh no they're… Diane?" Gordon could not believe his eyes, he had not seen Diane for almost a year. From the shocked expression on her face she had not recognised him either, probably because of the hat. He swiftly stood up and pulled a chair out for her, thankful she was alone. There was a long awkward moment then both of them spoke at once, the resulting laughter dissolved any tension. Before long Gordon had Diane laughing hysterically over the problems he had encountered with his father, specifically being mortified on learning his father had become a serial groper of the carers! He ended up crying with laughter too. They stayed talking until the restaurant called time. Both looked sad as they went their separate ways.

Weeks went by and Gordon was surprised he had not received any further correspondence relating to Diane's application for divorce. Then one day Anthony rang him and casually dropped it out that his mother was no longer seeing her colleague. That night Gordon wrote a letter to Diane telling her how much he had enjoyed their recent surprise encounter and shared laughter and that he would always be there for her. Although she already knew his mobile telephone number he added it at the end of the letter. A few days later Diane rang him, and that was their start of rebuilding bridges.

Nick

The taxi pulled up outside the house and Penny wondered who was visiting in the middle of the afternoon. She was surprised to see Nick climb out and she was horrified at his dishevelled appearance. He practically fell through the front door.

"What on earth has happened to you?" Penny enquired, her face tense with concern.

"I can't talk. I need to lie down," Nick snapped. "Just leave me alone," he shouted as he staggered off to the spare bedroom, slamming the door shut. Penny stood open mouthed in total bewilderment, staring at the door. The alarm on her wrist watch brought her to her senses, and reminded her that it was time to pick the children up. While waiting for them outside the school she rang her mother and told her about Nick coming home early, clearly upset.

"I bet it's got something to do with that murder," her mother replied.

"Murder, what murder?"

"A young girl has been murdered in the city centre, according to the local news she worked at the same firm as Nick."

"Oh my God, if you're right…" her words trailed off.

"You're going to have to confront him love. Bring the children around to me while you get to the bottom of things."

After dropping the children off Penny rang Jeremy Hall, who was her mediator, for advice on the best way to handle the situation. He thought for a moment then advised the softly, softly approach, i.e. do not get angry and confrontational, but say she realised something very bad had happened as he was clearly upset, then enquire if there was anything she could do. If he said no she just needed to reassure him that she was there to listen when he was ready to talk. He told her to make sure she was safe, certainly until she fully understood the situation, suggesting she take someone with her. Concerns regarding her personal safety alarmed her as up until then she had not given her own safety a thought. She toyed with the idea of asking her father to go with her but decided against it. She did not want to upset him, so she took a chance and went home alone.

She tried the door to the spare bedroom, it was locked. She knocked on the door, there was no answer. Through the door she repeated the words Jeremy had advised, still no reply. She sat in the lounge and waited. Nick surfaced at about 9.00pm. He poured himself a glass of water then sat at the far end of the room. She waited. Without looking at her, in a quiet voice he said, "One of the girls from work was..." he gasped, clearly fighting to regain his composure. Then, his voice cracking, he continued, "...murdered. The police found her in her apartment yesterday evening."

She waited, and focused on a point somewhere in the middle of the carpet.

"There is no easy way to say this. I will be a suspect because I was in a relationship with her."

She waited, still staring at the carpet.

"I had nothing to do with her murder." His voice became high-pitched, then in barely a whisper he confessed, "I loved her. I-I-I loved her, loved her so very much." He buried his face in his hands and sobbed.

Penny slowly rose and left the room, quietly closing the door after her. She collected fresh clothes for herself and the children and drove to her parents' home where she fell apart.

Let's Get Together

Although the Flakes quintet kept in regular contact through emails, telephone calls, text messages and Facebook, they had not actually meet as a group over the four years since Lucy and Ben had moved to London. Then out of the blue Lucy telephoned Bev.

"Hi Bev, Lucy here, hope you're well."

"Oh hi Lucy, this is a nice surprise. We're all okay, are you?"

"Yeah, we're good. Look this is just a quick call, I'm coming up to Manchester just after Christmas, I'm going to a family wedding. You enjoy organising things, how do you feel about organising a 10 year get-together of the birth of the Flakes on the same day we started, January 10th?"

"I can't believe it's been a decade since we started at Stepwells," Bev said. "Okay, leave it with me. I'll let you know if everyone can make it. As the 10th is a Sunday, what about Sunday lunch at The Toby Jug?"

"That sounds like a plan. Keep me posted please. Sorry but I must dash. I'll email you. Byeeee."

Reunion Continued

"We've certainly had an interesting time during our city years," mused Ben as he tucked into his steak and chips.

"Yes, we sure have, and met some weird and wonderful characters along the way," laughed Bev. She sipped her red wine before asking, "I wonder whatever happened to the likes of O'Dwyer, Richardson and the Husslebeas?"

"Well I had heard," said Lucy leaning forward in a conspiratorial way, elbows on the table, knife upright in her hand which she used like a conductor's baton, "when Richardson's youngest daughter started work O'Dwyer put pressure on him to leave his wife, but he finally grew some balls and finished with her instead!"

"No, you're joking!" exclaimed Rachel, putting down the fork of food she was about to devour. "What did she do then?"

"She telephoned his wife and told her all about their affair, dates, places, intimate details, everything." She waited to let the revelation sink in. "If she was hoping his wife would kick him out then she wasn't disappointed, but what did disappoint her, or should I say *devastated* her, was instead of going back to her with his tail between his legs, Richardson moved in with Maggie Rollaston and quit working at Stepwells!"

"Oh my God!" Rachel clasped her hand across her gaping mouth, eyes wide open in disbelief. After the shocking revelation had sunk in she continued, "I would love to have seen O'Dwyer's face when she found out, I never liked her but personal feelings aside you have to feel sorry for the poor cow. What a shitty way for Richardson to treat her! Unbelievable!"

"Yes, especially as he's since had a son by Maggie and there's another baby on the way!" Lucy then added, "O'Dwyer is probably too old to have children now. I haven't heard what's happened to her but she must be very bitter and twisted."

"Woman scorned and stalker comes to mind. I'd put money on her trying to get revenge. I wouldn't like to be in their shoes," said Ben. Then he asked, "Anyone know what became of the Husslebeas?"

"Apparently Hayden Husslebea had a breakdown and…" Piers smiled, "you're going to love this… he accused Paul Husslebea of stalking him!"

The group burst out laughing, then Piers elaborated, "He claimed he was making numerous silent phone calls to him at work, on his mobile and to his home address, that he was getting copious amount of junk mail, catalogues and goods he hadn't ordered. Of course, he couldn't prove anything and only scant interest was shown by the police because he'd been the bane of the local service for years with his steady stream of complaints and constant whinging."

Rachel shuddered at the memories of the silent phone calls she had endured and the distress they had caused her, but after years of practice she was able to quickly push them to the back of her mind and join in with the laughter, adding, "Well that certainly sounds like a clear case of karma!"

After finishing their main courses, while waiting for their desserts, Bev carried on with the stalker theme and asked, "Whatever became of your stalker Piers, Faye thingamabob?"

His face flushed and he remained tight-lipped. The group looked at him in bewilderment, surprised at the lack of a witty response. Eyes downcast he eventually spoke. "Well actually eh, I eh, I married her," Piers answered quietly, as if he was ashamed. Everyone was stunned into an embarrassed silence, each trying to think of something to say, then Lucy jumped in with both feet and asked the question they had all been dying to ask, but did not have the nerve to.

"So how on earth did you two end up together, and when?"

Piers looked at each of them in turn, he took a big gulp of his drink, before explaining. "The 'when' was a quiet, two witnesses off the street, registry office affair, Valentine's Day 2007, a Wednesday... So far as the 'end up together' was, as you know I moved to London in December 2005 to test the water at becoming a stand-up comic. Well, I'd been doing the rounds for about six months, trying different styles, working various venues and audiences, dying on stage more times than I care to remember and relying on my old friend a bit too much." He held up his 'old friend' his drink, took another big gulp before continuing. "One night I noticed a familiar face in the audience, it was Faye. I don't mind admitting that I was shocked to see her. We didn't speak to each other that night, or during the next four weeks I was performing. At first I was freaking out seeing her watching me night after night, but then I found I was actually looking for her amongst the audience. One night she didn't turn up and I had a panic attack! I kid you not; it was worse than any stage fright. Being on stage can be exhilarating but it can also be one of the loneliest places. The next time I saw her I sent a stagehand to ask her to meet me backstage, and, as they say, the rest is history. She is now my manager and my lovely wife, she takes good care of me." He went quiet after his update and then, as if thinking out loud, softly added, "I need her."

He looked into his glass for a long moment, aware that the rest of the group were watching and waiting for him to say something, so true to form he finished off with a joke. "Talking of Freudian slips, one day there was a priest sitting in a pew with a very worried and nervous look; another priest saw him and asked what was wrong. 'Well,' the first priest said, 'have you ever heard of a Freudian slip?'

'No,' said the other.

'It's when one slips and says something one is thinking, usually at the least opportune time.'

'Oh,' said the second priest, "so, what happened?'

'Today I performed a wedding and you know the part when you say 'I now pronounce you man and wife'?'

'Yes,' said the second priest.

'Well that is what I meant to say but what I actually said was, I now sentence you to death.'"

The group burst out laughing again.

After their laughter subsided Piers continued, "I'm actually surprised Faye accepted my proposal because I quoted one of my favourite Groucho Marx one-liners: 'Marry me and I'll never look at another horse!'" More group laughter. "Needless to say it didn't go down too well, so I ended up on bended knee making the usual pledges, and now, in all honesty, before you stands one happily married man."

He did not sound very convincing, in fact he cut a sad figure, a shadow of the exuberant, vivacious Piers they remembered and loved.

Ben turned to Rachel. "So Rachel, what's new with you? How long is it since you worked in the city?"

"Five years; I can't believe how quickly the time has passed. Unfortunately my job's on the line so I may have to return to city working, which is really annoying because I will have to give up my creative writing course, which I really enjoy. As a matter of fact I've written a novel."

"Oooh am I in it?" asked Lucy, eyes dancing with excitement. "What's the title?"

"You might be," Rachel teased. "I'll let you read it when it's been proofread. I haven't decided on its title yet."

"I'll proofread it for you, I'd love to," volunteered Lucy.

"I'm sure you would, probably sex it up too!" Rachel laughed, before adding, "Seriously, thanks for the offer, but someone has already agreed. She is an excellent proofreader and a dear friend. Someone I worked with fifteen years ago, before my Stepwells days."

"You said you're going to lose your job, why's that?" asked Piers.

"It's a small firm, badly managed, and recently past mistakes have come home to roost. At times it's a crazy place, like appearing in that classic old movie, 'One Flew over the Cuckoo's Nest', where the inmates take over. Anyway, a few have already gone and as I'm struggling for work I expect to be in the next round of redundancies. Frankly, although I'm upset about losing my job, part of me will be glad to go, particularly as I share an office with one of Gillian O'Dwyer's cronies, Carol Weddaburn and...'

"Carol Weddaburn? You never told me!" admonished Lucy.

"Oh sorry, I thought I had, well it gets better. At first I worked for a young chap, but after twelve months he moved on. I was flattered when he asked me to move with him but I had to decline, it wouldn't have been financially viable. Unfortunately, it was a decision I came to regret because shortly before he left the senior partner reassured me I wouldn't lose my job as he had his replacement already lined up. He described the replacement but didn't name him, he didn't need to, I knew instinctively who it was." She paused for effect. "It was Gordon Humphrys!"

"Humpty Humphrys!" Lucy echoed, "Good God, how weird is that?"

"Tell me about it! I've always believed things happen for a reason, so please, why him?" Rachel implored before continuing, "Why am I caught up in some sort of cosmic joke? I mean, of all the people I could work for…"

"That's unbelievable," said Lucy, "first Turner and the "I'll have the fish" fiasco, then Humpty Humphreys, and both of them had affairs with Jennie! Aw Rachel don't tell me you had an affair with Jennie too!" but when she saw the indignant look of horror mask Rachel's face she quickly added, putting her hands up in surrender, "Only joking, only joking I agree it's as if someone is having a big laugh at your expense."

"Want an even bigger laugh?" Piers piped up with a twinkle in his eyes. "I've just had a thought about the perfect title for your book Rachel," and in unison they both said, "I'll have the fish!" then all of them roared with laughter.

"Well that's definitely a quirky title, I'll see what the publisher thinks of it, if I ever get that far!" scoffed Rachel.